PRAISE FOR THE WRAITHWOOD TRILOGY

Roat weaves an emotional journey of coming-of-age that pushes Brinnie to dig deeper into her own power. *Mordizan* continues to weave an original perspective on Arthurian mythology.

— READER'S FAVORITE 5 STAR REVIEW FOR *MORDIZAN*

Alyssa Roat gives new life to Arthurian legend.
Portland Book Review

Immersive, atmospheric, and brimming with magic, *Wraithwood* presents a skillful take on Arthurian legends, harnessing a gothic manor and ensemble of enchanting characters to create an unforgettable read. A treasure for any booklover. Alyssa Roat is a wizard at her craft.

— CAROLINE GEORGE, AUTHOR OF *DEAREST JOSEPHINE* (HARPERCOLLINS)

The irresistible first book in a planned trio, *Wraithwood*'s world is both magical and familiar. Supernatural revelations enter the story in an unobtrusive way: chairs float in the air; a bedroom emerges from a blanket in a wizard's hovel; an impenetrable maze proves to be the best estate security. But it's Brinnie's empathetic search for answers, and for her own identity among the wizards, that will carry affectionate interest in her story forward into the trilogy's next volumes.

— *FOREWORD REVIEWS*

Wraithwood is a magical and notable retelling of Arthurian legend.

— *READER'S FAVORITE* 5-STAR REVIEW FOR *WRAITHWOOD*

An instant classic. You can't help but fall in love with all the characters, especially Brinnie. I'm incredibly picky with books I like, and I fell in love with this one. Arthurian legend like you've never seen it before, and all incredibly complex characters. You can tell the author threw her heart and soul into this book, and I cannot wait to find out what happens next in Brinnie's adventure.

— HOPE BOLINGER, AUTHOR OF THE *BLAZE* TRILOGY

In *Wraithwood,* Alyssa Roat strikes a balance between intrigue and whimsy just right for young teen readers. It's a perfect summer read!

— LINDSAY A. FRANKLIN, AWARD-WINNING AUTHOR OF *THE STORY PEDDLER*

MORDIZAN

Also by Alyssa Roat

The Wraithwood Trilogy

Wraithwood

Mordizan

Castelon

The Dear Series

Dear Hero

Dear Henchman

Dear Hades

MORDIZAN

THE WRAITHWOOD TRILOGY

BOOK TWO

ALYSSA ROAT

Vista, CA

ISBN: 978-1-61153-183-1 (paperback)

ISBN: 978-1-61153-184-8 (ebook)

ISBN: 978-1-61153-214-2 (large print)

Library of Congress Control Number: 2026934542

Mordizan is published by: Torchflame Books, an imprint of Top Reads Publishing, LLC, 1035 E. Vista Way, Suite 205, Vista, CA 92084, USA

Previously published in 2022 by Mountain Brook Ink under the Mountain Brook Fire line, White Salmon, WA U.S.A.

Scripture quotations are taken from the King James Version of the Bible. Public domain.

Cover Design: Indie Cover Design, Lynnette Bonner

Interior Layout: Jori Hanna

For every girl who sees herself in Brinnie
The shy girls, the bookish girls, the gentle girls
The ones who made it through Mordizan and came out alive
The ones with scars
You are strong, you are brave, you are enough

CHAPTER ONE

Brinnie glanced up from her math homework and then fixed her eyes back on the page. Yes, that girl was still watching her.

She shifted on the hard metal bench, trying to focus on her equations. The late afternoon sun beating on her back did nothing to make her more comfortable. Her few minutes of productivity before the after-school programming buses showed up were turning out to be anything but.

She darted another glance. The girl had plopped down at a nearby table fifteen minutes ago, and her eyes had been glued on Brinnie in an intense stare ever since.

Am I supposed to recognize you?

From quickly stolen glances, she knew she'd never met the girl. What with her short, light-brown hair that looked as if it had been hacked off with one swipe of an axe and her three-ring binder plastered with stickers, Brinnie was fairly certain she would have remembered the girl if they'd interacted before.

She took a deep breath. *Focus. It's just a teenager acting weird.* She fixed her attention on her math, readjusted the paper, and began making tedious calculations.

"Are you a vampire?"

Brinnie jumped. Her foot caught under the table, and she nearly fell over backward in her haste to leap to her feet.

The girl suddenly stood in front of her, binder clutched to her chest.

Sit. Breathe. Brinnie forced a smile and a slight laugh. "Funny."

The girl blinked at her, oversized circular glasses enlarging her brown eyes to owlish proportions. "Well? Are you?"

She forced the smile to remain pasted on her face. "If I had a dollar for every time someone made a vampire joke . . ." Dark hair paired with unusually pale skin and light eyes made her a prime target.

"I promise I won't tell anyone." The girl slid onto the bench across from Brinnie. She set down her binder and propped her elbows on it. "I've always wanted to meet a real one."

Brinnie glanced down at the binder. The stickers were all from various vampire shows and movies. *Oh, great.* She bared her teeth. "See? No fangs. I also happen to like garlic." Her gaze wandered to the gate. Any minute now, the buses would arrive.

"Oh. That's too bad." The girl sat back and pushed her glasses up her nose. "I thought I might have finally found a school that's actually interesting."

New and strange. She would probably need friends and might have trouble making them. Which meant, according to Brinnie's heart already swelling with sympathy, that was her job. *The weird ones always find me.* "When did you transfer?"

"Just got here two days ago from Colorado." She fanned her red face. "It's pretty hot."

"Welcome to Arizona." She chuckled, brushing at a tickle on her arm. "And today is a cool day."

She scratched the lingering itch, glancing at a group of boys who seemed to share the girl's sentiment about the heat and had decided to combat the issue by throwing water at each other. As a scowling aide strode by to scold the boys, Brinnie's fingers halted over her arm. Not an itch. The sensation that pricked her upper arm was something she hadn't felt in a long time—a strange coolness.

Her heart skipped a beat. *No. Not here.*

The chill crept deeper into her skin.

She shot to her feet and gathered her belongings, stuffing them into her backpack. "Well, I have to go. Nice to meet you."

The girl stood as well. "Where you off to?"

"I think I, uh, forgot something. I'll see you later." She slung her backpack over her shoulder while scanning the courtyard. Other than the boys being scolded about the water fight, she saw the usual stragglers hanging around from the after-school programs that had been let out early, some aides, and the occasional teacher. No one who looked particularly suspicious.

What do I do? Should she stand in plain sight, making her an impossible target? They wouldn't dare attack with so many witnesses. Or should she hide, before she was seen? It all depended on whether she'd already been spotted or not.

She glanced down at her arm. No light pulsing through the sleeve yet. They couldn't be too close. She had time to hide.

She attempted to stride casually across the courtyard. *Somewhere out of sight, somewhere I can call Mom.* She ducked around one of the buildings, pressing against the rough wall in a secluded corner barricaded on two sides by a fence and another by the building itself. Her only companion was a scraggly weed growing through a crack in the sidewalk. Reaching down, she wiggled her fingers into the lining of her sneaker and pulled out the thin pocketknife concealed inside.

It had taken months and several blisters to get used to the bulge in her shoe, and she'd reconsidered whether the weapon was worth it a few times. But now, she could hug past-Brinnie for sticking it out. She clicked the small blade open. With the knife in one hand, she pulled her clunky old phone from her back pocket with the other.

As she looked down to dial the number, she heard a scuffing noise beside her. On instinct, she whirled and slammed the person into the wall. The figure shrieked as Brinnie's knife pointed at their throat.

"Oh my gosh, don't kill me!"

Brinnie quickly stepped back and clicked the knife shut. She cursed under her breath. She was so done for. As soon as word got out that she had a weapon at school—once *Mom* learned about it . . . "What were you doing?" she demanded.

The vampire-loving girl readjusted her glasses with one hand, still clutching that stickered binder with the other. "You left so fast. I was making sure you were okay." She craned her neck. "Why do you have a knife?"

Brinnie stuffed the knife in her pocket. The online videos about self-defense hadn't covered what to do if you accidentally defended yourself against the wrong person. *Deflect. Redirect.* "I didn't even hear you come up. You've got some serious stealth skills."

No luck in distraction. "Knives aren't allowed on campus."

Mom would kill her. "I know. I'm sorry. Really, I should have left it at home. It's my bad." Her tone trembled with desperation. She cleared her throat, trying to wrestle back control of her voice. "Just please don't tell, okay?"

The girl scowled. "You almost killed me."

"No, I—" She stopped. How close vampire-girl had or hadn't been to death wasn't going to win this argument. "I'm really sorry. I totally overreacted." She offered a sheepish smile. "I'll leave it at home tomorrow. Can we act like this never happened?"

The girl pursed her lips, eyebrows raised. "I don't think—"

The familiar roar of the buses drifted from beyond the alcove. "Thanks. I've got to go." Brinne slipped past and darted for her bus, no other plan than *flee*. The coolness in her arm . . .

Mom might have to get in line to kill her.

Her bus idled in the middle of the line. She rushed up the steps, offered half a smile to the driver, and headed for the back of the mostly empty vehicle. She plopped into the cracked faux leather seat, her heart pounding. *Please drive away, please.*

After what felt like an eternity, the driver pulled out of the parking lot.

Brinnie sagged into the seat. She'd escaped. *Okay. Time to think logically.* The girl didn't know Brinnie's name. Didn't know her grade, her classes. Even if the girl reported her, how would she do it? Who could prove anything, if tomorrow she came to school without the knife? What would they do, round up all the black-haired blue-eyed girls in school like a police lineup?

She cringed. That couldn't be a very long list.

Gradually, the coolness in her arm faded. Brinnie got off at one of the stops farther from her house so she could clear her head on the walk home. It would be okay, she told herself. She would deny everything. And as far as she could tell, the person responsible for her tingling arm hadn't seen her. That was the more important issue anyway, even if it didn't feel that way at the moment.

She smiled ruefully to herself. Mom's wrath scared her more than any stalker.

She turned up her street and squinted at her sister's white Honda in the driveway outside their house. What was Anna doing here? *Right. Dang it.* Anna and her husband David were bringing David's sister over to meet the family. Apparently, the younger sister had gotten to be too much for the grandparents to handle, so she had come to live with her brother.

Brinnie wasn't in the mood to be polite and make friends. *But she's kind of like I was last summer, getting sent off to a relative's house to live. Of course, for me it wasn't permanent. And my parents are still alive.* Brinnie's need for space to think needed to take second place for now. She would have to be extra nice to the poor girl.

She took a deep breath, shoved down the stress of her latest escapade, and pushed open the front door with a smile on her face. But her expression froze when her eyes landed on the stranger inside.

There, shaking hands with her parents, was the girl she had almost stabbed.

CHAPTER TWO

"There you are, Brinnie." Anna switched little Isaac to her other hip and leaned toward Brinnie for an awkward hug around baby and backpack.

Brinnie returned the hug, pushing the door closed with her foot. She forced her gaze away from the girl standing in the front room next to David. The girl who had been at the end of her knife less than an hour ago. "Good to see you." She waved at the toddler on Anna's hip. "How's my favorite nephew?"

He grinned and reached for her. Anna handed him over, and Brinnie swooped Isaac around through the air, eliciting squeals of delight. She held him close, inhaling the sweet baby shampoo smell of the fourteen-month-old's golden curls. *Can I hide behind a baby and sneak out of here?*

She took a deep breath, shifting him to her hip. Isaac looked just like his beautiful mother. As usual, Anna was perfectly put together—honey-colored hair fashionably layered around her shoulders, flowy blue blouse matching a tasteful necklace. Confident, well-educated, successful.

And then there's me.

"Hey, Brinnie. This is my sister, Maddison." Anna's husband, David, wore his usual golden-retriever grin as he gestured to the vampire girl.

Brinnie set Isaac down to toddle back to his mother. Time to face the consequences of her actions. Hopefully Mom wouldn't kill her with everyone watching once the girl inevitably shared her near-death experience. Brinnie smiled and held out her hand, hoping it wasn't too sweaty. "Nice to meet you. I'm Brinnie."

Maddison raised an eyebrow as they shook hands. "Nice to meet you, too."

Nothing? No accusations? Brinnie's mind spun, searching for motives. Maddy's silence should have made her feel better, but her palms grew sweatier.

"You'll both be going to the same school," Anna put in, scooping up Isaac. "Maybe since Maddy missed the first month, you can introduce her to your friends and help her get settled."

Brinnie smiled. *Nope, nope, nope. Not happening.* "I'd love to, but I'm not sure how much that would help. You're a freshman this year, right?"

Maddy didn't break eye contact. "Yeah."

"There aren't a whole lot of classes with juniors and freshmen together. But you can hang out with us anyway, when you can."

Those owlish eyes narrowed, as if trying to figure out what Brinnie was up to. "Cool."

The men were already distracted. "So how about the game last night?" David asked Dad.

"Are you kidding me?" Dad grinned. That was his football face. *Oh boy.* "That was one heck of a throw."

Mom leaned over to Brinnie. "If you two want to go hang out, you can go ahead. You know, if you don't want to relive the game play by play."

Brinnie laughed, internally computing how she could avoid being alone with Maddy. Or maybe this was what she needed—a chance to hash things out, convince her not to tell. "Okay." She turned to the girl. "Come on, we can hang out in my room."

Brinnie had no sooner flicked on the light and dumped her backpack by the door than Maddy faced her with crossed arms and demanded, "What is wrong with you?"

Calm. Composure. Her gaze flicked from Maddy, to her own unmade bed—whoops—to her bookshelf, desk, and dresser that were luckily in order. "Is this about the knife thing?" *The "knife thing"? You mean when you nearly stabbed her?* "I got a little, uh, jumpy. I had no idea who you were. I'm sorry."

Maddy gave her a long, hard look Brinnie couldn't decipher. Then she backed up and plopped into Brinnie's desk chair. "Okay. You're crazy, though."

Just "okay"? Is that an "okay" of plotting my demise, or an "okay" of a person crazy enough to accept that I just casually had a knife? She eased into the next point. "Possibly, can we not tell my parents—or your brother—about this?"

She shrugged. "Sure."

Brinnie blinked. "'Sure'?"

"Yeah." She pushed the rolling chair away from the desk and spun it in a circle. "David said you were weird."

"He did?" Fantastic. Good to know her brother-in-law had such a high opinion of her that he felt the need to warn his sister.

"Yeah. He said you were nice, though." She looked around. "Nice room."

Oh, good, I'm a nice weirdo. She perched on the end of her bed. "Thanks."

"So you carry a knife around. That's kind of cool. Are you a zombie apocalypse nerd or something?"

Kind of cool? "Um, no."

Maddy fiddled with a charm on her black choker. "I had a friend back in Colorado who was obsessed with zombies. He had a giant stockpile for the apocalypse."

"Interesting." With Maddy's assurances of secrecy, Brinnie's heartrate had finally begun to slow, but she still needed to bring the topic of conversation around to safer waters. Away from knives. "So what do you like to do?"

"I study the supernatural." She kicked her legs, sending the chair spinning again. "Mostly vampires, aliens, that sort of thing."

Apparently, hobbies were *not* a safer topic. "Ah. Neat."

"Yeah. What about you?"

She shrugged. "I like to read. I'm not really that interesting."

Maddy crossed her legs in the chair and looked Brinnie up and down. "I think you're pretty interesting. You've got that look to you."

"What look?"

"I don't know. The intriguing look. Like that guy in Nevada." She leaned forward, lowering her voice. "I'm ninety percent sure he was a werewolf."

A little over a year ago, Brinnie would have dismissed Maddy as crazy. Now, she wondered if an ability akin to werewolves indeed existed. "Cool."

"Yeah." Maddy spun around again, making Brinnie dizzy. "What's this?" She reached up and grabbed a small object off the bookshelf from where it was nestled on a padded box with the books.

Brinnie sprang up, barely restraining herself from snatching it away. "It's nothing. But it's kind of fragile."

"Where'd you get it?" Maddy held up the marble-like orb between her forefinger and thumb so it caught the light.

Why? Why is that the first thing she found? "My uncle gave it to me."

"Neat." Maddy rolled the sphere between her fingers.

Brinnie flinched. "It's kind of special to me, so . . ."

Maddy could not take a hint. She squinted at the swirling mist. "What's that stuff inside it?"

"I don't know." *Put it down, put it down, put it down.* Visions of the orb shattering spun through her mind.

"What's so special about it, then?"

Brinnie took a deep breath. "It was the last thing my uncle gave me."

Maddy's eyes snapped up from the orb. "Oh. I'm sorry." She eased it back onto the shelf, placing it in the box. "How long ago?"

"That he gave it to me? A year, last month." *A full year.* Her chest squeezed.

Maddy nodded. "It's hard, thinking you won't see them again, isn't it?"

She winced. *Way to go, Brinnie.* She'd made it sound like he was dead, probably bringing up terrible memories for Maddy.

Although, she would never know if anything had happened to him. If the Maze had failed, or enemies had returned, or . . . She bit her lip. He might as well be dead to her. "He said we'd see each other again—in this world, or the next."

Maddy's gaze lowered. A line of tension appeared between her brows. "That's a nice thought."

How long ago had David lost his mom? Six years? Seven? And Brinnie knew his father had passed before that. It hadn't seemed important until now to know the exact timing. "So, do you want to see if my mom and Anna want to play cards?"

The vulnerability on Maddy's face evaporated. She smiled, but now, Brinnie suspected how much of it was a mask. *We're all hiding something.*

"Sure." Maddy hopped up. "But we better be on the same team."

"I know you're in here, Brinnie."

Brinnie sighed and waved away the shadows. So much for pretending the room was empty.

Sometimes she got away with it—reading in the dark, invisible—when she wanted to be alone. There was something comforting about sitting in bed propped up by pillows, covered in blankets both physical and ethereal, losing herself in a story where everything always worked out in the end.

She set down her book and focused on Mom standing in the doorway. "Yes?"

Mom's jaw tightened, holding back a scolding. *Surprising that she is.* Mom's ban against magic of any sort trumped all house rules.

Instead, her mother flicked on the light, stepped in, and shut the door. "What's wrong? You were on edge the entire time Anna and David were here."

Brinnie fiddled with the pages of her book. "I was fine."

"Did you not get along with Maddy?"

She took a deep breath, opting for honesty. "We got along fine. Maddy is just very . . . inquisitive." She uncurled her fingers, revealing the orb clenched there. Her only memento from Wraithwood. "I miss them."

Mom didn't ask who she meant. "It's for the best."

For the best. Always for the best. Brinnie looked up and met her mother's bright blue eyes, the mirror to her own. "I've tried so hard this past year."

"And you're doing well." Mom strode to the bed and put a hand on Brinnie's shoulder. "You've made some friends. You're a straight-A student. And you've only had a few slip-ups."

Slip-ups. Meaning times she used magic. *She means well. She's trying to protect us.* But the words escaped anyway. "Don't you ever wish you could just be who you are?"

Any softness in Mom's expression vanished. "No." Her irises glinted like ice, and she removed her hand from Brinnie's shoulder. "Never. Brynna, I know that was a hard summer for you. But you need to move on. This is your life."

Move on. This is your life.

In that moment, she decided not to tell Mom about what she had felt earlier that day. The last thing she needed was her mother worrying and pestering her about being more careful, looking out for herself, avoiding magic at all costs. "I know."

Mom smiled. "Remember the five rules?"

She held back an eye roll. "Lights on, sleeves down, stay visible, no helping, and don't play with shadows," she recited. "Got it."

"Right." Mom kissed her on the top of her head. "Goodnight. Try to get some sleep."

"Goodnight." As Mom closed the door behind her, Brinnie scowled. *Thanks for turning the lights out.*

She stomped to the wall and flipped the light switch off. For sleep, she was allowed to violate rule one—lights on. No one could suspect she had perfect night vision. She returned the orb to its spot on the shelf and flopped back into bed. She plucked at her pajamas, long sleeves despite the early September heat. Rule two—sleeves down. Hide the scar.

Rebellion surged within her, hot like her body temperature. She whipped off the stifling shirt and yanked on a tank top from the dresser beside her bed. Might as well break some more rules. *Goodbye, rule three.* She turned invisible and wrapped herself in a cloak of cool shadows.

It had been a shock, when she first returned home. She'd felt that after saving the world, something would be different. But it wasn't. No one had any idea how close they had been to destruction. Humanity around her went about their lives, completely unaware of everything her family had sacrificed to ensure that they could live another day. And that was the way it had to stay.

She snuggled deeper under the covers. She could accept that. She could accept a thankless job, and a hard one.

But all the pretending proved harder. Surface friendships, based on casual interaction, maybe some mutual book interests. She kept her distance. No sports, so adrenaline wouldn't lead her to accidentally unleash her power. She avoided sleepovers, fearing she would wake up invisible. And of course, even at home she struggled to hide her magical scar from her own father.

It had become second nature, now, to follow Mom's five rules, and to keep one eye out for enemies. She shouldn't be bothered by it anymore.

No such luck. Maybe because of her scar tingling, or because of Maddy's prying, or both, she missed Wraithwood. Loneliness ached in her chest.

Might as well break rule five, too.

Gathering the shadows with her mind, she worked them into the form of a dog. She focused on an image of her uncle's dog, Bruno, crafting his floppy ears and thumping tail. She patted the bed, and the dog jumped up beside her. She wrapped her arms around the shadowy creature and imagined its soft fur, basking in the comforting sense of company. The dog licked her chin, and for a moment she let go of the rational thoughts telling her this was merely a form created by her own imagination and brought to life by the power of suggestion. She imagined she was at Wraithwood, snuggling Bruno, and tomorrow she would awake to Mrs. Winslow cooking a ridiculously large breakfast. Maybe Quentin would have had a mishap and sent books flying around the library, or Marcie would want to practice Shakespeare, or Uncle Merlin might invite her to a game of Wizard's Chess.

She fell asleep with the shadow dog nestled by her side, a smile on her lips.

"Brynna Gwynneth!"

Brinnie bolted upright and snapped to visibility.

Mom stood at the foot of her bed, hands on her hips. "What is this?"

Brinnie looked down at her creation. It cocked its head at her, tongue lolling. "A dog."

"Don't have an attitude with me." Mom's jaw clenched. She waved her hand at the ephemeral creature, fingers passing straight through, as if she attempted to fan away smoke. "Get rid of it, now."

Brinnie raised her hand to disperse the shadows, but looking at the dog's bright eyes and panting tongue . . . "Could I keep it?"

"Brynna Lane."

She sighed and waved her companion into mist.

Mom stalked away and closed the bedroom door. Then she turned to Brinnie. "Young lady, this is getting out of hand. I gave you grace at first, while you were learning to control yourself, but now you're doing it deliberately. This has to stop. There will be absolutely no magic in this house."

"I'm sorry." She hugged her knees, trying to keep calm, to refrain from snarky comebacks. "I know I'm supposed to leave the shadows alone." *Keep your mouth shut. Don't say it.* "But I'm a shadowmaster. It's like telling a fish to stay out of the water."

A range of emotion played across Mom's face—anger, annoyance, fear, regret, resignation. She sighed and sat at the foot of the bed. "I know. I thought it would be impossible to leave ice and snow alone. But I've done it for years, and now it doesn't even occur to me to use magic." She fixed Brinnie with a hard look. "You can do it, too. Thinking about it and using magic in secret will only make it harder. You have to realize some hard truths. You don't live in a magical world anymore, and you never will." She pinched the bridge of her nose, closing her eyes. "Please. You need to forget that place. We can't . . ." She faltered. "We can't let it take away any more of our lives than it already has."

That place. Mom couldn't even bring herself to say the word Wraithwood. Brinnie forced herself to understand. Wraithwood, though freedom to her, served as a constant reminder of loss to Mom. A place of danger.

Brinnie inhaled, exhaled. "You're right." She slid off the bed and strode to her shelf. She picked up the orb in the nest she'd made for it and placed them in a desk drawer, out of sight. She shut the drawer. "No more magic."

She turned to see the relief in her mother's eyes. "Thank you. Now, you better get ready for school."

"But some people say that vampires actually suck the life force, not the blood of the victim. And—"

Isabel looked at Brinnie with wide eyes, as if to say, *Is this girl for real?*

Brinnie grimaced. *I'm sorry.* She had done the nice thing and introduced Maddy to a couple of friends, but the girl had spent the entire lunch period discussing the finer points of vampire diets.

Brinnie tried to focus on her lunch. She had a few bites of turkey and cheese sandwich and a few tortilla chips left. With luck, this ordeal would end soon.

Maddy ripped open her pudding cup without missing a beat. "Personally, I'm not sure vampires have victims at all. I think they might eat regular food. They're just immortal creatures that look like humans." She pointed her spork in Brinnie's direction. "You're kind of confirming that theory for me, Brinnie."

Brinnie choked on a mouthful of sandwich. "Me?"

Maddy ticked off points on her fingers. "You don't suck blood, or have fangs, and I'm pretty sure you don't have victims. You're too nice."

Her friends laughed, but Brinnie saw the earnest light in Maddy's eyes. *Someone save me.* "Just don't put a stake through my heart, okay?"

Why did it always have to be vampires? If she had to be mistaken for a mythical creature, an elf or fairy or something pretty and nice would be preferable. *Although I guess vampire is better than werewolf.* She suppressed a smile at that. She reached for another tortilla chip and coolness ran over her upper arm.

She froze, scanning the cafeteria.

Laughing and shouting teenagers crowded the long tables, most sitting, a few wandering to throw away trash or chat. She didn't see anyone unusual, but she felt far too exposed sitting in the middle of the room. Why did her friend group always insist on a middle table?

She stood and grabbed her tray. "Hey, I gotta run. I'll catch you guys later, okay?"

Without waiting for a reply, she went to put her tray in the receptacle, trying to act natural. Her arm burned cooler. They had to be close.

But who? She scanned the room again. How could she run if she didn't know who to run *from*?

She stepped out into the hall through the open doors leading to the cafeteria. Her gaze was immediately arrested by a tall man wearing a visitor's tag clipped to a leather jacket that seemed incredibly impractical for the weather. He towered over a staff member and rumbled a question Brinnie couldn't hear.

The middle-aged woman's eyebrows scrunched. She cocked her head, as if puzzled by his query. She wrung her hands, a fidgeting ball of anxiety before his rigid, militaristic stance, but he hardly seemed to notice her as his eyes roamed the corridor.

That's him.

As his head began to turn in her direction, Brinnie grabbed the nearest shadows and yanked them over herself. His eyes passed over her, then he returned his attention to the woman, offering a semblance of a pleasant smile.

Still invisible, Brinnie ducked back around the corner. She pressed herself against the wall, heart galloping.

After over a year, they'd done it.

They'd found her.

CHAPTER
THREE

Just around the corner stood exactly what Mom, what her uncle, what everyone had feared. *Focus, Brinnie.* Her cover wasn't completely blown—not yet.

Letting go of the shadows, she pulled out her phone.

"What was that?"

Brinnie jumped. None other than Maddy stood a few paces back, staring at her.

This girl. Brinnie couldn't think of a good response. "What was what?"

"You appeared out of nowhere. You were totally invisible!" Maddy squawked.

Brinnie cringed. "Please, lower your voice."

The squawking continued. "That was—"

She clapped a hand over Maddy's mouth, then instantly felt guilty. "I'm sorry. But you *have* to be quiet."

Maddy's eyes bugged.

Brinnie peeked around the corner. The man was still talking, for now. She glanced the other direction, where doors led to the outside. *That will work.* "Hey, Maddy?"

"Mmph?"

"Go back to the cafeteria."

She let go of Maddy and fled.

The doors swung open to a blast of hot desert air as she stepped out into the courtyard. She slipped around the side of the building, leaning against the wall.

The doors rattled open again. Brinnie felt magic tingling in her fingers, ready to fight. Slowly, she peered around the corner.

And stifled a groan. *Fantastic.*

Maddy, standing in the doorway, spotted her and scurried to her side. "How did you *do* that? What are you?" Her mouth formed an "o" and she pressed herself against the wall, lowering her voice to a whisper. "Are you hiding from something?"

Brinnie pulled her phone from her pocket and began dialing. She forced her fingers not to shake. This girl wasn't helping her stress levels. "Maddy, I'm kind of busy. You must have been seeing things. People don't turn invisible."

"But you did!" She bounced, short hair bobbing. "How? Could I learn? Are you a vampire? Or are you something else?"

Brinnie elected not to shake her brother-in-law's sister, tempting as it was, and instead held the phone up to her ear. "Not now."

It rang a few times before a deep voice responded. "Hello?"

She tensed. Not what she was expecting. "Dad? What are you doing home?"

"Forgot my lunch this morning. What's up?"

She glanced toward the door before striding across the courtyard and ducking behind another building out of sight, positioning herself so that she could watch the door in case the man came after her. Maddy trailed her like a pesky shadow—unfortunately one she couldn't control. "Is Mom home?"

"No, she's at Anna's, watching Isaac. Will your old man do?"

"Um, I kind of have a question for Mom."

Just then, the doors opened, and the man's broad shoulders filled the doorway. His eyes scanned the courtyard. Brinnie ducked out of view. "Actually, yes. I'm feeling pretty sick. Can you come get me?"

"I'm sorry, Brin. Did you go see the nurse?"

She chanced another look around the corner. The man glanced inside his jacket, and for a moment Brinnie glimpsed a long, metal object. "Um, yeah, she said I'm supposed to go home."

"Okay, kiddo, well, I have patients scheduled in half an hour, so I have to get back to work, but I'll give your mother a call. It might take her a little while to get over there from David and Anna's, though."

Brinnie retreated farther around the building. "I kind of need to go home now."

Maddy tried to peer around the corner. Brinnie yanked her back, giving her a glare she hoped conveyed *don't you dare get me caught.*

"I'm sorry, Brin. Ask the nurse for a place to lie down. She won't be too long."

Brinnie took one last peek and saw the man striding purposefully across the courtyard. Straight for her hiding place. "No, Dad, really. I need to leave. Now."

His voice grew serious. "You're not sick. What's happening?"

She couldn't keep up this conversation, these lies, and evade the man at the same time. "Just come get me. Fast."

She hung up and slid the phone back in her pocket. Keeping her back to the rough brick of the building, she rounded the next corner and ducked inside the first door she came across.

Maddy followed, sliding along the wall like a spy in a bad action movie. "What's going on?"

Brinnie clenched her jaw. "Go back to the cafeteria."

"What are you running from?"

Brinnie was contemplating whether it was possible, and not completely unethical, to tie Maddy up in a corner with shadows when the bell rang and the hall began to flood with students.

Maybe Maddy would be useful after all. "Do you want to help?" Brinnie whispered.

Maddy's head shot up and down.

"Good. Stand in front of me," Brinnie directed, pulling Maddy in front of her. She pressed against the wall and turned invisible, relying on Maddy to keep anyone from running straight into her. "Listen," she said in barely a whisper, "this isn't a game. There's a man out there who either wants to kill me or kidnap me—and I don't really want to experience either. He isn't after you, but there could be . . . collateral damage."

Rather than sober up, Maddy bounced on her toes with excitement. "So why don't you tell someone? A teacher?"

"Shh, you look like you're talking to yourself." Brinnie gritted her teeth. "I can't tell anyone, and I can't tell you why. You'll have to trust me for now."

Her attention turned to the door. The man in the leather jacket darkened the doorway, wading through the crowd, head and shoulders above the students. *Think. Where can you hide? Where can't he follow?*

Her frantic gaze landed on the sign for the restroom. *Perfect.* "Start walking toward the bathroom. I'll be right behind you. We'll hide in there until my dad comes."

"Ten-four," Maddy stage whispered.

Brinnie pressed against Maddy's back and they joined the crowd. An elbow connected with Brinnie's side, and more than one backpack made impact, but luckily the hall was so crowded that nobody seemed to notice they had bumped into empty space.

Finally, Maddy pulled open the heavy door to the ladies' room. After one girl exited, Maddy and Brinnie slipped inside.

The man wouldn't dare come after them here, or he would blow his cover.

I hope.

Brinnie took in their surroundings. The stall doors hung open, miraculously unoccupied. Before anyone else could enter, Brinnie returned to visibility. "Thank you. You can go to class now."

Maddy whipped around to face her, no longer staring at a blank wall. "No way. I've got to help you."

Give me patience. "I appreciate the thought, but I can take care of myself. You're going to be late."

"I don't care." Maddy gripped Brinnie's shoulders. "You've got to tell me. What are you? If you're not a vampire, are you a ghost?"

Brinnie couldn't keep the look of disbelief off her face. "If I were a ghost, why would I be concerned about someone trying to kill me?" She went silent as a girl entered the bathroom and shuffled into one of the stalls. Then she whispered, "Forget all about this, okay? Trust me, you don't want to get involved."

"But I do!" Maddy threw up an arm dramatically. "I've spent most of my life searching for something like this. Just tell me. I won't tell anyone."

"No."

She crossed her arms. "If you won't tell me, I'll tell your family that you threatened me with a knife and that you're running from a killer at school. I'll tell your parents, and your sister, and—"

"I get the point," Brinnie growled, glancing toward the occupied stall. *Hopefully she didn't hear that.* Hiding for her life, and this was what she had to deal with.

Maddy pushed up her glasses. "So at least tell me this—are you human?"

Brinnie glanced again at the stall. Maybe a tidbit of information would get Maddy off her case. And who would believe Maddy anyway? She leaned forward. "Promise you won't tell my family anything?"

"Yes."

Brinnie took a deep breath. "No. I'm not."

The words felt strange on her tongue. *Not human, not human, not human.* An anomaly. A danger to her family. The daughter who wasn't supposed to exist.

Her phone buzzed, interrupting her thoughts. She glanced at the screen. "My dad is outside." She hesitated. If Maddy refused to go back to class anyway . . . "Feel up to helping me one more time?"

Brinnie turned invisible once more and shadowed Maddy. The stream of traffic began to die down as students hurried to make it to their next class. The man stood in the hallway, pretending to look at a bulletin board, but his hand rested inside his jacket. Brinnie's heart pounded as Maddy walked by with exaggerated nonchalance and opened the door, stepping outside. It almost clipped Brinnie as it closed.

Maddy didn't stop until they'd reached the middle of the courtyard. Then she turned toward Brinnie's general direction. "How are you going to get out of the school?"

"Behind Building E. There's a fence that's pretty easy to hop." She put a hand on Maddy's shoulder, remaining invisible. The girl had proved helpful after all. She felt a twinge of guilt for her earlier uncharitable thoughts. "Thanks for the cover. Go to class and act normal. With luck, I'll see you tomorrow." She knew that was a slim hope, but she couldn't face the ramifications of her situation right now.

Something thudded behind her. Brinnie pivoted, heart sinking as the door swung open and the man stepped out. He pulled a long, glowing blade out of his jacket and balanced it on his hand.

It pointed directly at Brinnie and Maddy.

He looked at Maddy and grinned. "I've found you, shadow walker."

Oh, no.

Maddy's head cocked. "What? I'm—"

"Come on." Brinnie grabbed her wrist and towed her in a headlong run toward Building E.

Their feet slapped the concrete in a spastic rhythm as Maddy nearly tripped. "What are you doing?" she squeaked.

"He thinks you're me." Brinnie dragged her around the corner of Building E and slid to a halt in front of the chain-link fence. She shoved Maddy forward. "Climb it."

"I can't—"

"Just do it."

Brinnie spun, not waiting to see if Maddy obeyed. She settled into a defensive position, facing the man as he rounded the corner. "You're chasing the wrong person!"

He stopped, scanning the fence, the ground, adjusting his grip on the knife. "Don't play games with me, shadow walker. Show yourself."

The fence rattled behind her. If she could stall him long enough, maybe Maddy could get away, and then she could make a run for it as well, using invisibility to her advantage. "And why would I do that?" she taunted. "I think I have the upper hand here."

"I disagree." He reached inside his jacket, revealing another sheath. "Do it, or your human friend dies."

Brinnie glanced at Maddy, now over the fence, frozen and staring. *Run, you idiot.* "She doesn't know. You'll die, too."

"I don't believe you."

She faced him squarely, even though he couldn't see her, putting herself between him and Maddy. "It's the truth."

"I guess we'll find out." He flicked a small knife out of the sheath.

Great. Throwing knives. Did they all take the same how-to-throw-knives classes? Brinnie braced, ready to shield Maddy with her own body if she had to. She'd taken a knife before.

And nearly died.

The man pulled back his arm.

And from somewhere behind Brinnie, a ball of fire blasted toward him.

CHAPTER FOUR

Brinnie felt the heat as the fireball soared past her and exploded toward the attacker. He raised his hands, dropping the knife, and barely managed to deflect it with a burst of water in the shape of a protective shield.

Brinnie spun around to see a tall, broad-shouldered man with fiery eyes standing on the other side of the fence, arms outstretched, palms forward, like some sort of avenging Greek god—a god wearing khaki pants and a dorky button-down shirt dotted with tiny palm trees.

Brinnie's mouth dropped open. "Dad?"

He kept one palm facing the man and gestured with his other arm. "Get over here. Maddy, run for that car. Now."

Maddy took off, shoes crunching on gravel, heading for the silver Toyota parked and running on the street, driver's door thrown open.

Brinnie didn't have time to question it. She leaped for the fence, pulling herself up the chain link.

Dad and the man faced each other from opposite sides of the fence. She heard her father say, "Okay, let's break this up. This is no place for a fight."

The man hissed and thrust out his arm, shooting water the strength of a fire hose toward Dad. He ducked out of the way, and Brinnie saw the man start aiming for her as she swung her legs over the top of the fence. Dad must have seen it too, because he whipped a stream of flames toward the man, melting a hole in the chain link. "Brynna, get in the car."

She dropped over the fence, barely landing on her feet. She didn't look back this time, focusing on keeping her footing in the gravel. Ahead, Maddy peered from the backseat, so Brinnie rounded the car for the passenger door. Footsteps pounded behind her once she hit asphalt, Dad on her tail. She reached the passenger side, yanked open the door, and jumped in.

A fraction of a second behind, Dad leaped into the open driver's seat. He threw the vehicle into drive while slamming the door. "Brinnie, are you in here?"

She shook off her shadows, breathing hard. "Yes."

He didn't even flinch at her sudden reappearance. "Good."

She barely had a chance to pull her door shut as he stepped on the gas and the car shot forward.

Brinnie craned her neck over the headrest, trying to catch a glimpse of the attacker. Instead, she only saw Maddy's pale face.

"Is he gone?" Maddy asked.

"No." Dad gripped the wheel and spun it, taking a corner hard.

Brinnie clutched the seat, sliding into a more reasonable position than backward. She'd better put on her seatbelt if Dad was going to drive like a maniac.

He glanced in the rearview mirror, then slowed to only five over the speed limit on the open road. "I would have taken him out, but I couldn't risk prolonging the battle. It's a wonder no one saw what *did* happen." He sighed and sank back into the seat. "But he can't catch us now while he's on foot." His eyes flicked to each of them. "Are you both okay?"

Brinnie's mouth opened and shut. *Okay?* Sure, not physically banged up, but . . . "Dad! What *was* that?"

He ran a hand through his dark hair and took a deep breath before flashing a guilty smile. "I guess the secret is out." He gave a weak chuckle. "You didn't think you got shadow walking from your mother's side, did you?"

Her mind spun. All this time. The hiding, the lying, the lengths Mom went to . . . Did Mom know? *She couldn't.* But he knew about Mom? Nothing made sense.

Instead of asking the more obvious questions, she managed, "You knew I'm a shadow walker?"

"I knew before your mother did." He rubbed his face, suddenly looking older. "Now, how did that man find you?"

Right. Questions later, surviving first. "There's an enchanted blade, and it's tied to a scar on my arm. If it's close enough, it points toward me."

"How close would that be?"

"About a hundred leagues."

She watched his face for any sign of surprise, fear, worry, but his expression didn't change. "Do you think he'll call for backup?" he asked.

"Probably." She winced. "For some reason, Mordred's kind of obsessed with me."

He didn't ask who Mordred was, but she couldn't tell whether that was because he already knew or because he considered the information irrelevant at the moment. "Then we need to get far away, and fast. Do you still have that portal in your room?"

Brinnie hung onto the armrest as he took a hard turn. "What portal?"

"The one Merlin gave you."

Brinnie's brow wrinkled. He hadn't given her anything—except the bauble she'd shut in a drawer earlier. "You mean the orb?"

"Yes." He flicked on his turn signal for another right.

It took a few seconds for her mind to catch up. "So it's a portal?" She knew Uncle Merlin wouldn't have given her a useless trinket, but she'd assumed it would become a map, or release a clue, or *something* a little less dramatic.

She should have known better with Uncle Merlin.

Maddy handling it last night flashed through her mind, and she cringed at the thought of the orb falling, smashing to the ground. She wasn't sure what a portal was exactly or how they worked, but breaking one couldn't be good. "He didn't tell me that."

"Typical," Dad muttered. At Brinnie's questioning look, he shook his head. "Sorry. He probably didn't want you to use it if it wasn't an emergency."

"Okay, time out," Maddy butted in. "What are you people?"

Brinnie glanced at Dad.

"Unfortunately, that man saw her face." Dad sighed. "She's implicated. If they're after you, they may go after her to find you. And with the right resources, knowing her school and appearance, it shouldn't be hard to figure out her identity. I'd rather risk her knowing."

Brinnie closed her eyes briefly. Another person in danger because of her. "Wizards. We're wizards."

Maddy opened her mouth, but Dad interrupted. "We'll explain more later." He pulled out his cell. *Not* a smartphone, Brinnie noted. An old version with a flip-out keyboard, like hers. Another sign she should have spotted. Wizards tended to kill technology, and the newer the tech, the worse the results. "I better call in," he said. "I'm not returning to work today."

A few minutes later, Dad pulled into the driveway, phone still to his ear, and the three of them got out. Maddy shut her door and bounced on the balls of her feet, eyes wide, but with the hint of a grin flickering across her face. Of course now she would be excited instead of afraid. Brinnie wished Maddy would swing back to terrified. At least then she might make fewer decisions out of rash curiosity. *You better not do anything stupid.*

"I know. I'm very sorry. It's a family emergency." Dad pressed his lips together in annoyance but kept an even tone. "Have the nurse practitioner see them. I need to go. Goodbye." He hung up and slipped the phone back in his pocket. "Okay, Brin, where's that portal?"

She led them through the house to her room. Part of her resisted the idea of smashing her one memento of Wraithwood. If there had been any other way she could think of to get one hundred leagues away fast enough that she couldn't be tracked, she would suggest it, but nothing came to mind.

She flicked on the light to her bedroom and reached for her shoulder out of habit, ready to sling her backpack to the floor, but the familiar weight was missing. In her rush, she'd left it in the cafeteria.

She wondered if she would ever see it again.

Maddy hovered over her shoulder as she opened her desk drawer and pulled out the orb. The mist within swirled as she rolled the marble-like sphere in her palm. "So, Uncle Merlin said to smash it. But then what?"

"It will take you to wherever it was enchanted to go," Dad explained from the doorway. "I don't know where for sure, but I would assume Wraithwood."

Wraithwood. Her heart thumped. She could see them all again. Miss Burtle would critique her dusting technique in the library, and Mrs. Winslow would show her how to bake a new kind of pie, and Ms. Tynsdale would crack some sort of wry joke at Quentin's expense while Mr. Winslow pretended not to chuckle, and Uncle Merlin might take her by door to some far-off locale . . .

Focus, Brinnie. "Okay. Guess we'll hope for the best that it's Wraithwood and not the middle of the Atlantic."

"You should grab a few supplies in case." Dad turned, talking over his shoulder. He paused. "That is, in case it isn't Wraithwood. If it's the Atlantic Ocean . . . Anyway, I'll grab some snacks."

Brinnie followed him out, heading for the hall closet where she could find an extra backpack.

Maddy hovered between the two of them. "What about me?"

Dad halted halfway to the kitchen. "I'll explain more to you once we get Brinnie out of here."

Brinnie cocked her head. "Just me? What about you two?"

"They're not necessarily after us."

She paused with one hand on the closet doorknob and one on her hip. "You threw fireballs at him."

A knock pounded on the front door.

Brinnie froze.

Maddy jumped, then clutched her glasses, paling. Her swings between elated and terrified were starting to make Brinnie concerned for her mental health. "What's that?" she squeaked.

The pounding resumed. "Open up, shadow walker!" a deep voice boomed.

A second voice joined him. "We know you're in there!"

"That's bad news," Dad whispered. "Both of you, to the kitchen."

Maddy seemed frozen in fear, so Brinnie grabbed her and dragged her along. When her feet hit the tile, perfect for smashing, she realized why Dad had called them to this room.

The time for packing and preparing had passed with at least two wizards at the door.

"Here it goes." She threw the orb against the floor.

Glass shattered, tiny shards flying. The strange mist from inside the orb rose and swirled around Brinnie, Maddy, and . . . where was Dad?

She whipped her head around, trying to see through the mist. He guarded the doorway leading to the front room.

"Dad, get closer!" Brinnie reached toward him. "You're out of range."

He glanced over his shoulder, then back at the front door. "I don't —" His words were cut off by a splintering sound.

"Come on!" Brinnie grabbed his arm. The mist thickened, swirling around the three of them, obscuring everything from view.

"What's happening?" Maddy's fingers dug into Brinnie's arm like talons.

Both arms occupied, Brinnie reached out with her foot, feeling for the kitchen counter that had been there seconds ago. Nothing. "Um, I think we're all kind of in the portal."

Though she was gripping Dad's arm, his voice seemed to float from far away. "Stay close and walk forward. It will eventually recede."

Brinnie shuffled forward, easing into each step, until her toes hit something hard. She lifted the arm Maddy clung to and ran her fingers over the surface. It felt like polished wood. She moved her hand along the grain until she hit something metal. She explored the object with her fingertips—a brass knocker. "I think it's a door."

"Affirmative," Maddy chirped. "I also feel a door."

"I guess I'll knock." She lifted the knocker and let it drop three times.

Dad cleared his throat. "Just, ah, so you know—" he began.

But at that moment, the door in front of them swung inward, revealing high ceilings, a massive staircase, glossy polished wood—and a lanky man with a red-blond moustache and sparkling blue eyes.

Brinnie's heart caught in her throat. "Uncle Merlin!"

CHAPTER FIVE

Brinnie took two steps forward and threw her arms around her uncle.

"Brynna!" He caught her in a hug with a delighted chuckle. She inhaled the muted scent of his cologne as her cheek pressed into the soft fabric of his shirt. She could feel the vibrations of Wraithwood's magic on her skin, the hum of his familiar power. *Home,* a voice in her mind sighed. *Home, home, home.*

She pulled back. A smile danced in his eyes before his countenance morphed to concern. "If you're here . . ." He let go of her, all business and poise, his attention turning to the doorway. "Everyone, come in."

Maddy stepped through the door and promptly fainted face-first onto the hardwood floor of the great hall.

"Oh, dear." Uncle Merlin knelt. "She's human, isn't she?"

Brinnie rolled Maddy over onto her back. Remarkably, her glasses hadn't snapped. Nothing looked bruised or broken, but her eyes remained closed. "Yes. Is she okay?"

"She will be, as long as she's never done this before." Uncle Merlin felt her pulse. "A portal's the same as the Door. Humans aren't meant to travel by magic. Eventually they fall to pieces."

A quiet cough drew their attention back to the doorway. Dad stood outside in the mist, thumbs hooked awkwardly on his belt loops. "Pardon. I can't come in."

Uncle Merlin gave him a questioning look. "All humans are under blanket invitation."

Under blanket invitation. No one could get into Wraithwood without the invitation of the Master. A peace settled on her shoulders. Once last summer, Uncle Merlin had called Wraithwood the safest place in the world. Now, even with protection spells restored for estates around the globe, Brinnie couldn't help but think it remained true.

"So, it turns out he's not human," Brinnie explained.

Uncle Merlin's eyebrows shot up. He stood and adjusted his vest. "Well. Then, in that case, Andrew Lane, you are a welcome guest at Wraithwood Estate."

Dad took one tentative step forward but jolted as if stopped by an invisible wall. He grimaced.

Uncle Merlin frowned. "That's not your real name?"

Dad hesitated. For a moment, it almost seemed he would back away into the mist rather than answer the question. "No. It's . . . Antony Drakon."

Uncle Merlin's face drained of color.

Drakon. Brinnie tried to place the name, but she couldn't concentrate as the mist beyond the door began to fade. "Uncle Merlin, quick—it's closing."

For one horrible moment, he hesitated. Then, teeth clenched, he growled, "Antony Drakon, you are a welcome guest at Wraithwood Estate."

Dad stepped across the threshold, and the mist faded behind him. Beyond the door, the circular drive and hedges of Wraithwood came into focus, revealing a cloudy day.

"Thank you, Merlin. I—"

Uncle Merlin held up a hand to stop him, his jaw set. "Don't thank me yet." He jerked his head toward Brinnie. "You're still alive because of her—and because I want answers."

Brinnie gaped, ready to ask Uncle Merlin what on earth he was thinking, but Dad nodded stiffly. "I appreciate it."

Uncle Merlin's eyes that had sparkled moments before upon seeing Brinnie now held only ice. "Remember that you're on my estate, Drakon. Step out of line and I won't hesitate to end you—instantly."

Before Brinnie could demand answers, the dining room doors burst open. A familiar motherly form shuffled through, brushing her hands on her apron. She stopped in her tracks when she saw Brinnie, her hands flying to her mouth. "Brinnie! Is it really you?"

Thoughts of whatever glaring contest Dad and Uncle Merlin were locked in flew from her mind. "Mrs. Winslow!" Brinnie shot to her feet from her position beside Maddy and ran to wrap the housekeeper in a hug. "It's so good to see you."

"And to see you, dear."

Brinnie relaxed in Mrs. Winslow's warm, soft embrace. Tears pricked her eyes, but she held them back. The scent of cookies that always clung to Mrs. Winslow wrapped her in a secondary aromatic hug.

Mrs. Winslow held her out at arm's length. "Look at you! Sixteen, now? So beautiful and all grown up."

She felt her cheeks warm and forced herself to focus on the issue at hand. "Um, my friend—"

Mrs. Winslow peered past her toward where Dad knelt, reaching to lift an unconscious Maddy. "Oh, my! Is the poor dear all right?"

Uncle Merlin waved Dad away and muttered something that made him flinch. Uncle Merlin scooped her up instead.

What is wrong with those two?

Brinnie returned her attention to the question. "She's human, and we just came through a portal."

"Oh, a nasty feeling, I can tell you that, but nothing some hot tea can't fix, as long as it's her first time." Mrs. Winslow waved to the two men. "Come in, everyone, come to the kitchen. Shame on you, Merlin, leaving them all in the doorway."

His expression softened, and he smiled slightly. "Let's see if we can revive this girl. I suspect you have something in there to help."

Despite having fled from a dark wizard only moments before, Brinnie couldn't keep the grin off her face. Wraithwood was exactly as she remembered it. Every cornice and ornament in the wood felt familiar. As they passed through the dining room, where magic flickered in the chandelier, lighting the massive table, memories flitted through her mind like doves excited to take roost.

First through the door on the other side of the dining room, Brinnie stepped into the cozy kitchen with a small, crackling fire. Her gaze landed on a young man near the cupboards, his forearm buried in a porcelain jar. "Quentin!"

He snatched his hand out of the jar, dropping a cookie in the process, and spun toward her voice. "Brinnie?"

Mrs. Winslow bustled past Brinnie, pulling a wooden spoon out of her apron pocket and wagging it at him. "You stay out of my cookie jar, young man. You're the reason we never have any left after supper."

He hardly seemed to hear, still staring at Brinnie. "You look different. I mean, not in a bad way. I mean, it's great to see you. Um, what are you doing here?"

"A very good question, and one that hasn't been answered yet," Uncle Merlin observed. Brinnie stepped aside, and he settled an unconscious Maddy into a chair in the corner, propping her feet on the table and resting her head against the high back.

"One of Mordred's men found me." Brinnie scooted farther out of the way to make room for Dad to enter, shooting a questioning look at him as he hugged the wall, looking ill. "He had the blade. We had to get out of range, and the easiest way was by portal."

Uncle Merlin frowned, placing the back of his hand against Maddy's forehead. "That's unfortunate, but I suspected as much. A lot has happened since you left."

"But there's time enough for that later." Mrs. Winslow pulled open a drawer. "First, let's get this poor girl back to her senses. Where did I put the smelling salts?"

Within a few moments of administering the salts, Mrs. Winslow had Maddy awake. Maddy sat up, groaning and rubbing her head. "That was the worst thing I've ever felt." Her grimace morphed into a grin. "But it was awesome! We totally teleported!"

"Oh, wonderful, just what we needed," a dry voice said behind Brinnie. "Another Quentin."

Brinnie whirled toward the doorway to the dining room to see a familiar severe-looking woman. "Miss Burtle!"

"Indeed." She quirked an eyebrow. "And it appears the bookworm is back to mess up my library again."

Brinnie wrapped her in a hug. "Good to see you, too."

Miss Burtle stiffly tolerated the hug for a few seconds before waving her off. "Enough of that."

"Where are we?" Maddy asked.

"Wraithwood Estate." Brinnie spread out an arm in a grandiose gesture. She nodded to her uncle. "This is my uncle, Merlin. He owns the place."

"Sweet." Maddy tilted her head and blinked like an owl. "Are you a wizard, too?"

His moustache twitched. "Indeed."

She took in the crowded kitchen with wide eyes. "So, like, is everyone here a wizard?"

"Dear me, not everyone." Mrs. Winslow chuckled and waved a hand toward Miss Burtle. "Edna and I are human. I'm Mrs. Winslow. And who are you?"

Her gaze continued to rove the kitchen. "My name's Maddison, but everyone calls me Maddy. My brother married Brinnie's sister, so I guess we're kind of cousins."

Brinnie raised an eyebrow. "Not sure that's exactly how it works."

"Well, dear, how would you like some hot tea?" Mrs. Winslow patted Maddy's shoulder. "I know portals can be a bit uncomfortable."

"Yes, please." As Mrs. Winslow headed for the kettle, Maddy tilted her head upward. "Whoa! Is that magic, too?"

Brinnie glanced up at the bright orb floating near the ceiling, giving light to the room.

Quentin puffed up with knowledge. "Right. Wraithwood Estate lacks electricity, so we use magic." He bobbed his head. "Quentin, by the way. Uh, also a wizard."

"So cool." She pulled her feet down from the table and leaned forward. "I can't wait to write all this down in my Supernatural Sightings Compendium."

"Your what?"

Brinnie rubbed her forehead with her thumb. "That vampire-sticker binder. Of course."

Uncle Merlin frowned at Maddy. "You will not write any of this down if you value your life."

She put her hands up. "Are you threatening to kill me?"

Miss Burtle crossed her arms. "Threatening guests. A bit dramatic."

"*I'm* not threatening her, Edna." Uncle Merlin gave her a longsuffering look, eliciting as much of a smirk as Miss Burtle was likely to show. He turned back to Maddy. "I'm telling you what will happen if the dark wizards find out that you are associated with us."

He shot a glance at Dad. "They don't care if you're actually an enemy or not—they'll kill anyone."

Dad opened his mouth, but snapped it shut again, jaw tight.

"Take this, dear." Mrs. Winslow carried a mug to Maddy, steam wafting behind her, and set it on the table beside the girl. She headed back toward the stove. "I'll get mugs for everyone else, too. Now, Merlin, are you going to introduce our other guest?" She smiled at Dad.

Before Uncle Merlin could answer, a red-haired young woman stepped into the kitchen from the opposite entrance near the stairs. She halted, blinking. "What?"

"Marcie!" Brinnie swept her into a hug. *I've given more hugs in the past twenty minutes than the entire last year.* If she didn't watch out, she might become a hugger. "It's great to see you again."

Marcie clasped Brinnie's arms, smiling. "You too! But what, I mean, how—"

"A portal," Brinnie explained. She tugged Marcie toward the table. "Come join us."

"I can't." She looked over Brinnie's shoulder at Uncle Merlin. "She's awake."

He immediately disappeared.

Marcie patted her arm. "Don't worry, I can't wait to catch up. I'll be back in a moment." She ducked back toward the stairs, footsteps thumping on the steps.

Brinnie turned and focused her attention on Mrs. Winslow, who was pouring tea from the kettle into a teapot for the table with more concentration than the task warranted. Brinnie wrinkled her brow. "What's going on?"

Mrs. Winslow frowned, slowly setting the lid on the teapot and reaching into the cupboard for mugs. "It's Lydia Tynsdale, dear. They discovered her while she was spying at Mordizan. They decided to make an example of her."

"And?" Her heart thudded as she glanced around the room at the thin line of Miss Burtle's lips and Quentin's uncomfortable expression. "What happened?"

Mrs. Winslow hesitated, so Miss Burtle looked up at the ceiling and supplied, "They sent her mangled body to Castelon as a warning."

A mug clattered from Mrs. Winslow's hands onto the counter. "Edna!"

"I'm stating the facts."

"Is she dead?" Brinnie broke in.

"No, dear. Not quite. But." Mrs. Winslow fiddled with her apron. "She isn't doing well."

Brinnie's gut clenched. Her gaze met Dad's, and he looked away, expression pained. "So she's upstairs? Can I see her?"

The two women looked at each other. Mrs. Winslow spoke first. "Probably not a good idea, dear."

Miss Burtle frowned. "Her mind is in as poor of shape as the rest of her."

"She's gone mad," Quentin blurted.

Brinnie looked from one to another, blocking out Maddy's open stares and Dad's tense stance. Those were problems she could deal with later. "Uncle Merlin said a lot has happened. He didn't just mean Ms. Tynsdale, did he?"

Mrs. Winslow sighed. "No, dear. We've always been fighting. But now . . . well, you might say it's a full-fledged war."

CHAPTER SIX

At that moment, Maddy's mug crashed to the floor, shattering as she slumped forward.

Brinnie jumped toward her, grabbing one shoulder while Quentin grabbed the other, barely in time to keep Maddy from falling on her face. Brinnie leaned the limp girl against the seatback. "Is that normal?"

Miss Burtle pursed her lips. "She's human with no magic to protect her. Her molecules were thrown apart, transferred over a warp in space and time, and forced to come back together again. She's going to be having issues for the next couple of days, at least."

Brinnie winced. "Ouch."

Mrs. Winslow dabbed spilled tea from Maddy's lap with a dish towel. "We should really get her settled upstairs in a bed rather than a hard chair."

Dad pushed off the wall. "I can carry her." He slid one arm beneath her knees and another behind her shoulders and lifted. "Lead the way."

Mrs. Winslow gestured toward the stairs. "I'll show you to the guest room."

Brinnie watched them leave but didn't follow. Instead, she turned to Miss Burtle. "I know you won't waste time softening the blow. What's the situation?"

"I would tell you too," Quentin complained, opening the cookie jar again.

"And probably get the details confused." Miss Burtle gave him a disdainful look before returning her attention to Brinnie. She ticked off points on her fingers. "Mordred has grown more powerful. We haven't been able to get the Master Key's Case back. There are assassins and spies everywhere. The dark wizards are attacking all of our stability strongholds, so there's been constant fighting there." She pulled out a chair and sat. Even sitting, her posture remained rigid. "It could be worse, but it's certainly been better."

Brinnie took a deep breath. *This is normal for the wizard world. Relax.* "What are the stability strongholds?"

"No one ever explained that?" Quentin asked around a mouthful of cookie.

Brinnie narrowed her eyes. "Everyone spent most of the summer hiding everything from me and then shipped me home and told me to forget everything. My education is a bit spotty."

Miss Burtle raised an eyebrow. "Someone developed an attitude over the past year." She didn't seem displeased. "To answer your question, there are twelve strongholds around the world housing anchor points that help stabilize the protection spells and clearly define the limits of estates, so Masters' powers can't be used just anywhere. The Anchors are almost the opposite of the Master Key—the Key disables protection spells and throws magic into chaos, while Anchors uphold the protection spells and enforce the rules of magic."

Brinnie plopped into a chair across from Miss Burtle. "And they're attacking them why?"

"Because they're insane." Quentin shrugged.

"Because they're stronger than we are," Miss Burtle corrected. "Historically they've left them alone, since the Anchors protect dark estates as well. But with the strength they've been amassing under Mordred's leadership, they probably don't consider a lack of protection spells much of a problem."

Brinnie suppressed a wince. When protection spells had started fluctuating last summer, she'd witnessed secondhand the bloody effects of battle. She didn't want to imagine the fallout of the spells failing permanently.

Footsteps thumped on the stairs and Dad emerged into the kitchen. "I'd better call your mother." His shoulders tensed toward his ears, as if preparing for battle. "She'll need to know where we are." He glanced to Miss Burtle and Quentin. "Is there a phone I can borrow? Mine didn't survive the portal in working order."

"Here." Miss Burtle pulled an ancient cell phone out of her pocket.

"I'd go outside. Service is spotty in the house, especially with this many wizards."

He nodded. "Thanks."

As the door swung shut behind him, Marcie entered the kitchen. She cocked her head at Brinnie and hesitated. "She's asking for you."

Brinnie stood. "Who, Maddy?"

"No. Lydia Tynsdale."

Brinnie glanced back at Miss Burtle for answers, but the woman remained expressionless. "How does she even know I'm here?"

Marcie frowned. "I'm not sure if she does."

Quentin gave Brinnie a thumbs up. *Helpful, Quentin.* "All right, I'll go talk to her."

Brinnie followed Marcie up the familiar creaking stairs to the second floor. Marcie led her down the hall and gestured to the correct door. "I'll be downstairs if you need me."

As Brinnie stepped past her and entered the room, she had to stifle a gasp.

Ms. Tynsdale lay in bed with her golden hair spread out around her, its usual glossy sheen dimmed. Bruises mottled her face in shades of purple, yellow, and green, and a large cut slashed across her forehead. Matching bruises and what looked like burns covered what Brinnie could see of her twig-thin arms. Her sunken eyes roamed the room while her body twitched with tremors and shivers.

Uncle Merlin sat next to the bed, gently cupping one of her small, battered hands in two of his. He met Brinnie's horrified gaze and offered a small, grim nod in return.

Brinnie drifted closer, trying not to look too closely at the bandages wrapping parts of her arms, grateful most of her body was covered by the sheets. If Ms. Tynsdale looked like this now, presumably after the ministrations of a magical healer like Anika . . .

Ms. Tynsdale's roving eyes halted. Her gaze fixed on Brinnie, and her voice came out in a raw rasp. "Brinnie." She swallowed, choking on her words. "Brinnie, I'm sorry."

The words sent a chill down her spine. She took a hesitant step forward. "Sorry? For what?"

Brinnie glanced toward Uncle Merlin, but he shook his head and lifted a shoulder, brows furrowed.

The sheets jerked as Ms. Tynsdale shuddered. Her eyelids fluttered, eyes flicking back and forth. Then they flew open along with her mouth. A deep voice rumbled from her chest. "Brynna Ludovic. Give her this message." A wheeze. "I wait for you at Mordizan. I have made a discovery that will end the fighting once and for all. Meet me at the tenth stronghold on the ides of September if you wish to bring peace to the world. Tell her it is I, Mordred. Come alone. And tell her that if she does not, I know exactly where to find her family. I may not be able to kill some of them, but there are some fates worse than death." She shuddered again, her eyes shut, and she went limp.

Brinnie backed away slowly.

"Brynna," Uncle Merlin began.

She shook her head, turned, and fled from the room.

She'd made it halfway down the stairs before Uncle Merlin appeared in front of her. She tripped, slamming into his chest.

"Brynna, wait."

"Mom. Anna. Isaac. We have to find them. We have to make sure they're okay." She tried to push past him, but he held her firm.

"We will. Your father is calling them right now. Take a few deep breaths."

It was too much. Mordred knew her name. He knew her family. He had done . . . whatever he had done to Ms. Tynsdale.

"How? Why did he do this? I . . ." She gasped in a few ragged breaths.

"Good. Breathe." He slowly released her shoulders. "It's all right."

She closed her eyes, trying to shut out the sound of Mordred's voice emanating from Ms. Tynsdale's mouth, instead focusing on Uncle Merlin.

"We won't let anything happen to your family." He put an arm around her, and she sank into his embrace. "You don't need to listen to Mordred."

"But Ms. Tynsdale." She stepped back. "Has he possessed her?"

His brow wrinkled, then smoothed with understanding. "Do you mean the voice? No, of course not. She's a shapeshifter, reproducing his voice to relay the message." He straightened, morphing from consoling uncle to authoritative wizard. "He hasn't possessed her, and he doesn't know you're here. His threats are empty."

His confident tone soothed her ragged nerves. "Is it true, what Quentin said? Has she gone mad?"

He closed his eyes briefly and sighed, pinching the bridge of his nose. "No. She's perfectly sane, somewhere deep down. There are things the dark wizards can do . . . especially if Mordred has brought back the old dark arts. But she will recover." His expression hardened. "Darkness can't extinguish light."

Calm. Focus. Focus on the things you can control. "We better tell my dad so he can warn my mom."

As they entered the kitchen, Brinnie saw her father standing near the table with Mrs. Winslow. "Did you talk to Mom?"

His brow creased in worry. "No. She didn't answer her cell, or Anna's home phone. Anna and David aren't answering either."

Brinnie's heart seemed to stop. "Uncle Merlin, do you think . . . ?"

"There's one sure way to find out." Uncle Merlin regarded Dad for a moment, expression guarded. "Antony, if we travel to your house, can you lead the way from there?"

Dad winced a bit at the name—his wizard name, apparently. *I'm interrogating him thoroughly later.* "Yes, of course. But have you been to our house before?"

Uncle Merlin's cold demeanor broke for a moment, and he looked slightly guilty. "It was a long time ago."

"Then let's go."

Brinnie could feel the tension crackling between them. Dad's broad shoulders leaned inward, as if he was attempting to avoid conflict, but the room's temperature seemed to drop as a result of Uncle Merlin's icy bearing. She couldn't imagine how awkward the atmosphere would be between them without the buffer of another presence. "Can I come too?"

"I can only take one person at a time," Uncle Merlin said. "If we end up in a sticky situation, I wouldn't want to leave someone behind alone until I could return." He gave Dad a look that made it eminently clear exactly who he would leave behind. "Stay here. We'll be back soon."

"Okay." She looked from one to the other. Whatever feud they had going paled in comparison to what might be happening to Anna and Mom. "Be careful. Bring them here safe."

"We will." Dad kissed the top of her head, then tweaked her nose. "Behave yourself, Brin."

She glanced at Uncle Merlin, and for a moment she saw a flash of such anger in his eyes that her heart thudded.

But it disappeared as quickly as it came. "This way," he said.

They exited through the dining room door.

Brinnie watched the door swing behind them for a moment, then mentally shook her head. Worrying would do no good. She turned to Mrs. Winslow, whose gaze also remained on the door. Brinnie searched for a change of subject. "So where is Mr. Winslow?"

Her brow smoothed as her attention turned to Brinnie. "Up to no good, I'm sure. He went out to the barn a couple hours ago with Jerry. Those two spend every spare moment out there tinkering. You should see some of their inventions."

"So Jerry's still here?"

"Oh, yes." She beamed. "I forgot you didn't know, dear. He and Marcie renewed their vows a couple months ago. He's a changed man."

"That's wonderful." *At least something is going right.* Her smile slowly melted. "When is the ides of September? It's a thirteenth in September, right?"

"I haven't heard that term in a long time, but I believe so." Her eyebrows rose. "Why do you ask?"

"Just wondering."

Before Brinnie had to explain herself, the dining room door burst open and Miss Burtle strode through with a phone to her ear. Her eyes locked on Mrs. Winslow and Brinnie. "Just missed those two as they stepped through the door. You need to hear this." She pressed a button and held out the phone. "All right, Eira, I've got you on speaker. Tell them what you told me."

Mom's voice crackled from the device. "I was at Anna's babysitting Isaac when the house was attacked. I held them off long enough so that I could run outside and get in the car. I kept driving until I was sure I'd lost them. I'm at a gas station right now, using their pay phone. I have Isaac with me. Brinnie, are you okay? Edna said you're there."

She couldn't decide if this was good news or bad news. "I'm fine,

Mom. I'm just glad you are, too. Uncle Merlin and Dad went to find you when you didn't answer your phone."

"I left it behind. I'm running out of change for this phone. You need to call your father and tell them not to go to Anna's house. They'll be walking into a trap. Wait." A pause. "Your father. What does he think of all this?"

"Um." Brinnie exchanged looks with Mrs. Winslow and Miss Burtle. "I'll tell you later. Have you talked to Anna or David?"

"No." Anxiety tinged her voice. "Why?"

"We haven't gotten hold of them yet."

"I'm sure they're just busy." The tremor in her voice belied her true suspicions.

Brinnie bit her lip. "Probably."

"So what are you going to do?" Mrs. Winslow asked.

"Not sure what I can do. Isaac and I will stay here for now. We can't go back."

"Maybe Uncle Merlin could bring you here," Brinnie suggested.

"Isaac hasn't been to Wraithwood, honey. It would take a portal to get him there by magic."

"Oh." Her memory of the rules of Wraithwood's magic, with its complexities and quirks, had faded over time. "Right."

"At least give us the address of the station, dear," Mrs. Winslow said. "Merlin can come and check on you and let you know what's happening, if nothing else."

Mom rattled off the address. "Okay, I've run out of time. I—" Her words were cut off.

Miss Burtle clicked the phone shut. The three of them stood in silence for a moment. Then Miss Burtle flipped the cell open again. "Well. What's your house phone number, Brinnie? Maybe we can catch those two before they leave."

As Miss Burtle went off to make the call, Brinnie's rocked on the balls of her feet. Energy—she needed to do something, fix something. She turned to Mrs. Winslow. "Ms. Tynsdale gave me a message from Mordred. He said if I don't meet him on the ides of September, he'll do horrible things to my family. Step one would be kidnapping them."

Mrs. Winslow patted Brinnie's arm. "Your mother is fine." Her hands dropped to twist in her apron. "With any luck, your sister is, too. Don't pay any attention to that horrible man."

From the magical blade connected to her scar, to wizards bursting into her sister's house, Mordred didn't exactly make it easy to ignore him. But she refrained from voicing those thoughts and nodded. Instead, she lifted the teapot and poured a mug.

Not even back a day, and I'm coping with stress through tea.

A few moments later, Miss Burtle strode through the door once more. "Caught them, just barely. They're not going to Anna's house. They called her husband's work. Apparently, he went out for lunch a few hours ago and never returned."

Brinnie's heart sank. "What about Anna?"

"Your father said she's at a conference a couple of hours away. They're going to try to find her there."

On the other side of the house, a door slammed.

Miss Burtle nodded. "And there they went."

Brinnie's fingers flexed, tingling with tension. "Is there anything we can do?"

"Just wait."

Brinnie scowled. That was what she'd been afraid of.

Half an hour later, Brinnie jiggled her knee, perched halfway up the steps facing the front door. Her pacing had led her here, where she finally plopped into awkward vigilance.

More than just learning Anna's fate, she had questions for her father that demanded answers. Questions born of realizations she'd come to during her pacing.

I just hope I'm wrong.

A click echoed in the hall. She jumped up as the knob turned and the door swung open. She made it to the bottom step in the time it took her to demand, "Did you find her?"

The two men stiffly unhooked their arms, stepping apart. Dad straightened his windblown shirt, tossing back hair as he shook his head. "She never arrived at the conference."

Brinnie clutched the banister. "Oh, no."

Uncle Merlin pushed a stray lock off his forehead, the only sign he and Dad had been warping around the country. "It appears that Mordred has been busy."

"How are we going to find them?" Brinnie asked. *Please have a plan.*

Uncle Merlin hesitated. "We will find them, but . . ." He slowly began to pace. "We have no idea where they were taken."

My fault, my fault, my fault. The chant screamed in her mind. Her family had been living a normal life, minding their own business, and because of her, now were thrust into this mess.

Dad frowned. "Well, we know that Mordred's at Mordizan. Wouldn't that be where they would be taken? We could try to intercept them before they get there."

"But we don't know what direction they would be coming from, or when." Uncle Merlin paused his pacing, turning to Dad. "Have you been there before?"

Dad gave him a look, as if the answer should be obvious. "Yes. Many times."

The words hit Brinnie like bricks, though she had expected them.

Uncle Merlin shook his head. "We're only two men. The chances of us intercepting them would be slim, but if you're welcome at Mordizan . . ."

"Unfortunately, that was rescinded a long time ago."

Uncle Merlin sighed and brushed his hands together. "Of course. Well, we can try the interception method. I'll be back momentarily. I'm going to pop over to the gas station and update Eira—and advise her to get here as quickly as possible." He paused. "Should I tell her—"

"No," Dad interrupted before he could finish the sentence. "I will. Later."

"Very well." He gave him a hard look. "But if you don't tell her soon, I will."

With that, he disappeared.

Dad turned to Brinnie. His shoulders relaxed, and he offered her a rueful smile. "You okay, kiddo?"

"I am." She let go of the banister and stepped forward. "But Anna's not."

His forced smile melted. He put a hand on her shoulder. "We'll find them. Remember, they're human. Right now, there's not much Mordred can do to them."

"Are they?" Brinnie pulled away. She kept her expression carefully neutral. "Until today I thought you were, too. If you and Mom are both wizards, isn't Anna one, too?"

"No." To her irritation, he didn't have the decency to recognize the question as an accusation. "Children of wizards aren't always wizards. Neither your mother nor I are full-blooded wizards. No one really is, these days. Anna just didn't get the magic genes. Think Punnett squares."

She resisted the urge to clench her fists. *This is a life and death situation, not freshman biology*. "How do you know?"

"The same way I knew that you were a wizard. Wizards are born with the mark of the Enchantment in their eyes—enchantment wizards, at least. It fades quickly, but you had it, and Anna didn't."

She flashed back to a memory—two years old, sitting on the floor, Uncle Merlin looking at her eyes the one and only time he visited when she was a child. The day he'd made a deal with her mother to send her to Wraithwood.

And Dad had known the entire time.

"By the time she was a teenager," Dad continued, "I knew she wasn't a dark wizard, either. No trace of magic."

Brinnie took a deep breath to keep her voice from shaking as she asked her next leading question. "Why would she be a dark wizard?"

His feet shifted. His gaze drifted to the chandelier above. "Because I was a dark wizard." His eyes finally found hers. "You heard me say that my name was Drakon. Does that name mean anything to you?"

She pressed her lips together. She'd been hoping for some sort of alternative explanation than the one she had arrived at during her half hour of waiting. The one that explained Uncle Merlin's open animosity. "Goran Drakon. Ms. Tynsdale's father. He burned down the town at Wraithwood."

Pain shone in his eyes. "No. He didn't. I did."

CHAPTER SEVEN

Brinnie stepped back, a hand to her stomach as if she'd been punched in the gut. This was even worse than she'd anticipated. "Not Goran. You."

"Me." He looked green.

"What are you talking about?" Sudden anger flared through her. "You wouldn't do that. You're a *doctor.* You heal people, not hurt people."

He scrubbed a hand over his face. "Partially to make up for what I've done."

Her mouth opened and shut. She didn't know what to say, what to think. "It was an accident?"

He shook his head. He squared his shoulders, as if steeling himself for his next words. "No. It was a deliberate attack. I didn't let anyone escape alive."

A shiver ran down her spine. His brown eyes, usually so warm, were distant. Visions of the fireball he'd thrown at school replayed in her mind. *No, no, no.* The coincidence was too terrible—here he stood, married to the woman whose life he had destroyed.

A sinking feeling settled in her chest. Or was it coincidence at all?

"You have to say more than that," she managed.

He slowly walked past her, leaning on the banister without making eye contact. "Goran insisted I be the one to do it, to win glory for myself. But after that happened . . . I couldn't live with myself. I left the dark wizards. I first tried to join the enchantment wizards, but they didn't believe me. They wanted me dead, and who could blame them?" He ran his hand along the handrail. "Eventually I ended up on the run, living in a barn. It happened to belong to your grandparents' dairy farm. They found me, and I ended up working on the farm in return for a bed."

Adopted. She knew that about him. But she'd never realized just how old he'd been when it happened. His late teens, maybe twenties.

"Your grandparents taught me a different way of living, even introduced me to the church. Eventually I told them everything. They let me legally take their last name to hide my identity—and because they told me I was their son." He blinked. "They helped me to get into college and make a new life for myself."

He faced her fully, brow knit. "I'm not that man anymore, Brin. But nothing can change what I did. I just thought I was rid of it." He laughed without mirth. "It seems all roads lead back to Wraithwood."

His expression was so agonized, she felt tears forming in her eyes. She'd seen the destruction, the crumbling ruins, the rows of graves. The anger she'd felt toward Goran Drakon, the way she'd despised the evil man . . . and he hadn't been the one to do it after all. Her mind swirled with questions, how it was all connected, how they'd ended up here, how anyone could do something so horrible.

But the man in front of her was still her father, the one who had patched up her childhood scrapes and bruises, let her dress him up as the evil queen to play princesses, slipped her chocolate under the table, acted as a buffer when Mom only had criticisms and critiques.

She didn't know the man who had burned Wraithwood, but she did know the man who had raised her.

She stepped forward and wrapped her arms around him, leaning her head against those stupid palm trees on his shirt. Her head still didn't even reach his chin. Did he dress like a dork on purpose? A way to play down his otherwise potentially intimidating physique? To detract from any dark-wizard-ish vibes? *More secrets, more hiding.*

It didn't matter. "I love you, Dad. Still. Always."

He hugged her back, not speaking for a moment before he cleared his throat. "Thank you, Brin."

Brinnie stepped back. "But I have a lot of questions. First, if you're a Drakon, are we related to Ms. Tynsdale?"

He nodded. "Yes. Lydia is my half-sister." He hesitated, then added with a grimace, "Goran was my father."

Despite everything, Brinnie almost smiled at the familiar

expression of disgust. It seemed all three of Goran's children held a similar dislike of their father. Her eyes widened. "Then Nimue is your sister. Your full-sister?"

"Yes. My little sister." His breath hitched. "You've met her?"

"Last summer. She was working with Mordred, but she was at least a little nicer than he was."

"How was she? Did she look . . ." He waved a hand. "I don't know. Tell me more."

The thought of Nimue as a "little sister" made her snort. "I guess she seemed fine—I mean, besides being a dark wizard. She tried to kill me." *Positive things, Brinnie.* "But she seems to be the one person in the world Mordred cares anything about, so I guess she's got that going for her."

"Merlin told me about Mordred." He rubbed his chin. "It would make sense that she and Mordred are close, if he really is Mordred from Arthurian times."

"Why?"

"Well, she would be his, let's see, great-great-great-granddaughter?"

Brinnie's eyebrows shot up. "How is that possible? He's been asleep for more than a thousand years."

"Yes, but his wife wasn't."

She should be more concerned about descendants of Mordred, but she only blurted, "Someone actually married him?"

Dad laughed. "Yes. The powerful wizard Nimue, who our Nimue is named after. When the fighting at that time got really intense, Mordred put her under the same sleeping spell he later used on himself to keep her and his unborn child safe, since you can't kill someone under the spell. Of course, he never came back to wake her up. She was kept in a tomb at Mordizan until a thousand years were up around five hundred years ago and the spell was broken. Mordred's daughter ended up marrying the Master of Mordizan, and their only child was my great-grandmother. Mordred's daughter died, so the Master of Mordizan remarried and had other kids, and Mordred's line only carried through my great-grandmother. She married a lesser Master and had one surviving child, my grandmother."

"Let me guess. Your grandmother only had one surviving kid as well."

"Close. My uncle hated people and lived alone in a cave until he was eaten by a bear in '89."

Brinnie's mouth dropped open.

Dad laughed. "Kidding. You're right. Just my mother, who broke the cycle and had two children, but everyone at Mordizan most likely assumes I'm dead. So as far as Mordred's concerned, Nimue is all that's left of the wife he froze fifteen hundred years ago."

Brinnie slapped a palm to her forehead. "Great. So to top everything off, I'm related to that wacko."

Uncle Merlin sprang into existence in front of the door. Brinnie jumped.

Dad smirked. "Well, look on the bright side. You're also related to that one." He turned to Uncle Merlin, expression serious once more. "Well?"

Uncle Merlin had discarded his more formal attire in favor of high boots, a cloak, and what appeared to be far more battle-appropriate clothing, with a large knife strapped at his hip. "Eira is on her way here, and I made a couple calls for backup lookouts at key points. We had better get going."

Brinnie blinked. Only Uncle Merlin could have managed a complete wardrobe change and organized a team in such a short time.

Dad nodded. "All right, Brin. Hopefully we'll be back soon."

He turned to go, but she grabbed his arm. "Let me come. I can help. We can spread out, cover more ground."

"A good thought, but no." Uncle Merlin checked the knife at his hip and adjusted another small sheath strapped to his inner forearm before pulling down his sleeve. "If that blade is anywhere nearby, you'll lead them right to us. We need the advantage of stealth." He reached into his pocket, pulled out another sheath, and tossed it to Dad. "With your talents, you shouldn't need it, but just in case."

Dad caught the knife and detangled his arm from Brinnie. "Don't worry too much, kiddo."

"Be careful." She gave Uncle Merlin a stern look. "Both of you. And please don't kill my dad."

Uncle Merlin's stiff demeanor softened for a moment and his moustache twitched. "Yes, ma'am." Then he glanced at Dad and his expression sobered. "If I planned to kill him, he would be dead already. I'm leaving that decision up to Eira."

Dad swallowed. "Noted."

The two of them linked arms, stepped through the doorway, and were gone.

Each minute felt like an hour that afternoon and evening. Brinnie tried to take her mind off the situation by touring Mr. Winslow's and Jerry's barn full of crazy contraptions, from suction cup launchers for catching objects that Quentin accidentally levitated to an automatic corn husker that was more likely to chop off the user's hand than actually husk corn. She tried to muster enthusiasm for their demonstrations, but she knew her smiles and applause fell flat.

After dinner, Marcie brought out the pieces for Wizard's Chess and tried to teach Brinnie the official tournament rules, but somehow Brinnie ended up with her army riding into battle on cows while wielding pitchforks. She lost.

As the night wound down and everyone began to disperse for bed, Brinnie excused herself, claiming tiredness.

She ascended the stairs. The room from last summer was hers once more, the familiar blue linens and gauzy curtains beckoning her back. Instead, she passed it and slipped into Ms. Tynsdale's room, pulling the door shut behind her.

Ms. Tynsdale's closed eyes didn't even flutter as the latch clicked behind Brinnie, her chest barely rising and falling. Brinnie drifted closer.

Last summer, when Brinnie glimpsed her in her true form, she had thought Lydia Tynsdale the most beautiful woman she'd ever seen. But now, all Brinnie saw were bruises, wounds, and protruding bones.

Brinnie bit her lip. This was Mordred's doing.

He'd do the same to Anna and David if Brinnie didn't do as he said.

Three days. Three days until the ides of September. With a team of wizards at their side, she hoped that Dad and Uncle Merlin might find her sister and David. She hoped they could fight off whatever dark wizards came their way.

But hope didn't win battles. She had to come up with an alternate plan.

She doubted that Mordred wanted to kill her. From the beginning, he'd been more interested in turning her to his side. Even now that he knew of her descent from Arthur, he seemed more intent on capturing her than on revenge. She couldn't guess why. She was a shadowmaster, yes, a rare talent, but he had plenty of wizards at his disposal.

Ms. Tynsdale's breath rattled. Brinnie scanned the room and swiped an extra pillow from the top of a nearby dresser. Like all the rooms at Wraithwood, this one was outfitted for noble visitors, with grand, heavy furniture. She slid an arm under Ms. Tynsdale's thin shoulders, eased her up, and nestled the extra pillow beneath her head to prop her up.

Her breathing evened, and Brinnie hovered near the edge of the bed, watching for signs of discomfort as her mind drifted back to her ponderings.

If not because of her shadow walking abilities, perhaps Mordred wanted her because of her abilities as a helper, a catalyst for the magic of others. Perhaps he wanted to magnify his own powers. Though her knowledge was frustratingly limited, she knew helping was a rare talent as well. *Lucky me, two rare talents.* How many other helpers were there? Was she simply the most convenient one to capture?

To help her think, she began speaking aloud. "In that case, I could meet him. He would release Anna and David, and then I would, I don't know, pretend to help him. Maybe I could even do some spying or something while I was at it. Then I could escape, and come back here, and everything would be good, right?" She paced. "I mean, what's he going to do to me? If he gets mad and wants to kill me or something, I'll just tell him, 'Guess what, I'm your great-great-great-great granddaughter,' and he'll give me the Nimue treatment."

"No."

Brinnie gasped as a hand clasped around her wrist.

Ms. Tynsdale's eyes shone luminous in the muted moonlight, staring straight at Brinnie. No, not at her—through her, as if looking at something Brinnie couldn't see. She opened her mouth, and quivering words spilled out. "Myrddin's flesh and Myrddin's blood shall destroy the world he built."

Brinnie shivered at the piercing gaze. "What do you mean?"

Her eyes flicked away, gaze bouncing around the room. Her breath came faster. "Mordred's bane, his final doom, the heir of Arthur doth supply."

"Calm down. It's okay." Brinnie patted the hand clutching her wrist, wincing as Ms. Tynsdale's nails dug into her skin. "What are you trying to say?"

"The line of Myrddin here must die, or all we wrought shall be in vain."

Brinnie's heart beat faster. "Okay, you're quoting something. What are you quoting?"

Her gaze wandered, then settled back on Brinnie. Her eyes cleared and focused. "Brinnie? Is that you? What are you doing here?"

The confusion in her voice cracked Brinnie's heart. She knelt, clasping Ms. Tynsdale's hand with both of her own. "I'm listening to you. What were you trying to tell me?"

She blinked. "Tell you? I wasn't saying anything." Her brow furrowed. "Where are we?"

"We're at Wraithwood." Brinnie squeezed her hand. "You were saying something about Myrddin, and Arthur." *Please, please remember.*

For a moment, she seemed about to answer, but then her eyes unfocused and wandered. "Tell Merlin that I'm going to the Academy. Mom won't like it." She looked back at Brinnie. "Eira, do you think they'll take a Drakon?"

Her heart sank. Brinnie forced a smile. "I'm sure they will. You should go back to sleep."

"Right." Her eyes drifted shut, and her breathing deepened.

Brinnie disentangled her arm and backed away. The shapeshifter didn't stir.

She slipped through the door and closed it behind her.

In the hall, Brinnie leaned against the door and clenched her fists. Nothing would have pleased her more than punching Mordred in the nose. She looked up at the ceiling and took a shuddering breath.

What did the words mean? *Mordred's bane, his final doom.*

If the words were anything more than the ramblings of a broken woman, they could be the leverage she needed against Mordred.

CHAPTER EIGHT

I'm exhausted. Maybe I'm overthinking this.

Brinnie pushed off the door to Ms. Tynsdale's room. If the words did mean anything, she wouldn't figure it out tonight. She'd wait until morning, then ask around. For now, she should go to bed.

In her room, she put on the oversized t-shirt and pajama shorts Marcie had lent her and brushed her hair. She really needed a shower. *Tomorrow.* Her appearance had been the least of her worries.

Those worries kept her mind spinning long after she'd climbed beneath the covers. She tossed and turned for an hour before giving up on sleep. With a sigh, she rolled out of bed and padded down the hall to the grand staircase. She descended to the bottom step, propped up her feet, and fixed her gaze on the front door. At least she could make herself useful. She would know the instant anyone returned.

Instead, she awoke with a terrible crick in her neck, blinking up at the chandelier hanging high above.

She pushed onto her elbows, wincing at all the places the steps had dug into her. At some point in the night, she'd sprawled on the stairs. She sat up and rolled her shoulders, working blood back into her muscles. She groaned as she stood and hobbled to look out the window. The bright blue sky indicated morning. Stretching while rubbing her dry eyes, she passed through the dining room and into the kitchen.

The door swung open to reveal two occupants. "Hey!" At the table, Maddy greeted her by waving a forkful of pancake in the air. "Guess what? Magic food is delicious. Of course, you probably knew that already."

Mrs. Winslow carried a cup of tea to the table and sat across from Maddy. "It's not magic, dear. It's just normal food." She smiled at Brinnie. "Good morning."

"Good morning." Brinnie scanned Maddy head to toe. The girl sitting at the table seemed no worse for the wear. "You look like you're feeling better."

"Feeling great. This is awesome." Her large eyes sparkled as she stuffed another forkful of pancakes in her mouth. "Will you teach me magic?"

Brinnie slid into a chair at the table and reached for the pitcher of water sitting in the middle, pouring herself a glass. "I can't do that."

"Please? I promise I'll use it only for good and not evil, and all that sort of thing."

Brinnie rubbed her eyes again, but the sandy feeling didn't dissipate. She probably looked like a half-dead scarecrow. "You don't teach someone magic. You're either born with it or you're not."

Maddy grinned. "Then maybe I was born with it!"

Please. Not first thing in the morning.

She must have thrown a pleading look toward Mrs. Winslow, because the housekeeper smiled at her knowingly and stepped in. "What Brinnie is trying to say, dear, is that you can't do magic. You're a human, like me. If you were a wizard—well, you would know by now. Brinnie and her father and Merlin—they're not human. They're wizards. Only wizards have magic."

Maddy scowled. "That's not fair. I hate those kinds of fantasy novels. I don't see why Brinnie gets to be some sort of immortal elf creature and I have to be a hobbit or something."

Brinnie snorted and choked on her water. Mrs. Winslow laughed. "Maybe so, dear. But that's how it is."

"So where is everyone?" Brinnie asked.

"Oh, off and about. You two were late risers. I kept some pancakes warm for you near the stove."

"Thanks." Brinnie headed for the cupboard to grab a plate. "Any word from anyone?"

"Oh, yes! Your mother called a couple of hours ago. With luck, she'll be in Lyle late tonight. Poor thing. She's been driving all night."

Brinnie raised an eyebrow. "Hopefully she's had lots of coffee." She lifted the lid above the pancakes and forked a few onto her plate. As she headed back to the table, she glanced toward Maddy. "Did you tell her about the, uh, situation?"

"How an evil wizard captured my brother and your sister in order to force you to do what he says?" Maddy took a swig of milk. "Yeah, she told me. Pretty awesome."

"Awesome?" Brinnie's plate clattered onto the table. "Not awesome! That's really bad."

Maddy wiped her mouth. "Well, yeah, that part is, but an epic battle between good and evil? So cool."

Brinnie just stared, hands on the back of her chair. "Aren't you worried about your brother?"

She shrugged. "Yes, but the good guys always win, you know? The innocent bystanders always get saved by the good guys."

Brinnie shook her head and slumped into the chair. Maddy had to be bluffing, right? Putting on a brave face? "What do you think this is, a Disney movie?"

"What's a Disney movie?"

Brinnie looked up to see Quentin enter the kitchen. "It's, um, never mind. Good morning."

"Good morning." He lifted the lid off the plate of leftover pancakes. "Mmm. Does anyone want these?"

Mrs. Winslow laughed. "You just had breakfast half an hour ago."

"But then I had to go fulfill my taxing and important duties as Protector of the Master Key," he protested.

Maddy leaned forward. "Ooh. What's that?"

"He walked downstairs and looked to see if the Key was still there," Brinnie said flatly. Then she grinned. "Nice try, though."

"And it was there. See?" He shook a flopping pancake at her. "I've done my job well."

"Behold, Castelon's finest," Brinnie said with a dramatic flourish.

"But of course!" He struck a pose. "Remember who it was that single-handedly turned the tide of the Battle of the Master Key."

"Is that seriously what they call it now?" Brinnie laughed. "It makes it sound so dramatic."

"It was dramatic. The Master of Castelon himself said that the world owed me a great debt." Quentin winked, sliding into the chair next to Brinnie.

"Oh, shut up." Brinnie gave him a playful shove. "Last I checked, you weren't a helper or a shadowmaster."

"No, no, it was my wonderful levitation magic that saved the day."

She wished she could bottle this moment, ignore the looming threats. "Soon you'll be believing your own lies."

"That's what you get for not taking the credit."

"I don't know," she teased. "Mordred knows who I am now, and it looks like my family's back into magic whether they want to be or not. Maybe I'll reveal myself and steal your glory."

He shrugged and reached for another pancake. "Go ahead. As long as I get to stay here and eat Mrs. Winslow's cooking."

"Which reminds me." Brinnie sobered, light mood crashing to earth like a deflated blimp. She turned to Mrs. Winslow. "How *did* Mordred find out who I am?"

"Who knows, dear? He's had over a year to search. Or it's possible that he tortured it out of Lydia."

Brinnie closed her eyes briefly, trying not to imagine what sort of abuse had inflicted those wounds on Ms. Tynsdale. Trying not to feel guilty that many of them might be from Ms. Tynsdale refusing to expose her. "With Mordred, it could be anything." She took a deep breath. "So, what's on the agenda for today?"

"Fighting dark wizards in an epic battle against the forces of evil?" Maddy made finger guns at her.

For once, Brinnie was glad of Maddy's insane optimism.

"Dear me, I hope not." Mrs. Winslow chuckled. "There's nothing in particular planned for today. We were going to go to the grocery store, but with Merlin away, there's no one to lead us through the Maze."

"The Maze? Can we try it?" Maddy asked.

"No!" the three of them said together, then looked at each other and laughed.

"I got us all in a whole lot of trouble last summer when I went in there," Brinnie explained. "It's magic. Unless you're Uncle Merlin, you get hopelessly lost."

"Maybe you and Quentin can show Maddy around," Mrs. Winslow suggested. "Keep your mind off things while we wait."

Brinnie raised an eyebrow at the thought of all the trouble Maddy could get herself into, but she said, "Sure. After I clean myself up, how would you like to meet the animals?"

"Or we could go chair-flying," Quentin suggested.

"Do you think that's a good—" Brinnie began.

Maddy's hand shot up. "I vote chair-flying!"

Quentin grinned. "Good choice."

Two chair collisions, three runaway chickens, and one hole in the wall later, Brinnie escaped to the rose garden. She didn't think she could take any more of the stress of watching Quentin and Maddy together. They were both disasters waiting to happen.

She sat on a stone border and Bruno trotted over to lie next to her, eyes half-closed in the sun. She rubbed his ears, and his tail thumped. "How's it going, old fellow? Have you been chasing any more rabbits into the Maze?" His tail thumped harder, and his tongue lolled. She smiled. "I missed you, too, buddy."

Her mind wandered back to the night before and Ms. Tynsdale's strange words. She could almost dismiss them as the ramblings of a poor soul out of her mind, but Ms. Tynsdale seemed to be trying to convey something through them. The meaning on the surface seemed clear—a descendant of Myrddin would destroy all he had built, presumably the current system of magic, and Arthur's heir would bring about Mordred's doom. But where did the words come from? Were they history, from Arthur's time, or poetry, perhaps the wizard equivalent of Shakespeare? And why did she need to know them? Why should they keep her from confronting Mordred?

"I know next to nothing about any of this," Brinnie mused to Bruno. Her education in magical history was sadly lacking. "But I know exactly where to find out more."

Bruno loped behind her as she went up the drive, rounded the house, and climbed the steps of the portico. He lay under the porch swing as she opened the double doors and entered.

She closed her eyes and inhaled the musty scent of books, engulfing her senses like a healing elixir. The library was exactly as she remembered it. Rich, gleaming wood, soft sunlight from the roof's dome, shelves drawing the eye upward. She ran her fingers along the spines of the books on the nearest shelf and pulled one out just to feel the pages, breathe in its smell, and hear the crackling of the binding. There were no books like these in the school library—old, proper books that were delicious to hold and look at.

But she had a mission. She slid the book back into place and began perusing the shelves on the first floor, which was reserved for nonfiction. She smiled to herself at some of the titles like *Magic in the British Isles, 1500-1600*. How hadn't she noticed such things last summer before she knew about magic? Maybe because she spent most of her time on the second floor, in the fiction section. She'd learned last summer that a lot could happen under a person's nose without their noticing. She continued scanning the shelves for anything concerning Arthurian times.

After about five minutes of searching, she found a book titled *The Song of Morgana.* Close enough. She took it down and plopped the tome on the conference table that dominated the center of the library.

When she opened the book, familiar but illegible text sprawled across the page. She huffed. The ancient language. *A little deceptive to put the title in English and write in another language.* She remembered the translating glass Uncle Merlin had given her when they were searching the Wraithwood Scrolls that allowed her to read the ancient language. *I wonder . . .*

She looked up at the third floor and then shook her head. Even if it did await there with all the other magical objects, digging through the collection of largely contraband magic on the third floor was asking for trouble. Especially as a helper, her magic was sure to make everything go crazy. She preferred not to be dismembered or caught up in a tornado.

On the other hand, what Ms. Tynsdale said might be important. Brinnie took a deep breath and shook herself. *Okay, no magic, no magic, no helping, no shadows, don't think about the shadows . . . aaaand now I'm thinking about the shadows.* Shadows danced in the corners of the library, begging to come out to play. She huffed in frustration. *You would think after a year I'd be able to control myself a little better.* Of course, Mom never let her practice. "Okay, stop. All of you. Sit!"

Around the room, shadows coalesced into the forms of wolves and sat. Tails wagged, and obsidian eyes blinked expectantly. *What is it with me and canines?* "Stay there. I'm going up."

She took the stairs, carefully thinking about anything but magic. *Think about books. Good books. Treasure Island. Oliver Twist. Little Women. Around the World in Eighty Days. Uncle Merlin could do that in two seconds.* She clenched her teeth. *Wrong train of thought. Okay, The Scottish Chiefs, The Lord of the Rings . . .*

Soon she had reached the third floor. Her gaze traveled over the scrolls to the shelves of magical objects. She tried to look from afar, but the shelves were anything but orderly. She ventured closer and scanned the shelves. Amongst the jumble of rings, medallions, boxes, and stones shone a few glass circles and orbs. She pursed her lips. Any one of them could be the correct stone, or none of them. *And who knows what would happen if I touched the wrong one?*

She heard a clacking sound. Her gaze swept up to a broomstick clattering about on the shelf over her head. *Great.*

At the same time, a shriek rang out below. She jumped, and the broomstick responded to her mood spike. The broom shot off the shelf. She barely snatched it, wood scraping her palm. A split second later, she realized her mistake. Before she could react, the broomstick yanked her off her feet.

Brinnie yelled as it carried her over the railing. She held on for dear life as it shot in circles near the second floor. She looked down to see Quentin and Maddy standing near the conference table, gawking at her with their mouths open.

"I don't think that's how you're supposed to ride a broomstick!" Maddy called.

"No kidding." She gripped tighter. "Help, please, Quentin?"

"What am I supposed to do?"

"I don't know." She swung her legs to avoid crashing into the railing. "Levitation is your thing, not mine."

"But I didn't make it do that! You'll have to let go."

"I'd rather not break a leg."

Her shadow wolves' eyes tracked her, watching her fly with their heads cocked sideways. An idea sparked—a risky idea.

She didn't know much about shadow magic, despite her attempts to research it at the end of last summer. Shadow magic was a nebulous art. Despite a few secretive attempts, she'd never been able to manage the solidity of the wolves she'd summoned last summer, which had inflicted real pain on her enemies. Occasionally, she could feel the shadows, touch them, as if they were physical things. Usually, they passed through her fingers like smoke.

She'd have to risk it.

She gathered shadows to create a large cloud over the conference table, compacting as many as she could. She imagined them forming a fluffy cotton-like consistency. Then she took a deep breath and let go of the broomstick.

She clenched her eyes shut, braced for impact.

The fall was over in a second. Her feet hit first, sinking through shadows of cotton batting consistency, and slowly came to rest.

She opened her eyes and let out a sigh of relief. She waved the shadows away and stepped down from the table. Meanwhile, the broomstick began to waver without her magic, then fell to the ground.

"Sweet!" Maddy ran over and grabbed the broom. "Can I try? That looks even better than chair riding."

"Probably not a good idea." Brinnie took it from her carefully and laid it on the table. "For all I know, it might be cursed or something."

"Imagine if you rode to school on a broomstick. You could have your own reality show." She spread her hands out, forming an invisible banner. "Brinnie the Teenage Witch."

"There's a big difference between a witch and a wizard—" Quentin began.

"I'd be dead," Brinnie said flatly.

Maddy's smile faltered. Brinnie winced. When did she become so harsh, so cynical?

Quentin glanced back at the broom. "Why did you have that anyway?"

Brinnie pointed at the book on the table. "I was looking upstairs for that translator glass thing, where you look through it and you can read the ancient language. I jumped when someone screamed down here, and that set the broom off."

"Oh, sorry." Maddy raised her hand. "That was me. Your wolves scared me."

Brinnie glanced at her shadowy guardians ringing the room. "Oh." She waved at the wolves, still sitting where she had placed them. "Shoo!"

They dissolved into the corners and crevices, only shadows once more.

"What are you trying to read?" Quentin asked.

Brinnie slid the book toward him. "This. I'm trying to research some stuff about Arthurian times."

"Research?" Maddy leaned across the table, squinting at the book. "Meaning that's real, too?"

"Yeah."

"Cool!"

Quentin picked up the book. "*The Song of Morgana*. Ouch. We were supposed to read that in school."

"You were?" Brinnie leaned forward. "Do you remember it saying anything about Mordred's bane?"

He flipped through the pages, nose wrinkled. "Note that I said 'supposed to.' I only read the first few pages before I decided I didn't need to pass that test. I had a high enough score in other things."

Just her luck. "Can you read the ancient language, at least?"

"Of course. I am a wizard." He seemed to realize what he had said. "I mean, because all wizards, you know, in our world, I mean, not that I'm saying—"

She bit back a smile at his stammering and waved it off. "It's fine. How would you like to help me with a project?"

He glanced at the book. "Um, I'm thinking I'm not going to like it very much."

"Great. So we're looking through the books to see if we can find anything about Mordred's bane, the heir of Arthur, the line of Myrddin —that's Arthurian Merlin, Maddy—Mordred's final doom, or the destruction of the world Myrddin built."

He raised his eyebrows. "Should I be concerned?"

She hesitated. She'd been afraid to speak the words aloud, afraid someone would dash her small hope, call her silly for thinking random phrases could mean anything. "It's probably nothing. Just something Ms. Tynsdale said last night." She looked up, trying to recall the exact wording. "Myrddin's flesh and Myrddin's blood shall destroy the world he built. Um . . . Mordred's bane, his final doom, the heir of Arthur doth supply. And . . . The line of Myrddin here must die, or all we wrought shall be in vain."

Maddy crossed her arms. "That doesn't rhyme."

Brinnie gave her a questioning look. "Why would it rhyme?"

"It's a prophecy, isn't it? They're supposed to rhyme."

A prophecy. Her blood chilled. Her mind drifted back to the dying words of an ancient woman. "I never said it was a prophecy."

"I'm more confused by how you remembered that." Quentin fanned the pages of the book in an irreverent manner that made Brinnie wince. "Did you write it down or something?"

"A bookworm has to remember the important words. They might be clues for later." She raised an eyebrow. "So what do you think? Is it a prophecy? Is that a thing with magic?"

He shrugged. "Possibly. Not really in the way you usually think of prophecies, as predicting the future, but more of telling how magic works."

"Ms. Tynsdale acted like it was important." She strode toward the shelves.

Quentin shifted uncomfortably. "You realize she's out of her mind?"

"Maybe partially." She pulled another book off the shelf, this one titled *Masters Genealogies*, and thumped the heavy tome onto the table. "But I'd sure like to find out what Mordred's bane is."

Maddy slid the book toward herself and began flipping through the genealogy. "Isn't the internet pretty much made for this sort of thing? There are whole sites with this family tree stuff."

"Wizards don't generally use computers," Quentin explained, regarding the first page of *The Song of Morgana* dubiously. "Magic and modern technology don't mix very well. We tend to accidentally destroy things."

"I always wondered why my mom refused to give up her old flip phone before I knew she was a wizard." Brinnie scanned the shelves.

"I understood when I crashed Isabel's new phone trying to take a picture."

"Besides, most of us don't legally exist, unlike Brinnie here." Quentin gestured toward her. "There wouldn't be any wizard genealogies or histories on computers."

Maddy looked up from skimming the lists of names. "Isn't that tax evasion?"

"What's tax evasion?" Quentin asked.

Brinnie paused dead in her tracks and choked on a giggle. "Never mind that. I think the loss of a few tax dollars is worth our keeping the human population of the world alive."

Maddy grinned. "Cool. Hero outlaws."

Brinnie pulled out *Pre-William Britain* and flipped through the pages. "This one's in English. Maddy, do you want to help?"

She took the book and scanned the table of contents. "Absolutely. This is like a history book married a fantasy novel and had an awesome baby."

Brinnie settled into a chair with the genealogy. "Then let's get reading."

Hours passed as they pored over books. Quentin sighed often and rubbed his eyes, making slow progress through *The Song of Morgana*. Brinnie skimmed page after page looking for anything having to do with Mordred's bane or the heir of Arthur. Finally, in a thick book handwritten in ink, she found something. "Guys, listen to this."

Maddy rolled over from her position sprawled on the floor. Quentin's head jerked up, as if he'd almost been caught napping.

Brinnie read, "'And Arthur did perish upon the plain, and the golden age of Albion that had been foretold he failed to bring about. Therefore, Morgana did go unto Gwenhwyfar, and thus foretold that the heir of Arthur should bring about the age. And so they did flee with the only son of Arthur, that he might bring about the age. But a king he never became, and thus it has been said that perchance the magic of Myrddin was the Albion that was spoken of."

They both stared at her blankly. Quentin cleared his throat. "What exactly does that tell us?"

"I don't know. But it mentions the heir of Arthur."

He shook his head. "I'm thinking this is a lost cause."

Brinnie sighed, slumping back into her chair. "Are you sure you've never heard anything like what she said before?"

"No."

"Well, it seems pretty clear to me." Maddy shut her book with a thud.

Brinnie rubbed her sore temple, squinting at Maddy. "What?"

"Whatever it is, you can't find it here." She leaned on her elbows and propped her chin on her fists. "She learned about it at that Mordi-place. It must be a well-kept secret of the enemy that she risked her life to obtain."

Brinnie ignored the dramatic tone and focused on her words. "That actually makes sense." She tapped her fingers on her book. "Ms. Tynsdale never gets caught. She's been searching for the Case for over a year. For them to catch her now . . . maybe she learned something even more important." She finally voiced the idea that had been rattling around in her head. "Maybe she found the prophecy in Mordizan that Morgana told me about. The one that would tell us how to defeat Mordred."

"Wouldn't they just kill her, then?" Quentin stretched with a wince.

"You would think." Brinnie stood and paced. "But we're talking about Mordred. This is all part of his plan. He sent her back to give me a message." She clenched her jaw. "He knows I would want to find his bane. He wants me to go to Mordizan, for whatever reason. And this would be the perfect reason for me to go. It's all a plot."

Maddy raised an eyebrow. "Isn't that what kidnapping your sister is for? And trying to kidnap *you*? That sounds like overkill."

"Actually, you might be onto something." Quentin pointed to *The Song of Morgana*. "As someone who was forced to study magical history—it sounds like typical Mordred. He was known for hedging his bets, so that even if one plot didn't go to plan, there would be backups. And backups to the backups—like reawakening over a thousand years later."

"Like when you trap someone in Tic-Tac-Toe." Maddy drew X's in the air. "They block you one way, but it just leads to you winning another way."

"Uh, sure." He looked at Brinnie. "But you can't do what he wants.

You'll be playing right into his hands. For all we know, he made up the whole prophecy to draw you in."

She scowled. The thought of a fake hadn't even occurred to her. "Ugh. You're right." She pushed her hand through her hair, no doubt messing up her ponytail. "But if it is real, can we take that chance?"

A rumbling sound interrupted her train of thought. Maddy stared at Quentin's stomach. "Was that you?"

He ducked sheepishly. "It's almost dinner time."

They'd spent hours and hours researching for her, with only good-humored complaints. Brinnie's scowl melted. "All right. Why don't we leave off for now and go get some food?" She reached for a stack of books to put away. "But please don't say anything to anyone about all this."

"Why not?" Quentin thumped a tome closed and tilted his head. "Couldn't they help?"

She hesitated while scooping books into her arms to re-shelve. Could either of the two keep their mouths shut?

But if she didn't tell them why to be quiet, Quentin would talk. She took a deep breath. "If Uncle Merlin and my dad don't find Anna and David, I'm going to meet Mordred. But I can't tell anyone this plan, because they aren't going to let me go. So they need to think I'm not even considering going."

Quentin paused, leaning against the table. "Um, I think that's a bad idea."

Maddy stood and stretched. "Agreed, actually."

See? Sensible responses, her gut screamed. Mordred was trying to trap her with a three-pronged approach. She'd only escaped last time due to a heavy serving of luck, and the fact that Mordred had been unprepared for her, hadn't known who she was. Facing him on purpose was a fool's errand. But . . .

"I can't let what happened to Ms. Tynsdale happen to my sister." She glanced at Maddy. "And to your brother." She shut her eyes briefly, pushing down the waves of guilt threatening to crash. "I brought this on them, and I'm going to get them out of it."

"It's not your fault." Quentin clenched a fist on the table. "You can't help it that Mordred's a—a filthy scumbucket."

Brinnie's eyebrows rose. "A *scumbucket*?"

He tried to suppress a smile, turning his attention to the books. "It was the first appropriate word that came to mind."

She slid one of the titles in her arms back onto the shelf. "Scumbucket or not, I'm going to make sure Anna and David are safe."

"Fine." He sighed and hefted *The Song of Morgana*. "I won't tell, at least for now. But you're crazy."

"We already knew that," Maddy said with a shrug. "Good thing I like crazy. Now let's go get some food."

CHAPTER NINE

"I don't like all these official rules," Brinnie complained. "I like Uncle Merlin's version better."

Quentin and Brinnie sat across from one another at the game table on the third floor. Maddy lounged nearby, watching them settle in for a round of Wizard's Chess. Light orbs bounced above them, staving off the darkness as dusk fell, or so Brinnie assumed.

Quentin arranged his pieces. "But how is anyone supposed to win if you don't have set resources? You could go back and forth forever. It's supposed to be a battle strategy game."

"I just like playing pretend." She committed the positions of the pieces on the board to memory. Ignoring his protests, she swept the pieces off the board into a drawer, closed her eyes, and concentrated. She waved her hand over the table, replacing the game pieces with shadow replicas improved to look more like real people. "There. The brave knight of Calidin charged at Sir Olav and ran him through with his spear." One of the shadows galloped on a nebulous four-legged form across the board and impaled another mounted knight, who fell dramatically from his equally ill-defined horse. *Canines remain my specialty, apparently.*

"You can't do that!" Quentin exclaimed.

"Why not?"

"They were at least a hundred yards apart. Olav would have seen him coming."

"Okay, valid." The vaguely humanoid shadow-Olav jumped up. "Hooray, I'm not dead!" Brinnie said in an attempt at a masculine voice as he climbed back onto his horse. "Now can the knight of Calidin charge at him?"

"Sure."

Maddy shook her head. "This game makes absolutely no sense."

"That's because we don't have an actual enchanted board," Quentin said. "And because *someone* keeps cheating." He looked down. "Hey! Why are your knights killing my knights?"

Brinnie smirked, fingers twitching toward the shadowy pieces. "Because you're not paying attention."

"That's *not* how it works."

"But this way is more fun."

"For you! I don't have shadow magic."

An idea formed. She held the image in her head, concentrating. She drew her arms apart and the shadowy outline of a sword materialized between them. The form was blurry, and the grip didn't feel quite solid, but it would do. She handed it to Quentin. "Here. Fight me."

He took it reflexively, and as Brinnie let go, it remained in his hand. *Fascinating.* "What? No, I—"

She drew her arms apart again, creating another for herself. She jumped up and waved it at him. "You're Olav, and I'm the knight of Calidin."

Maddy thrust her hand in the air. "Ooo, can I have one, too?"

Brinnie tossed the second sword to her, and Maddy snatched it as if it were real. Brinnie then formed a third for herself. Each shadowy blade formed more easily, the lines less blurry. "And you're a rogue. You want us both dead."

"Wizard's Chess is strictly composed of two sides," Quentin protested.

"We're not playing chess anymore." Maddy jumped into a fighting stance. "Die, fiend! I shall slay thee!" She swiped at Quentin's head.

The blade shape passed over him like ordinary shadows, but he yelled anyway. "You decapitated me!" He raised his sword. "That isn't very nice."

"Guess you'll have to make me pay."

Blades collided with the impact of pool noodles, barely solid. Brinnie wondered if she could make the shadow blades fully materialize, but she wasn't about to try. Her heart thumped at the idea. She suspected making them deadly would be a lot harder than compacting shadows into springy, vaguely sword-shaped forms.

Maddy whirled toward her, blade swinging, and Brinnie blocked. Magic sang through her veins, thrilling at the impact.

She'd never had a chance to explore what she could truly do. She knew her shadows could become nearly solid, knew she could form suggestions of shapes, especially canine creatures, but how far did her powers of creation go? Here at Wraithwood, her powers seemed stronger. She could touch shadows here, and Maddy and Quentin could as well—but could shadows hurt, the way they had seemed to last summer, when her wolves chased away enemies?

How much of a weapon did she truly hold in her hand? Only illusion, or the real thing?

"Team up!" Maddy shouted. She and Quentin descended on Brinnie.

Brinnie shook herself out of her reflective mood. "Excuse me, rude!"

Chaos ensued. Quentin managed to "decapitate" Brinnie as the shadow sword passed through her neck, so she fell to the floor and yelled, "Argh, thou hast slain me!"

Postmortem, Brinnie ran Maddy through.

Maddy clasped her hands to her stomach. "Ah! My guts!"

"I shall avenge you," Quentin cried, performing an elaborate spin. Mid-twirl, his arm thwacked into something solid.

Uncle Merlin, having appeared in the doorway, looked down at the shadow sword protruding from his chest. "What on earth is going on here?"

Brinnie and Maddy scrambled up from the floor. All three swords disappeared. "We were, um, trying to keep our minds off the situation," Brinnie explained.

Quentin turned red, dropping his outstretched hand, now empty. "Er, sorry about slaying you."

Uncle Merlin's eyebrows rose. "Forgiven." He cleared his throat and adjusted his lapels, rumpled from being slain. "Brinnie, your mother is in Lyle. Do you want to come with me to lead her through the Maze?"

The fun of the fight faded. "Yes, but weren't you and my dad looking for Anna and David?"

"Your father still is. We've seen no sign of them yet." His face betrayed no emotion, despite her attempts to read whether she should be concerned. "I'll rejoin him after we retrieve your mother."

She bit her lip. "Okay. Let's go."

She cast a look back over her shoulder at Quentin and Maddy. Quentin righted a chair that had been knocked over in the fight, and Maddy gave her a thumbs up.

On the way downstairs, Brinnie asked, "Why do you want me to come? I thought I was a beacon for the knife."

Uncle Merlin turned the corner at the next platform. "You would be, near Mordizan, which would make it difficult for us to find Anna through stealth. But I assume Mordred knows you're at Wraithwood. Five minutes outside the estate or the Maze isn't much of a risk."

His shoulders remained tight, and he didn't look directly at her. She filled in the blanks. *And you don't want to be alone with your sister when you have to explain how we all got into this mess.*

Sometimes, everyone needed a buffer around Mom.

After linking arms and stepping through the front door, they appeared on a narrow, roughly paved two-lane road between tall trees. In the distance, Brinnie could see a few buildings in what she assumed was Lyle, the nearest town.

Uncle Merlin frowned. "I should have brought a light of some sort."

Brinnie looked up at the stars beginning to speckle the sky. "Oh. It's nighttime."

He nodded. "Just tell me if I'm about to run into something."

The crunching of their feet seemed to echo over the chirping of crickets and whisper of leaves. "Closed" signs hung in the shop windows lining the empty street. The small town shut down with the sun.

As they approached the gas station, Brinnie spotted a familiar gray car sitting alone near a pump. "There she is."

She took a step forward, but Uncle Merlin held out a hand. "Wait. What's that?" He pointed off to the side, around the corner of the building near an outdoor icebox.

A figure hovered in the shadows, pressed against the side of the building. It could be a worker on break, but Brinnie's crawling skin didn't seem to think so. "A person."

"What sort of person?"

"Kind of a tall guy, wearing mostly black. Oh." She paused, seeing something long glint at his side. "Yeah, it looks like he has a sword."

"Stay here," Uncle Merlin instructed. He disappeared.

The figure peered around the corner of the building right as Uncle Merlin appeared right behind him. Before the man could react, Uncle Merlin kicked in the back of his knees while grabbing his sword arm and twisting. The man grunted. Within a second, Uncle Merlin had wrested the sword from the man's grasp and held it against the man's own throat. He pushed him forward into the dim lights of the gas station.

Brinnie's eyes widened. She'd seen Uncle Merlin fight before, but it was always jolting to see her usually calm, poised uncle engage in combat. She headed toward Uncle Merlin and the man.

A car door slammed shut. Mom strode forward, Isaac clasped protectively to her chest. Her tousled hair stuck out in all directions, and a half-asleep Isaac clutched her wrinkled shirt with one grubby fist, but she held her shoulders straight, a stormy look on her face. "Merlin, what do you think you're doing?"

"He's a dark one." Uncle Merlin shoved the man into the middle of the lot and pushed him to his knees, halfway between the door to the closed convenience store and the two pumps. He stepped to the side of the man and pointed the tip of the sword under his chin. "What are you doing here?"

The man gave his head a cocky tilt, straw-like hair flopping to the side. "That's no business of yours."

Brinnie slowed to a halt a few paces away.

Uncle Merlin stepped closer, and the man was forced to straighten as the blade tilted up. "I believe the person holding the sword decides whose business is whose."

The man rolled his eyes. "Or what?"

"Fine." Uncle Merlin raised the sword. "If you won't speak, then there shall be one less of your sorry kind on this earth."

"Merlin!" Mom snapped. Brinnie winced at the mom-voice. "You can't just kill people."

"This is war." He swung downward.

Time seemed to slow. Brinnie couldn't move, couldn't force her feet forward to stop what was happening.

"Wait!" The man threw an arm over his face.

The sword stopped mid-swing. "Talk."

"I'm a spy for Mordred." He lowered his arm. "I followed that woman here to be sure the shadowmaster was here as well."

The relief coursing through her turned to ice. He had Mom followed, but hadn't taken her? Just to get to Brinnie? What was this sick game?

Uncle Merlin easily flipped the sword in his hand and pointed it back at the man. "And did you learn whether she was?"

He smirked at the less threatening tone, straightening. "Why else would her mother come here? Mordred has a message for the girl." He looked past Uncle Merlin, gaze settling on Brinnie. "I assume that's you. Your sister and her husband are being held at an estate of one of the Allied Masters. They will be released if you meet him at the tenth stronghold by the ides of September. But if you don't . . ." He flashed a wolfish grin. "Lydia Tynsdale's wounds will seem as nothing to theirs."

Ice turned to fire. She glared at him, clenching her fists to keep from shaking. "And which estate are they at?"

"I didn't need to know, so I wasn't told." He looked from Uncle Merlin to Brinnie and back again. "That's all I know." He held out a hand. "My sword, please."

Uncle Merlin shook his head. "I'm keeping it." He lowered the weapon. "Go. Leave before I change my mind about killing you."

The man grinned cheekily while climbing to his feet. He tucked his hands in his pockets and sauntered away. Right before he turned the corner of the gas station, he offered a mocking salute.

Mom whirled on Uncle Merlin, clutching Isaac to her chest. "What is going on here? What's happened to my family?"

Uncle Merlin deflated with the threat out of sight. "I'm afraid it's what has happened to wizard families for centuries. They got caught in the crossfire."

"They've been *kidnapped*?" Mom's eyes flashed. "How? What do they have to do with anything?"

"Mordred wants me," Brinnie forced herself to explain. The buzz of a flickering light above kept time to the chant in her head. *My fault, my fault, my fault.* "He's using them to make me to come to him."

Instead of turning on Brinnie, Mom stared at Uncle Merlin. "And so you did nothing about this?"

His jaw tightened almost imperceptibly. "I've been searching for them ever since Brinnie turned up here."

"And Andrew?" Mom threw out an arm. "Where is he? Don't tell me he's been kidnapped, too, and you've just conveniently forgotten to tell me."

Uncle Merlin's eyes darted to Brinnie. The weight of secrets hung heavy in the air. "He's outside of Mordizan," he said. "We thought Mordred would most likely bring Anna and David there, so we were waiting in hopes of intercepting them."

Mom's mouth dropped open. "And you left him there?"

"He's perfectly capable of taking care of himself." He stepped past her. "Now let's get to Wraithwood before someone else comes along. Do you have room in the trunk for a sword?"

Her mouth opened and shut like a fish before she finally bit out, "Fine."

As they walked back to the car, Mom shifted Isaac to her hip and put an arm around Brinnie's shoulders. "Are you okay, honey?"

No scolding yet. Impressive. "I'm fine, Mom." She wanted to say more, to assure her mother that Uncle Merlin was handling the situation as best as possible, but she didn't want to disturb the tenuous peace.

Brinnie took a back seat with Isaac, shoving aside fast-food wrappers—out of character for neat-freak Mom. Such a long drive had taken a toll.

After buckling Isaac in, Mom slid behind the wheel and turned the key in the ignition while Uncle Merlin took shotgun. She pulled out of the gas station without saying a word.

Trees blurred past, the modern car driving much faster down the road than the Model T had ever gone. Brinnie thought she would explode in the suffocating silence that dragged on for several minutes, interrupted only by occasional sleepy noises from Isaac.

Finally, Mom broke the silence. "This is your fault."

Uncle Merlin didn't respond for a moment. "Pardon?"

The glow of lights on the dashboard highlighted Mom's clenched jaw. "I entrusted you with my daughter. Just for one summer. One." She pounded a palm against the steering wheel. "And what happened? She was kidnapped. Lost in a maze. Almost killed. Given the mark of the dark wizards so they could hunt her down."

Uncle Merlin remained silent.

Mom took that as an invitation to continue. "And because of all that, my oldest daughter is being held prisoner by wizards she didn't even know existed, my husband is alone outside the dark wizards' capital, and the daughter I entrusted you with can't leave Wraithwood for fear of being kidnapped." She threw a hand in the air. "Well done, Merlin. Your plan worked out so well, didn't it? I knew I shouldn't have listened to you. I should have kept her home. I knew better. I know what magic does. It's evil. There's no such thing as dark wizards and light wizards. You destroy things, kill people—"

"Eira." His quiet voice broke her tirade. "Do you really think we are all evil?"

Brinnie's chest tightened. She didn't want to admit to herself how much she hung on her mother's next words. *Do you think* I'm *evil?*

Mom hesitated. "I don't know," she said finally. "What difference is there between you? You were going to kill that man."

Uncle Merlin waited for her to make a turn before speaking. "I would have stayed the blade whether he gave the information or not. It was a ploy. I wouldn't have killed him." He sighed. "The difference is that we're forced to fight. Not just to defend ourselves. To defend the world."

She stared straight ahead. "That doesn't change the fact that you caused all of this."

He winced. "Eira—"

"Honestly! How bad can your judgment be? You left my husband alone at Mordizan. He's a wonderful man, but he's human. How do you think that would work out if he ran into a wizard? You might as well have left him in a shark tank!"

"Mom." Each berating word pounded into her skull, into her memory, until Brinnie couldn't stand it anymore. "Uncle Merlin's done everything anyone could possibly do. Dad is fine. He's a wizard, too."

Mom stiffened. "What are you talking about, Brynna?" Her voice strained. "Stay out of this."

"It's true." Uncle Merlin's words were delivered in a carefully maintained monotone. "The man you married?" The calm tone slipped, and his voice took on an edge. "He's Antony Drakon."

Frost sparked across the steering wheel. The car engine sputtered and died. Mom pumped the brakes and the vehicle shuddered to a halt.

Mom stared at the steering wheel for a moment before slowly removing her hands. She didn't look at them as she spoke. "Great. Thank you, both of you. We've wrecked the car. Because that's what magic does."

"It's a wonder it made it this far with three wizards, anyway." Uncle Merlin unbuckled his seatbelt. "It's only about a five-minute walk to the Maze from here. We would have had to leave it soon."

Mom threw the door open, stepped out, and yanked open the back door, reaching in for Isaac. "I don't know what kind of sick joke that was, Merlin." She pulled Isaac out and shut the door with her hip.

Uncle Merlin stood outside the car as well. "It's true. He's not really Andrew Lane. He's Antony Drakon." The next words slipped out of his mouth as if unintended. "If my judgment is bad, I don't know what to call yours."

They stared at each other over the roof of the car. Brinnie could almost feel ice forming between them, though she didn't see any more of Mom's magic manifesting. She slipped out of the car and shut her own door, feeling ill.

Mom's words came out clipped. "Let's get through this maze." The temperature around them dropped. "I want to talk to my husband."

CHAPTER TEN

The kitchen buzzed with voices and activity despite the late hour. Isaac laughed and shrieked as Mr. Winslow bounced him on his knee. Mrs. Winslow fussed over Mom, exclaiming that she hardly looked different at all, asking about everything that had happened in the past thirty years, and introducing her to the new members of the Wraithwood household—Marcie, Jerry, and Quentin. Uncle Merlin had gone to find Dad and call off the interception team, since Anna and David wouldn't be found at Mordizan.

Brinnie leaned against the wall, watching the chatter. From Mom's smiles and the Winslows' enthusiasm, it would be hard to guess that Mom and Uncle Merlin had spent the entire trek through the Maze in stony silence. Apparently the Winslows weren't on Mom's hate-list.

Miss Burtle pushed through the dining room door and her gaze settled on Mom. "Eira. You're back."

Mom smiled. It almost looked sincere. "Not exactly under the circumstances I would like to be. But it's good to see you again, Edna."

"Likewise." She scanned the room. "But I'm afraid I have bad news."

Mrs. Winslow straightened from baby-talking to Isaac. "What is it?"

"The eleventh stronghold has fallen. It's in enemy hands."

Quentin dropped the lid back onto the cookie jar and looked up from his not-so-sneaky thousandth attempt at pilfering. "That's bad."

"Thank you for that illuminating remark." Miss Burtle pressed her lips together.

"Have they destroyed the Anchor?" Jerry asked. He brushed

nervously at the fine coating of sawdust still clinging to the front of his jeans.

"No. They can't destroy one at a time. They all have to be destroyed at once in order for it to work."

"So we're still safe for now." Marcie sat back in relief. "There are eleven more."

Miss Burtle frowned. "For now. But our forces are outnumbered. We need more fighters."

"I should go," Jerry said bitterly. His shoulders hunched inward. "I should be fighting. If it hadn't been for me, Mordred would be dead and none of this would be happening."

"Don't say that." Marcie scowled.

Mom reached for Isaac, and Mr. Winslow passed him over. "What do you mean?"

"Last summer Mordred almost killed me. I didn't know about magic then." He glanced toward Brinnie, expression pained. A pain she knew all too well. "Brinnie helped save my life, but if I had died, Mordred would have, too."

If you had died. If I had never been born. So many ifs.

"*Maybe* Mordred would have died," Mrs. Winslow said sternly. "But at that point, you knew enough that it might not have mattered. We don't let people die around here, especially not on the off chance that it will kill someone else."

"Besides, you can't go." Miss Burtle waved a hand. "The strongholds are in the Alternate."

Maddy's hand shot into the air.

Brinnie bit back a laugh. "This isn't school. You can just ask."

"What's that?"

"It's like the double space in the estates," Quentin offered.

"Shockingly, that doesn't explain anything."

"So we're telling her everything, too?" Mom glanced around the room.

Miss Burtle shrugged. "From what I understand, there wasn't another good explanation for fireballs."

Mom sighed and turned to Maddy. "When Myrddin set up the new system of magic, there were some places he left in an alternate existence," she explained. "They exist over the same space as what is ordinarily there, as a double space. But with the strongholds, there are no gateways like there are to the estate double spaces. If a wizard walks in, they go to the Alternate. If a human does, they stay in what is there, here."

Maddy wrinkled her brow. "Sorry, but that made about as much sense as Quentin's explanation."

"It's a confusing concept," Brinnie put in. *And yet another fact no one bothered to tell me.* "The point is, Jerry can't get there because he's human."

"And so our pool of possible defenders is even smaller," Miss Burtle concluded.

A door slammed in the front of the house. All heads turned toward the dining room door.

It swung open a few seconds later and Uncle Merlin stepped through, followed by Dad.

Dad's eyes locked on Mom. He froze in the doorway. Brinnie could see his Adam's apple bob. No one spoke—only Isaac's babble broke the silence.

Mom patted Isaac's back, not taking her eyes from Dad, and took a step forward. "Andrew? Is it true?"

His weight shifted subtly, and for a moment, Brinnie thought he might turn and run. "Yes."

Mrs. Winslow brushed her hands together. "Well, we had better head to bed." She started across the room, grabbing Mr. Winslow by the arm and pulling him with her. "Goodnight, all."

"I'll get the baby settled," Marcie offered. She slid Isaac from Mom's arms and gave Jerry a pointed look. The two slipped away.

Quentin stuffed a cookie in his pocket and headed for the door. "I think this is probably a family matter."

Miss Burtle sighed and left wordlessly.

Maddy saluted. "I think Quentin's right. Technically I'm not related to you guys, so." She made herself scarce.

Uncle Merlin looked from one to the other, jaw tight. "Try not to destroy anything." He glared at Dad. "Don't give me an excuse to do anything I wanted to do thirty years ago." Then he disappeared.

The two hardly seemed to notice him, eyes locked on one another.

With no one looking at her, Brinnie grabbed some shadows and settled in to watch.

You have no right to be snooping on this private moment.

She shoved that thought down.

Mom's knuckles whitened as she gripped the back of a chair. "You're Andrew Lane. The man I married."

"Yes. And no." He took one step closer. "Before that was my name, my name was Antony. Antony Drakon."

She shook her head. "No."

He held out his hand, palm up. A flame sprang to life, dancing over his fingertips.

Mom's hands trembled.

He closed his fist and dropped his arm. "Eira, I'm sorry."

Her voice was barely a whisper. "Did you know?" She gained volume. "Did you know, when you married me?"

"I had no idea. I didn't even know you were a wizard." His voice cracked. "All I knew was that I loved you."

"Stop." Her already pale face drained of all color. "You want me to believe that, completely by chance, I married the man who killed everyone I knew? The man whose fault it is that my parents died?"

He opened his mouth, but no sound came out. He closed it again and gave one short, stiff nod.

"Do you know what that was like?" Tears formed in her eyes. "We had to bury them all ourselves. We did our best to give each one a headstone, even if it was the wrong name. Even if there was nothing left to bury. And then my parents . . ." She put a hand over her face, unable to continue.

Chills ran down Brinnie's spine. The rows of headstones flashed through her mind. How long had that taken? How many days had they combed through rubble?

His eyes squeezed shut, and a tear slipped out. "I'm so, so sorry," he said softly.

She looked up. "How." She gritted her teeth, a sob escaping. "And why?"

He took a deep breath. "I left everything. Made a whole new life. I never thought I would encounter magic again. And when I met you . . . I didn't know you were a wizard until Brinnie was born with the Enchantment." He ran a hand through his hair. "But I never saw a trace of magic from you. You said your parents died when you were very young, so I thought you must not have known what you were."

She hugged her arms around her torso. "I lied."

"I know." He sighed. "When you wanted to send Brinnie away last year, I finally guessed that you did know about magic. I was so close to telling you about myself—I was about to—but then you told me your brother lived at a place called Wraithwood."

Mom's fists clenched. "And did that bring you a sick sense of joy, to send a Drakon child straight into Wraithwood?"

Brinnie flinched.

"Nothing about it made me happy." His voice dropped. "I was afraid for Brinnie. I didn't know Merlin—I didn't know what he might do to my child if he found out. But what else was I supposed to do? I'd hoped she could learn about her powers here, safely. Then she would never have to know. And . . ." He hesitated. "And you would never have to know either. I'd never have to find out if you would be able to forgive me." He looked away. "That's terrible, I know. I'm so sorry."

She sank into a chair with her elbows on the table and dropped her head in her hands. "Do you remember when we met? It was at a soup kitchen. You were serving the soup. And I . . ." She looked up with tears rolling down her cheeks. "I was the dirty homeless woman in line."

Brinnie's eyes widened. That was a new part of the story. Mom and Dad never talked about when they met.

When Mom had gone on the run, she'd really taken nothing with her.

"And I hated whoever was the reason such a beautiful, sweet woman ended up in that position." His jaw clenched. "Turns out, it was me."

"Andrew, I tried so, so hard to get away from magic. I thought I succeeded, until Brinnie was born." She threw out an arm in his direction. "But I married a wizard without even knowing it. All these years, I just wanted to keep my family safe. I didn't want my children to ever have to go through what I went through. And now . . ." She gazed at the kitchen table with a vacant stare.

He circled the table and reached out to place a hand on her shoulder, but she pulled away. He let his arm drop. "I know. It's horrible, all of it. But do you think, maybe, this was meant to be? The odds, the chances of this—"

"Don't try to put a positive spin on this." She glared at him. "I've been cursed with bad luck my entire life."

"Not many people find themselves in the position we're in." His gaze took in the light orb floating near the ceiling, the walls of Wraithwood. Brinnie pulled her shadows tighter, even though she knew he wouldn't see her. "But many wish they had the opportunities we do."

"Opportunities?" She laughed harshly. "To do what?"

He held her challenging stare. "To do something about the darkness in this world."

A heavy silence filled the room. Brinnie took shallow breaths, afraid they would hear her thumping heart in the quiet.

Mom shoved back her chair and stood. "Bold words from a mass murderer, Antony Drakon."

She turned and stalked out.

Dad opened his mouth as if to say something as she walked away, but he didn't. Instead, he heaved a shuddering sigh and leaned on his hands against the table, head bowed. Brinnie had never seen him look so defeated.

She skirted the room and slipped into the storage area, taking the stairs slowly. On the second floor, she headed for her room until she noticed that the door of Ms. Tynsdale's room stood halfway open. She tiptoed down the hall and peeked in to make sure everything was all right.

Sitting by the bedside, Uncle Merlin held Ms. Tynsdale's limp hand. Ever so gently, he brushed a stray lock of hair from her forehead. "I'm sorry, Lydia," he whispered. "I've made a mess of everything." He clasped her hand in both of his. "I need you to wake up so you and Eira can yell at me together."

For some reason, the scene felt more private than the entire conversation Brinnie had spied on between her parents. The raw emotion in his words turned Brinnie right around again, headed back for her room. She couldn't watch anymore.

Mordred was tearing her family apart to get to her.

Then you can have me. But not them.

She swiveled, a new destination in mind. Bed called to her after an exhausting day, promising better sleep than her perch on the step the night before, but it could wait. Hopefully Uncle Merlin was distracted enough not to be paying attention to where everyone was in the house. That Masters' power still disconcerted her.

She descended the stairs and passed through the kitchen and dining room, the great hall, and the office, pushing open the doors to the library.

Strongholds. Anything about the strongholds. She scanned the shelves. She pulled out several books, but they only explained or described the strongholds. They never gave their location.

She huffed. *It's probably classified information.* They wouldn't want just anybody waltzing up to the strongholds protecting all of the estates. That meant the only place she might find something was in the Wraithwood Scrolls.

She climbed to the third level, too engrossed in seeking information to think about magic. She rifled through the scrolls, kicking up dust. Her eyes burned, begging for sleep, but she ignored them until finally she found something of use.

A snippet of a map caught her eye. She snatched up the scroll, glanced around, and spread it out on a nearby table.

"Estates and Strongholds," read the handwritten caption. She placed paperweights on the edges of the map while scanning its contents. It displayed the full world, but instead of countries and cities, the map's legend revealed that blue markers identified the sites of estates that answered to the enchantment wizards' headquarters of Castelon, and red dots indicated the possible locations of dark estates.

But what interested her the most were the X's scattered across the map. Each had a number scrawled above it. She scanned the map until she found the X labeled with a ten. Her eyes widened.

So that was why Mordred had chosen that one. It was only a few hundred miles away.

With a road map, or a GPS if she could manage not to kill it, she could get there within a matter of hours. And Mom had left a car right outside the Maze—the very vehicle in which Brinnie had passed her driver's license test not even a month ago. If she could get it to restart . . .

She began to plot.

CHAPTER ELEVEN

The ides of September is tomorrow.

Tomorrow. Tomorrow. Tomorrow.

The words echoed through Brinnie's mind like a chant, drowning out the awkward silences at the breakfast table, distracting her from analyzing the looks various family members shot at each other. Instead, she focused on keeping her knee from bouncing or her fingers from tapping as she waited for the perfect opportunity.

With so many people, they had to use the dining room table instead of the smaller table in the kitchen. Which she didn't mind—when everyone dispersed, she might be able to snag Uncle Merlin alone more easily.

"When do you leave?" Mrs. Winslow asked Uncle Merlin.

He pulled out his pocket watch. "In about twenty minutes."

"Where are you going?" Mom handed a piece of fruit to Isaac.

"Council meeting in Castelon." His gaze swept the table. "There will be some important talking points on the floor today in light of the recent fall of the eleventh stronghold."

Mom gave him a sharp look. "You're not going to tell them who Anna is, are you?"

"I've kept your secrets for decades, Eira. That isn't ending now."

She turned to Dad. "And you?"

"I'll be spending the day tying up loose ends in Arizona, with the help of Miss Burtle." He nodded to the secretary. "I hear she's good at helping people disappear."

Mom clenched her fist on the table. "We're not disappearing. Once all this blows over, we're going back."

Her stare challenged anyone to disagree with her. Brinnie averted her eyes.

Dad maintained an even tone. "Simply taking some precautions." He stood. "In fact, we should probably get started. Can I take anyone's plate?"

Awkward conversations buzzed as people began to leave the table. Brinnie slid into a seat next to Uncle Merlin.

She kept a nonchalant tone. "Do you think we should go move Mom's car off the road?"

He set down his fork and reached for a glass of orange juice. "I don't see why. No one comes to Wraithwood these days, so no one will need to use the road."

"But won't they be able to track Mom here?"

"I suppose, but it doesn't matter." He took a sip of his drink, eyeing her sidelong. "They can't come after her here, and this is the only logical place she would have gone anyway."

Brinnie tried to think of something else. "What about the human police? Even with Dad's precautions, eventually someone will wonder what happened to all of us, and there might be a missing persons case. We don't want them to see it and find Wraithwood. Now that the Maze is up, it can't pass for just a strange old mansion."

"I suppose it wouldn't hurt to be cautious. Perhaps this afternoon, once I return from Castelon."

She nodded. "Cool. Can I come with you?"

"To the council meeting?"

"No, to move the car." She noticed her hand fidgeting and tucked it under the table. "Maybe we should fix it too, while we're there."

He raised an eyebrow. "Why? So you can steal it and drive off to the stronghold?"

Her mouth opened and shut. She darted a glance toward Mom, still feeding Isaac at the other end of the table, but she didn't seem to have heard. "Wha—no, that's not—"

"I understand," Uncle Merlin broke in. He smiled slightly. "I would have thought up something similar. But that's a no."

Her cheeks burned. "You won't tell Mom, will you?"

"Wouldn't dream of it." He took a last swig of his OJ and stood, giving her a wink. "But next time you might want to think up a better excuse. Your lying could use some practice."

After Uncle Merlin left, Brinnie helped Mrs. Winslow tidy up the kitchen, mulling over options in her mind.

She could try the front door. If she opened it and stepped through, she didn't know where she would end up, but it would be outside the Maze. From there, she could figure out a way to the spot where the map marked the tenth stronghold. If she had any idea what she was looking for.

She needed more information. And there was only one wizard who could give it to her.

After helping Mrs. Winslow with the dishes, assisted by a talkative Quentin and Maddy, Brinnie managed to catch Quentin alone outside the washroom. "Quentin! I want to talk to you."

He glanced toward the door to the kitchen. "Haven't we been talking all morning?"

"Not alone." She sidled her way in between him and the door. "I wanted to ask you if you've ever been to the tenth stronghold."

He took a step back. "Nope. No way. I'm not helping you with this."

"It's my only option." She glanced toward the door, making sure no one could hear them. "They have Anna and David on an estate. No one's going to be able to get them."

"And you think if you turn yourself in, he'll actually let them go? Does that sound like Mordred to you?"

She scowled. It didn't, but she wasn't about to admit that. "It's a trade. That's how trades work. If things go wrong, I'll turn invisible and run."

He shook his head. "I'm not telling you anything. Honestly, I should tell your parents what you're planning." He stepped around her and began marching for the door.

"Wait." She shot out her hand to stop him.

Shadows flew from their posts clinging near the foot of the wall and beneath the steps, crisscrossing the door like overzealous guards.

Quentin jerked to a halt. "Are you . . . are you threatening me?"

She yanked her hand back. She hadn't meant to do anything, but the shadows had leapt to her unconscious bidding. She held her fist against her chest, willing the shadows to dissipate. "No. Of course not. I mean, not intentionally."

He gave her a strange look. "I think you should let me go now."

She nodded numbly. "Okay." Then she straightened her shoulders. "But promise not to say anything."

"Or what? Will you summon a shadow wolf to go after me?"

The words punched into her heart like a knife.

He must have seen the hurt flash across her face. "I'm sorry. I won't tell them. But please don't do anything stupid."

She didn't know what to say. "I'll try."

He gave her one last cautious look and headed for the door.

That final glance twisted the knife already in her chest.

Quentin hadn't experienced much of her power last summer. She'd hardly known it existed. But she'd learned from Uncle Merlin that, strangely, the most powerful wizards tended to develop their abilities as teens, instead of mid-childhood like most young wizards. He'd warned her that her power might continue to grow.

Like a bizarre magical puberty talk.

The voices screaming that all of this was her fault added a new worry to the mix. Was even her magic threatening?

How similar were she and Mordred, really?

She pivoted and headed for the library. It didn't matter. She would find out more about the stronghold herself, and she would get her sister back.

"Fools. Complete fools." Uncle Merlin paced through the kitchen.

Miss Burtle crossed her arms, leaning against the wall. "We already knew that."

As soon as Uncle Merlin returned, everyone had gathered to hear what news he brought from Castelon. Brinnie had abandoned a stack of books in the library scattered across the table in a way that would make Miss Burtle cringe.

She scooped up her toddling nephew and bounced him on her hip, the movement as much an outlet for her anxiety as a way to entertain Isaac. A much less obnoxious outlet than Quentin's bouncing leg as he perched on a stool in the corner. Miss Burtle shot him a look, and he stopped, leaning over to whisper to Maddy instead. Probably explaining what the council was, or some other wizard tidbit that Brinnie herself may or may not know.

"Apparently the fall of the eleventh stronghold was an 'unfortunate anomaly,'" Uncle Merlin was saying. "And Mordred, it seems, is just some impostor dreamt up to scare us."

Mrs. Winslow worried a dishrag between her hands. "But the crypt is empty."

"According to them, the body was stolen by dark wizards." Brinnie didn't know if she'd ever seen him so agitated. He threw out an arm. "You should hear the things they're saying in the council chamber. The attacks on the strongholds are being dismissed. The assassinations and missing persons? Not even mentioned. They're lulling everyone into a false sense of security."

"And so of course you told the chamber of the true enormity of the situation," Miss Burtle said.

"Naturally."

"And?"

He stopped pacing and turned to face them. "And I was told to stop fearmongering and leave the council chamber."

Dad leaned forward in his chair. "Can they do that?"

"They did."

Mom's eyebrows rose. "How can they kick a council member out of the council chamber?"

He sighed and ran a hand through his hair. "I'm not a council member."

"What do you mean?" Her brow furrowed. "Ludovic is one of the hereditary seats."

"Was," he corrected. "That was revoked a long time ago when I stopped playing by Castelon's rules."

Miss Burtle cleared her throat. "Though I did tell you after last summer that you should put in for one of the electoral seats."

"Yes, I suppose. I was trying not to stir up even more trouble after the treason scandal."

Dad's fingers drummed on his knee. His expression remained calm, but Brinnie recognized the motion as one of his anxious tells. "So are they even sending more reinforcements to the strongholds?"

"Oh, yes. They have to give the appearance of caring, after all. They're sending four score defenders."

Quentin sat up straighter. "For each? That's not bad."

Brinnie bit her lip to keep in an untimely laugh. Apparently even after everything that had happened, Quentin maintained his irritating respect for Castelon's authority.

"No," Uncle Merlin said flatly, "to share between all of them."

Mrs. Winslow made a noise of dismay, and Miss Burtle rolled her eyes.

Dad shook his head. "Stupid, but not surprising."

Mom waved her hand, as if shooing away irrelevant concerns. "Can they do anything about Anna and David?"

Uncle Merlin frowned. "I was told to leave before I could bring it up."

"Merlin!"

"Without disclosing their identity, the council wouldn't have helped anyway. Why would they be concerned about two unknown humans? Unless, of course, I said that they were being held hostage to lure in my niece, whose mother is, in fact, alive, and whose father is Antony Drakon . . ."

"I get the point," Mom broke in.

Miss Burtle uncrossed her arms. "Luckily, Merlin has his own network of spies."

"I wouldn't put it that way." He glanced at Quentin. "There are simply spies that I know about that Castelon does not." He pointed in Quentin's direction. "You didn't hear that."

He put his hands up innocently. "I watch the Key. Everything else is none of my business."

"In any case, I've sent the word out to be looking for Anna and David." Uncle Merlin pulled out a chair and sank into it. "If they're being held at any of the estates we have people in, hopefully we'll know within a few days, and we can come up with a rescue plan."

"We don't have a few days." Brinnie didn't realize the words had come out of her mouth until everyone turned to look at her. *Well, no turning back now.* "The ides of September is tomorrow."

"I'm sorry, Brynna." Uncle Merlin rubbed his temple. "There's nothing else we can do."

Her conscience made a plea for honesty, and she decided to give in. She would at least give them a chance to agree to her plan before she did it on her own. "I think I should go."

"Absolutely not." Mom gave her *The Look*. "I won't have both of my daughters held captive by Mordred."

Brinnie refused to be cowed by the mom look. "It won't be both. It will be a trade." *A trade of the daughter you don't want for the one you do.* "Mordred wants to hurt Anna. He's threatened them with a fate worse than death. As far as I know, he doesn't want to hurt me. I'll meet Mordred, make the trade, and escape later."

"You make escaping Mordizan sound easy." Dad shook his head.

She straightened her shoulders. "I can turn invisible. That's a big advantage when it comes to escaping."

"He will have thought of that," Uncle Merlin said.

She steeled her spine. *For Anna.* "I need to get into Mordizan. Ms. Tynsdale was telling me about something. I think it's a prophecy." She recited the three lines. "Maybe that's how she got caught. She found the prophecy Morgana told me about. The one that tells how to defeat Mordred."

"Lydia's not in her right mind, dear," Mrs. Winslow said gently.

"She seemed to know what she was saying this time. If I go with Mordred, maybe I can find the prophecy and learn how to defeat him."

The words sounded ludicrous. Her, a sixteen-year-old, defeat a fifteen-hundred-year-old wizard? *Not defeat. Just figure out how, so someone else can do it.*

"I think it's a good idea," Maddy said from the corner.

Brinnie had almost forgotten she was there, listening to them all discuss the fate of her brother. The two made eye contact, and Maddy gave her a subtle nod.

"If he doesn't kill you first." Miss Burtle sniffed.

"We all want them back, but we won't sacrifice someone else to do it," Dad agreed. He rubbed his chin. "But I might have another idea."

"Launch a full-frontal attack?" Maddy guessed.

"No. Pretty much the opposite, actually. With my father gone, I'm the Master of Dirklon." His fingers drummed. "What if I recently escaped from where I had secretly been held captive by the enchantment wizards, and came back to claim the estate?"

Uncle Merlin snapped his fingers. "Right. You ally yourself with Mordred, gain his trust . . ."

"And eventually use that against him to rescue Anna and David," Dad finished. "He doesn't know what happened to me all these years. For all anyone at Mordizan knows, I've been rotting in a dungeon."

"That will take a long time," Mr. Winslow spoke up. "Might not have that long."

"Then it's a two-part plan." The gears turned in Brinnie's mind. "I'll go, and we'll make the trade like I said. Mordred will release Anna and David. But then, after Dad gains Mordred's trust, he can get me out of there. I should be able to keep up a bluff, at least until then."

Silence.

Her plan made sense. No other plan would rescue Anna and David while still giving her a hope of escape. But no one wanted to admit it.

"A lot could go wrong," Mom said hesitantly.

"And a lot could go right."

Uncle Merlin sighed. "I don't think we have a choice if we want to get them back safely."

Mom scowled. "I don't think that after what you've already done you have any right to send her into more danger."

Did she really care? Or was it a matter of disagreeing with Uncle Merlin on principle?

Stop thinking like that, Brinnie. Mom did love her—in a strange, controlling way. "He's not sending me. I'm volunteering."

"Maybe someone could, like, follow you," Maddy suggested, "and they could climb up a tree, and when Mordred comes out—bang!—they could snipe him off, and then just take David and Anna and everyone's happy. Except Mordred, because, you know, he's dead."

"Wizards can't use firearms with any hope of accuracy." Uncle Merlin made eye contact with Brinnie. "But I won't let you go alone."

"Mordred specifically told me to come by myself. We can't risk him doing something to them if I disobey."

"I won't join you for the trade, but I'll escort you there and be on hand if something goes wrong." He glanced at Dad. "I'd say both of us, but . . ."

"I can't be seen with you. I know."

Brinnie looked from one to the other, one brow raised. When had the two of them formed an alliance?

Her heart warmed as the truth occurred to her. They had united in a common interest—her.

"Okay." She took a deep breath. Her heart pounded. *We're doing it. It's actually happening.* "Tomorrow it is."

CHAPTER TWELVE

Plotting lasted another four hours, laying out plans for Dad's takeover of Dirklon, Brinnie's trade, Uncle Merlin's scouting. Parties that weren't directly involved came and went. Mrs. Winslow kept them supplied with tea and snacks while they hunched over papers, maps, and lists littering the kitchen table. Brinnie's head ached with schematics and contingencies.

Finally, Dad slapped his pencil down on the table. "Enough for one night. We won't remember anything else in the morning if we keep going."

Brinnie rubbed her temples. "Agreed."

Uncle Merlin shuffled the papers into piles. "Brynna and I should get some rest before tomorrow. I think we should start out early."

Brinnie pushed back her chair, stood, and stretched her aching back. She focused on those sensations, instead of the fear that made her heart want to race.

Last summer, she'd had no choice in the matter. She'd been lost in the Maze by accident and ran from Mordred because she couldn't do anything else. Now, she was willingly walking right into his clutches. Part of her thought she had to be crazy.

She shook those thoughts away. "Do you know where Quentin is?"

Uncle Merlin's eyes unfocused for a split second. "He's heading down to the cellar."

"Thanks. I need to talk to him." She waved, leaving the table. "I'll see you tomorrow morning."

She passed into the storage room off the kitchen. Beneath the stairs, a small door was propped open a few inches. It creaked in protest as she pulled it open just wide enough to slip through. She ducked through the low doorway and descended a narrow flight of stairs into the unknown below.

She had never actually been in the cellar. She knew the Key was kept there, in a magic-proof room, but she didn't know what else she would find.

Chill air drifted upward, prickling goosebumps on her arms. At the bottom of the stairs, she emerged into a cramped room with stone walls. A couple of crates in the corner looked like they hadn't been disturbed in decades, but the room stood otherwise empty. In the opposite wall, a barred metal door, like one to a cell, hung open. She stepped through into the passage beyond.

Heavy barred doors studded the stone walls between unlit sconces. Brinnie peered through one to see a cell containing chains and manacles. She shuddered. No wonder the cellar had been closed off.

At the other end of the passage, a door of solid metal seemed to glow. A feeling pulsed from it, and her vision seemed to flicker. *Darkness*, she realized. The Key affected her power in this underground chamber with no light source. She grasped the massive handle and dragged it open, then pushed the door shut again after her.

She turned to see Quentin facing away from her, illuminated in the glow of a strange bluish light. It came from a pulsating orb, roughly the size of her head, on a stone stand in the middle of the room.

The orb swirled with a rainbow of color, slow, slipping one over another, giving Brinnie the feeling that if she stared at it long enough, it would suck her in and she would become one of the many churning colors.

She began to feel lightheaded and leaned against the door. She sank to the ground, but she couldn't tear her eyes away. Around her, the room grew darker, but the orb became brighter and brighter, filling her field of vision.

"Brinnie! Stop it." Quentin stepped in front of her, blocking the orb, and snapped his fingers in front of her face. "You can't stare at it like that. You'll kill yourself."

She jolted back to her senses. Her head spun, and she rubbed her eyes. "I . . . I didn't mean to."

"It does that to you." He kept his eyes averted from the orb, fixed on the floor nearby instead.

She stood, blinking to clear her head. "That's the Key?"

"Yes." His voice was reverent. His eyes drifted to the sphere, then away again, focusing on her.

She glanced at the Key, but not for too long. "It doesn't look like a key."

"Well, it's not like a house key or something."

"I know." She turned sideways, trying to stifle the urge to stare, to lose herself in those colors once more. "I . . . I'm not sure what I expected."

He turned his back to it but didn't meet her eyes. "Sometimes I like to come down here when things seem crazy. It's peaceful. I don't have any magic here, and neither does anyone else."

Brinnie winced. "Quentin, I'm really sorry about what I did earlier." She hesitated. "I really didn't mean for the shadows to do it—it was like they anticipated my desires and acted before I could veto them."

He leaned one shoulder against the rough stone wall. "That's a dangerous power not to control."

She grimaced. "I know."

He sighed, looking up at the ceiling. "I get it. And I forgive you. But I still don't think you should go with Mordred."

"We have a plan. My parents even approve."

"It's not that." He hesitated, picking at invisible lint on his sleeve. "Did you know that I had an older sister?"

She shook her head. Actually, she realized with a pang of guilt, she really didn't know anything about his family.

"Her name was Alana. She was a spellcaster, a really good one. She thought she could infiltrate Mordizan, bring back information." He stopped.

"And? Did she?"

"Sure, she infiltrated Mordizan. But then we didn't hear anything from her for months." He released a breath in a whoosh. "And when we finally did . . . she had joined their side."

"Oh."

Images flashed through her mind. Mordred holding out a hand, offering for her to join him. *"Together, we can bring about the world that should be."*

"I'm so sorry, Quentin. That's terrible. But you know me. There's no way I'd ever join Mordred."

"That's just the problem. I do know you. And you're a lot like my sister." He hugged his arms around his middle. "No one ever would have thought she would change sides. But she did." He sighed. "I know I won't be able to talk you out of it. But please be careful. Falling into darkness is easier than you think."

"Whoa! That thing's cool!"

Brinnie whirled to see Maddy standing in the doorway, glasses gleaming in the light of the Key. It took a moment for Brinnie to collect her thoughts. "Close the door. We don't want the magic to leak out."

"Whoops." She shut it behind her. "Is this that key thing?"

"Yes." Brinnie cocked her head. "Why are you down here?"

"Wanted to see what you were up to." She drifted toward the Key. "What happens if you touch it?"

"For humans?" Quentin shrugged. "Nothing, really."

"Cool." She reached out an arm and poked it. The colors swirled away from her finger in mesmerizing eddies.

Quentin nudged Brinnie. "Stop staring."

"Oops." She fixed her eyes off to the side.

"It's like a lava lamp or something." Maddy swirled her finger on its surface, causing the colors to spiral.

"Be careful," Quentin was starting to say, when the Key tipped off the pedestal and crashed toward the ground.

Brinnie dove forward to grab it, but Quentin shoved her away. "Don't touch it!"

She fell on her hip, rolling sideways with the momentum, and Quentin jumped backward, pressing himself against the wall as the orb rolled toward him. His eyes went wide. "Quick, Maddy, grab it."

"You don't need to freak out." She picked up the Key and settled it back on the stand. "See? Not broken or anything."

"Okay, no more touching." Quentin released a breath, taking a tentative step forward. "That was way too close."

"Why?" Maddy knocked on the hard surface. "It's not going to break."

Quentin flinched at her actions. "No, but if it made contact with us—a wizard's bare skin—it could kill us."

Her eyes widened. "Oh. Yeah. That's kind of bad."

Brinnie pushed herself up from the floor. "Maybe we should all get out of here."

As they filed out and closed the door, Brinnie blinked, trying to make out the passageway. "I can't see anything."

"Welcome to our world." Quentin flicked on a flashlight. "This way."

Once they reached the top of the stairs and the storage room, Quentin turned off the flashlight.

Brinnie resisted the urge to rub her eyes. Her sight would return eventually. "I never noticed how dim it is in here." She forced a smile. "Maybe this will help me sleep."

It did not.

She tossed and turned, plans and details and worries running laps in her mind. The next morning passed in a blur. Mrs. Winslow was sure that they needed a massive supply of food to take with them, Miss Burtle told Brinnie every random fact about Mordizan that she could possibly need to know, Maddy asked questions about everything, and Quentin hovered, getting in the way.

Before she knew it, she stood in the great hall, a small backpack slung over one shoulder, with everyone gathered around to say goodbye.

She hugged everyone from Wraithwood. Mom gripped Brinnie's shoulders with tears in her eyes. "I can't believe I'm letting you do this. What kind of mother am I?"

Those tears sank into Brinnie's soul. Not scolding. Not a million instructions. Just worry.

For a moment, she wondered if in some strange way, part of Mom's constant nagging and scolding came from a love she didn't know how to express.

Brinnie gave her a squeeze. "Don't worry. I'll be fine. In and out."

Dad was next. He wrapped her in his arms. "Be careful, kiddo. I'll do everything I can to get you out of there as quickly as possible."

"But not too fast." She winked, forcing a levity she didn't feel. "Got to do some spying first."

She nodded to Uncle Merlin. He tightened the belt around his waist, from which hung a sword in a sheath. *A sword.* This was no pleasure trip.

He offered his arm, and she linked hers with his. Then they stepped through the doorway.

They landed near the gas station, behind an old Dodge Caravan that looked at least twenty years old. Uncle Merlin unlinked his arm and reached under the body of the minivan, feeling around. Tape ripped, and he pulled out a set of keys stuck to duct tape.

Brinnie's eyebrows shot up. "You're stealing a car?"

"Of course not." He turned the key in the passenger side door, then rounded the vehicle to the driver's side. "I bought it this morning and had it delivered here. Now let's hope I can drive it."

She decided not to press the issue. She knew next to nothing about wizard finances, but she'd gotten the impression Uncle Merlin had enough money and connections to pay some human enough not to question dropping off an old vehicle at a remote gas station. But a more worrisome thought struck her.

"Hold on. What do you mean you hope you can drive it?"

"Well, I asked for an older vehicle on purpose, but what with being a Master, the more magic present, the more likely things are to get destroyed." He opened the driver's door. "This is a bit different from the Model T, but it should be all right."

Brinnie got in on the passenger's side and buckled her seatbelt, checking to make sure it was secure while Uncle Merlin tossed his sword in the back. She hadn't thought getting to the stronghold would be a life-threatening situation, but watching Uncle Merlin turn the key in the ignition three times before the vehicle actually started didn't give her much confidence.

When it finally rumbled to life, he shot her a smile. "There we go. That's a very good sign. I have a particularly poor track record with modern inventions, so only three tries bodes well for us."

Oh wonderful. I'm glad the car barely starting bodes well.

The vehicle's suspension seemed to be shot, and every rut and pothole of the old roads jostled them in their seats as they bounced over hills along tree-lined back roads.

They rode in silence. Brinnie watched the trees blur past,

reminding her of her first trip to Wraithwood with Bert the shuttle driver. She'd had no idea then what awaited her.

Would she have run the other direction if she did?

To distract herself from thoughts of Mordizan, she gathered some shadows in her hands and began molding them, attempting to form a bird. *I should know how to do something beside canines.* She imagined the mourning doves that sat outside her window in Arizona, cooing at unholy hours of the morning when she wanted sleep. She formed the plump body, the round head with slightly protruding eyes.

Her hands were clumsy. She'd never been much of an artist. The bird looked cartoonish, so she closed her eyes and imagined the birds, letting her mind mold the shadows instead, feeling them bend to her bidding.

When she opened her eyes, an all-black shadowy form of a mourning dove sat on her lap.

Uncle Merlin nodded to the dove. "You're very talented, you know."

Brinnie blinked, shaking herself out of her trance-like creative state. "What?"

"This sort of magic." He gestured to the dove. "It's been thought to have been dead for decades."

"Well." She looked down at the bird as it pecked her leg. "I guess it's not."

He remained silent for a moment, eyes on the road. "How was it? Your year without magic, that is."

"Sometimes it felt like last summer was only a dream." She watched the trees, trying to form thoughts. "But then I would look at my scar and know that it was real. It's strange, how people just live their lives, completely unaware. No idea that all that's standing between them and destruction is a few good wizards." She paused. "Imagine how much differently they would live if they knew."

"Or would they?" He shook his head. "Human nature is a terrible thing. Look at the wizards. Bickering and political wrangling in Castelon, wizards who won't fight, innocent people hurt." He slowed and put on his turn signal. "There's only a fine line between Castelon and Mordizan."

Brinnie's head whipped toward him. "But we're defending the world. The dark wizards are trying to destroy it."

"Indeed. For that reason, there is a line. But Castelon's tactics can be every bit as brutal as Mordizan's." He completed the turn, then glanced at her, expression serious. "It's easy to be sucked into doing things you never thought you would if you can convince yourself that the end justifies the means."

The hours passed. Brinnie's head bobbed, but anxiety kept her awake.

Eventually, Uncle Merlin slowed and pulled onto a dirt road. "This road leads to the stronghold. We'll have to leave the vehicle here."

They stopped to eat a lunch of sandwiches packed by Mrs. Winslow, though Brinnie had to force hers down. Her stomach felt like a knot, responding to the plans running on repeat through her head.

They hiked along the dirt path for nearly an hour. Trees shaded them from the late summer sun, but Brinnie cursed the humidity. The path continued to narrow, too small for a vehicle. She doubted many humans ventured this way.

The sound of burbling water reached her ears. Uncle Merlin stepped into the trees and gestured for Brinnie to join him off the path.

He pointed. "There's the entrance."

A stone bridge wide enough for four or five pedestrians to pass side by side arched over a stream with grassy banks. Moss climbed up the sides of the weathered gray stone. On the opposite bank, the dirt path lined with trees continued.

"We must part here." Uncle Merlin stepped deeper into the underbrush, a hand on his sword hilt. "Are you ready?"

She took a deep breath. The plan called for Uncle Merlin to oversee the proceedings from a distant, secretive location, while Brinnie would boldly confront Mordred on the bridge to make the trade. She hated the idea of parting, but . . . "Yes."

"Good. You are a powerful wizard, and I trust you to accomplish the mission." He put a hand on her shoulder. "But as my niece . . . I must be insane to let you do this. Promise you'll stay safe. You're more important than anything you might learn. You're here to free your sister. Anything else is extra."

She nodded and gave him a shaky smile. "Nothing too risky."

"Exactly." He stepped away. "Godspeed."

Uncle Merlin melted into the trees, and Brinnie continued along the path.

CHAPTER THIRTEEN

Crunching dirt gave way to rough stone as Brinnie stepped onto the bridge. The stream burbled beneath her, leaves twirling in the eddies, the woods serene.

The calm before the storm.

Brinnie fixed her eyes ahead. As she reached the middle of the bridge, she felt something like a ripple.

Where trees had once lined a dirt path on the other side of the bridge, a grassy plain stretched before her. In the distance, a stocky castle of the same stone as the bridge rose on the top of a hill, pennants flying from the battlements. Brinnie could just make out forms stationed on the wall. Ringing the castle from a safe distance were the tents of an enemy.

And in front of her, a guard station squatted at the other end of the bridge, manned by two sentinels in black and red livery.

Welcome to the dimension of magic. It appeared not much had changed in the past millennium. She was completely out of her depth. What did she know about any of this? Her heart beat faster.

"Halt." The two sentinels lowered their spears.

She put her hands in the air, not moving from the center of the bridge. "I'm here to see Mordred."

"Are you the shadowmaster?" the one on her left called.

"Yes."

"Prove it," the other growled.

Hands shaking, she drew shadows to her and let them swirl into her hand, an eddy of darkness.

The first nodded and gestured toward their end of the bridge. "This way."

Brinnie remained firmly in place. "Please tell Mordred that I'll meet him here. And tell him to bring his prisoners for the trade."

The first man laughed. "You didn't think it would be that easy, did you?"

Leaves rustled behind her. She whirled to see six armed men emerge from the trees, two dropping from branches above.

Her heart pounded. *A trap.* They'd watched her approach. For how long? Did they know Uncle Merlin was here?

She forced her voice not to waver. "I was told this would be a peaceful exchange."

The sentinel stepped forward. "You were told wrong."

Brinnie backed away, arms out. She felt the shadows dappling the bridge around her beginning to stir. *Good.* She felt the ripple again—she'd backed out of the Alternate, but now, she could still see the landscape of that dimension. Evidently, once crossed, the Alternate became clear. *Also good.* The plan could still work. "You don't want to do this," she warned.

Her words went ignored. The men behind her strode forward, and the sentinels in front of her approached.

A hair-raising howl floated through the trees from outside the circle of men. The soldiers exclaimed as a dozen shadow wolves broke from the forest and wove between them to surround Brinnie in a circle, facing outward and growling.

She patted one with relief. *Thanks, guys.*

"Still have your little pets, I see." The familiar voice sent chills up her spine.

Brinnie turned back toward the guardhouse. The sentinels stepped aside to let a tall figure pass. His black robes rippled, like some gaunt, dark priest. "Brynna Ludovic. A pleasure."

The wolves snarled.

"Mordred." She gestured to the men encircling her. "What is this?"

"A misunderstanding, I believe." He glared at the sentinel on his right. "Under whose orders have you accosted my guest?"

The man shrank away. "Master Vorath's, sir."

"Does he so fear a young girl that he would send half an army against her?"

The two sentinels exchanged nervous glances. "No, sir, but a shadowmaster—"

"So he fears one wizard?" Mordred's gaze bored into him. "I didn't take Vorath for a coward." He waved a hand at the men advancing on Brinnie. "Dismissed."

The soldiers stepped back, fading into the forest once more.

As they dispersed, Mordred smiled at her, revealing too-white teeth. "What would Arthur have thought if he knew that his line would give rise to a mistress of shadows?"

She kept her chin up. "Where is my sister?"

"In time." He brushed past the sentinels, approaching within feet of her wolves. "Have you come as a student, to learn? Or as an exchange, a prisoner for a prisoner?"

"I thought we've had this conversation. Why would I want to learn anything from you when you keep doing things like this? You kidnapped my sister."

Mordred sighed and folded his hands in front of him, looking down on her like a frustrated adult to a naughty child. "We have indeed had this conversation. I may have kidnapped her, but she was not harmed, nor did I intend to harm her. It was the only way to get your attention." He snapped his fingers and gestured to the woods to Brinnie's right. "See for yourself."

Twenty yards away, on the bank of the stream opposite the fortress, six soldiers tromped through the underbrush, two figures between them.

"Anna! David!" Brinnie rushed to the edge of the bridge, hands on the wall. "Are you okay?"

Anna waved. "We're fine! Completely fine."

The guards parted to give a better view of the couple. Their clothes were clean, and from where she stood, Brinnie couldn't see any blood or signs of physical harm. No shackles, no ropes. "They didn't hurt you?"

"No." Anna glanced at David. "We were worried when they came and said we had to go with them, but we haven't been harmed."

Their guards led them forward until they reached the bridge.

Brinnie scrutinized them. "They didn't threaten you? Anything?" She shot a glance at Mordred, but his expression gave away nothing.

"No. Oh, Brinnie, I'm so glad you're safe." Anna ran a few steps past her captors, holding out her arms, then hesitated, looking at the wolves. "We went willingly. They said you were in trouble."

Her relief they hadn't been hurt warred with her feeling that something wasn't quite right. But Anna and David were on the correct side of the boundary to the Alternate, free to walk away if the soldiers allowed them.

She turned from Anna's waiting arms to Mordred. "Call your soldiers onto your side of the bridge. And I want to watch Anna and David leave. No double crossing."

"Very well." He gestured to the men. "As I have stated, I have no interest in your human relatives. But your wolves must allow my men to pass."

Reluctantly, she dismissed half of her pack, but kept a few surrounding her, pressed in tightly. The men skirted her, keeping to the sides of the bridge, before converging behind Mordred.

"What do you want with me?" Brinnie tried to read Mordred's face. "Why me?"

"I want you to know the truth. I want your help in changing the world." He shook his head. "I can see you still doubt me. Once again, I ask you to consider. Have I ever done anything that was not for the purpose of bringing about the world that should be?"

She glanced at Anna and David, still standing behind her on the bridge. "So if I go with you, they're completely free."

"Of course."

"And if I don't?"

"I will still let them free. As I said, I have no desire to harm them." He nodded to the two. "Go."

Anna hesitated, but David took her arm, drawing her toward the path.

Very un-Mordred-like behavior. Unless that was his plan. He wanted her to think that he was the good guy. Well, she could play along. "You said you'd found a way to bring peace."

He nodded. "Indeed I have."

"If I go with you, you won't kill me?"

"Of course not. I never tried to do that, and I never will."

She stepped closer, but still outside the Alternate. "I don't know if

I believe you or not about everything else, but I know you're telling the truth about that. So maybe . . . maybe I should find out."

He smiled. "It gladdens me greatly to hear you say so. If you are ready, I would like to bring you to Mordizan at once."

She waved away the last of her shadow creatures, removing the barrier between them. "Okay."

"Good." He reached into his cloak and pulled out a vial the length of his index finger. "All I ask is that you drink this."

She took a step back, attempting to lead Mordred forward. "What is it?"

"It is a potion to put you into a deep sleep. It will ease the trip to Mordizan."

She shook her head. "I think I'll be fine without it."

"Unfortunately, it is a safety precaution." He advanced. "The location of Mordizan isn't meant to be known to all."

"Oh." She held her arm out to take it, shuffling one step forward. *Come on, Mordred. Come to meet me.*

In their planning, Uncle Merlin had explained that he couldn't transport into the Alternate from outside of it. Early planning suggested he sneak through the border somewhere else, but the strongholds could only be accessed through specific entry points. But if Brinnie could lure Mordred past the border, Uncle Merlin could appear on the bridge with her and make a surprise attack.

Mordred took a few steps forward to hand the vial to her. Was he out of the Alternate? She couldn't quite tell.

She took the glass container and pretended to struggle to uncork it. *All right, Uncle Merlin. Right now would be a great time for the sneak attack.*

Nothing. No movement.

She put the tincture to her lips and slowly drained it, grimacing at the taste. *Come on. We're running out of time.* Where was he? She put the cork back in and made as if to hand the vial back to Mordred but held it just out of his reach so that he had to take one step closer.

A yell sounded behind her. Brinnie whirled as Uncle Merlin appeared beside Anna. Wait, when had Anna drawn closer? Why were she and David only a few steps behind Brinnie?

Uncle Merlin grabbed Anna by the arm and swung her past Brinnie, shoving her. Anna cried out and rolled, jumping to her feet behind Mordred.

Brinnie shrieked. "What are you doing?"

Mordred ducked as Uncle Merlin yanked the sword from his sheath and swung right where Mordred's head had been. In one quick motion, Mordred reached beneath his robe and whipped out his own blade just in time to parry a second blow. "Ludovic. I wondered when you might turn up."

Brinnie stumbled back, heart sinking. Uncle Merlin couldn't win a full-on duel with Mordred. Why had he attacked Anna? Why had he destroyed all element of surprise?

"Let her go, Mordred," Uncle Merlin demanded.

"Let her go? I'm not holding her prisoner. She may leave if she wishes."

"You know that's a lie." He held his sword at ready, angling himself between Brinnie and Mordred. "Brynna, get out of here. That's not your sister."

"What?"

This time Mordred struck, and Uncle Merlin was forced to defend himself. The blades met and metal crashed on metal. "Let her make her own decisions, Ludovic."

Uncle Merlin shoved Mordred back with their locked blades. "Brynna, that's not Anna. It's a trap."

Her thoughts swirled like molasses, fuzzy, too slow. She tried to process, eyes going to Anna, backing away behind Mordred as soldiers advanced. "But she's right there . . ."

"Humans can't enter the dimension of magic. You shouldn't be *able* to see her."

Swords clashed again. "Silence," Mordred growled.

Uncle Merlin gave Brinnie a glance that begged her to understand. "They're not your family. They're shapeshifters. Ru—"

Time slowed. His words cut off in a grunt as something long and glinting grew from his stomach. A blade. A blade from one of the soldiers behind him.

The man yanked the sword out. Uncle Merlin stumbled.

Brinnie heard herself scream. She tried to run to him, but the ground seemed to be rolling beneath her feet. Her legs gave out, knees cracked against stone, palms scraping. So much blood, Uncle Merlin on the ground, Mordred with his sword raised . . .

The potion took effect, and all went black.

CHAPTER FOURTEEN

"Did you hurt her?"

"No. I only gave her a sleeping potion."

"So I'm in charge of her? Even after last time?"

"Yes. She knows you. She will be more inclined to trust you."

Voices echoed as if from a distance. Brinnie tried to swim upward into consciousness. A strange taste in her mouth. A spinning feeling. But something soft beneath her. A bed? She forced her heavy eyelids to open.

Two people stood at the foot of the bed. A woman with long black hair tied in a ponytail—Nimue—and . . . Mordred.

Everything came rushing back. She shot upright, then clutched her head, room spinning and blackness threatening to engulf her once more. "Uncle Merlin!"

"It is good to see you awake." Mordred folded his hands in his robes.

She searched Mordred's face for an answer—or tried to. He seemed to have two heads. "My uncle. Is he alive?"

"I am not certain. He disappeared after attempting to murder me."

She opened her mouth to argue, but what he said was technically true. "Anna and David? What have you done with them?"

"As you saw, I set them free."

She shook her head, then instantly regretted the movement. "That wasn't really them." The room continued to spin, the wooden beams crisscrossing the stone ceiling seeming to rotate like a ceiling fan. *Get up. Find them. Get out.* "Where are they?"

"Those were, in fact, your sister and her husband. Under ordinary circumstances, humans cannot enter the dimension of magic. However, these were not ordinary circumstances."

Brinnie squinted at him. "How so?"

The woman beside him put a hand on her belted hip. "He's not an ordinary wizard."

How had Brinnie never seen the striking resemblance before? Brinnie herself looked similar enough to her, though Nimue's skin was darker than Brinnie's alabaster complexion, and Brinnie's blue eyes didn't match her brown ones, but she was a near perfect match for the female version of Dad. Nimue and Dad could be fraternal twins. "Can I talk to them, then? Make sure they're okay?"

"And how do you propose to do that?" Mordred asked. "Shall we track them down and bring them back here?"

"Oh." Brinnie rubbed her temple, trying to clear her mind. How indeed? Could she trust that Anna and David had truly been released? She didn't know enough about magic to know if Uncle Merlin had been mistaken, if Anna really could have passed into the Alternate under special circumstances.

She didn't even know if Uncle Merlin was alive.

She had too little information, too little power—too much of a headache. She winced, looking around the small room with dark stone walls. "Where am I?"

"Where do you think?" Nimue gestured dramatically. "Welcome to Mordizan."

The stone walls, Mordred's robes, Nimue's gray tunic with knives tucked into a leather belt—she'd taken a step back in time.

Mordred nodded once. "Nimue will take care of you. I have other things to attend to, but I expect to see you tonight." He turned, strode three steps to a heavy wooden door, and exited the room.

Brinnie eased one leg, then another over the edge of the bed. "What happens now? A dungeon?"

Nimue crossed her arms. "That depends on what you do. Either we can be civil, or you can try to run away like last time."

"*Me* be civil?" Brinnie crossed her arms as well. "You tied me to a banister last time."

Her eyes narrowed. "You brained me with a frying pan."

"*After* you tied me to a banister."

They glared at each other until the corner of Nimue's lips twitched. Then she laughed, and Brinnie broke a half-smile.

"I like you, kid." Nimue walked to the other side of the room and the small wardrobe standing against the wall. "Don't do anything stupid, and I think we can get along."

"I'm giving this a chance. Maybe Mordred is right."

Nimue snorted. "You're awfully combative for giving this a chance." She pulled open the doors of the wardrobe.

"I want to make sure my family's okay." Brinnie craned her neck to see Nimue around the nearest wardrobe door.

Nimue appeared to be shuffling through clothes hanging inside. "Hate to tell you, but if you do the right thing and join us, the Ludovics aren't your family anymore. They're your enemy. And you better hope Merlin is dead."

He's not dead. She barely kept the words from bursting out, an emphatic declaration. Maybe if she repeated them, she could be sure they were true. Instead, Brinnie planted her feet on the floor and tested her legs. A bit wobbly, but they would hold. "Well that certainly make switching sides sound enticing."

"I just want you to be informed." Nimue pulled out a garment and threw it on the bed. "Family doesn't mean anything. You saw my own sister threaten to kill me. Not that I blame her. I would have done the same."

Brinnie took a few shaky steps toward the article of clothing on the bed. "She wouldn't actually have killed you."

Nimue closed the wardrobe doors. "Of course she would have." She pointed at the bed. "Some clothes for you there. Make yourself decent and I'll be back for you in a bit."

Brinnie considered sharing the tidbit that she'd later overheard, how Ms. Tynsdale told Uncle Merlin she'd prayed Mordred would buy her bluff. *"I can't stand the sight of her, but she's still my sister."* Nimue was never truly in danger.

But she didn't. "Decent?" She looked down at herself. Grass stains streaked her jeans and shirt, and brown dried blood crusted the denim of her pants. "Ah. Decent."

Nimue quirked a thumb over her shoulder toward the wall on the other side of the wardrobe as she left. "Washroom over there. You've got thirty minutes." She stepped through the door into the hall beyond and paused. "And do a good job. You're having dinner with the

Master of Mordizan."

The door slammed behind her.

She wanted to exclaim something about the Master of Mordizan, but all Brinnie squeaked out was, "Do a good job? Am I five?"

Nimue was already gone.

Brinnie turned to the bed and picked up the outfit Nimue had selected. Her eyebrows shot up. It was a long black dress of some sort of soft material. She held the dress up against her. The hem brushed the floor, and the fitted sleeves went down to her wrists, while the bodice laced up in front. *What on earth am I supposed to look like? A witch princess?*

No time to waste on clothing. Before Nimue returned, Brinnie scoped out the room. The walls were all stone, as was the floor. A light orb floated near the ceiling, she assumed to make up for the lack of any windows. The furniture consisted of only the bed and the wardrobe, and iron bands stretched across the heavy door.

A guest room for prisoners.

Just to make sure, she twisted the doorknob. Locked.

She tried to control her breathing. *This is what we wanted.* She'd made it into Mordizan. She'd made the trade for Anna and David—hopefully. And no one else had been harmed . . . except Uncle Merlin. Who at least was still alive.

She hoped.

She collapsed onto the edge of the bed. Nothing went according to plan. Anna and David might not be free, Uncle Merlin might be dead, and she might be a prisoner for nothing.

Not nothing. No matter what else had or hadn't happened, she had a purpose here. She needed to gain Mordred's trust and find his bane.

Wobbly legs carried her to the narrow door to the washroom. Beyond, she discovered a standard bathtub, sink, and toilet. She decided not to question the arrangement. They probably had some unfortunate water-controlling wizards in charge of their sewers.

Towels hung on a stand near the bathtub, and the water actually came out warm, so she took a soap-less bath to get rid of the dirt and blood. As the red flowed off from her, she shuddered.

He's alive. He has to be.

Strength returned to her limbs as the potion lost effect. Once she toweled off, she returned to the chamber, leaving her dirty clothes in a heap in the corner. She wriggled into the dress and laced up the bodice.

With her hair still wrapped in a towel, she began examining the room, searching for weak points in case she needed to escape. She guessed she probably had at least another ten minutes before Nimue returned. She was feeling along the wall for imperfections in the stonework when she heard the doorknob rattle.

She yanked open the wardrobe and pretended to be looking at the clothing inside.

Nimue entered dressed in similar attire to Brinnie, with a long black skirt trimmed in dark green. She'd also exchanged a ponytail for a more elaborate updo.

Nimue looked Brinnie up and down. "Good. It fits. Here." She tossed her a hairbrush.

Brinnie fumbled to catch it. "We're having dinner with the Master of Mordizan?"

"He let you come here." Nimue shut the door and leaned against it. "We have to convince him that it was a good idea."

Brinnie dumped the towel on the bed and dragged the brush through the tangles in her hair. "And if we don't?"

"He kills you." Nimue fiddled with a slim dagger the length of a finger, testing the edge. *Where did that come from?* "A threat neutralized."

Brinnie's eyes widened. "So how do I convince him?"

Nimue pointed the dagger at her in approval. "Good. Asking the right questions." She pushed off the door. "Mordred and I both know you're on the fence about all this, and that's a risk he's willing to take, but the Master is not. Your job tonight is to convince him that you are loyal to Mordizan. You're not questioning whether you're on our side or not. You're sure. The hardest part will be convincing him that you aren't loyal to the Ludovics anymore."

Brinnie's heart thumped. Her first test as a spy, and already at the highest level. "How?"

"He's paranoid about spies, and rightly so—you probably think that's what you are right now." Nimue rolled her eyes. "You'll get over that quickly. For now, you need a convincing reason why you have completely turned your back on the enchantment wizards."

"Wait." Was her mind still addled from the potion? "You think I'm a spy, and you want to help me convince your leader that I'm not?"

Nimue sighed. "Mordred has other plans for you. It's all politics. Do you want to spend your time up here, or in the dungeons?"

"Okay, reasons." Brinnie thought for less than a second. "Probably because they lied to me for fourteen years. And wouldn't let me use magic even when I found out the truth." The reasons continued to roll off her tongue, and she ticked them off on her fingers. "And I want to be who I am without anyone telling me to hide it or that it makes me evil. And I believe that with our magic, we really are capable of bringing about a better world, but no one was willing to let me try."

Nimue nodded along.

She tried to stop herself, but the last reason tumbled out of her mouth. "And my mom never wanted me anyway, so I might as well go someplace I'm wanted."

Nimue raised an eyebrow. "That'll work. You've half got me convinced." She held out a hand. "Give me that brush. We've got to do something decent with your hair before we go."

Nimue's brush strokes were surprisingly gentle, but Brinnie hardly noticed. Her mind replayed her blurted words, appalled. The lies had rolled off her tongue so easily—almost like they had been waiting. *Watch yourself, Brinnie. You might start believing your own lies.*

After Nimue finished twisting Brinnie's hair into a braided bun, somehow securing it with a long black stick, she set aside the brush. She reached into the wardrobe, pulled out a pair of black flats, and tossed them in front of Brinnie. "All right, put your shoes on and let's get going. And in case you were wondering, this hair stick is blunt. If you try to kill someone with it, you'll just look stupid."

Brinnie gaped, feigning surprise as she stepped into the shoes. "I wasn't planning on trying to attack anyone with a *hair accessory*."

"Too bad." Nimue grinned. "That would be my first thought."

As an avid reader, it had been Brinnie's as well. But Nimue didn't need to know that.

After exiting the room, they emerged into a long hall with a high stone ceiling. More heavy wooden doors led off from it every twenty feet or so. Nimue led the way to a staircase at the other end. No windows illuminated the spiral staircase, only light orbs in sconces.

They descended and entered another hall, then a wider room, then what seemed to be a courtyard. She looked up, trying to discern the time of day, but she saw neither sun nor stars, only walls studded with windows rising high on all four sides.

Brinnie tried to keep her bearings, but as they continued, she became completely lost. They passed through so many halls, rooms, and staircases that she lost all sense of direction, and everything was made of the same dark gray stone.

Occasionally, Brinnie spotted figures crossing ahead of them, or heard voices behind doors. The farther they went, the more frequently other denizens made appearances. Their attire seemed a mix of medieval fashion and modern practicality. She imagined the various tunics, robes, and insignias meant something, but for now, she felt like an extra on the set of a fantasy film. Some stood and talked, others strode by with purpose, and every so often, a guard in what she was beginning to recognize as the black and red Mordizan livery stood posted at a crossroads.

Wherever they went, those they encountered dipped their heads in various levels of respect to Nimue, from full bows to deferential nods. She nodded back, leaving a wake of whispers behind them.

Brinnie's heart raced. Why hadn't she considered this? Why had she imagined Mordizan to be the size of Wraithwood? There had to be hundreds of people just in this fortress, and they all seemed to know Nimue. Her aunt wielded power here.

A house in a hedge maze seemed like child's play in comparison.

They turned a corner, and Brinnie's breath caught. She found herself in a long hall with high ceilings. Massive chandeliers hung above them, casting shadows on obsidian columns leading to two enormous double doors. A red carpet led to the doors, and red, black, and gold tapestries blanketed the walls. Between the columns, guards stood at attention, spears erect.

Nimue slowed to a regal walk. Her lips barely moved as she spoke to Brinnie. "The dining hall is in there. Mind your manners and remember your story."

Brinnie nodded. She tried to match Nimue's pace. As they drew near, two men stationed outside the doors bowed and pulled them open.

Head up, Nimue strode through the doors onto a wide floor. On either side, tables lined the room. However, Brinnie's eyes were drawn forward. There, an arrangement of three huge tables of dark wood, probably capable of seating forty-some people, loomed above the rest on a slightly raised dais. Candles in candelabras flickered on the table among leafy garlands and shining dinnerware, and voices echoed in the vast room from the occupants of the center tables. Music seeped from an alcove Brinnie couldn't see.

Voices quieted as the two of them entered. Heads turned their way. As if on cue, the music trailed off, reaching the end of a song.

Nimue's heeled boots echoed on the stone floor as she and Brinnie continued forward. They stepped up onto the dais and walked between the two flanking tables like a gauntlet, diners staring.

Closer and closer to that central table. To the ornate chair in the center, where a broad-shouldered man with dark brown hair and a well-trimmed beard watched them approach impassively, elbows resting on the armrests of the thronelike seat. A gold signet ring gleamed on his right hand.

Mordred sat beside him, a brooding figure in dark robes. His eyes bored into Brinnie, warning. *Don't step out of line.*

Ten feet in front of the central table, Nimue stopped and curtsied. "My lord."

Brinnie swallowed, tucked in her shaky arms, and bowed to the Master of Mordizan.

CHAPTER FIFTEEN

The Master nodded to Nimue with a slight smile. "Nimue Drakon. Always a pleasure. And who do you bring with you?"

She stepped to the side, gesturing to Brinnie. "May I introduce Brynna Ludovic."

Brinnie tried not to fidget as whispers erupted from those seated at the tables and curious eyes fixed upon her.

"Brynna Ludovic." The Master sat back, giving Brinnie a better view of the intricate gold embroidery across his scarlet waistcoat. An irrational urge to giggle burbled up in her. The Master of Mordizan and Uncle Merlin apparently had similar senses of style. "So young, this shadowmaster I've heard so much about." His voice snapped her back to sobriety. He stroked his chin. "Tell me, Brynna, how does a descendant of Arthur come to possess such dark power?"

Tread carefully. "I don't know, but I imagine my ancestors are rolling in their graves."

A few chuckles gave her hope she'd effectively deflected the question.

"Indeed." The Master raised an eyebrow. "And with such a . . . *noble* lineage, why do you desire to join our ranks?"

She glanced at Nimue, who gave a subtle nod. "I may be a Ludovic by blood, but not by heart. They lied to me and hid my heritage, forcing me to live as a human. I'm done hiding." She took a step forward, emphasizing her words. "I believe there's a better way for wizards to live. I want to live in that world where wizards are free. The world Mordizan stands for."

Scattered applause behind her gave her hope, but the Master remained nonplussed. "Are you willing to back up these claims?"

Her heart pounded. "Of course."

"Then you will give up the Enchantment?"

She'd been warned this might happen. Though the Enchantment protected humankind by tethering itself to wizards, Uncle Merlin had explained that Castelon sometimes gave spies approval to give up the Enchantment when needed for going undercover among dark wizards. "Gladly."

"And you will join us in battle to capture the strongholds?"

Brinnie's heart skipped a beat. This, she hadn't anticipated. "Whatever is required of me."

For a moment, he simply regarded her, and she feared he would call her bluff and it would all be over. But at last he nodded. "Join us. Let us eat."

A small sigh of relief escaped from her lungs.

The music started again, and conversation picked up. She followed Nimue around the table to two empty seats on the right of Mordred. Nimue sat beside him, and Brinnie wrangled her skirt into the other.

Servers brought out plates of food, revealing such ordinary dishes as chicken and fish. *Significantly better than the blood of children.* At least the meals weren't evil.

Brinnie tried to copy everything Nimue did, so she wouldn't accidentally commit a faux pas. She spread out her napkin, picked up the same fork.

"Any word about Ludovic?"

The name pricked Brinnie's ears toward the Master of Mordizan, who addressed Mordred.

Mordred wielded his fork and knife with extreme precision, cutting a tiny piece of chicken. "None."

Nimue took a bite of what looked like potatoes, and Brinnie copied her.

"Then we may assume him dead." The Master smirked.

Nimue swallowed, reached for her glass. Brinnie did the same.

"I do not believe that would be wise." Mordred shaved off another tiny piece. "We must not underestimate him."

Nimue dabbed her lips. Brinnie echoed the motion. Nimue shot her a look. "Quit that," she hissed. "Eat like a normal person." When Brinnie gave her a wide-eyed look of innocence, Nimue added, "You look psychotic."

Meanwhile, the Master laughed. "Ah, Mordred. Always fearing the worst. He was run clean through. By now, Wraithwood has no Master."

The words punched through Brinnie. She stared down at her plate. *Don't react.* She blinked to keep tears from coming to her eyes.

"No Master, perhaps, but a mistress." Mordred folded his hands into his robes. "Eira has returned. If she inherits his power, she will be even more powerful than he."

"Interesting." The Master of Mordizan leaned forward to address Brinnie. "How much do you desire to prove yourself to me?"

She managed not to choke on her water. "Very much, sir." Was "sir" the right honorific? Dad and Uncle Merlin had neglected to mention how to address a dark Master. She took another sip of water to soothe her dry throat.

"I had hoped you would say that." A smile snaked across his lips. "I need you to eliminate Eira Ludovic."

This time, she did choke. "You want me to kill my mom?"

"Who better?" He dug his fork into fish gleaming with a red sauce that reminded Brinnie of blood. "You shall 'escape' from Mordizan, return to Wraithwood, and when she is unsuspecting, you shall neutralize the threat."

The meager food in her stomach churned at his calm, professional demeanor as he spoke of murdering her mother.

Before she could speak, Mordred broke in. "That may be too much to ask of her so soon."

"Of course." The Master chuckled. "I'm not a fool, Mordred. She'll have months of training first. She'll need to be ready to rule as the Master of Wraithwood as a member of the Allied Masters."

Nimue gave Brinnie a raised eyebrow, no doubt thinking of their previous conversation. Brinnie took a deep breath. "I'm sorry, I was just a little surprised at first at that level of responsibility. Of course I'll do it."

Mordred shot her an approving glance.

The Master of Mordizan nodded appreciatively. "Good. Nimue will have you enrolled tomorrow." He addressed Nimue directly. "We'll expedite the process, of course. We need her in place in a matter of months, not years."

Before Nimue could reply, the great doors swung open, sending a chill sweeping through the room.

Candles flickered, and conversation faltered.

A bent figure hobbled through the doorway, leaning on a staff. *Thump. Thump. Thump.* The airy music continued, an absurd counterpoint to the off-beat thud of the staff. The ragged ends of the figure's long gray robes dragged along the floor. *Swish. Shuffle. Thump. Swish. Shuffle. Thump.*

The hair on the back of Brinnie's neck prickled.

As the person drew closer, Brinnie made out long, matted gray hair peeking from beneath the figure's hood, along with a face etched with nearly as many wrinkles as Morgana's once had.

The old woman came to a stop before the Master of Mordizan and pointed at him with one gnarled claw. "I have come to claim what is mine."

Her rasping voice sent chills down Brinnie's spine.

The Master of Mordizan looked at her impassively. "And what would that be?"

Her trembling finger wandered to her left, until it pointed directly at Brinnie. "I claim the right to an apprentice."

A murmur rippled through the room.

"Do you know who that is?" The Master of Mordizan addressed the woman. "Brynna Ludovic. A descendant of Arthur. You would do well to choose a different apprentice."

The old woman shook her head and smiled to reveal blackened teeth. "There is no other. I claim the mistress of shadows."

Nope. Big nope. She forced herself to stay in her seat, even though the woman's eyes on her made her skin crawl. She felt shadows stir around her, responding to her spiking heart rate.

Mordred shook his head. "I have already designated Nimue as her mentor."

The old woman laughed, a creaking, grating sound. "Mordred. All your power, yet you still fear me."

"I don't fear you." His voice dripped with disgust. "What you practice is not magic."

"Enough." The Master of Mordizan held up his hand. "Your claim is valid, Keilrie. But first she must be trained and rid of the Enchantment."

"One month." She held up one shaking finger. "One month, then she is mine."

"Objection," Mordred said. "She has other obligations."

The woman smiled slowly, mouth cracking open like a shriveled pumpkin splitting in the sun. "Then you will have to share." Her gaze drifted until it met Brinnie's.

Brinnie recoiled from the woman's black eyes, a darkness with depth that seemed to try to pierce to her soul. Even the shadows clinging to Brinnie shrank away.

The woman raised an eyebrow and cackled. "Not all is as it seems."

Then she turned, raised her staff, and shuffled away. *Swish. Shuffle. Thump.*

The song from the alcove came to an end. All remained in eerie silence as the woman hobbled through the doors. A concerned buzz filled the room as they shut.

Brinnie leaned over to Nimue. Her voice shook. "Who was that?"

Nimue frowned. "Someone we weren't counting on."

CHAPTER SIXTEEN

Brinnie huddled in bed, a blanket wrapped around her shoulders. She stared across the room, trying to let her mind figure itself out.

Eventually, tears began to fall. Though she tried to stop it, the horrible image of the sword piercing through Uncle Merlin replayed over and over in her mind.

He couldn't be dead. He held them all together, the one steady factor in the strange confusion that was the world of magic.

I never actually said goodbye.

I never told him I love him.

She took a shuddering breath and wiped the tears from her face. No. He wasn't dead. She wouldn't believe it. No matter what the dark wizards said.

Her heart burned against Mordred with loathing. The Master of Mordizan was just as bad, expecting her to murder her own mother. How on earth could she even pretend she agreed with them? Especially for the weeks it might take Dad to rescue her.

Weeks. That amount of time hadn't quite sunk in before.

Not even Mordred is as bad as that creepy lady. Brinnie cringed at the thought. Dad or no Dad, she might need to get out of there within the next few weeks if it meant working with Keilrie.

She wrapped herself in shadows and snuggled into the hard mattress. Soon, the long day took its toll, dragging her into sleep.

Sometime in the middle of the night, she awoke, confused.

A scratching sound emanated from near the wardrobe, like something brushing against stone. She clenched the blankets. Were there rats?

Something scraped again, almost like stone on stone.

That would have to be a huge rat.

She eased out of bed, drawing shadows to her, trying to form a weapon. She looked down at what she'd made.

Apparently her subconscious thought a frying pan would be the best defense against giant rats. *Fair enough.*

She bent and peered under the wardrobe. Nothing. She swung it open. Clothes, shoes, but no rats. Finally, she checked the bathroom, but nothing looked out of place there.

She heaved a sigh. *I hate this place.* Then she stumbled back to bed.

The scraping never returned.

The next morning, Brinnie began another inspection of the room. The door remained locked, and a search of the wardrobe yielded no bobby pins or other tool with which to attempt to pick the lock. Not that she knew much about it—her knowledge of lockpicking came entirely from novels. The hinges must have been on the outside of the door, so she couldn't try to pull those apart, and the pipes in the bathroom were much, much too small for a human.

Defeated for now, she rifled through the wardrobe and pulled out some simple black pants and a loose black shirt. *Why always black?* After brushing her hair with the flimsy hairbrush Nimue had left and tying it back with the singular hair tie she'd been allowed—what was she going to do with a hair tie?—she sat on the edge of the bed swinging her legs.

About five minutes later, the doorknob rattled.

Nimue entered wearing a similar outfit to Brinnie, but with a belt around her waist holding a knife sheath. She looked Brinnie up and down. "Good. You're awake. Come with me."

Brinnie pushed off the bed. "Where are we going?"

"First things first. You need to get rid of the Enchantment."

She swallowed hard. She'd taken comfort at times in the idea that her passive existence in carrying a shred of the Enchantment helped protect humankind. Especially when all she could feel was the shame of being the unwanted daughter. *But plenty of other wizards also carry the Enchantment.* As long as even one wizard lived with the Enchantment attached to their magic, the human world remained safe.

Brinnie followed Nimue into the hall, between two guards with spears standing to either side of the door. Nimue waved them away. "You're dismissed. We'll be out for a while."

Brinnie gave Nimue a questioning look. "Are they always there?" She looked over her shoulder as the two men in familiar Mordizan livery headed off in the other direction. "Were they there yesterday?"

"Of course. Just a precaution. I dismissed them when I was taking you to dinner."

The thought of guards standing outside her door all night made her cringe. Maybe they had been the source of the strange noises? But the noises hadn't seemed to come from the hall.

Once again, the corridor was empty. Brinnie wondered if they were keeping her in a deserted area of the fortress. They traveled such a confusing route she would have felt like she was in the Maze all over again if not for the people they passed, some dressed as guards, some carrying books, others strolling through barren stone courtyards, talking. She thought she might recognize some of the locations from the night before, but she couldn't be sure.

As they descended a flight of steps, Brinnie's stomach rumbled. Nimue chuckled. "I agree. But this isn't something you want to do with food in your stomach."

Not comforting. What did extracting the Enchantment entail?

Nimue led the way to an ordinary-looking wooden door without any marking and knocked.

A few seconds later, it swung open to reveal a wiry man with a shock of tousled curly hair and magnifying spectacles that enlarged his eyes to three times their size. He clicked the sides of the spectacles, lifting the magnifiers to reveal his natural eyes. "Yes? Can I help you?"

"Good morning, Aron." Nimue gestured to Brinnie. "She's here for an extraction."

He rubbed his hands together. "An extraction!" He waved the two of them forward. "Come in, come in."

His obvious excitement made Brinnie a bit worried. They stepped into what seemed like a magical lab, with wands, stones, and papers littered across a large desk and table. An open space in the center of the floor was covered with what looked like chalk markings. Brinnie shuffled sideways to stand next to the wall, trying not to disturb a pile of books stacked on the floor.

Aron scurried about, shuffling papers and examining wands, casting one aside in favor of another, clicking the magnifiers on and off to examine them. He looked up at Nimue standing in the doorway. "Why are you here? Out!"

Nimue put her hands on her hips. "She's my charge."

"She'll be fine." He waved his arms at her. "Out, out! You're throwing off the balance of magic."

Nimue raised an eyebrow. "Fine. Brinnie, I'll be outside."

Brinnie nodded, and Nimue exited, shutting the door behind her.

Aron continued his squirrel-like search. "Age?"

Brinnie glanced around, before realizing he was asking her. "Oh. Sixteen."

"Good, good." He grabbed a pen from behind his ear, shuffling through papers. "Lineage?"

Did that mean last name? Wizard family? "Um, Ludovic?"

He stopped short and whirled, eyes enormous. "You're the shadowmaster."

"You know about me?"

"Everyone does. We've all been talking about you."

"Oh." Word traveled fast in Mordizan. Unsettling.

He gestured with a wand. "There, stand there. In the middle of the circle. Are you sure you want to do this?"

Brinnie followed his instructions, stepping into the middle of the chalk outline. "Yes, of course."

"Good. Because if you're not sure or you resist, we're going to have a terrible time." He examined the chalk circle, tapping some sort of powder in worn spots. "Containment powder," he explained. "Keeps all the spells from bouncing around the room. Are you ready?"

No. What needs to be contained? What sort of ritual is this? "I think so."

"Not good enough." He pointed to his head. "Know so. I'm going to extract the Enchantment, but it's woven into your magic. Bad things happen when you don't fully surrender. Tearing magic. Killing you. Killing us both." He shrugged. "I'd rather not die, personally."

Her heart thumped. "I'm sure that I'm ready." *I really want this. This will let me find Mordred's bane. It's good. No doubts.*

"Then stand right there, don't move, and whatever you do, don't move out of the center of that circle." With that, he extended his arm with the wand and closed his eyes.

Suddenly, he gave the wand a jerk. She felt a tug inside of her, somewhere deep in her core. It took all of her self-control not to clamp down and resist.

The next tug took her breath away. The shadows within her hissed. Then it changed. Instead of tugs, he pointed the wand straight at her, and she gasped as the tugs became a constant pull.

It felt as if her soul was being vacuumed out. Within her, a shining, burning thread began to rip from the weave of her magic. Her vision became fuzzy, and she clutched her chest, gasping.

A bead of sweat rolled down Aron's temple. "Don't resist," he warned.

Her legs gave way and she fell to her knees. She couldn't suck in a breath. The thread clung to her magic. *I can't do this. This Enchantment is all that stands between humanity and destruction.* The thoughts came almost unbidden. As they did, pain exploded in her temples, and she cried out.

"Don't resist!" Fear tinged his voice.

Let it go, let it go, she begged the magic. Her shadows threw themselves toward Aron, but they rebounded off the invisible walls of the containment circle. Pain shot through her limbs, her mind.

Aron gripped the wand with both hands, teeth gritted. He stepped forward, one foot crossing the line.

Her magic lashed out. Instead of attacking, it grasped the magic flowing from him, yanking it away. He yelled. "Stop it!" His eyes widened. "Are you a helper, too?"

"Yes," she gasped. She cried out as something inside her ripped again. "Why does it matter?"

"No no no no." His breaths came quick and shallow. "Not good." He grimaced, adjusting his grip on the wand. "I'm sorry, but I'm not dying today."

Like a fisherman hauling in a big catch, he yanked the wand back.

Tension snapped through Brinnie. With a pop that resounded like an explosion, that golden thread of the Enchantment ripped free.

She screamed. It felt like every cell inside her had exploded. She felt herself hit the ground. Something had gone terribly wrong.

All went black.

CHAPTER SEVENTEEN

"I will personally gut you," a female voice growled.

Fingers at Brinnie's neck. A hand slapping her cheek.

"You didn't tell me she was a *helper*." Aron's voice.

"Why does it matter?" Brinnie placed the female voice now. Nimue.

"Why? Because she nearly killed us both! Do you know how dangerous she is?" His tone slipped toward awe. "My mentor would give anything to study her."

Brinnie's eyes blinked open just in time to see Nimue shoot to her feet and grab Aron by the front of the shirt. "If you tell *anyone* about her, you are dead." She gave him a shake and let go. "And depending on *who* you tell, I'll decide whether that's by my hand, or if I'll give you to Ignatius as a little gift. Got it?"

He went pale. "Yes, my lady. Forgive me, my lady."

Brinnie rolled onto her side, grunting at the ache in her bones.

Nimue instantly knelt. "Brynna. Are you okay?" As Nimue touched her shoulder, Brinnie felt a spark go out from her. Nimue exclaimed and snatched her hand away. "Aron, call a physician."

"I'm fine. Really." Brinnie pushed herself up. At first she thought she was just dizzy, but then she realized the swirling effect came from shadows racing in frantic circles around the room. She waved her hand at them. *Stop that. Settle down.*

Nimue sighed. "At least your magic is still intact."

"Too intact," Aron grumbled, rubbing his wand hand. Nimue glared at him, and he shrank away.

Feeling returned to Brinnie's limbs. She stood slowly, and her legs held.

Nimue looked relieved. "Good. Thank you, Aron."

"I'd say it was a pleasure, but." He frowned, shaking out his hands.

"Sorry." Brinnie offered a sheepish smile.

"Well, if you're feeling all right, we have a lot to do today." Nimue hesitated. "Are you? Because if you're not . . ."

Something inside of Brinnie felt raw, like road burn on her soul. But if she wanted to find Mordred's bane, she needed to know this fortress inside and out, learn how everything worked. "I'm fine. What's next?"

Nimue grinned. "That's what I like to hear." She nodded to Aron. "We're out. Come on, kid."

Brinnie followed her into the corridor. What would Nimue say if she knew her half-sister's favorite nickname for Brinnie was the same? *Just a dark-haired Ms. Tynsdale.*

They would both want to kill her if she said that out loud.

"So where are we going?" Brinnie asked.

"Masters' heirs usually have years of training. Vorath—you know, the Master of Mordizan—wants you trained properly in order to take over Wraithwood." Nimue sighed. "Mordred wants you trained too, of course, but we were hoping to give you a bit more time to acclimate. Unfortunately, Keilrie has claim to you after a month, so we need to get you a solid start before she starts taking your time."

Brinnie shivered. "Why? Can't we just say no?"

"I would, but *some* people are a stickler for the old laws." Nimue rolled her eyes. "Our law states that every master wizard has the right to an apprentice. It's a tradition that's faded with the years, and with the streamlining of the University, but it used to be that if you wanted to learn to be a good wizard, you apprenticed yourself to an older wizard. As the only living shadow walker, Keilrie has first dibs on training you."

Brinnie grimaced. They turned a corner and wove around a pair of wizards who nodded to them politely. One carried a stack of papers, while another lugged a satchel that looked to be either full of books or bricks—Brinnie guessed the former. She wished she could be lugging books instead of getting handed off to a creepy lady.

Nimue laughed at Brinnie's expression of distaste. "Hopefully we'll be able to keep you in the field so often that you won't have time to see her much."

They approached a walkway with a raised portcullis guarded by two sentinels and emerged into a wide courtyard, where Brinnie could see clouds above. She turned, walking backwards, and her mouth fell open.

Behind them loomed the fortress of Mordizan—or at least, part of it. A grand castle of dark stone with soaring towers and crenellated battlements blocked out the sky. The courtyard they stood in seemed to ring the massive structure. Slitted windows high up stared down at them like squinting, judging eyes. The courtyard stretched for about half a football field before it reached a second circle of structures, these also decked with towers and wall walks.

Nimue didn't share Brinnie's awe, striding ahead. "I don't want to take you all the way to the University and back, so you're doing assessments here. We have some scholars within the fortress, and they're able to run the academic tests."

Brinnie hurried to catch up. "Academic tests?"

"For the University. We have to see where you are, to place you in classes."

Classes? Classes in what, murder?

"Lucky for you, we can get everything done in one day." Nimue led the way through a doorway into the next circle of structures. "They're having combat assessments in the west courtyard at eleven, so we can squeeze in the academic portion this morning."

Brinnie stopped just inside the doorway. "Combat assessments?"

Nimue didn't seem to hear. She passed a line of busts of what Brinnie assumed were prominent wizards lining the foyer and approached a woman sitting at a semicircular desk to the right. "I registered someone for a nine-thirty evaluation this morning."

The woman shuffled her papers. "Nimue Drakon?"

"Yes."

Brinnie set her feet moving again and joined them at the desk. The woman squinted at her, then looked back down at the papers. "Milady, it seems we have a problem. The person you registered is sixteen."

Nimue leaned a hip against the desk. "Yes?"

"The University does not accept students under the age of eighteen."

Nimue waved off the objection. "She's an exception."

The woman folded her hands on the desk. "Milady, we of the Order of Scholars have been entrusted with the running of the University by the Master of Mordizan. Our rules can't be bent."

"Unless he says so. Which he did." Nimue hooked a thumb at Brinnie. "That's Brynna Ludovic. The shadowmaster? Vorath wants her trained."

The woman pursed her lips, but nodded. "Wait here."

As the woman left through a door behind the desk, Brinnie turned to Nimue. "'Milady'?"

Nimue raised an eyebrow. "Drakon?"

Brinnie just looked at her. Was that supposed to explain something?

"You know, a Masters family?" Nimue sighed as Brinnie continued not to track. "It's polite to call a woman from a Masters family 'milady' and a man 'my lord'."

The Masters and estates were reminiscent enough of lords and fiefdoms, but now Brinnie really felt like she'd gone back to feudal Europe.

The door behind the desk opened and a woman with brown hair pulled back in a severe bun stepped through. Her face was expressionless as she looked down at her clipboard. "Brynna Ludovic?"

"That's me."

The woman turned and waved Brinnie with her. "Come back."

Brinnie glanced at Nimue, who nodded. "I'll see you later. I'll have someone come get you and bring you where you have to go next."

Brinnie followed the woman through the door. No guards? No one watching her? Weren't they afraid she would escape?

To where? If she bolted, she would get nowhere. She had no idea how to leave this fortress. Schematics of the interior of Mordizan that she'd studied at Wraithwood had been spotty. Especially with the blade, they would find her before she found an exit.

They didn't consider her a threat. It was almost insulting.

The woman led Brinnie to a study with one large desk covered in papers and one small, bare desk surrounded by bookshelves. She took a packet of papers from her clipboard and set it on the small desktop. "Take a seat." She placed a pencil next to the packet.

Brinnie sat in a hard wooden chair, trying not to giggle. In the fortress of the dark wizards trying to destroy the world, and where did she find herself? Taking a test in a classroom.

"You have thirty minutes." The woman sat at the other, larger desk and turned over an hourglass. "Time starts now."

Brinnie picked up the pencil and looked at the first page. *Name the three divisions of aqua wizards.*

She blinked and looked up at the test proctor, but the woman already had a book open. Maybe the next question was easier. *Conjugate the verb meaning "to work magic" in the ancient language.* Her eyebrows rose. *This will be interesting.*

She flipped through the packet, trying to find questions she could answer—few and far between. She had returned to the beginning and was imaginatively conjugating the unknown verb for working magic—*I magicado, you magicadee, he magicadoodles*—when a shadow fell across her paper. She looked up to see the proctor paused in carrying more books over to her desk, looking down at Brinnie's paper with a raised eyebrow. When she made eye contact with Brinnie, she turned and walked away shaking her head.

After a series of questions regarding divisions of magic, wizard history, the ancient language, and how magic worked, Brinnie finally came to a question she might actually know the answer to. *A traveler can move from any distant point to another in less than a second. What limitation is there on this ability?* Feeling very knowledgeable, Brinnie wrote, *The traveler has to have been to that place before.*

By the end of the test, Brinnie concluded that she knew absolutely nothing about anything. As the last of the sand fell through the hourglass, she set aside her pencil. Good thing Master Vorath wanted her trained for battle, not for the classroom. *But I am demanding more thorough lessons when I get back to Wraithwood.* Failing a test was just embarrassing.

She handed the test over to the woman, who set it in a basket on her desk, hardly looking up from her work. "Tell Marta to have someone send you to Gerd. I assume you're off to combat assessment."

"Uh, yeah, I guess so." Brinnie backed toward the door. "Thank you."

The woman didn't respond.

Brinnie hoped Marta was the lady at the desk, or else this was about to get awkward.

Marta, who did in fact turn out to be the desk lady, gave Brinnie a series of confusing directions to the west end of the fortress, where she would find this Gerd.

"Nimue didn't send anyone to show me how to get there?" Brinnie asked after listening to the instructions for a second time.

Marta frowned at her, pointedly focusing on her papers. "No."

Okay, then. If she knew where to even start, she would have taken the opportunity to snoop around for Mordred's bane. But she needed to learn the ins and outs of the fortress better first. "Thank you."

Marta didn't respond.

Why so grumpy? They get to read and study all day. They're living the life. And Brinnie was interrupting that. Well, made sense. She hated being interrupted when reading as well.

She did her best to follow instructions, but she'd never been good at navigation. Soon, she realized she had no idea where she'd gone wrong, but she didn't know where to go next. And she hadn't passed another person in about five minutes now.

She spun in the long hall with stairs there, a door there, a window there . . . a window. Maybe if she looked out, she could get her bearings.

The narrow window opened three feet over her head, clearly not designed for the viewing pleasure of shorter people. Or anyone, for that matter—it had probably been included as a vent to allow air flow. She jumped, caught the sill with her fingers, and pushed her way up the wall with her feet until she could get her elbows on the sill.

She scanned the grounds outside. At some point, it appeared she'd ascended to a second or third floor. The stone of the courtyard lay several yards beneath her, and the scenery gave no indication of where she'd wandered to. *Great.*

"See anything interesting?" a male voice asked.

She jumped and tilted backward. Her feet and fingertips scrambled for purchase, forearms scraping against the ledge, but she missed and fell.

Hands wrapped around her waist, and before she could register that the person was helping her, she whipped her elbow around and struck him in the nose.

"Gah!" The person let go, stumbling away, and Brinnie teetered into the wall.

Back against the wall, she now had a view of the speaker who had startled her, and she was glad he wasn't actually an attacker. The young man in front of her holding his nose had to be as tall as Dad, with shoulders like a quarterback. He pushed back dark, curly hair with the hand not holding his nose, eyes wide. Blood dripped onto his red shirt.

Brinnie clapped her hands over her mouth. "I'm so sorry." She patted her pockets. "I'd give you a tissue if I had one. I really didn't mean to."

He reached into his own pocket and pulled out a rag, holding it to his nose. "I guess I deserved it for startling you."

Was his nose crooked? The gushing blood didn't fit his calm demeanor. *What do I do?*

He glanced at her scraped arms. "It looks like you took some damage as well."

"It's no big deal." *Great. Wonderful. Good job, Brinnie.* Her first full day at Mordizan, and she'd accidentally accosted a denizen. From the crest of Mordizan stitched on the right shoulder of his shirt, probably someone who worked for the Master.

He pulled out another rag, replacing the one filled with blood, hardly seeming bothered. "I got the impression that you're lost. Are you trying to go somewhere?"

"To someone named Gerd, and combat assessment, apparently."

He smiled, which would have been more comforting without blood on his face. "Seems appropriate after the martial prowess I just witnessed."

She felt her cheeks go red. "I'm so, so sorry."

"It happens. But you don't want to show up like that." He gestured to her arms. "He'll never let you hear the end of it, and you'll get sand in the wounds from the training pits." He adjusted the rag beneath his nose. "If you want, you can come with me to see Leslie. We'll both get patched up, and then I'll show you how to get to combat."

Brinnie narrowed her eyes. Could she trust him? What if he planned to kidnap her or something?

With blood pouring from his nose?

"Okay. Thanks." She hesitated. "But I'm more dangerous than I look."

She expected him to make a quip about dangerous elbows. Instead, he nodded, meeting her eyes with a solemn gaze. "I believe it."

She fell into step beside him, feeling awkward. He directed them toward the opposite end of the hall, down a flight of stairs, and through another hall.

They emerged into a wider room with a door leading to the courtyard. Here, guards and soldiers clanked through with weapons and armor, men and women in white shouted to each other, and college-aged people scurried back and forth, carrying out orders.

The bloodied young man lurked around the corner, watching the chaos. Was he hiding? He nodded toward a wooden door to the side, where a man had just exited. "This way."

He slipped around the corner, knocked, and let himself in. Brinnie scurried inside behind him.

A woman in white with a messy blonde ponytail turned around from wiping down a metal table and jumped. She let out a breath in a puff. "What if I was with a patient?"

"Sorry, Leslie. Trying to avoid attention, and I watched the last one leave."

She took in his bloody face and cracked a smile. "I can see why. What did you do?"

He gestured to Brinnie. "I startled a dangerous warrior."

Her face heated again.

The woman, Leslie, pulled out a drawer from a series of cabinets along one wall of the small room. An examination room, Brinnie realized. This was some sort of clinic. Leslie retrieved a wad of gauze and pointed to the table. "Hop up."

He shook his head. "You can do her first. She needs to be patched up before combat assessment."

She advanced. "Your face is covered in blood."

"I just need some fresh rags." He backed away.

"Let me see your nose, you big baby." Brinnie giggled to herself as

Leslie cornered him and pinched his nose with two fingers. Something popped, and she released. "There. You were going to walk around with a fractured nose." She grabbed a cloth, ran it under a sink set into the cabinets, and handed it to him. "Here. To wipe off the blood."

"Thank you." He began scrubbing his face, heedless of the apparently broken nose.

Oh. Magic. His nose wasn't broken anymore. Leslie must be a healer.

Leslie turned to Brinnie with a bright smile. "Excuse us. I only treat Marcus that way because he's my cousin and chronically ignores injuries. Real patients get treated nicely." She raised a hand, fingers splayed. "May I?"

"Uh, sure."

"Now all I'm going to do is put my hand on your head to give a basic assessment." She reached out, touched Brinnie's forehead, and closed her eyes. Her eyebrows rose. "You've been in battle already. What happened to your side?"

Brinnie glanced toward the young man, Marcus. He leaned against the wall, arms crossed, looking amused. "Yeah. A guy stabbed me with a knife last summer."

Leslie nodded, fingers still resting against Brinnie's skull. "You were fixed up by a skilled healer." She opened her eyes. "What's that on your arm?"

Brinnie hesitated, but what did it matter here? She pushed up her sleeve. "A scar from an enchanted blade."

Leslie frowned, leaning forward. "Who holds the blade?"

Brinnie noticed Marcus's eyes also fixed on the mark. His amusement seemed to have been replaced with cold, calculating interest. His face looked older, sharper, without the humor. "Mordred," Brinnie responded.

"Oh." Leslie smiled. "Good. Not the enemy then."

It took Brinnie a minute to understand. *Oh, yeah. The good guys are the enemy.* "Nope."

"Here, let me see your arms." Leslie ran her hands over Brinnie's raw forearms, and the skin smoothed in their wake. "There. Other than that, you seem to be in excellent health, good shape. Marcus said combat assessment. Are you looking to become a fighter?"

Nope, just looking to get out of here ASAP. "I'm not sure."

"You're a little small, but I could see it." Leslie glanced at a ticking clock on the wall. "You should probably hurry to the practice arena if you're part of the eleven o'clock trials."

Nimue had mentioned eleven. "Right. Umm."

"I'll take you there." Marcus pushed off the wall. "The duels should be starting soon."

Brinnie's eyebrows shot up. *Duels?* "Okay. Well, thank you, both of you."

Leslie gave a cheerful wave. "Good luck!"

Fabulous, Brinnie thought as they exited. *Time to go fight some people. And hopefully not get killed before the real fighting even starts.*

CHAPTER EIGHTEEN

The practice arena was enormous. Open at the top, with stands ringing it like a stadium, the arena featured giant circles filled with sand like a multi-ring circus. Along the walls that separated the stands and the arena floor on the nearest side of the stadium, racks held every weapon imaginable—swords, spears, axes, bows and arrows, and more. Firearms were noticeably lacking. Brinnie thought of Quentin's pistol exploding in his hand and smiled to herself.

"This is where I leave you." Marcus nodded to her. "Good luck."

"Thank you." Her voice echoed in the wide entranceway. "For everything."

"Of course." Marcus sauntered away to the right.

Brinnie scanned the arena, looking for direction. Standing near a rack to her left, a blonde girl who seemed a year or two older than her sat on a stool, sharpening a sword. The only other person in the room was a stocky man sitting in a chair to the right of the door. He slouched back with his thick, muscled arms crossed over his chest.

He raised one eyebrow at Brinnie, causing one of his many scars to pucker. "You going to stand there, or are you going to prepare?"

She forced herself not to fidget, watching Marcus stroll away with longing. *I wish I could walk away.* "Um, how should I prepare?"

His look made her feel incredibly stupid. "If you don't know how to prepare for battle, then why are you even here?"

Okay, then. "Can I use whatever I find?"

He barked a laugh. "Good question. Can you?"

She pressed her lips together and went to browse through the racks of weapons. Her knowledge of how to wield them came exclusively from books. The online self-defense classes hadn't covered medieval warfare. She found a short, light sword and decided it would do for . . . whatever was coming. Hopefully she could use magic instead.

She stood next to the racks uncertainly until the man burst out, "You're making me crazy. We can't start until everyone's here. Go find something to do."

"Sorry." She forced a polite tone. "Do you have any suggestions?"

"I suggest you get out of my sight."

Brinnie scowled. Her stomach groaned with hunger, her magic ached from the extraction, and she'd had a long day all before noon. She promptly turned invisible.

She heard laughter from the blonde girl. The girl put away her sharpening stone. "She did what you said, Mr. Gerd."

He glowered and grumbled, "Don't you start with me, or I'll start docking points."

Brinnie sat by the wall and waited, trying to ignore her rumbling stomach. On her left, the girl strapped on light leather armor. On the right, past Mr. Gerd, she noticed Marcus making his way down the racks, perusing the armory. Occasionally, he picked up a weapon, tested it, gave it a swing. Most he put back, but a few he left leaning on the ground against the racks. Inspecting them, Brinnie realized. Those were the defective ones.

She realized she knew nothing about the random young man who had startled her then escorted her around the fortress. Mr. Gerd didn't seem to mind him poking around. Marcus wore boots, fitted pants, and a loose shirt that looked appropriate for training. Maybe he was a soldier. The broad shoulders and what she could see of his toned forearms supported the theory.

One by one, other young people trickled in until there were eight others besides Brinnie. Mr. Gerd scowled at the last boy to come in. "Finally. You have thirty seconds to pick a weapon and get back over here." As he scurried away, Mr. Gerd stood. "Gather round, all of you! Here's the rules—no killing, no maiming, no magic, and you don't win until I say you win. Got it?"

Brinnie turned visible. "Excuse me," she blurted. "No magic?"

The girl she had appeared next to jumped and swore. *Whoops.*

Mr. Gerd glared at her. "Are you deaf as well as stupid? You heard what I said."

Brinnie felt her cheeks burning. As she looked down, she heard someone say, "I think what she meant to ask was why."

He turned to the blonde who had spoken to him earlier. "Why? Because I said so. And because you won't always be able to use magic in battle. You have to have combat skills as well." He glared at them all. "Got it? Now pair off. You two, you two, you two . . ."

Don't pick me last. Please. At nine, they had an uneven number. She didn't want to be awkward number three in a group.

His pointing finger swung in Brinnie's direction dead last. "And you two." His finger flicked toward someone behind her.

She glanced over her shoulder, and her heart thudded. *You've got to be kidding me.*

Marcus stood behind her, sword in hand and a shield propped against his leg.

He was part of the trials too? She scanned the group. Of course. Of course they were paired together. He was the tallest and brawniest young man in the group, towering at least a foot over her. Mr. Gerd wanted her to die.

He pointed at her and Marcus. "I want to see you two first. Get in the ring."

This is quite possibly the stupidest thing I've ever done. The group gathered around one of the circles, and Brinnie hopped into the sand pit opposite Marcus. His sword was much larger than her own, and the shield . . . *A shield. Duh. That would have been a good idea.*

Mr. Gerd grinned, as if anticipating the prospect of Brinnie getting her head chopped off.

Marcus removed the shield from his arm and set it outside the circle. "It wouldn't feel fair." He strode forward and stuck out his hand. "A pleasure to duel with you today."

She shook it. "To be honest, I can't say I feel the same way."

"Let the duel commence!" Mr. Gerd yelled.

Marcus waited a few seconds while Brinnie set her feet, then came in swinging. She ducked and darted to the side. She felt the air swish above her head and her heart rate kicked into overdrive.

As he swung again, she barely held her sword up in time to fend off his blow. Metal crashed, jarring her wrists. He gave his sword a twist and her blade wrenched from her hands, thumping into the sand. He flicked up his sword, the tip at her throat. She put her hands up in surrender.

Marcus let his sword drop and smiled. "Not too bad."

Mr. Gerd scowled. "Pick up your sword, girl." As Brinnie did what she was told, he said to Marcus, "Don't go easy on her."

That was going easy?

Marcus swung at her again. She managed to block the blow and hang on to her sword, but suddenly something hit her legs and she was on her back, staring at the sky with his sword to her throat once more.

He'd kicked her feet out from under her. She looked like an idiot.

"Get up," Mr. Gerd growled.

Marcus offered her a hand. Brinnie took it, stood, and dusted herself off. Picking up her sword, she stood in a ready position, knees bent, on the balls of her feet, like she'd read about.

Marcus turned to Mr. Gerd. "This doesn't seem fair."

Maybe she could impress them with stealth, strategy. She leaped forward while he wasn't looking.

Almost too fast for her to see, he grabbed her wrist and plucked the sword from her grasp. His brown eyes sparkled with amusement. "That wasn't very nice."

His humor stung more than her bruised backside. She bit her lip as she heard snickers around the ring.

Mr. Gerd rolled his eyes. "Fine." He waved at Brinnie. "Get out of there. You're done." He pointed to another pair. "Your turn."

Brinnie trudged out of the ring. She watched as the others dueled, amazed at how quickly their blades moved and how long the duels lasted. Especially the blonde girl. Brinnie imagined she must look like a bug, her eyes went so wide at the girl's whirling blade and quick attacks. It looked like a dance—a lethal, powerful dance.

What was she doing here? How had she thought she could infiltrate this foreign world of war and wizards? She knew nothing, could do nothing. Every synapse in her A-plus-student mind buzzed with shame.

Mr. Gerd watched all the duels with a scowl. At the end, the combatants gathered around. He jabbed his finger around the circle. "You, your form is sloppy. Did you train with a noodle?" His finger stabbed again. "You, you would lose a race to a snail. Where is your footwork?" His gaze passed to Marcus. "You could do better." The two shared a strange, knowing half-smile. "And you." He looked at the girl who had stood up for Brinnie earlier and hesitated. "You didn't disappoint." He crossed his arms. "I guess we'll see if you lot are any better with magic." He pointed at Brinnie. "Especially you. I've never seen anything that bad in my life."

She swallowed and nodded.

"Now for round two, no weapons allowed. Just magic. Got it?" Everyone nodded. "Good." He smirked at Brinnie. "How about you go first again?"

She gritted her teeth. If he intended to laugh at her again, he would be disappointed.

She re-entered the ring. Marcus stepped in from the other side. Like before, he strode forward to shake her hand. "A pleasure to duel with you."

She suppressed a smile. "A pleasure."

He raised a brow. "I look forward to this one."

"No talking," Mr. Gerd bellowed. "Duel!"

As with the sword duel, Marcus attacked first. His hand scooped through the air and he flicked his wrist, sending a ball of fire spinning toward Brinnie's head. She ducked and turned invisible. *A fire wizard, like Dad.*

He turned in slow circles, scanning the ground. Looking for footprints, she realized. Well, she didn't need to move. She called to the shadows lurking in the corners of the arena. They swept forward along the ground, slithering tendrils of darkness. Someone shrieked in surprise.

When they reached the circle, the shadows coalesced into three wolves. Marcus shot a stream of fire at one, but a second rammed into the back of his legs, knocking him over. The third jumped on his chest, jaws around his neck, teeth barely resting on skin.

Marcus, the bizarre weirdo, grinned as he put his hands up.

Brinnie turned visible once again and turned to Mr. Gerd.

His mouth hung open. He closed it, opened it again. Finally, he barked, "Let him go." He gestured to Marcus. "You, out." He pointed to someone behind Brinnie. "You, get in!"

Brinnie dismissed the wolves. Marcus stood and gave her an approving nod before stepping out of the ring. She watched him with confusion. Hadn't she just given him a terrible score in the trials? Why didn't he seem bothered?

Her attention turned to her next opponent as the lanky young man stepped into the ring. She sized him up, waiting for him to strike first so she could learn his power. When he didn't, she shrugged mentally, turned invisible, and sent a shadow wolf toward him.

Vines burst out of the ground and entangled the wolf by its legs. *Plant wizard. Got it.* She summoned another two wolves. Vines burst up to entrap them as well. *Good. Focus on those.* While the boy was busy with her wolves, she skirted the vines, tiptoeing behind him.

She jumped up and wrapped her arms around his neck in a chokehold. With her legs dangling off the ground, she took a page from Marcus's book and kicked the backs of the boy's knees. He stumbled and fell into a kneeling position, yanking at her arms as she tightened her hold. He ripped her arms away and she fell backward, but before he could recover, Brinnie's three wolves escaped the vines and pounced. Brinnie rolled out of the way and let them take him down.

His voice squeaked. "I surrender!"

She called off the wolves, clambered to her feet, and turned visible, panting. *Did I really just do that?* She offered the boy a hand. "I'm so sorry, I didn't mean to be that aggressive."

He didn't take her hand, instead standing on his own and stomping out of the ring.

Gerd stabbed his finger at another wizard. "You next!"

Brinnie opened her mouth to protest. This wasn't how the duels were supposed to work. Before, each person only had to fight once. She closed her mouth again. Arguing would be pointless. Best to just get it over with and try not to hurt anyone.

Her next opponent was an aqua wizard, whom she defeated by evading the streams of water. A bystander wasn't so lucky, getting drenched by a rogue blast. After that, the next girl she faced tried to attack her with beetles that came crawling out of the ground. Brinnie emitted an embarrassing number of shrieks in the short time it took to send her wolves to take down the girl and put an end to the duel.

Mr. Gerd nearly growled. "Lana! Into the ring."

The blonde girl with the exceptional sword skills strode forward. She smiled at Brinnie. "You've been amazing."

"Thanks." Brinnie smiled back. "You were amazing with the sword."

"Thanks." She bounced on her toes. "Shall we duel?"

She didn't want to attack this girl who had been so kind to her, but Lana seemed excited. "Sure." Brinnie turned invisible and conjured a pack of shadow wolves. She sent them toward Lana, expecting an easy victory once again.

Instead, the corner of Lana's lips quirked up and she threw out her hand. Blinding light flashed from her fingertips, scything through the wolves.

Brinnie gaped, struggling to hold the shadows together. For a moment the wolves flickered, but then they dissolved, shadows blasting away.

New plan. Brinnie skirted the outer rim of the circle, trying to sneak up behind Lana. The girl threw out her arms and spun. Light flew from her fingertips in a circle. The beams pierced through Brinnie's simple shadow covering, leaving her in plain sight. She hadn't needed to reinforce her invisibility before. That was always a given.

Cheers erupted from the spectators, some for Lana, some for "shadow girl." Before Brinnie could recover, Lana shot a bolt of light toward her. Brinnie threw up her arms, forming a shield of shadows to defend herself. As she frantically gathered more and more shadows to strengthen her shield, Lana's beam of light grew brighter and took on an almost solid quality.

Shadows streamed to her from all around the arena, roiling about her in a great, dark cloud. She thrust her arms forward, pushing them toward Lana, trying to quench the light. As shadow and light collided, lightning sparked. The onlookers shouted, scrambling away.

Lana didn't let up. Brinnie held out both hands, channeling the shadows, pushing against the light. Lana did the same, light flowing from both palms. Brinnie called all the shadows at her command, but she could feel them being eaten away.

I'm actually going to lose.

With a sudden burst, the light broke through and slammed into Brinnie's chest. She felt herself go airborne, then slam into the sand. She blinked, trying to regain her vision, blinded by the light.

A knee rested on Brinnie's chest. "Do you admit defeat?"

"Definitely." The knee released, and Brinnie sat up blinking, trying to make out anything around her. Her eyes felt like marshmallows over a campfire. Lana's form swam in her vision. "Nice work."

Lana gave her a hand up. "You too." She held on until Brinnie gained her balance. "Unfortunately, light always beats darkness."

Brinnie squinted. She wished she could make out Lana's expression. Was she talking about the duel, or something else?

Had she found a fellow spy?

"All right, all right, that was a pretty show." Mr. Gerd's rough voice cut through their conversation. "You two out, give someone else a chance to duel."

Brinnie's vision began to return as she tromped through the sand out of the ring. As they stepped out, Lana held out her hand to shake. "I'm Lana."

She took it. "Brinnie."

"I've never met a shadowmaster before. Are you new to Mordizan?"

"Yeah." Brinnie hesitated. That would be normal, right? "I just got here a couple days ago. You?"

"Same. I got here yesterday for the trials. I'm from Ariondam."

"Oh, cool." Brinnie tried to act as if she knew what that was.

Lana laughed. "It's okay. You don't have to pretend you've heard of it. Most people haven't. It's a really small estate, only a few dozen people. The only reason I know Mr. Gerd is because he used to live there, too."

"You caught me." Brinnie smiled. Could Lana really be a dark wizard? Her chipper mood didn't seem to fit. "So you're here to go to the University?"

"That's the goal, as long as I pass all the trials and tests. I want to be a warrior." She cocked her head. "What about you? I'm guessing something having to do with magic."

Brinnie relaxed. Lana didn't seem to have any idea who she was.

They could just be two students, talking about college. A strange, dark wizard college. "Preferably. And not having to do with sword fighting."

Lana laughed, setting her long ponytail swinging. "Have you ever used one before?"

"Not really. My training is a bit lacking."

She shrugged. "It's okay. Your magic should get you through. You can learn everything else. Look out!"

They both ducked as shards of ice went flying over their heads. "Pay attention!" Mr. Gerd bellowed.

"Catch you later at the dining hall?" Lana whispered.

Brinnie had no idea where that was, but she would find out. "Sounds good."

As Lana turned her attention to the ring, Brinnie felt eyes on her. She looked over her shoulder to see Marcus lurking in the doorway to the arena, watching with his arms crossed. When their eyes met, he gave her a nod and strode away, disappearing through the doorway.

Brinnie sensed she wasn't the only one with secrets.

CHAPTER NINETEEN

Nimue frowned at the paper in her hand. "Did they not teach you anything at Wraithwood?"

Brinnie attempted to shovel food into her mouth at a respectable rate. "By the time I found out about magic, I was a little busy with the whole Maze thing. I didn't have much time to study."

The two of them sat at a table in what seemed to be a communal mess hall not far from the arena. At three in the afternoon, the hall was empty other than the two of them and a few people wiping down the long tables.

Nimue shook her head. "Well, you didn't pass the University exam, that's for sure. Luckily Vorath's having them train you regardless. You should feel honored. It's every young wizard's dream to go to the University."

Brinnie popped the last bite of her sandwich into her mouth. The cooks had given her leftovers, and she had no complaints. "So is it just battle training, or other stuff, too?" Maybe she could learn something that could lead to the prophecy and Mordred's bane.

Nimue folded the paper. "History, politics, magic theory—you need everything. All expedited and all rudimentary, but you're no use completely clueless." She puffed out a breath and pushed back hair that had escaped her ponytail. "Against all common sense, you're being moved over to the University dorms. It will be easier for you to get to classes, I suppose, but I hate to have you that far away. Then if all goes as planned, we'll have you sent out in the field."

Brinnie's eyes widened. "Like, in the field, fighting?"

"Ideally. Probably to one of the strongholds. Give you some practice with actual battle."

Her heart sped up. "Oh. You, uh, trust me with that already?"

Nimue laughed. "Not for a second. At least, not yet." She sat back. "But that's okay. I think you'll come around in time."

Brinnie blinked. "So you don't trust me, but you're going to let me wander around? You're not going to throw me in the dungeon?"

She snorted. "Of course not. Even if we did, what would that accomplish? Reinforcing Enchantment propaganda about us?" She sighed. "I'll admit, I worried a little when the person I sent to pick you up from the testing didn't find you that you'd done something stupid and made a dash for it. But it looks like Marcus got you where you needed to go."

"The ladies told me you didn't send anyone."

Nimue rolled her eyes. "Scholars. Don't listen to a thing you say." She slid a satchel across the table to Brinnie. "I packed you clothes, toiletries, that sort of thing, and some money if you need to buy more stuff when you get there."

"Oh!" Brinnie accepted the bag and peeked inside. "Thank you."

"Don't sound so surprised. You're our key to taking Wraithwood and the Master Key. Not to mention Mordred's taken an interest in you as his protégé."

Brinnie dropped the bag. "Mordred's protégé?"

Nimue heaved a sigh. "Really, kid. Why did you think we did all this? We worked hard to get you here. You're worth a lot to us."

The words shouldn't have struck such a deep chord, but she found herself speechless. She didn't know why she had thought they wanted her—perhaps to keep her in a dungeon out of the way, perhaps to exact revenge on the descendants of Arthur. It hadn't mattered in her desperation to free Anna.

With a jolt, she realized she wasn't used to someone . . . wanting *her*.

"We haven't seen someone like you in centuries. The last thing we want to do is waste your talent in some dungeon." Nimue tilted her head, setting her chin on her fist. "This isn't Wraithwood. We embrace magic here—fully."

The skin on Brinnie's arms prickled. *No, stop it. Don't let her trick you.* They only wanted to use her.

Nimue stood. "Anyway, I have a slew of incredibly boring meetings to attend, so I can't personally take you to the University." She addressed someone behind Brinnie. "Thanks for taking over."

Brinnie turned. None other than Marcus strode across the mess hall, now in a new, unbloodied shirt. He nodded to Nimue. "No problem at all."

Who is *this guy?* Maybe he was heading to the dorms too after the trials?

Nimue slid off the bench and gave a wave. "Have fun." She pointed at Marcus while walking backward. "You lose her, I'm blaming you."

He half-smiled. "Got it."

As Nimue exited, Brinnie scrutinized Marcus. No satchel or bags to bring to the dorms, only what looked like a hooded jacket hanging over one arm. Was he even the right age for the University? She was horrible enough at human ages, but with wizards who could apparently live hundreds of years . . .

"So? Are you ready?"

"Right." Brinnie grabbed the satchel and slung a strap over her shoulder while standing. She picked up her tray to carry it to the crates near the exit.

Marcus led the way toward the doors. "Sorry about the sword duel, by the way. Gerd would only have sent someone else in to fight you if I'd gone easy. I hope I didn't hurt you."

Her cheeks flamed. She would prefer never to remember the humiliation again. "I'm fine." She slid her tray into one of the racks of crates. "I don't know what I did to make him hate me."

"He hates everyone." Marcus shrugged. "We just put up with it because he's the best battle instructor the University has. He trained me as a child."

As a child? Why are children swinging swords? "So you've, uh, been here a long time?"

"I was born here. But from what I hear it's pretty new for you." He looked at her sideways. "I don't think we were ever properly introduced, Brynna Ludovic."

"Brinnie is fine."

They passed into another courtyard—the same one from earlier? She couldn't keep it straight.

"So what brings a descendant of Arthur to Mordizan?" He shrugged on the gray jacket he'd been carrying.

A jacket in summer? "Oh, you know, fighting for a better world, that kind of thing."

He snorted, flipping up his hood. "Right. Why are you really here?"

"I'm not lying." He gave her a look, and she sighed. "First, it was to save my sister. A prisoner exchange, I guess. But then, well, I'm starting to think maybe Mordizan isn't the evil place everyone made it out to be."

He remained silent as they passed a few people headed in the opposite direction. Then he said in a low voice, "Maybe that's because you don't know it well enough yet."

Her heart thumped. "What do you mean?" Had she found an ally?

They turned a corner, emerging into a wider part of the circular courtyard. Marcus led her toward a gate between the buildings. He hesitated, then shook his head. "Nothing. Just keep your eyes open. And be careful what you say."

Conversation ceased as they passed the guards at the gate and emerged into another ring-like courtyard between the buildings and a massive wall many times Brinnie's height. Offset by several yards from the interior courtyard's entrance, an enormous iron gate was set in the wall, flanked by two guards each way. More watched from the battlements, monitoring the flow of traffic through the entrance as the guards stopped each person who passed.

Brinnie's heart sped up irrationally. *Chill. You're supposed to be here.* But guards still made her twitchy.

They fell into line and soon reached the two guards. Marcus nodded to them.

"Name and destination?" one of them asked.

"Marcus Vorath. University dormitories."

"My lord." The guard half-bowed and turned to Brinnie. "And you?"

"Um, Brynna Lane, I mean Ludovic, and same." *Wow, that didn't sound suspicious at all.*

But the guards didn't bat an eye. "Do either of you have anything illegal to declare?" the second guard asked.

"No," Marcus said, and Brinnie followed suit.

He nodded. "Go ahead."

A portcullis hung above either end of the passageway through the wall. Brinnie glanced up to see gratings far above. She knew enough about castle design to know that this central portion was designed to trap enemies and pelt them from above with arrows, boiling oil, or tar. She shuddered.

"What was the point of that?" she whispered to Marcus, gesturing behind them. "We could have completely lied."

He tugged his hood lower as they passed pedestrians coming the other way. "No, we couldn't have. The guards of the gate can tell if you're lying. It's a strange sort of magic."

"Oh." *Good to know.* And unfortunate if she ever wanted to sneak around.

They emerged from the passageway, and her attention was immediately arrested by her surroundings.

Buildings with brightly painted signs and intricate facades lined the wide, busy street crowded with the oddest people Brinnie had ever seen. She spotted wizards in stereotypical robes and pointed hats, people with birds on their shoulders or objects floating along behind them, passengers flying overhead seated on broomsticks, and children playing catch with a light orb.

Magic. Magic everywhere, out in the open, as a way of life. Despite the dark stone construction of so much of the fortress, streets, and buildings, color burst vibrant from storefronts, outfits, flares of magic. Smells of cinnamon and spices and something baking wafted through the air. It felt like what a renn faire tried to be, perfected and magnified.

Marcus motioned to her. "Come on. We'll catch a broom."

She realized she'd been standing in the middle of the road, blocking the way. She hurried after him.

Marcus led the way along the sidewalk of the crowded street. Brinnie stared at the shop windows, spun in a circle to see higher buildings rising beyond, gaped at what appeared to be messenger birds gliding overhead.

Marcus took her arm as she almost ran into a couple strolling by with a child. His lips twitched in a smile. "Come on. You act like you've never seen magic before."

"Not like this." Never like this. How did something so beautiful exist in the shadow of Mordizan?

They came to a platform set off from the street and stepped into a roped line. Broomsticks carrying passengers glided onto the raised platform, ten feet above the street. The riders hopped off, new ones got on, and the next broom came swooping in.

As they joined the line, Brinnie thought her eyes would pop out of her head. "People seriously ride broomsticks."

"We tried to do benches for a while, but they were too heavy for the levitation spells to last very long. Broomsticks seem to work the best."

A memory made her grimace. "My last broomstick experience wasn't exactly pleasant. Are you sure this is safe?"

"People use these all day, every day." He stepped into one of four new lines where the original branched. "Here, this is the line for the western quadrant brooms."

Within a few moments they arrived at the front of the queue. As a broomstick came to a halt in front of them and let another wizard off, Marcus grabbed hold and straddled it like a horse. "They can carry two, if you don't want to ride alone your first time."

If she was going to die by broomstick, he was going down with her. She climbed on behind him and gripped the broom with white knuckles.

"Are you ready?" When she nodded, he lifted his feet from the ground, and the broom took off.

She clutched the broom, crossing her legs for extra grip as they flew over the heads of the people below. "How far is it?"

"Not far." To her horror, he swung one leg over to sit sideways so he could see her, holding on casually with one hand. "About a five-minute ride. The brooms are pre-programmed with destinations."

The broom didn't waver, and though a breeze flowed by, they didn't hit any turbulence. As she began to relax and realize she wasn't going to fall off, Brinnie's mind started turning. "Wait a minute. When we went past those guards, what did you say your last name was?"

He was quiet for a moment, looking out over the rooftops of the city. "Vorath," he admitted finally.

"As in, Vorath, the Master of Mordizan?"

"Yes."

That explained the Mordizan crest and the . . . lurking. "Are you related?"

"He's my father."

Brinnie's eyebrows shot up. The dots connected. How he and Gerd knew each other, why Marcus had been inspecting the weaponry, why he seemed to be hiding his face as they wove through the street. "Well, uh, that's cool."

He kept his eyes on the skyline. "Just please don't start calling me 'my lord' and agreeing with everything I say."

"Whatever you say, my lord."

His head whipped toward her, and she tried to keep a straight face. A grin broke out in spite of herself, and he shook his head with a chuckle.

They rode on, past what seemed like a residential area. "How big is Mordizan?" Brinnie asked.

"You mean how many people? Around eight or nine thousand that actually live here. But there are always people visiting from other estates or attending the University. So probably double that." He nodded toward a platform ahead. "Here comes our stop."

They disembarked at a platform similar to the one where they had boarded. The buildings here were smaller, more like hole-in-the-wall establishments. They passed primarily college-aged pedestrians, talking, laughing, toting books or weapons. Marcus led the way toward a collection of tall buildings with towers that matched the architecture of the Mordizan fortress on a smaller scale. Brinnie followed him past a series of more ornate, presumably academic buildings until they arrived at a simple, rectangular building of four stories.

Marcus halted outside. "And here you are. Someone in there should be able to direct you to your room."

"Thank you for all your help." She cocked her head. "It seems like a lot of trouble to bring me all the way here."

"Not a problem." He tucked his hands in his pockets. "I have some business in the area anyway. I'll see you later."

Before she could ask any more questions, he strode away.

The son of the Master of Mordizan had nothing better to do than escort a new student to her dorm? *Maybe he's bored.*

She opened the door and went inside. She found herself in a lobby with a collection of chairs, sofas, and tables, with a desk at one end manned by a curly-haired young woman with her nose in a book.

Brinnie approached the desk. *As if I didn't hate talking to human strangers enough.* She fidgeted, unsure if she should interrupt the young woman's reading.

The reader glanced up and raised an eyebrow. "Yes?"

"Hi, um, I'm new, and I think I'm supposed to find my dorm room."

She set down her book and grabbed a clipboard. "Name?"

"Brynna Ludovic."

Her eyes darted up from the paper, looking Brinnie up and down with interest. Then she looked back down at the paper, running her finger along the list. "Fourth floor. Room two. Stairs are back there." She pointed.

"Thanks."

Brinnie's legs burned more than they should have once she reached the fourth floor. *I am embarrassingly out of shape.* She found a simple wooden door with a number two on it, so she tried the handle and stepped inside, only to see someone sitting within, their back to her. "Oh, sorry. I didn't know anyone was going to be in here."

The girl sitting at a desk turned around, blonde ponytail swinging. None other than Lana grinned at her. "No way. Have you been assigned to this room too?"

Brinnie relaxed. "Yes—are we roommates?"

"Yes! What are the odds?" Lana laughed. "I'm so glad. I was worried I was going to get stuck with that other girl. You know, the one with the beetles?" She shuddered. "I'd be worried about waking up with beetles in my hair."

"Ick!" Brinnie felt her mood rising. If she had to attend a dark wizard university, at least she had a friendly light wizard roommate.

Lana swung her legs over the back of the chair, leaning against the desk. She threw her arms out. "Welcome to home sweet home. We got two beds, two desks, two trunks, and not nearly enough natural light." Lana scooped her hands through the air, conjuring two balls of light, and tossed them toward the ceiling where two others already floated, making up for what Brinnie assumed was the lack of light from the window slit above the desks. Brinnie noticed a couple daggers and a sword lying on Lana's desk next to a polishing rag. "Anyway, want to go to the dining hall? I'm starving."

"Oh, sure." Brinnie glanced at the beds and set her satchel on the one without Lana's bags tossed onto it. She hadn't eaten that long ago, but maybe socializing would lead to learning more. Who knew so much of spying was socializing? They really needed to come up with some better tactics for introverts.

"Great." Lana hopped up. "Come on, I've already scoped out where it is."

A few minutes later, they entered a long, squat building and gave their names to a woman at the check-in before proceeding to the long tables and buffet lines of the dining hall. "This is strangely normal," Brinnie observed under her breath.

"What do you mean?" Lana grabbed a tray.

"Well, I mean." She fumbled for words. "It just looks like a cafeteria from back home."

Lana laughed. "What else would it look like?"

Once again, Brinnie, dark wizards don't feast on children. They went through the line and sat at the end of one of the long tables with their food. Brinnie focused on her plate, trying not to say anything else awkward.

After a moment, she realized Lana had been strangely quiet. She looked up to see Lana giving her a questioning look. "What?"

"Why is everyone looking at you?"

Brinnie scanned the dining hall. Groups and individuals spread throughout the room cast furtive glances her way. She saw a few look at her, then lean forward to whisper with their companions. A pit formed in her stomach. "Um . . . are you sure they're looking at me?"

"Well they're certainly not staring at me."

A girl who seemed to be a few years Brinnie's senior stood up from a nearby group and slid into a seat near Brinnie and Lana. "Hi. Are you new here?"

Lana smiled, peppy as ever. "It's our first day."

"Well, welcome to the University." The girl pushed short brown hair out of her eyes. "I'm Erin."

"Lana. And this is Brinnie."

"Hi." Brinnie gave a small wave.

Erin leaned forward. "Brinnie, as in Brynna? Brynna Ludovic?"

Oh, no. Where is this going? "Yeah."

Erin's eyes widened, and Lana's mouth dropped open.

Erin scooted closer. "So you're really Merlin Ludovic's niece?"

"Yes." Brinnie raised an eyebrow. "Does he have a reputation around here?"

Erin gave an uncertain laugh. "The one responsible for thwarting our advance last summer? And for like half our failed attempts in the past decade? The only wizard Master Vorath wanted dead more than him is the Master of Castelon himself."

Brinnie felt a surge of pride. She hadn't realized how much Mordizan hated her uncle. "Sounds like him."

"When were you going to tell me this?" Lana demanded.

Brinnie put her hands up. "I don't know. It never really came up." She turned to Erin. "How did you know?"

Erin gave a thumbs up to her group. The students immediately began buzzing with conversation Brinnie couldn't catch. "Word travels fast." Erin shrugged. "My aunt was at the dinner last night. We've all been talking about it."

Brinnie scanned the room. Not just Erin's friends, but half the dining hall seemed to be watching. "And is the general opinion favorable?"

"Of course." Erin laughed. "You literally escaped *Wraithwood*. Everyone thinks you're something of a hero, escaping the enemy, offering your services to Mordizan."

Escaping? An interesting twist to the story. *Well, this is unexpected. How am I supposed to sneak around if I'm a celebrity?*

Erin leaned forward. "Can I ask you a question?"

"Um, sure."

"Is it true that you killed Merlin Ludovic?"

Brinnie's heart froze. She could feel eyes on her from all directions. She cleared her throat. "Is that what they're saying?"

"Rumor has it you lured him into a trap, made him think you were on his side, and bam!" She clapped her hands together. "Right when he was distracted, you ran him through."

Brinnie's throat clenched. She forced the words out. "I didn't kill him."

Erin looked disappointed. "So it was Mordred, then. Well, either way, you did get him there."

You did get him there.

You did.

You did it.

The urge to flee coursed through her. Brinnie stood. "It's nice to meet you, but I'm really tired from assessment. I think I'll go."

"Oh, okay." Erin cocked her head. "See you around?"

"Yeah."

With controlled steps, she walked over and placed her dishes in the receptacle. Then she directed her feet out the door, back to the dorm, and up the steps.

It wasn't until she got to the room and shut the door that she finally sank onto the bed and put her arms around her knees, staring at the opposite wall.

A knock sounded at the door. "Brinnie?" Brinnie turned invisible, but not before Lana opened the door and spotted her. "What's wrong?"

Brinnie remained invisible to give herself time to compose her expression. "Nothing. I'm fine. Tired, is all."

Lana sat on the bed opposite Brinnie's. She cocked her head, gazing toward the empty space near Brinnie's head. "I know we just met, but we are roommates now. Want to talk about it?"

I wish I could. If you knew who I truly was, what I've come here to do . . . you'd be forced to kill me. "I appreciate it, but I'm really okay."

Lana leaned against the wall, feet hanging off the bed. "This is about your uncle, isn't it? You cared about him, didn't you?"

Great. Good job, Brinnie. Cover blown already. "No. I hate them. I hate what they did to me."

Lana shook her head. "Maybe he's the enemy and you hate what they did, but you still don't hate *him*."

Brinnie didn't respond.

Lana crossed one leg over the other. "It's okay. I know how it is." She looked down, lacing her fingers in her lap. "My best friend went over to the enemy, almost a year ago. And I want to be a warrior, always have, but . . . I'm afraid, if I ever face her in battle, I won't be able to fight her."

Brinnie slowly dropped the shadows shielding her. "I hate war. People who would be your friends, or even your own family, all fighting, trying to kill each other."

"Exactly." Lana threw her hands in the air. "If those blasted enchantment wizards would just give up the Enchantment, we could end this whole thing right now."

Brinnie kept tears in check. Lana definitely wasn't a fellow infiltrator. They weren't allies, not yet. Not if Lana still thought the enchantment wizards were at fault. "Or we could stop trying to kill the enchantment wizards. But we won't. Both sides are too stubborn to stop."

"It's different." Lana scowled. "We're fighting for what's right. We can't stop. We're fighting for freedom, and a better world."

She might regret the words, but she let them fall out anyway. "That's exactly what the other side says too."

Instead of arguing, Lana only sighed. "And that's why there's a war."

For the first time, Brinnie wondered if there ever could be a winner.

CHAPTER TWENTY

"Strike. Return. Strike. Return. Keep it going." The hard-faced sword instructor stalked the rows. "Alston, watch your feet." She paused in front of Brinnie, sighing. "Ludovic, you're attacking, not giving them a friendly tap. Put some force into it."

Brinnie swung harder, her arms burning. She wished she could exchange at least a few of her battle classes for normal ones, like history or language studies. From knife work, to archery, to battle fitness, and now to sword study, her day seemed designed to kill her. Maybe that was the evil plan. They would kill her through physical exercise. She just had to get through this class, and she would be on to battle strategy, a rest at last.

"Ludovic, please." The instructor crossed her arms, biceps rippling with muscle. "Where on earth is your foot pointing?"

Brinnie looked down and bit back a sigh. "Sideways?"

"Thank you. Now fix it."

Apparently, Mr. Gerd only taught advanced battle classes, to Brinnie's relief, but this instructor didn't seem to like her much better. She'd never had a teacher dislike her before.

Hold on. Am I a teacher's pet?

"At ease."

The class of about fifteen people stopped and lowered their wooden swords. Brinnie stuttered to a stop along with them.

"You have ten seconds, then we're returning to block stances." The instructor looked at her watch.

Brinnie started to count to ten. When she got to eight, the instructor shouted, "Weapons at ready."

I hate this place.

"Block one. Block two. Block three. Return. Block one. Block two . . ." She stalked the rows again with an eagle eye. "Morris, clean up that form. Igard, you're off balance. Ludovic . . . what are you doing?"

She had no idea. "I'm sorry." Maybe she was doing the wrong block on the wrong beat? She tried the other one.

The instructor sighed and ran a hand over her close-shaven scalp. "Your hands are reversed. Switch them."

"Oh." Brinnie moved her right hand up to below the hilt and slid her left toward the pommel. "Oops."

She walked away shaking her head. Brinnie glanced over and saw Lana waiting outside the practice field, stifling a smile. *That's it. If I ever have to use a sword instead of magic, I'm dead.*

At the end of class, after shelving her wooden sword, Brinnie found Lana leaning on the fence. "Hey." She waved at Brinnie. "Ready for battle strategy?"

"Yes. Thank goodness. I'm dying."

Lana laughed. "I'll trade you. I was bored out of my mind in history this morning."

Brinnie fell into step with Lana. Two days of classes had passed, but she hadn't had this class yet. "What even do we do in battle strategy? Play Wizard's Chess?"

"I wish. My brother and I used to play for hours. He drove me crazy though, always breaking the rules."

Brinnie laughed. "You'd hate to play with me. Last time I played, I turned it into a real-life sword fight."

"A sword fight? Let me guess—you lost?"

"Hey!"

They entered the classroom laughing and sat at one of the long, thin tables set up in rows. About twenty more students entered, and a stocky man whom Brinnie assumed was the teacher began thudding thick, worn tomes onto the tables in front of the students. "Welcome. I'm Mr. Morton. I've only got six copies, so you're going to have to share. Master Ortgard Vorath's *History of Enemy Battle Strategy.* Who here has read it?"

Only two hands went up. Mr. Morton nodded. "As I expected. Who here is familiar with the Battle of 1812?"

All hands went up, including Brinnie's. Brinnie leaned over to Lana and whispered, "Doesn't he mean the *War* of 1812?"

"You, in the front." He pointed to Brinnie. "Summarize it for me."

Nothing like putting someone on the spot to summarize an entire war. "Essentially, America got tired of the British messing with their trade and stealing their sailors to impress them into the British army, so they went to war. Of course, it was also a good opportunity for a land grab into Canadian and Native American territory. Nobody really won, and they signed a treaty in 1814."

She became aware of everyone giving her strange looks. Mr. Morton squinted. "Er, no. Nice try. You in the back."

A young man with long hair lowered his hand. "That was when our forces took over Baronstead."

"Indeed." Morton looked relieved. "And how did they do that?"

"The Master of Baronstead and his only son were both killed in battle."

Brinnie's cheeks heated. She hadn't even been close.

"At Baronstead?" Morton asked. He nodded to another student. "You."

The girl shifted in her seat. "No, they were killed in a previous battle."

"And why is that significant?"

"Because that allowed our forces to get into Baronstead."

"Why?" He pointed to Lana.

Lana shot Brinnie a pitying look. "The Master of Baronstead had no other family, so the estate didn't have a Master. Anyone could get in."

"Precisely. Thank you." Mr. Morton paced in front of the class. "You all know the rules. The Master decides who can and can't enter the estate. This is why we can't launch frontal attacks on enemy estates. We can't get to them in the first place. Baronstead stands out as the best possible case scenario. Take out the Master, take out the estate. So how do we do that? Yes, you."

"Espionage, assassination," the long-haired guy answered.

"And?" Someone else raised their hand. "You."

"We lure the enemy off of the estates."

"Yes. How?" He pointed again to Lana.

"By stirring up the humans to violence. The enchantment wizards can't stand it and come to stop us."

Brinnie tried to contain her horrified look at Lana.

"Right." He strolled between the tables. "So we work our way into places of leadership, mess with human wars and politics. But that isn't the goal. In fact, we're happiest if the enemy intercepts us before we ever get there. Then we can fight them directly. But we all know this is not ultimately effective. What problem do we still face concerning Masters? You."

A young woman jumped, startled from taking notes. "Oh. Uh, they almost never leave their estates."

"Precisely." He leaned against his podium. "And that is where, as someone mentioned, assassination comes in. That has historically been our double-pronged approach—luring enchantment wizards off their estates and assassinating them on their estates. But who can tell me what our third prong initiative is? You."

"Attacking the strongholds," Lana responded.

"Right. And why haven't we done so before?"

Lana almost bounced in her chair. *Do I look like that in classes?* "Our forces were weaker than they are now. If we did succeed in taking the strongholds and destroying them, our estates would be just as vulnerable as theirs, and it was a toss-up who would win."

"And what changed?"

"The balance shifted. Our numbers are vastly greater than theirs."

"And we have Mordred on our side," someone from the back put in.

"Exactly. So, as we've discussed, our overarching battle strategy is simple—luring them off their estates, assassinating their Masters, and attacking the strongholds." He tapped the book on his podium. "But strategy for individual attacks is far more complex. The best way to learn that is to learn by example. That's what the books are for. I want you to break off into groups and spend the rest of our time reading the first chapter. Expect to discuss it tomorrow. Questions?"

Brinnie's stomach clenched. She felt like she would be sick, sitting through a dry academic discussion of how to kill people. She raised her hand.

"Yes?"

"What is the end game? Why are we trying to kill the enchantment wizards?"

Once again, everyone looked at her strangely. A few students muttered derogatory comments. Mr. Morton held up his hand. "No, it's a fair question. Can anyone answer it?"

"Humans are backwards and barbarous," the long-haired boy said. "They've completely messed up the world, while we hide in dark corners trying not to be caught, since we wouldn't be able to do a thing to protect ourselves, considering we would die if we killed them. Meanwhile, with the effects of Myrddin's curse, with each generation our magic grows weaker and more specialized. Soon we might even start aging and dying like humans. The enchantment wizards are driving all of us to our deaths. By destroying the Enchantment, we liberate wizardkind."

Mr. Morton nodded. "Well said, young man."

Brinnie knew she should stop. *Keep a low profile.* But she needed to know the logic. How did they justify this to themselves? "Maybe I'm missing something here, but why not just tell the humans about wizards? Once they believe, the Enchantment has no effect, right? We could defend ourselves."

A couple of students groaned. Mr. Morton waved them off. "I appreciate the dedication to starting off the class on a solid logical foundation." He turned to Brinnie. "Belief is a difficult thing to be certain of. Hearing and believing are not one and the same."

"Fair." She took a breath. *One last question.* "So once we eradicate the Enchantment, then what?"

Lana gave her a warning nudge. "We're free."

"To do what?"

"To build a new and perfected world." Mr. Morton shifted, as if finally growing sick of Brinnie's questions.

"A world without humans."

He pressed his lips together. "If necessary, yes."

Shut your mouth, Brinnie. She didn't listen to herself. "So then that's why we can't tell them, really. Not because of the whole hearing versus belief thing. But because we would lose the element of surprise if we want to wipe them out."

Uncomfortable silence reigned. Brinnie could hear her own heart beat. Would anyone contradict her?

"Throughout pre-Myrddin history, humans have sought to kill all wizards, seeing us as a threat." Mr. Morton's voice was hard. "They massacred us, forced us into hiding. They would do it again if they knew we existed."

So that's a yes. Brinnie opened her mouth but thought better of it. She nodded. "I understand."

"Good." He sighed, turning back to his book. "Now all of you, turn to the first chapter. I want it finished by the end of class."

Brinnie lay draped across her bed, staring at the ceiling. "I'm going to die."

Lana wriggled into pajamas. "Can you do it somewhere else? I don't want to have to deal with a dead body."

Brinnie threw a pillow at her and groaned as her muscles twinged. "There's a reason I've always been more of a book person than a sports person."

She'd been in the University for five days, each day packed with conditioning and battle training. Her only respites were the battle strategy and magic lessons.

"Before you know it, you'll be graduating." Lana flopped into bed. "That's what my mom always told me. She said to enjoy every minute of it."

"I don't think I'm graduating." Brinnie rolled over and looked at Lana. "I'm pretty sure they're sending me off to war as soon as possible. This shouldn't be allowed. I'm only sixteen."

"Yeah, yeah, because you got in early and all that. Rub it in." Lana stuck out her tongue and pulled up the blankets. She'd told Brinnie she signed up for the trials the second she turned eighteen. "I'm a little jealous."

Brinnie reached to put a bowl over the light orb that acted as a nightlight. "Of getting in early?"

"Well yeah, that too, but I mean being on the front lines, attacking the strongholds, leading the charge."

Brinnie shook her head. "Have you ever seen a battle?"

"Well." Lana cleared her throat. "Not technically."

She stared up at the ceiling. "There's nothing fun about it. You're scared. People die. Getting stabbed hurts like nothing else. You lose people you care about."

Lana remained quiet for a moment. "You were in the Battle of the Master Key, weren't you? I heard that you turned the tides. That you won the battle for the enemy."

No sense in lying. "Yes."

Lana sat up and looked at her. "Why are you really here?"

Brinnie's heart skipped a beat. "What do you mean?"

"Come on. You can't stand people talking about your uncle's death—"

Presumed death.

"You ask questions in battle strategy that no one else would ask—I'm just not convinced you had some heroic change of heart." She scrutinized her. "Why are you here?"

Brinnie hesitated, buying time by sitting up. She could try to lie, fake her way out of it. But she doubted she could be convincing. "The truth is, I'm here for my sister. Mordred kidnapped her. The only way he would let her free was if I came to Mordizan. So I did."

Lana spun her legs around so she was facing Brinnie. "Then why are you still here?"

"I can't very well escape."

"Of course you can. You can turn invisible, for goodness' sake. Tell me the truth."

Brinnie thought quickly. "Honestly, I don't think he let my sister go. I think he lied. And I'm afraid that if I leave, he might kill her. But as long as I'm here, he'll keep her alive for leverage." Maybe that was true, maybe it wasn't, but it gave her a reason beyond *why yes, I'm here to destroy Mordred.*

Lana shook her head slowly. "I should report you." She sighed. "But I won't. You remind me of my friend. She was the nicest, sweetest girl. She had so much potential. But she started talking with one of our prisoners . . . She's not my enemy. She's just confused. You're here for your sister, and I'd do the same thing for my brother."

Brinnie's heart warmed. Not for the first time, she wondered how Lana ended up on the wrong side of the war. "Thank you."

"But please understand." Lana fiddled with her blanket. "I can't cover for you. If you get yourself in trouble . . . I have a duty to Mordizan."

Brinnie nodded. "I couldn't ask for more."

Lana lay back down and let out her breath with a whoosh. "Okay. Good. We won't speak of this again."

Life settled into a strange routine. By day seven, Brinnie began to feel more confident. Though her battle training was still taxing, the instructors called her out a little less often. She could move from class to class without getting lost, and she was intimately familiar with the dining hall. But time grew short before she would have to study with Keilrie as well—and who knew when Vorath would send her into the battlefield? She needed to find the prophecy. Luckily, she had a lead.

"Dismissed."

As the students filed out, Brinnie approached the front desk and addressed the magic theory teacher. "Excuse me."

She looked at Brinnie over her wire-rimmed glasses. Brinnie was still getting used to the aging process in humans versus wizards, but she had to guess this wizard was old—at least over a hundred. "Yes?" the teacher asked.

Brinnie gathered her courage and blurted out her spiel. "I know we're supposed to be working on a project about one of the divisions of magical powers, and the book is very good, but I was interested in doing a report on the anomalous division." She took a deep breath and plunged ahead. "I was wondering if there were some other resources I could use, since those powers aren't as extensively covered in the book."

The instructor smiled, wrinkles crinkling in delight. "Of course. I've always found the anomalous wizards to be the most fascinating. I'll give you a pass for the Great Library of Mordizan." She shuffled papers aside, reaching into a small drawer. "It's in the fortress itself, but they'll let you in with the pass. There should be more than enough for you there."

"That sounds wonderful. Thank you." Inwardly, she did a happy dance. Once she'd heard a couple of classmates talking about the

Great Library, she had begun to think that if an ancient prophecy would be anywhere, it would be there.

As she nearly skipped back to the dorm, pass in hand, she recited Ms. Tynsdale's words in her head. *Myrddin's flesh and Myrddin's blood shall destroy the world he built. Mordred's bane, his final doom, the heir of Arthur doth supply. The line of Myrddin here must die, or all we wrought shall be in vain.*

She was so caught up in her musings as she opened the door to their room that when she saw someone sitting in Lana's chair, it took her a moment to register that it wasn't Lana leaning against the desk with an arm propped on the back of the chair, one tall boot crossed over the other. "Nimue?"

"Glad you're back. Came to check on you but wasn't sure if I'd catch you before I need to leave." Nimue stretched, revealing the usual daggers strapped to her sides. "How are the classes going?"

"Good, I think." Brinnie edged into the room and set her satchel on her bed.

"That's what your instructors say." Nimue swiped a pencil from the desk and fiddled with it. "Apparently, you're picking everything up pretty fast. Mr. Morton says you've been asking some interesting questions though."

Oh boy. Here we go. Brinnie tried to casually take a seat on the edge of the bed. "I'm trying to figure everything out."

"Figuring things out is fine. Asking questions is fine. But Brynna." She put down the pencil and leaned forward, elbows on her knees. "You can't do that in front of a whole class. Word is going to get back to Vorath."

So Nimue isn't the only one monitoring me? She probably should have expected that. "I'm sorry. My bad."

"Just be careful." Nimue stood. "If you have questions, ask me." She hesitated. "Is there anything you want to talk about?"

"I don't think so." Should there be?

"In that case, I'd better get going." She made her way toward the door. "I have a few more calls to make this evening."

"Okay. Take care."

"You too." She hesitated for another moment, then stepped out and closed the door after her.

Weird.

Brinnie sighed and pinched the bridge of her nose. Especially now that she had the library pass, she needed to blend in. She might be getting close to a lead.

A few seconds later, Lana threw the door open, eyes wide. "Was that Nimue Drakon I just saw leaving?"

"Yeah. She came to check in."

"What?" Lana tossed her books onto the desk and plopped on her bed. "You know her?"

"Yeah. She got me set up here at the University and all that."

"No way!" Lana shook her head. "You know all the coolest people."

"I guess." She redirected to more pressing concerns. "Hey, I got a pass for the Great Library. Do you happen to know how to get there?"

Lana threw her hands in the air. "And you get to see all the coolest places." She grinned. "That's awesome. But unfortunately, I have no idea. I'm as new here as you are."

"That's okay." Brinnie shucked off her shoes and sat cross-legged. "I can ask around at dinner."

Lana's grin faded. "Oh, um, I'm not all that hungry. I think I'll stay here. Want to join me?"

Brinnie looked her over. No dark circles under her eyes, paleness, flush. "Are you feeling sick?"

"No, I just ate a lot at lunch." She fidgeted with the blankets, not making eye contact.

Suspicious. "Okay. Well, I'm starving, so I'm going down. Do you want me to bring you anything?"

"No, I'm fine. Actually, I think I have a couple apples up here." She rolled over and pulled open her trunk, rooting around. "You want one? We could turn in early."

Brinnie gave her a look. "Why don't you want me to go down?"

Lana didn't emerge from her upside-down dive into the trunk at the foot of her bed. "I never said that."

"You didn't have to. What's going on?"

"Nothing. But I'd like you to stay here with me. I want some company."

Brinnie put a hand on her hip. "Lana, what's wrong? Are you really okay?"

"I'm fine—it's not me." She let out a puff of breath. "It's you."

"What about me?"

She hesitated, wriggling back onto the bed and into a sitting position. "I think it's best if you don't go down there tonight. I can bring you something back, but . . . they're all celebrating. Apparently the word came in early this morning, and it's spread like wildfire. Our spies from Castelon sent news. Number two on Mordizan's hit list was confirmed dead."

Brinnie felt like she was missing something. "Okay . . . And I shouldn't go down there because?"

Lana bit her lip. "Merlin Ludovic was number two. It's confirmed. He's dead, Brinnie."

CHAPTER
TWENTY-ONE

Time paused. Her ears seemed to ring. Brinnie stared at the floor. "No. It can't be. He survived. He always does."

"I'm sorry." Lana hugged her abdomen. "I'm really sorry."

"Tell me what happened," she managed.

Lana took a deep breath. "When he disappeared, he transported himself to a healer."

"Anika?"

"I don't know what the name was. But she couldn't do anything. It was an enchanted blade. They took the body back to Wraithwood. Eira Ludovic was acknowledged as the interim Master of Wraithwood in a ceremony at Castelon this morning."

Reality felt like a fog, but she grasped an incongruency. "Interim?"

"Yes. She didn't inherit the Mastership powers." She hesitated. "Everyone's saying that you must have."

Brinnie shook her head and stood up. "I'll be back."

Lana shifted uneasily. "Where are you going?"

"I don't know. Out."

"Brinnie, I'm sorry."

She stopped at the door and turned toward her friend. "I know. And thank you. I just need some time."

The dorm passed in a blur. On the street, she noticed some students looking at her curiously, but she ignored them. Her legs kept moving, carrying her until she found herself in a small, empty courtyard.

She sank onto a stone bench and gazed up at the sky as the sun sank and the stars crept out.

"Tell him I love him," she whispered to the air. "And tell him I'm sorry."

She didn't know how long she stared at the stars with tears rolling down her cheeks, but at some point, the black hole of loss inside of her sparked and flickered into rage. This was Mordred's doing. It was Vorath's doing. Even Nimue had a hand in it, and she hadn't even had the decency to tell her what happened when she came to visit.

But above all, Mordred was to blame. He had as good as killed Uncle Merlin himself. He had Anna and David locked up somewhere —she knew it.

She would find them. She would avenge her uncle. *Forget Mordred's bane. I'll kill him myself.*

A plan began to formulate. She had the pass. She could get into the fortress. Then she would find him, and kill him.

She stood and strode back toward the dorm with purpose. *Get the pass. Get to the fortress. Track him down.*

Intent on her goal, she hardly noticed as someone came up beside her. "Hey. I guess you heard about what happened."

She glanced up. Marcus. *Of all people. Thank your lucky stars you are not your father, or you would have a wolf at your neck.* "About Merlin Ludovic? Yes."

He easily kept stride with her aggressive pace. "I wanted to say that I'm sorry."

She looked at him skeptically out of the corner of her eye. "Why?"

"Because I know it must be hard for you." His tone remained calm. "I wanted to see if you were okay."

Her anger flickered. "I'm fine. What's good news for Mordizan is good news for me."

He took hold of her arm to stop her. "Is it really?"

She glared down at the hand on her arm, and he quickly removed it. She composed herself. "Of course."

He didn't reach for her again, but he didn't break eye contact. "Don't let anyone think differently. Now isn't the time to do anything rash."

"Is that a threat?"

"No. A warning." He glanced toward the surrounding buildings. No one else roamed the streets at this time of night, but the darkened windows seemed to watch them. "There are eyes on you everywhere. Right now would be a terrible time to make a wrong move."

Her heart thumped. "And you're telling me this why?"

"That's my business." He stepped back, glanced once more at the nearest windows. Then he nodded to her. "Have a good evening."

He melted into one of the side streets between the shuttered shops, most likely invisible to anyone who didn't have Brinnie's night vision, and turned a corner, disappearing from sight.

As she watched him walk away, she began to return to her senses. If it was that easy to waltz in and kill Mordred, someone would have done it already. And after Marcus's warning, it seemed that they might be expecting her.

Fine. Not tonight. She set her course back to the dorm. *But I swear to you, Uncle Merlin, I am going to find his bane. He's going down.*

The next day after classes finished, Brinnie hopped on a broom heading for the fortress. It had been easier than she'd expected to get directions. Everyone wanted to talk to her, ask her if she'd heard the news, and ask if she was there when it happened. They were only too happy to help after she gave away fascinating tidbits about how her uncle died, stabbed from behind. Hewn down without honor, ambushed by a much larger force.

No one seemed to care about that part.

As the broom halted at the platform near the fortress, she climbed off and patted her pocket to make sure she still had the pass. At the gate, she waited for three people in front of her to enter before reaching the guards. "Brynna Ludovic. I have a pass to go to the Great Library."

"Anything illegal to declare?"

"No."

"Have a good day."

I will not, but thank you anyway.

The library was apparently on the southeast side of the fortress, opposite anywhere Brinnie had ventured before. She tried to keep her head down and avoid interacting with anyone she passed. She followed the circle of the inner courtyard, skirting the main fortress, until she turned a corner and directions were no longer necessary.

On the other side, steps of dark, polished stone led up to a massive structure lined with gothic pillars, like a creepy version of the British Museum.

She ascended the steps and grasped the massive spiral handle of one of the heavy doors, pulling it open.

Inside, a woman holding a wand stood in front of an opening in the middle of a wooden rail stretched across what appeared to be a lobby. "Pass?"

Brinnie handed her the rectangular piece of parchment. She waved the wand over it, then proceeded to wave the wand in front of and behind Brinnie. "Clear. Go ahead." She handed her the pass. "And don't lose this."

"Thank you."

As Brinnie stepped through the next set of wooden doors, her eyes widened and her mouth fell open. The library was enormous. She counted six stories rising above her, ascending to a dome. Around the central circle beneath the dome, which housed tables and chairs, shelves filled the entire ground floor. The library at Wraithwood would fit in here at least four times over.

Books. So many books. She forced herself not to bounce up and down in excitement.

Near giddy, she browsed the shelves, trying to figure out how they were organized. The books didn't have stickers with call numbers on the spines like normal libraries. She deduced that everything she saw was nonfiction, but that wasn't surprising. What use would the dark wizards have for fantasies? They lived in one.

"Can I help you?"

Brinnie turned around to see a bent old woman leaning on a cane at the head of the aisle. Perfect, a librarian to direct her. "Do you work here?"

"No, but I'm rather familiar with the place." She gave a close-lipped smile. "What are you looking for?"

Close enough. "I'm doing a project about anomalous wizards. Do you know where I would find books about that?"

"Second floor on the left, you'll find books on the divisions of magic." The old woman hobbled closer, then pointed upward with her cane. "If you want to learn about significant anomalous wizards in history, I'd look on the third floor."

"Thank you." Brinnie decided to take a chance. "I'm also doing some research on the subject of prophecies. Do you know where I would find books about that?"

"Prophecies?" The woman tugged at her shawl. "What do you mean?"

Maybe mentioning it was a bad idea. "You know, like predictions of the future."

She huffed a chuckle. "You young wizards and your fascination with the future. You're wasting your time. Magic has many uses, but predicting what is to come is not one of them."

"Oh, I'm not trying to predict the future. I'm studying early attempts. Like those of the Myrddin Era?"

"I don't know if there are any books on the subject." The woman tapped a finger to her lips. "If anything, there might be some ancient scrolls . . ."

If she'd learned one thing in Wraithwood's library, it was the importance of scrolls. "Can I see them?"

"Of course not." She offered another close-lipped smile, her considerable wrinkles crinkling. "They're far too fragile to be open to the public."

"Oh, okay." Brinnie tried not to look too disappointed. "Well, thank you. I'll go check out those books upstairs."

"Good luck. In a library, you never know what you might find." She chuckled to herself and shuffled away.

Brinnie headed toward a twisting staircase until she was sure the old woman was out of sight. Then she began scouring the library for where scrolls might be hiding.

The first four floors offered no answers. Only books lined the shelves, and all doors simply led to study rooms, maintenance closets, or other equally unhelpful places. She was about to ascend to the fifth floor when she heard an amplified voice saying, "The library will be closing in fifteen minutes. Please make your way to the doors."

She glanced up the stairs and back down. *I can do this in fifteen minutes.* She hurried up the staircase and began a fast-paced search.

Nothing but shelves lined the walls. She found no doors, no

windows. At the foot of the stairs to the sixth and final level, she heard the voice again.

"The library will be closing in one minute. Staff will now begin a search of the building to help escort all guests out of the library."

Brinnie took the stairs down two at a time. At the second floor, she slowed her pace so she wouldn't look suspicious. She passed a man coming up the stairs and gave him a friendly nod. She exited the library without ado, as the woman passed the wand over her and motioned her through.

Once in the courtyard, she began making her way around the fortress. Lights shone from the narrow windows high above, but she passed few denizens in the courtyard. A couple of soldiers gave her odd looks but didn't stop her.

At the gate to the inner circle, guards waved her past impatiently and closed the doors after her. She turned the corner into the yard in front of the main gate and came to an abrupt halt.

The massive doors were closed.

She approached one of two guards that still stood posted at either side of the gate. "Excuse me, I need to get back to the University."

"Sorry, miss." His posture remained rigid, eyes forward. "The gates are closed for the night. They'll open at five o'clock sharp tomorrow morning."

"Oh, sorry, I understand. I don't expect you to open them just for me. But is there another exit I can use?"

He turned a bored gaze on her. "You know the rules. Everyone out by ten o'clock. No one enters or exits."

She bit her lip. She could try to find Nimue, maybe spend the night in the room from before. "Okay, thank you. I'll go find someone to stay with for tonight."

He raised an eyebrow. "Inner gate is closed too. You have friends in the barracks?"

"I was visiting the library. I don't actually belong here." She didn't know what else to say. Would she have to spend the night huddled in the outer courtyard somewhere?

He sighed and hooked a thumb to his right. "The guardhouse is that door. You can stay there until the gates open. Just be more careful next time."

"Thank you. I appreciate it."

He nodded, looking bored again already.

The wooden door to the side of the gate opened into a room set off from the wall housing a vast array of gears, chains, winches, pulleys, and ropes stretching up at least a few stories. Sitting at a roughhewn table beneath the hanging gears, two men played a game of cards by the light of a lantern. They looked up as Brinnie opened the door.

She hesitated in the doorway. "Hi. I got shut in. The guard out there said I could wait in here until the gates open, but if you're busy . . ."

One of the two, a broad-shouldered man with a beard, pulled out a chair at the table. "Come sit. You can join the next round." He looked back down at his oval-shaped cards.

She paused for a moment before starting forward, surprised at his casual demeanor. She crossed the cramped room, ducking under a pulley, and sat. "Do people get stuck in here often?"

"Often enough." The other man, a younger, lanky fellow, shuffled through his cards. "Usually University students who lost track of time." He snorted. "Not exactly great security." He finished rearranging his hand. "Hit me."

The bearded man dealt him another card from one of three piles in the middle. "I'm Betram. That's Stephan."

"Brinnie."

"So let me guess—library?" Betram tossed a card into the center of the table.

"Yeah." Brinnie gave a sheepish smile. At least her predicament wasn't unusual. "I was working on a project."

"Lie." Stephan looked up from his cards. "Am I right?"

Brinnie shrank back from his inquisitive gaze. "Who, me?"

"Yes. That was a lie."

Her heart beat faster. "Um . . ."

Betram chuckled. "Don't let him get to you. He's just learning the ropes." He addressed Stephan. "It wasn't a lie. It was a truth, intended to mislead."

Stephan shrugged. "That's the same thing."

"No." Betram tapped the side of his nose. "An outright lie isn't helpful, but you can learn a lot from a truth intended to mislead."

Right, the guards' talent Marcus mentioned. Living lie detectors.

Betram laid his cards face up one by one—a seven, a fourteen, a twenty-one, and a face card with an "M" Brinnie didn't recognize. Maybe a Master? He grinned at Stephan. "I think you owe me a drink."

Stephan tossed his cards in—five, ten, seventeen, twenty. "Looks like I do."

"I'll let you know a little secret," Betram said to Brinnie while shuffling. "You may have heard that we detect lies with magic."

"Yes."

"Well, we don't." He chuckled. "Truth is, we're not even wizards."

She clasped her hands beneath the table, trying to remain casual. If she could figure out the secret of the guards, it might come in handy. "Then how do you do it?"

"Training. Years of training." He stacked the cards in a pile on the edge of the table. "Once you know the signs, no one can hide a lie."

"What are they?"

Both men laughed. "Can't very well tell you," Betram said. "Who knows what mischief you might get up to?"

"Fair enough." She couldn't help smiling.

Betram pulled a second deck from one of his deep pockets, this one the usual black and red playing cards Brinnie recognized. "Here. I'll deal you in." He cut the deck. "Stephan and I know plenty of human games we can teach you. I hear they're the new cool trend with cultured young wizards these days. Ever played BS?"

She snorted. "Yeah right. I'm not playing that with you two."

Betram guffawed and slapped his knee while Stephan chortled. "The girl knows her card games. How about pitch then?"

Brinnie didn't know what she would do all night, but she might as well entertain herself. "Deal me in."

After a few hands, she couldn't stop yawning.

"Two," Betram bid. "Long day?"

"Yeah." She arranged her cards. "Three. My class schedule is insane."

"Non-literal truth," Stephan said with a smile. Then he frowned at his cards. "Pass. It's all yours."

Brinnie tossed out the ace of hearts. Stephan groaned and threw out the jack.

"Tell you what." Betram added a three. "We've got a cot back there, for when one of us gets a little too sleepy."

"Or tipsy." Stephan pushed the trick toward Brinnie.

"Right." He winked. "If you don't tell anyone about our little naps, we'll let you use it for the night."

"I really appreciate it. I might take you up on that after this hand." She tossed the king of hearts into the center. "You've been awfully nice to someone silly enough to get shut in for the night."

Betram shrugged. "We get bored."

Stephan groaned again. "I'm starting to regret it." He threw out the two of hearts. "There's your third point."

"Quit your whining and bellyaching." Betram added a six of spades to the stack and pushed it toward Brinnie. "I've been here fifteen years, and no one's ever tried to break in and open the gates." He patted his ample belly. "As you can see, I wouldn't be much use if they did."

"You could sit on them," Stephan suggested.

After taking the next three tricks for a whopping score of five—much to Stephan's dismay—Brinnie left the two guards to a friendly banter about Betram's girth. She found the narrow cot in a back corner and sank onto its hard surface. It smelled a bit like unwashed man, but at that point she wasn't too picky. Within moments of her head hitting the flattened pillow, sleep overtook her.

"Brinnie."

It seemed like only a moment had passed as she opened her eyes.

Betram stood near the cot. "Gate's opening in two minutes."

"Oh. Thank you." She sat up and yawned as Betram left. As the thought of how many classes she had that day came into her mind, she sighed. Today would be a long day.

Betram and Stephan rolled up their sleeves, positioning themselves near the levers and gears. Stephan saluted. "Best of luck, even if you are ruthless at cards."

Brinnie thanked them profusely before exiting into the courtyard, where the gate opened with much groaning and creaking. She took a broom back to the University and arrived at her room just as Lana was waking up.

When Lana saw Brinnie, she sat bolt upright. "Where were you?"

Brinnie stumbled straight to her trunk and pulled out some clean clothes. "I got shut inside the fortress. Apparently, the gates close at ten."

Lana squinted at her. "Got a little carried away in the library?"

"It's huge!" Brinnie spun around with a grin. "You should see it. So many books . . ." Her smile faded under Lana's scrutiny. "What?"

"I thought about reporting you missing." She crossed her arms and leaned back against the wall. "You were gone all night. What was I supposed to think?"

Brinnie deflated. "I'm sorry. I had no idea I would get shut in. But I see how that might look." Like she'd made a run for it.

Lana sighed, sliding out of bed. "Please don't put me in that position again." She reached for her clothes. "I don't want to have to make a choice. But I will choose Mordizan."

Brinnie swallowed. "Got it."

"We better get going, or we'll be late to class."

That afternoon, once Brinnie had survived all of her classes, she again set out for the library. This time it wasn't to search for the prophecy—she needed to actually do some research to make her project believable.

As she sat at one of the tables in the library taking notes from a heavy, musty tome, she heard a voice say, "Did you find what you were looking for?"

She looked up to see the old woman from the day before hobbling slowly toward her. "Yes, I did. Thank you."

"Fascinating, isn't it?" She leaned against the chair opposite Brinnie. "When we look at the anomalous wizards, everyone always talks about spellcasters and detectors, but I find helpers the most interesting. There's so much more to them than just amplifying the magic of others."

Brinnie turned back a page and ran her finger along a passage. "And they're the only wizards who are capable of having abilities from more than one division. They can be helpers as well as just about anything else." *Like me.*

"Indeed. It's such a rare power, though. The last helper at Mordizan died over two decades ago." She clutched the back of the chair with both gnarled hands. "You know, they didn't used to be called helpers. Early post-Myrddin wizards called them *liniadi*."

"Meaning 'rulers' or 'governors' in the ancient language." Brinnie leaned forward, more than happy to nerd out about research with someone willing to listen. "I was reading about that. One source said that they could not only amplify magic, but also stifle it."

The woman nodded. "And some of the earliest sources claim that they could even absorb the magic of others and use it for their own purposes."

"Really?" Her blood chilled. That seemed like too much power for one wizard to have. "I haven't read that."

"Ah, but that's just speculation." The woman pointed at the text with one crooked finger. "The early writers were prone to exaggeration."

Something about the action prodded Brinnie's memory. She cocked her head. "Do I know you from somewhere?"

"You might." The old woman smiled, but unlike when she had smiled before, this time, she revealed her teeth—blackened teeth. "People aren't always what they seem."

"Keilrie." Brinnie pulled back. How hadn't she seen it? The old woman had ditched the cane and cloak, and her wild hair had been tamed into a thick, messy knot, but all else remained the same. How had she not noticed the dark eyes? Or had they never made eye contact at all?

Keilrie cackled. That grating noise was certainly familiar. "Hello, Brynna. Don't feel too badly. A cloaking spell has fooled many a wizard before you."

"Why are you here?" she asked warily.

"To see you, of course. I wanted to meet my soon-to-be apprentice."

Brinnie tried to give her the benefit of the doubt. She had been helpful here in the library, after all. "So you're a shadowmaster."

"No. I am but a shadow walker. You, however." She leaned forward. "I have waited decades to find one such as you." She grinned. "A mistress of shadows. A true being of darkness."

Brinnie suppressed a shudder, trying to keep from shrinking away. Answers first, being creeped out later. "So what does it mean, that you're only a shadow walker?"

"I see the shadows, and darkness doesn't hinder my vision. I can cloak myself in darkness. But, unlike you, the shadows do not obey my command."

"Oh." Brinnie glanced around for anyone who might interrupt the uncomfortable conversation, but she'd picked an especially secluded spot to immerse herself in study. "I thought I had a couple more weeks before I became your apprentice."

"Yes. I'm just here to observe my future student." She pulled out a chair with an agonizing screech of wood against stone.

This time, Brinnie couldn't suppress a wince at the noise. "And what do you observe?"

"Very powerful, of course, though untrained." Keilrie eased into the chair. "You have no idea what you're capable of. The only shadowmaster, the only *liniad*. But that's not what interests me. I'm most concerned with your soul." Her dark eyes bored into Brinnie's. "Does it, too, dwell in darkness?"

Creepy, creepy, creepy. "Of course not. I'm here fighting for the good side, the side of Mordizan, doing what's right."

Keilrie barked a laugh. "You know as well as I that this is the side of darkness. You can justify your actions, tell yourself lies, as so many of the others do, but sooner or later you must come to terms with it."

Shadows stirred at Brinnie's discomfort. "If you think it's wrong, then why are you here?"

"Wrong? I never said it was wrong. There is no right and wrong. That is a construct of the light." She grinned. "I revel in the darkness."

Brinnie's stomach clenched. Shadows flickered. "Why would anyone knowingly do that?"

Keilrie reached out a claw and Brinnie recoiled, barely snatching her hand away in time. "Your heart, child. Like mine, like every shadow walker before you, it's dark at its core. You can try to suppress it. But in the end, you are darkness. I have simply embraced what I am." She smiled. "And you, mistress of shadows. Your darkness could be like none the world has ever seen."

Brinnie slammed her book shut. "I think that's irrelevant. This whole battle is about protecting the human race versus destroying it and building a new, magical world order. Not about this dark and light thing." She stood. "I need to get going."

Keilrie's cackle sent chills down Brinnie's spine. "Is it not? But why shall we destroy humanity? Is it not to banish them to darkness, to feed the void? To spite the one who made them?"

Brinnie's mouth dropped open. "Mordred said that what you practice isn't magic."

"My power extends beyond magic." She folded her hands, sitting back in her chair. "Even Mordred fears me, and he does well to do so."

Brinnie picked up the book and shook her head. "I don't think this apprenticeship is going to work out. Have a nice day." She turned and walked away.

She heard Keilrie's voice behind her. "On the contrary, this is your destiny. You *are* darkness. You can't escape what you are."

Brinnie kept walking. "Goodbye."

"For now."

So you think. No way would she train with Keilrie. She would find a way out of this, even if that meant she needed to convince them she was ready for battle.

And if I can't find the prophecy, then with any luck I might learn something that can help me kill Mordred.

CHAPTER TWENTY-TWO

Swords clashed. As her opponent threw his weight against her sword, pressing her own blade toward her, Brinnie used the opportunity to kick him in the gut. He grunted and stumbled back, allowing her to swing for his head. He managed to block just in time, but it was only a diversion. She landed a solid kick in his solar plexus and he nearly dropped his sword. She took advantage of the momentum to slam into him with her shoulder, knocking him to the ground. She pounced on top of him, pinning his sword arm down, and held her blade to his throat.

Her lungs burned as she gasped in air, pushing herself up. She offered the young man a hand, but he stood on his own. Probably a good thing, considering his greater height, though he had the physique of a bean pole.

He glared at her. "You cheated."

Mr. Gerd snorted, entering the ring. "That was a disgrace."

Nimue crossed her arms, standing at the edge of the sandy circle. "Pardon?"

"Not her. You." He pointed at the boy Brinnie had just bested. "She just picked up a sword less than a month ago, and because of a couple unconventional tactics, she made a fool of you. You've been training for how long now?"

He turned red. "Uh . . ."

"Rhetorical question. Go." Mr. Gerd pointed toward the rest of the open practice field. "I want ten extra sets from you."

As the boy left, Brinnie winced. Maybe she shouldn't have been so aggressive. But when Nimue had requested to watch a sparring match, and Mr. Gerd had pulled Brinnie out of her intermediate classes for that purpose, her focus had turned to impressing them both—

especially after she'd made such a fool of herself with the sword her first time in front of Gerd.

Brinnie looked apprehensively from one to the other. Nimue raised an eyebrow. "Well, blade master? What's your expert opinion on her progress?"

Mr. Gerd scratched the back of his neck. "It was rough. Not pretty. But it was vicious." He crossed his brawny arms, feet apart in a military stance. "I've always thought there were two kinds of fighters —the kind that master the form until they fight like a machine, and the kind that throw themselves in there and attack so hard you don't know what hit you. I'd say she's the second." The corner of his lips twitched in what Brinnie might have thought was a smile. "Bloodthirsty little thing."

Nimue laughed. "Wise observations. Thanks for your help. I'll take it from here and send her back to class."

Back to class? Brinnie's muscles groaned in protest.

Mr. Gerd gave a sharp nod, then turned and marched toward his more advanced students on the other end of the field.

As Mr. Gerd left, Brinnie headed for the racks to hang up her blunted metal sword and exchange it for the wooden practice weapons her class had been using before she'd been pulled out. Nimue fell into step with her. "Nice job, kid."

"Thanks. It's been a crazy few weeks."

"Crazier than they had to be." Nimue gave her a sideways glance. "I was told you've been spending your evenings training the past two weeks."

She shrugged. "Yeah. I figured I needed a lot of work."

After her encounter with Keilrie in the library, Brinnie had determined to do anything to avoid being forced into apprenticing to the creepy old lady. However, her studies in the library had yet to yield results on the bane of Mordred and the prophecy, so between classes and trips to the library, she had begun practicing and conditioning outside of class, often with Lana.

She hated every minute of it. She would take burning eyes and a tickly nose from dusty tomes over burning lungs and noodle arms any day.

They reached the racks, and Brinnie exchanged weapons, wishing she hadn't left her water on the other end of the field nearer her class.

Nimue put her hands on her hips and looked Brinnie up and down. "Is there anything you want to tell me? Where did all this come from?"

"I've decided which side I'm on." Brinnie smiled at the irony.

Nimue raised an eyebrow. "Oh, yeah?"

Brinnie's heart clenched with a familiar pain, one that no amount of study or sprints or swinging of swords could take away. Her gaze swept the field, full of students who had cheered her uncle's death. Them, she didn't resent. They hardly knew better. But Mordred, and Master Vorath . . . "The next person with my blade at their throat isn't getting up afterward."

Nimue shook her head and grinned. "I knew it. You've got that look."

"What look?"

"The anger. A need for vengeance. We've all been there. You don't become a fighter for no reason."

Brinnie paused. *Vengeance? No. Justice.* She smiled grimly. "I've certainly got my reasons."

"Well, Miss Bloodlust, I have to get back to the fortress." Nimue glanced toward the sun, high in the sky. Its bright rays cut through the chill that had clung to the morning mid-October breeze. "But I'll be seeing you there soon."

Brinnie firmed her jaw. "I'll be there this evening."

"Good. Your first assignment is waiting for you."

Her first assignment as a member of Mordred's army. And her escape from Keilrie.

After her classes, Brinnie headed through the main courtyard of the University back toward her dorm on wobbly legs. Students still clustered around the announcements board in the center, buzzing about the newest addition.

Lana had pointed it out early that morning.

"Isn't that a new announcement?"

The two had drifted closer to read the paper.

Lana gasped. "No way. Has the war gotten to that point?"

Brinnie scanned the poster. *University students . . . draft . . . early graduation*. "So they're taking some of the best fighters early?"

Lana bounced on her toes. "I hope that includes me. I hear the eighth stronghold needs reinforcements."

Brinnie's stomach had knotted. More war, more death, as she continued her futile search for Mordred's bane.

But soon, she saw an opportunity. If she could be drafted into Mordred's army, she could get into the fortress. So far, guards had barred her from going anywhere but the library. And if she had the excuse of battle, she could escape Keilrie. Maybe she could even sabotage Mordred's war on the front lines. But she wouldn't get ahead of herself.

Now, passing the students thronged around the board, she thanked the heavens for the good fortune of Nimue showing up for that very purpose—drafting her into Mordred's army two days before Keilrie's claim.

She hadn't even made it up the steps to the dorm before Lana threw open the door and came barreling toward her. "Guess what?"

"Seems like something good." A smile blossomed at Lana's enthusiasm.

"They sent me through." Lana grasped Brinnie's shoulders in excitement. "Mr. Gerd said I don't need history and ancient language studies to fight. He's passing along all the good fighters for the offensive."

"No way!" Brinnie exclaimed, unsure of how she felt. "That's great."

"We can go to the fortress together. I won't have to sit here being sad and lonely without a roommate." Lana bounced back up the steps and pulled open the door. "Come on, we better pack."

"Good news for me as well," Brinnie said as they ascended the stairs. "I'm drafted too."

Lana stopped mid-step and whirled toward Brinnie. "No way."

"Yes way."

Lana squealed and hugged her. "We're going to storm some strongholds together!" She spun and darted up the stairs.

After packing, as Brinnie followed Lana toward the broom stop, she tried to sort through her feelings. On the one hand, having a familiar face in the army was an unexpected blessing. On the other, she had hoped that Lana would stay behind for at least a year, out of harm's way, giving her enough time to kill Mordred and end the fighting.

Brinnie and Lana hopped on a broom together. "Can you believe it?" Lana threw out an arm. "Both of us get to go off to the front lines. Together!"

"It's crazy," Brinnie agreed.

Lana grinned. "I'm so glad we ended up roommates. I didn't think I was going to find any friends here, at least not so quickly."

"Me neither." *I didn't think I was going to find friends at all.*

Which makes this all so much more complicated.

The man with a buzzcut at the desk looked at them without expression. "You're here for the army."

Lana clasped her hands behind her back. "Yes, sir. University recruits."

He sighed, shuffling through his papers. "Names?"

"I'm Lana Arion, and this is Brynna Ludovic."

He flipped through until he apparently found what he was looking for. "It appears they think we can build an army of young girls," he muttered. Then he shoved the papers toward them and pointed to a few lines. "Your assignment is the fifth fortress, both of you. Your detachment leaves tomorrow morning at six-thirty. Be in the west outer courtyard by six to get your gear. The barracks are full, so you're on your own until then."

"Full?" Lana's hand perched on her hip.

He ignored her and pulled two metal necklaces, like dog tags, out of a drawer. He tapped the papers and then the tags with a wand. "These are your I.D.s, letting the guards know you're supposed to be here."

"Thank you." Brinnie swiped the tags for both of them off the counter before Lana could argue with him. She gave Lana a nudge, leading the way out of the office.

Once they had exited into the corridor, Lana huffed. "Well, he was pleasant."

Brinnie shrugged. "We don't look like much." She handed Lana her necklace. "Anyway, we can ask Nimue about someplace to stay."

"That's because he hasn't seen what we can do." Lana looped the tags over her neck. "Do you know where to find Nimue? Who you just so casually know and can ask random favors of?"

Brinnie laughed. "Yes, as we've established. And unfortunately . . . I have no idea."

"All right, then. We better start searching. She's probably with all the important people, right?" She pointed. "East is that way. I think most of the council chambers and things are on the east side."

"If nothing else, someone there might be able to point us in her direction."

They exited the outer ring of buildings and crossed the outer courtyard toward the main one. Not surprisingly, they were stopped by a guard not far from the entrance and asked for identification. "Where are you headed?"

"Perfect, we need directions." Lana gave him a dazzling smile. "Do you know where we can find Nimue Drakon?"

His eyes narrowed. "For what purpose?"

"Sorry." Brinnie lifted her necklace. "I'm Brynna Ludovic. Nimue is my, uh, mentor."

He fidgeted with the scabbard at his hip. "Well, I don't know exactly where she is. But the public council chamber is that way." He hooked his thumb over his right shoulder. "I think public meetings are closed for the day, but—"

"Perfect, thank you!" Lana grabbed Brinnie's arm and pulled her along. "We won't trouble you any more."

Brinnie stumbled after her, offering the guard an apologetic smile.

They had rounded the corner of the fortress when a figure stepped out in front of their path. Brinnie's heart sank when she saw the bent old woman with wild gray hair. "Hello, Keilrie."

The old woman shook her finger at Brinnie. "You thought you could run away? You're my apprentice now, not some fighter."

"Well, not according to this." Brinnie held up her I.D. "Master

Vorath wanted me to fight. I'm off to the strongholds. I can learn all the apprentice stuff when I get back."

"No. You were promised to me. His month is over. If he wanted you to fight, he should have sent you then." She took hold of Brinnie's arm with her clawed fingers. "You're coming with me."

"No." Brinnie shook her off. "I'm not."

Lana tugged on Brinnie's other arm. "Come on, we have places to go." Her eyes darted toward the old shadow walker with trepidation. She'd heard enough about Keilrie's creepiness from Brinnie.

Keilrie glared. "I'm going to talk to Vorath about this."

"Please do." Brinnie stepped past her. "Good day."

Two more guards wearing the Mordizan emblem and swords at their hips emerged from around the corner. Keilrie bared her teeth. "I meant now."

She wasn't about to start a fight. Brinnie and Lana glanced at each other, then fell into step with Keilrie and the guards. One of the guards glanced at Lana. "Who are you?"

"Brynna's, uh, battle partner. Whatever happens to her affects me too."

He hesitated for a moment, then shrugged. "Fine."

As they marched across the courtyard, Brinnie hissed to Lana, "My partner?"

"Just go with it. I want to see what happens. And I don't want to wander this fortress by myself."

The guards led them into the main fortress, Keilrie hobbling behind.

The passages they took were grander, wider. The wizards they passed wore fine robes, dresses, or uniforms, with guards stationed in alcoves periodically. Brinnie felt awkward in her plain school clothes, but at least she looked better than Keilrie, who seemed to have woken up in the morning and rolled out of a dumpster.

They entered a wide foyer featuring a massive chandelier and lined with six guards on each side. Two guarded tall wooden doors studded with ironwork.

One of the guardsmen leading their small party spoke to the guards at the door. "Keilrie Shadowwalker and Brynna Ludovic, as summoned by Master Vorath."

The men flanking the entrance gripped Frisbee-sized iron rings and pulled open the groaning doors.

Their party entered, affording Brinnie a view of a semicircular table in the center of an official-looking room with emblems hanging from the walls. In the middle of the table sat Vorath, and to either side of him sat people she didn't recognize, presumably his main council. Smaller, empty benches fanned out in front of the elevated table, probably for lesser members. A walkway led through the smaller benches from the door to the table where Vorath sat.

The man beside Vorath pointed to something on a map sprawled across the table. "My lord, you can see here that the wall is a good five feet shorter on this side. With the help of siege towers, we could easily get over the wall and take the stronghold."

"Yes, but how do you propose to build siege towers there? It's the middle of a plain with no timber. Carting in supplies would take far too long." Vorath looked up toward Brinnie's group standing awkwardly inside the door. "Keilrie," he sighed. He waved them forward. "Come in, I don't want to have to shout."

Keilrie blazed a trail up the aisle. "My lord, you promised me this girl as an apprentice."

Brinnie summoned her courage and followed Keilrie, taking a place beside her in front of the table. "With respect, sir, I've been assigned to leave tomorrow morning for the fifth stronghold."

"And therein lies the problem." He looked bored. Brinnie couldn't blame him—siege towers were far more interesting than this magical custody dispute. "I recognize your value as a fighter. But Keilrie has convinced me of your value as an assistant to her work as well. What say you?"

Brinnie chose her words carefully. "I'm honored to be considered of value to Keilrie, but I also desire to fight for what I believe in and prove myself to you, especially if I am to one day inherit Wraithwood. Whatever your decision, my lord, I'll consider it just."

He nodded. "Wise words. Hear me, both of you. Keilrie, I recognize your claim. You shall have her as your apprentice." Brinnie's heart sank. "But, this is also a time of war. I need skilled wizards. You may have her for one week. Then she will leave with the next detachment."

Keilrie scowled. "There's little I can do in just a week."

"Then I suggest you get busy." He waved them off. "Now go. I have more pressing matters to attend to."

"Excuse me, my lord, but can I stay until the next detachment too?" Lana piped up.

He squinted at her. "Don't I know you from somewhere?"

"Lana Arion, my lord. I came with my father to the last Masters' Gathering."

"Ah, yes." He nodded. "Why do you wish to stay?"

"I'd rather go with Brynna. We've been roommates, and we fight well together."

He shrugged. "Yes, that's fine." He turned to a young man waiting off to the side. "Have someone inform their commander, and secure them a place to stay." The errand boy ran off, and Vorath's attention returned to them. "Anything else? Good. You all may go."

As the doors closed behind them, Brinnie whispered to Lana, "We've never fought together before. You can't just lie to the Master of Mordizan!"

Lana grinned. "Oh, really?" she whispered back. "What was it you said? 'I'm honored to be considered of value to Keilrie.'"

"That's not lying, that's diplomacy."

Lana feigned confusion. "Wait, aren't they the same thing?"

"Brynna!"

Brinnie made a face at Lana and turned around. "Yes?"

Keilrie scowled and motioned to her. "Come with me. We have much to do." She waved Lana off. "You go with the guards. I've no use for you."

Brinnie forced her expression to remain neutral. "Yes, ma'am." To Lana, she muttered under her breath, "Wish me luck."

Keilrie shuffled off, not waiting to make sure Brinnie followed.

Lana wrinkled her nose. "Have fun with her. She's a ray of sunshine, isn't she?"

Brinnie started walking backwards. "Should I find that offensive?"

"You can take it however you want, oh mistress of shadows." She waved. "See you 'round."

With that, Brinnie grudgingly followed after Keilrie.

CHAPTER TWENTY-THREE

They descended into the depths of the fortress. No one crossed their path, and the passageways became dank and chill. The ceilings grew lower, the stone rougher. Somehow, Brinnie could sense that they were underground.

Strange chimes hanging from the ceiling clacked together with the wind of the opening door as they reached their destination, and a pungent aroma assaulted Brinnie's nose. A chill ran up her spine and she stopped in the doorway.

Keilrie turned and grinned at her. "What's the matter, child? Come in."

Brinnie took a hesitant step inside, her shadow flickering on the walls from the light of a handful of dripping candles in the small, cell-like room. She felt something brush her ear and whirled around, but there was nothing there. She could almost hear voices, strange whispers. Even the shadows felt unfamiliar. "What are we doing here? It must be night by now."

Keilrie nodded. "Indeed. But we are creatures of the night, are we not?"

The door swung shut behind Brinnie as if of its own accord, closing with a dull thud. Keilrie struck a match and lit the incense sitting in the center of a low table. Its strange, sickly-sweet smell made Brinnie queasy.

Keilrie sat on a pillow on the other side of the table and gestured to a cushion opposite her. "Sit."

Her legs screamed at her to run, but Brinnie forced herself to proceed forward, hesitating to step over the chalk lines and runes drawn on the stone floor. She sat on the crumbling cushion, every muscle tense. "Well?"

"Give me your hand."

"Okay . . ." Brinnie held out her hand. Keilrie took hold of it. In one swift motion, she slashed Brinnie's palm with a small knife. "Ow! Why?" Keilrie held on so that Brinnie couldn't pull away, holding her hand over a smooth black stone so that the blood dripped down her palm and onto the surface.

Keilrie released her and held her hands up. "Here, oh dark ones, we offer the blood of Brynna Ludovic. As her blood paints this rock, let your darkness paint her soul."

Brinnie started to stand. "Yeah, I don't like where this is going."

"Sit!" Keilrie's dark eyes fixed on Brinnie's own and she felt the will to move leaving her. Keilrie closed her eyes, raised her hands once more, and began to chant words Brinnie didn't understand.

Brinnie tried to get up, but she found that her legs wouldn't move. Keilrie's chant grew to a keen, and her words became unintelligible.

Brinnie's heart raced, and she tried to keep her limbs from trembling as an unreasonable terror welled within her. Somewhere beyond her waking senses, she could feel them—the shadows that weren't shadows, dancing, swirling, shrieking with screams that she heard not with her ears, but heard nonetheless. And within that shrieking, she could almost hear a voice that was not a voice, but rather a knowing, a transmission of thought.

Embrace the darkness, mistress of shadows. We can make you more powerful than you've ever dreamed.

She shot to her feet, sweeping out an arm to knock over the candles, the incense, the black stone. They clattered to the floor, hot wax flying, fire flaring onto oil.

Keilrie hissed, throwing a bucket of water onto the flames, plunging the room into the sort of darkness that affected neither of them, but was a welcome relief from whatever it had become seconds ago. "What have you done?" the woman demanded.

Brinnie's chest heaved with gasping breaths. "That is *not* magic."

"Of course not." Keilrie dropped to her knees, scooping up the black stone. "There are powers far beyond magic. And you have shunned them."

Brinnie planted her feet. "As any sane person would."

"You fool." Keilrie glared up at her. "They could have made you the most powerful wizard in the world. You're a *liniad.* You know what it's like to supply others with strength. They could do that for you. You could be even more powerful than Mordred."

"Then why don't you accept their offer yourself?" Brinnie clutched her stinging hand. Blood stained her fingers.

"They don't want me. They told me long ago that my role was to bring the one to them who was truly a creature of darkness, whose mind and body could contain their power without being destroyed." She nodded. "That's you."

Brinnie backed away. "You're wrong about that."

Keilrie laughed. "Mistress of shadows. Creature of darkness. Vessel of the dark ones. Those are your names. You will join us."

She shook her head. "No deal." She turned for the door. "I'm out of here."

"You can leave. You can try to run away from your fate." Her grin grew. "But you can't. Bit by bit, you'll become darker and darker, until one day you realize that I was right—you are the darkness."

She yanked open the door. "I don't think so." Then she slammed it behind her.

It took her many purposeful angry strides before she realized she had no idea where she was. She stopped to get her bearings, but dank passages with the mildew smell of underground tunnels stretched in either direction with no indication which way led up. Without any sense of direction, she decided to go right.

She wandered for quite a while without making any progress that she could discern. *Story of my life. Getting lost.* The halls remained empty. As she came to the end of a passageway, she arrived at steps leading downward. She hesitated. She wanted to go up, not down. On the other hand, she was fairly certain she had been traveling in circles. Maybe someone down there could give her directions.

She descended the narrow, twisting stairs. At the bottom, she arrived in what seemed to be a small antechamber. A light orb hovered near the ceiling above a doorway in the opposite wall. *Well, light orbs are a good sign.* Someone had to have been here recently. She passed through the doorway into a hall lined with several heavy doors. She tried to open them, but they were locked. She stopped in the middle of the passage and blew out a frustrated breath. "Hello? Is anyone down here?"

Behind her, she thought she heard footsteps. She started to turn, but a hand clapped over her mouth from behind. She struggled and tried to break away, but whoever it was yanked her backward into one of the rooms and closed the door.

She wriggled, trying to kick the person, trying to bite, trying to scream, but the arms around her held like steel bands. "Shh! It's me," a voice hissed in her ear.

She kicked out her feet one more time before the voice registered. She paused, and the hand eased away from her mouth. "Marcus?"

"Yes." He let her go and she turned to face him as he pressed his ear to the door and listened. She opened her mouth, but he held up a hand for silence. "It's clear," he said finally. He stepped away from the door. "Now what are you doing down here?"

"Me? I got lost. I think the better question is what on earth you're doing sneaking up on me like that."

"I heard you calling out." He kept his voice low, glancing toward the door. "You can't be found down here. It wouldn't go well for you."

"Why not?" She looked around the empty room, about ten-by-ten feet. Holes in the wall indicated that at one point, something may have been bolted there, but now the space stood bare.

"You got lost and just happened to end up in the depths of the fortress?" He procured fire in his palm. "I hardly buy your story myself."

"Well, it's the truth. Do you know how to get back up to the main fortress?"

"Right now I get to ask the questions." The fire grew, presumably so he could better see her face. "Why are you here? What are you doing at Mordizan?"

This again? She tried to keep her expression neutral. "I'm attending the University. Currently, I'm apprenticed to Keilrie."

"That's not what I mean. You can tell the truth. There are no ears here."

What was his deal? Was this some kind of trap? "I'm here to fight on the side of Mordizan."

"Are you?"

"Of course."

"Then there's something you might want to see." His fire dimmed, and he opened the door. "Follow me."

She didn't have much choice if she wanted to find her way out, so she followed.

In the hall, he grabbed a torch from a sconce and lit it. Then he continued, holding the torch aloft.

He led her down the hall to a bare spot on the wall, where he paused. He reached up and pressed one of the stones, and it sank in. "Stand next to the wall and be ready to move," he directed.

A secret passageway? She decided not to ask questions. She did as he said, and he pushed in another stone near the floor with his foot. A section of the wall began to rotate. Brinnie followed as he slipped through the opening before the wall rotated shut once again. He held up the torch and illuminated a rough flight of stairs. "This way."

Brinnie shuffled forward, stirring up dust. "What is this? Where are we going?"

"Mordizan has all sorts of secret tunnels, rooms, passageways. Perfect for spying, or hiding things you don't want to be seen." She noticed his all-black garb, dusted slightly with dirt—as if he'd been lurking in these very passages. He started down the stairs, turning sober eyes on her over his shoulder, expression grim. "I warned you before—there are eyes and ears everywhere."

She ducked under a spiderweb, following him down the uneven steps. "Where are we going?"

"Mordred told you he released your sister and your brother-in-law?"

"Yes."

"He lied." Marcus turned a corner at the bottom of the stairs and stepped through a small opening to the side that Brinnie wouldn't have noticed.

"So those *were* shapeshifters." Her heart sank. "Then where are they?"

"That's what I'm showing you. Hold this." He handed her the torch and pulled himself onto a shelf halfway up the wall leading to a tunnel. He reached down and she handed him the torch before clambering up herself. Brinnie could just barely stand without her head hitting the ceiling, but Marcus was bent over. "Down this way. Be very quiet."

They continued down the tunnel's passage. Eventually, Marcus cupped his hand over the torch, smothering the flame. Brinnie gasped, expecting him to burn himself, before remembering magic.

He smiled, held out his unscathed hand, and whispered, "Fire wizard, remember?"

She nodded and followed as the passageway narrowed and the ceiling grew lower until they were crawling on hands and knees. Her hands ached from the rough stone. By the way Marcus felt his way through the passage, Brinnie guessed it must be pitch dark.

However, he soon began crawling with more confidence. Was there a light source? Marcus held up a hand for her to stop and gestured in front of them. There, blocking the way, were metal bars. He crawled up next to them and plastered himself against the wall so she could join him in peering through. She wriggled her way forward until they were wedged with their faces against the grate.

The opening looked out over a room from near the ceiling, and Brinnie realized that they must be in a ventilation shaft. The room housed four tiny, barred cells, and a guard stood watch in front of them. Two cells stood empty, but the other two each housed an occupant.

The dark-haired prisoner on the right lay slumped against the wall, one hand clutching his bloodied upper leg. *Please no.* But as Brinnie watched, the blonde prisoner in the second cell lifted her head, and Brinnie's hand shot to her mouth.

Anna and David.

"Please." Anna shoved tangled hair out of her face, manacles clacking, as she appealed to the guard. "He's hurt. Just let me help him. All I need is some antiseptic and gauze. Or send a doctor with the proper supplies."

The guard looked bored, as if they'd had this argument many times. "Maybe you shouldn't have tried to escape."

"It's infected. He's going to die if you leave him like this."

The guard shrugged. "That's not my fault, is it? The infection will kill him, not me."

Brinnie's stomach sank. A loophole to the rules of the Enchantment. They could let David die on his own.

"What is wrong with you!" Anna's voice cracked. "What's the difference? Why let him die when I could fix it so easily?"

The guard ignored her.

"Why? What have we ever done to you?" Anna shrieked. "To any of you?"

"It's okay, Anna." David raised his head, grimacing. "I'll be fine. Really."

That's it. Brinnie leaned away from the bars and raised a hand to summon the shadows. Marcus glanced over and shook his head emphatically. She nodded back just as emphatically and pressed her hand against the grating to form shadow wolves in the room below.

Marcus grabbed her arm and pinned it to her side. She reached to throw out her other one, but he grabbed that too, wrestling them both behind her back. She wriggled, trying to yell at him wordlessly through her glares. But he pulled her back along the passageway as she put up a futile fight.

Out of sight of the grating, he hissed, "Stop it. You can't do anything."

"Marcus, I don't want to hurt you, but I will." She gave her arms another yank. "I have to save my sister."

"And how exactly are you going to do that? Sure, you can take down one guard, but can you take down the entire fortress? Do you even know your way out? You may be able to turn invisible, but those two can't."

Her raging heartbeat began to calm. It almost made her angrier that he was right. They made eye contact, and she nodded. He released her and retreated as much as the small space allowed.

"Fine, then." Brinnie shot another glance back up the tunnel. "Then what *are* we going to do? Or did you just show me that to taunt me?"

"We're going to take down Mordred."

"What?" Brinnie searched his face for any signs of joking or deception, but his jaw had set in grim determination.

"I know that's why you're here." He shifted in the passage.

"Luckily for you, that's what I want too. Let's get out of this shaft, and we can talk."

What was he trying to do? Get a confession out of her? It had to be one of Mordred's tricks.

She followed him, crawling up the shaft until they reached where Marcus had left the torch where the passage widened. He lit the torch and turned to her. "Let's talk."

She crossed her arms. "You first."

"Fine. My father is blind. He doesn't see what Mordred's doing. Mordred is rallying everyone to the cause, bringing in new strategies, making himself popular. What do you think is going to happen once the strongholds fall?" Marcus adjusted his grip on the torch. "Everyone is going to look to Mordred as the leader. And you can bet that pretty soon he'll come up with the brilliant idea of becoming the Master of Mordizan himself so that he can be a better leader." He leaned against the wall, head still bent in the tight passage. "Only problem is, there's already a Master, and the Master's son, and the only way Mordred can become the Master is for both of them to die, a sacrifice that will clearly be in the best interest of the people, and one he will make."

Brinnie's eyes widened. "You think Mordred is going to kill you?"

"I know he will. Nimue told me so. We've been good allies for a while, and she wanted me to leave, before it comes to that."

Brinnie shook her head. She had to admit, it sounded plausible. "And so, if I actually was an enemy of Mordred, how exactly do you think we would take him down?"

"I don't know," he admitted. He switched the torch to his other hand. "That's why I'm asking you. I assume you came here with a plan."

"And why would I trust you?" She crossed her arms.

He gestured down the passageway. "Didn't I take you to see your sister?"

"Sure, but let's think about this for a minute. Even if you're telling the truth about the whole Mordred scenario, what happens after we get rid of him? Our alliance is over? We start trying to kill each other?" She moved her hands to her hips. "Or are you planning to kill me as soon as I tell you what I know?"

He ran a hand through his hair in frustration. "Why would I want you dead?"

"Oh, I don't know, maybe because I'm a Ludovic infiltrator—at least in your mind—and you're the heir of Mordizan."

"I don't want you dead, but I realize there's no good way for me to prove that." He sighed. "I'm not concerned with killing enchantment wizards. I would rather not kill anyone. I only want Mordred gone. And I think, in that, we have a common goal."

Brinnie hesitated. It was possible that he felt the same way she did when she thought of the normal people she had met, like Lana and, maybe, Marcus himself—she didn't want to hurt them. Just Mordred.

Or maybe he would turn on her the moment she revealed her plan.

Unfortunately, she was getting nowhere. The inside knowledge and connections the heir of Mordizan could afford . . . She came to a decision. "Okay, then. We work together against Mordred. We're allies until he's dead. I'll tell you what I know, we'll take him down together, and after that . . ."

"After that, we go our separate ways. You can go home with your sister, or whatever it is you want to do. And we hope never to meet each other on the battlefield."

Brinnie took a deep breath. "We have an understanding."

"Good." He stuck out his hand.

She shook it. "Now can we maybe discuss this somewhere a little less cramped?"

CHAPTER
TWENTY-FOUR

"The library, tomorrow at noon."

Marcus already began to fade down the hall with silent footfalls. Brinnie imagined he would soon disappear into some hidden alcove or tunnel. "Got it." She waved. "Thanks for helping me get back to my room."

He nodded and melted around the corner.

Brinnie eased open the door and winced as the hinges squeaked. She entered a room similar to their dorm, with a bed on either side—and Lana sitting on the left bunk, arms crossed. *Oh, no.*

As Brinnie shut the door, Lana demanded, "Explanation?"

Brinnie attempted to dance around the question. "What are you doing up? It's got to be three in the morning."

"Me? What about you? I was starting to think Keilrie ate you or something."

"Apparently she really likes working at night." Brinnie flopped onto her bunk. Not bad. Softer than the one at the University.

"Doing what exactly? You were gone for hours and hours."

"Oh, you know. Summoning the darkness." *Spying on the dungeons. Plotting Mordred's demise.* "Fun stuff like that."

"Ugh." Lana lay back and pulled the blanket over her head. "I'm just glad you're not dead."

"Debatable. I'm certainly dead tired."

Within seconds, she was out like a light.

She was in a strange place with a red sky. Trees lined the path, obsidian trees with no leaves. The black path, dark and twisting, led away into the distance.

Strange music floated on the wind, horrible in sound. No, not music at all—it sounded like the clacking of bones. Lightning flashed, and in that split second the trees were illuminated, revealing the skeletons of massive beasts, their bones shaking and clattering together.

A loud banging awoke her. "Brynna!"

She shot upright and looked at the door in confusion, trying to remember where she was.

Lana groaned. "Why? It's five in the morning."

Brinnie stumbled out of bed and opened the door to reveal Keilrie's scowling visage. *Great.* "What are you doing here?"

"We have things to do." Keilrie tapped her fingers on her staff. "Come."

"Let me get dressed." Brinnie closed the door before Keilrie could protest. Part of her winced at being rude to an old lady, but Keilrie defied a lot of norms.

As she wriggled into clothes, Brinnie tried to clear her head. It had just been a dream. A strange, unsettling dream. The strains of skeletal music echoed in her mind, stirring a feeling of panic in her chest. She hummed a tune to try to drown it out.

Lana turned toward the wall, pulling the blanket over her head. "That woman is crazy."

Brinnie looked up and realized that she was trying to put her shoes on the wrong feet. "What? Oh. Agreed."

Properly shod, Brinnie followed Keilrie. "Where are we going?"

"Your magic needs work." Keilrie's staff *thump-thumped* a determined rhythm. "We're going to practice."

In an exhausted fog, Brinnie hardly registered their path until Keilrie led her to a large, open room with a weapons rack in the corner. Another training area, apparently.

Keilrie turned to face her. "I want to see you hide yourself with shadows."

"Okay." Brinnie promptly turned invisible.

Keilrie reached out. Her fingers twisted, and she pulled. Brinnie felt the shadows rip away, leaving her exposed. Keilrie scowled. "That was terrible."

Brinnie couldn't move for a moment in shock. No one had ever been able to touch her shadows. She snapped her mouth shut. "I mean, you are a shadow walker."

"But I'm not the only one who's going to be able to see you. A wizard of skill can learn to look for anomalies in the shadows." Keilrie leaned on her staff. "Now that the enemy knows about you, they will certainly start training to do so. Light wizards especially, like your friend, will see right through you."

"Okay, so what do I do?"

"Don't be so sloppy. Don't throw shadows over yourself. Drape them to match the surrounding shadows."

Brinnie looked up at the large light orbs floating near the ceiling. "There aren't exactly many shadows where we're standing."

"So what does that tell you?" Keilrie asked with surprising patience.

"I should use as little as possible."

"Exactly."

She tried again, this time with only a thin covering of shadow. Keilrie nodded. "Better."

Interesting. She'd never thought of the density and direction of shadows mattering. Maybe something good would come from training with Keilrie after all.

"Now, you're not only a shadow walker. You're a shadowmaster. I want to see your creations."

Brinnie summoned a wolf to her side.

Keilrie peered at it. "They can do physical damage?"

"Yes."

"Solid to the touch? Not just for you, but for others?"

"They have been when I've needed them to be." No need to admit she didn't know much of how that worked.

"Direct it to kill me."

Brinnie blinked. "What?"

"You heard me. Direct it to kill me." Keilrie grinned. "Don't worry, you won't succeed."

Was this some sort of trap? Brinnie hesitated, then waved the wolf forward. "Get her."

The canine sprang at Keilrie's throat, snarling. But to Brinnie's surprise, the wolf passed right through her. It whirled, leaping for her back, but passed through again, landing in front of Brinnie. It snapped its teeth right through Keilrie as the old woman stood smirking.

Brinnie called off the wolf, waving it out of existence. "How did you do that?"

"I didn't believe." She cackled. "You know how it works. You create using your imagination, and all physical sensations are the result of the power of suggestion. You are capable of suggesting so strongly that it becomes like reality—you can wound your enemies with nothing. But, if someone doesn't heed your suggestion, if they truly believe that what they see is only a shadow, an illusion . . ."

"Then it becomes one." Brinnie's mind spun. "But what can I do about that?"

"Make me believe."

Brinnie summoned another shadow wolf. "Okay. So how do I do that?"

"You need to convince me that this is real. Imagine the small details of how it looks, how it moves. Make it seem as lifelike as possible. Think of what its teeth can do—imagine how its weight can knock over a grown man when it springs. Believe in your own creation. If you truly believe that it will rip out an enemy's throat, so will your enemy." Keilrie spread her arms wide. "Now direct it again. Tell it to spring at me, pin me down."

Brinnie held the images in her mind, imagining the individual hairs of the wolf's thick pelt, each sharp tooth that it bared. Solid, real. She held the image in her mind of her wolf knocking Keilrie to the ground. She opened her eyes, waved to the wolf, and it pounced.

But once again, it passed right through. Keilrie cackled.

"Why didn't it work?" Brinnie waved the wolf back to her side.

"You don't believe that it's real."

Brinnie stuck her hand through the wolf. "Well, of course it isn't. It's a shadow."

"That is your problem. This is not a shadow. This is real."

Brinnie put her a hand on her hip. “How am I supposed to believe that when we both know it isn’t true?”

Maddeningly, Keilrie grinned. “Until you know that the shadows are real, anyone can escape your power simply by disbelief.”

Brinnie scowled. “Then I better hope everyone believes.”

“Or, you could fight with shades that are real in truth.”

Brinnie had a feeling she wouldn’t like where this conversation was headed. “What do you mean?”

“You fight with shadows when you could fight with darkness.” Keilrie leaned forward. “Imagine if instead of sending shadow wolves, you sent the dark ones forth in canine form.”

Brinnie sighed. “Dark ones as in last night’s creepy dark ones? We’ve already had this conversation. It’s a no.”

“Then I suppose you had better start believing.” Keilrie straightened. “Try again.”

Half an hour after noon, Brinnie finally handed her pass to the woman at the library. She found Marcus sitting at one of the ground floor tables in nondescript clothes, flipping through a book.

He looked up as she approached, a teasing grin quirking the corner of his lips. “Did you get lost again?”

“I wish. I was busy driving Keilrie crazy with my incompetence. She finally let me go.” She plopped down in the chair across from him. “Find anything?”

He glanced around, then slid the book toward her and pointed to an empty space as if showing her something. “Yes. My father said there’s a door by the entrance to the library. You can hardly tell it’s there. That’s where the sensitive material is kept.”

She almost felt annoyed that he’d learned in one morning what she’d been trying to discover for a month. “And he just told you this?”

“It took a little more than flat-out asking, but the point is, if we get through that door, we can look for the prophecy.”

A pang of trepidation ran through her at his words. They had spent at least an hour last night discussing plans and pooling information, but the fact that Marcus of all people knew about her flimsy hope for destroying Mordred . . . "Okay. Any ideas how to do that?" She glanced toward the woman manning the entrance. "Security is literally standing right in front of it."

"You can turn invisible."

"Sure, but it's got to be locked, right?"

A woman carrying a stack of books walked by and Marcus shook his head and said, "No, it says here Sir Eirlen was a fire wizard." As soon as she had passed, he continued, "I have the key. I think." He pushed his shirt aside a few inches to briefly reveal a key ring attached to his belt, crowded with keys of all sizes. "It has to be one of these."

She refrained from asking where he had gotten that key ring. "Nice. Okay, so I take the keys and start trying them in the lock. What about when the door opens? We need a distraction, or she'll notice that."

"I'll take care of the distraction. You go in and find the prophecy. I'll be waiting out here."

"Good. And how do I sneak out again?"

"Oh. I didn't think of that. Hmm."

They sat in silence for a moment, thinking. Finally, Marcus said, "So what if she sees it open and close on its own? You'll be leaving. They'll search the place and find nothing."

"But they'll know something's up. And they'll know that besides Keilrie, I'm the only one here who can turn invisible. I would think they'd come to the obvious conclusion that it was me." She thought. "Unless . . . what if I hid in here until the library closes? Then once everyone's gone, I can sneak in and out."

"Only one problem. I have to get the keys back into my father's room before tonight, or he'll notice they're missing. But what if you went in, and left the keys outside the door? I'll pick them up, and you wait until the library closes to come out."

She nodded. "That could work."

"Good." He pulled the book back toward himself, propping it up as if reading. "You ready?"

She ran through the plan in her head. "Hold on. These are old scrolls, right? Are they written in the ancient language?"

"I would assume so."

"I can't read the ancient language."

He looked at her over the top of the book for a moment. "What?"

She shoved down embarrassment and bookworm pride. "I didn't even know wizards existed a year and a half ago. Do you have a translator stone?"

"No. They're not common, since most people don't need one." He set down the book and closed it. "But I think I know where we could find one."

"Lead the way."

They left the library and went out into the courtyard, taking a familiar route. "Are we leaving the fortress?"

He smiled. "You've learned your way around. Yes, we need to go to one of the shops."

Before they reached the gate, Marcus stopped in a passageway and glanced both directions. Then he reached behind a pillar and pulled loose one of the stones in the wall to reveal a small cavity. He placed the key ring inside and replaced the stone. "Can't lie to the guards," he explained. Then he flipped up his hood, his tall frame seeming to shrink. "Let's go."

Once they had passed through the gate, Marcus led the way down the busy street to a broom stop. Brinnie ducked as a distracted wizard trailing a floating wooden chest turned and swung the heavy trunk behind him. "Where are we headed?"

"The shop is past the University, near the artisan's quadrant. If anyone has a translator stone, it's Oswald Goddensfeld."

Something seemed familiar about that name, but Brinnie couldn't place it. Once they took a broom over the roofs of the city, she followed Marcus to a shop front with an eclectic assortment of wands, broomsticks, stones, and trinkets in the window and a sign declaring it to be "Oswald's Emporium".

A bell jangled above the door as they entered a crowded store with the musty smell of an antique shop.

A short, balding man behind the counter wearing a porkpie hat turned as they entered and smiled jovially. "Welcome!" His eyes swept over them, and he grinned even more broadly. "Ah, Marcus! What can I do for you today?"

After a quick glance around the shop, Marcus removed his hood and gave an easy smile, striding toward the counter. "Hello, Oswald. I'm in need of a translator stone. Do you happen to have any?"

"An unusual request, but as you know, that's my forte." He brushed his hands together. "Let me go look in the back."

As Oswald passed through a swinging door behind the counter into a back room, Brinnie wracked her brain for where she had seen him before. Her eyes widened as it hit her. He had been at Wraithwood last summer. He was the strange man who called Uncle Merlin away the day she first met Ms. Tynsdale. Her powers had acted on him without her control, showing him to be some kind of shapeshifter.

Marcus browsed the shelves as they waited, holding up a wand of reddish wood, what looked like a piece of blue quartz, a pocket watch. "You'll find a lot of counterfeits in these sorts of shops, but Oswald is an honest man. I've never been disappointed."

"That's good." Brinnie glanced toward the swinging door. If she'd spotted Oswald Goddensfeld at both Wraithwood and Mordizan, she had her doubts about him being as honest a man as Marcus thought.

He came trundling back a few moments later with a small box in his hand. He set it down on the counter, and Brinnie and Marcus drew close to observe.

He opened the box with a flourish to reveal a rounded glass. "Here we are. One translator stone, slightly used, but in good condition."

"Once again, you have exactly what I need." Marcus nodded to the stone. "We'll take it."

Oswald closed the box. "One thing you should know. It only works on the ancient language. If you want to read Chinese, I'm afraid I can't help you."

"No, that's exactly what we need."

"Excellent." He pulled a piece of brown paper from below the counter and began wrapping the item. "And who is your lovely friend?"

"Sorry, this is Brynna. Brynna, Oswald." He gestured between them, and Brinnie gave a small wave. "We're doing some research, and unfortunately she never learned the ancient language."

"A pleasure to meet you, Brynna. Oswald Goddensfeld." He offered his hand.

She shook it, trying to make eye contact with a questioning look. But his expression didn't change. Did he not recognize her? They'd only met briefly, after all. Or was she wrong about him?

He finished wrapping the box and tied it with a piece of string. "There you are. That will be five coin."

"Oswald." Marcus pulled a coin purse from his pocket. "I know it's worth more than that."

"Ah, maybe six, but consider it a discount for a loyal customer."

Marcus shook his head and laughed. "You're a generous man." He slid two large coins across the counter. "Here's ten and I'll take it. I'm sure that's still a swindle." He picked up the box.

"Always a pleasure." Oswald tipped his hat. "Have a wonderful day."

As they turned to leave, Brinnie glanced over her shoulder one last time. Oswald raised a brow and put a finger to his lips. Brinnie's eyes widened, and she whipped her head back around. She'd been right. But whose side was he on? Was he spying on Mordizan, or Wraithwood?

The door jangled as they exited. "Now that that's settled, back to the library?" Marcus's voice brought her back to the present.

"Yes." She fell into step next to him. Another question niggled at her brain. "Why did you haggle the price *up*?"

"Unfortunately, no one wants to be accused of swindling the heir of Mordizan." He sighed, adjusting his hood once more. "I've made it clear that I won't take things for free, but I still have to work to give shopkeepers a fair price. There's no reason why I shouldn't pay like everyone else."

"Oh." Brinnie took a few more steps before she blurted, "Are you sure you're Vorath's son?"

He laughed. "As far as I know."

While he kept his eyes forward, weaving around a group of oncoming pedestrians, she scrutinized his face. The way the Master of Mordizan ruled over the dark wizards like a king, Marcus could be walking through these streets like a prince. Instead, he hid his identity and overpaid at stores. He'd warned her to lay low after news of Uncle Merlin's demise, taken her to see her sister. It could all be for selfish reasons, but what if it wasn't?

She dodged the oncoming traffic and leaned closer, keeping her voice down. "I know you're doing this to keep Mordred from killing you and your father. But . . . is that the only reason?"

He didn't turn to look at her. "Not wanting to die isn't reason enough?"

"I don't know. Is it?"

He stopped under an awning, out of the way of the sidewalk, and took a deep breath. "What if there's another way? What if we could get rid of the Enchantment without killing the enchantment wizards?"

"But I thought either they give it up willingly, or you have to kill them. And they're not going to give it up."

"I know." He frowned. "But I think we're going about this all wrong. All wizards are in the same boat. Magic is decaying, we're stuck in hiding, and we're trapped in an endless cycle of war. If we could only stop fighting for a moment, maybe we could figure something out."

Brinnie blinked. "So, you don't just want to get rid of the Enchantment and wipe out humankind?"

"You think I want a genocide?" He grimaced. "Some might, but I don't. I want the Enchantment gone, but I want magic to be the way it used to be. When wizards and humans lived together."

"From what I've heard, wizards enslaved humans and acted like gods and there was constant war. I don't really think your father would put aside his newfound universal power to cure cancer in favor of world domination."

He started walking again. "I know. And I know it sounds ridiculous. But with Mordred gone, once I become the Master . . . maybe we can make peace." He glanced at her, and she could see the tiredness in his eyes. "If we're going to live like this, at least we can stop killing each other."

They didn't speak as they reached the broom stop and waited for their turn, leaving Brinnie alone with her thoughts.

For the first time, she thought she might be able to trust someone in Mordizan.

CHAPTER
TWENTY-FIVE

Back in the library, shielded by the stacks, Marcus unwrapped the box, took the key ring off his belt, and handed the keys and the translator stone to Brinnie. "Okay. I'm going to go talk to her. Once she's distracted, you turn invisible and get in there as quickly as you can."

"Got it."

Marcus peered around the shelf, then straightened his shoulders and sauntered toward the woman guarding the entrance. Brinnie glanced around as well before turning invisible. She followed him as he approached the woman with a friendly wave.

"It's Kepler, right?" Marcus leaned on the bar between the doors and the library. "Alison Kepler?"

"Yes." Her stony expression stopped just short of a glare. "Can I help you?"

Brinnie skirted them and began feeling along the stone and wood paneling for the elusive door.

"Marcus Vorath." He stuck his hand out and shook hers. "You've been working here a long time, haven't you?"

"Near twenty years."

"Wow." Marcus hopped onto the bar, taking a seat and maneuvering himself so that Kepler had to turn away from Brinnie in order to talk to him. "How has it been? Do you like it?"

"Can't complain." Brinnie could hear the barely controlled annoyance in her voice. She held back laughter, imagining the poor woman's struggle not to scold the heir of Mordizan to get off the partitions this instant. *Well done, Marcus.*

Brinnie felt along the wall until her fingers ran over a small crack. Upon closer examination, she saw the outline of a door, and a small keyhole the same color as the wall. She pulled out the key ring and tried the first key.

"Are there ever any problems?" Marcus asked. Out of the corner of her eye, Brinnie could see him lean back and casually cross one leg over the other, as if settling in for a long conversation. "You know, security issues?"

She tried another key, attempting to keep them from jingling.

"Not really. University students trying to sneak books out for late-night studying, but that's about it. Why do you ask?"

"Oh, I'm just curious." He propped a foot on the security partition. "With everything that's going on, it's made me interested in fortress security."

"Well, if you want my opinion, I doubt any enemy infiltrators are interested in a bunch of books."

Little does she know. Brinnie tried the sixth key in the lock and scowled as it didn't go in.

"True enough," Marcus said. "Are you much of a reader?"

"Not really."

Brinnie shoved in another key as Marcus struggled to make conversation. "Interesting. How did you come to get a job in a library if you don't like books?"

Brinnie celebrated internally as one of the keys finally fit into the lock. She turned the key and the door popped inward with a click. She slipped through the crack, careful not to cause any creaking. She looked back briefly to see Marcus still engaging in chatter, the security guard oblivious to what Brinnie was doing. Then she eased the keys to the ground and closed the door after her.

She turned to see a room, about fifteen feet square, filled with honeycombed shelves brimming with scrolls.

This was going to take a while.

She started at the first shelf to the left, pulling the translator stone out of her pocket and running it along the ribbons to read the names on the scrolls. The first several she came across were guides to dark magic and curses. At least she could rule those out. But many of the titles were vague, giving little hint to their contents. She would have to do some reading.

Time had lost meaning by the time she made it a third of the way through. Her rumbling stomach said hours, but she wasn't sure whether night had fallen. She had yet to find anything of use, though she now knew more about ancient magical techniques than she ever wanted to know.

She pulled out another scroll and rubbed her eyes. Her lack of sleep the night before was catching up to her. *You just have to do this two more times. You got this.* Yeah, right. She doubted she could stay awake for another two-thirds of a room.

A rattling sounded behind her, then a click. She dove behind a shelf before realizing she could turn invisible. The door swung open, but she cast aside the shadows when she saw who it was. "Marcus? What are you doing here?"

He scanned the room before his eyes landed on her. "The library's closed. I came to get you. I received a message saying that Keilrie is looking everywhere for you. You have to get back before they find out what you're doing."

She shoved her current scroll back into its place. "But the keys, your father . . ."

"I'll come up with something. You have to go."

Brinnie quickly exited the room and Marcus locked it behind her. He led the way past the security railing. He cracked open the front door, peered outside, then opened it wide enough for them to exit. "Did you find anything?"

"No. Not yet. I'm not even halfway through."

He locked the door behind them, gesturing her into the shadows near the walls of the fortress. "We'll get back in another time. It's almost midnight. We need to think of a reason to tell Keilrie that you weren't in your room."

"Okay. Um . . . I was in the bathroom?" Speaking of, she could use a visit to the facilities after that long in the library. And a drink. And a meal. And a long, long night's rest.

"All day? She told my father that Lana told her you had been gone since this morning."

"She went to your father?" Brinnie half-jogged to keep up with his pace.

"She's convinced you ran away."

"A little paranoid." Brinnie searched for an excuse they could use.

"How's this. Tell them you were with me, touring Mordizan. No one has seen much of me all day, since I've been sneaking around through the secret passageways stealing keys and such. I haven't seen my father or Keilrie."

"Okay, good." Brinnie breathed out a sigh of relief. "Then you can back up my story, make me sound more believable."

"Right. We'll confront her together. One moment." He shoved aside a decorative piece of stonework to reveal a small door in the wall. "Quick detour. I have to put the keys back."

Brinnie followed him in ducking through the door. They scurried through the cramped tunnels and up and down narrow stairs, Marcus lighting the way using his hand as a human torch. *Which paranoid former Master of Mordizan built this many escapes and spyholes into his own fortress?*

When they reached a small wooden door, Marcus stopped and snuffed out the flame. "Wait here," he whispered. "I'll be right back."

She stepped back, and he slipped through the door.

A few seconds later, he returned. "No good. My father is in there."

"Let me go." She wouldn't let their cover be blown by a set of keys. "I'll turn invisible."

He nodded. "There's a peg by the door. Hang the keys there."

"Got it."

She took the key ring, covered herself in shadows, and ducked through the door.

It opened into an alcove with a tapestry hung over it. Gingerly, she pushed back a corner of the tapestry. A short wall blocked her view of the rest of the room, so she slipped out, pressed against the wall, and peered around the corner. Perched on the edge of an armchair, looking over maps laid out on a low table, was Vorath.

She scanned the room for the peg. It didn't take long to spot it right next to the door—straight across from Vorath. *Fabulous.*

Stepping carefully, she made her way across the room. It seemed to be the entryway to Vorath's chambers, with one open door revealing what seemed to be a bedroom and another that must lead to a bath. A fire flickered behind a grate, and she avoided passing too close. She had just started to reach up to hang the keys on the peg when a knock sounded at the door. She jumped, almost dropping the keys, before jerking them back into the cover of her shadows.

"Mordred to see you, my lord," a voice called.

Vorath sat back. "Send him in."

The door swung open and Brinnie jumped out of the way as Mordred entered, robes sweeping behind him. Her scar instantly went cold.

Great. Could Mordred have worse timing? She heaped shadows over her arm to cover the glow that would soon emanate from her scar. The blade hung from Mordred's belt in a scabbard. *Please don't pull that out, please, please, please . . .*

"Mordred." Vorath rested his elbows on the arms of the chair. "What is it?"

Mordred took up a stiff stance on the rug before the low table. "You didn't tell me that we have a new prisoner."

Vorath leaned forward and shuffled the papers and maps. "We've taken many prisoners. I didn't know you needed to know about all of them."

Brinnie sidled back toward the hook.

"Really?" Mordred's jaw tightened. "You found the return of Antony Drakon not worth mentioning?"

Brinnie's eyes widened.

Vorath looked up. "Ah, yes. Drakon."

"It simply slipped your mind? Why don't I believe that?"

Brinnie slowly reached toward the peg.

"It didn't slip my mind." Vorath ran his fingers through his beard. "We don't know if he is who he claims to be. I thought it best to wait until we're certain."

"For what reason?" The edge to Mordred's voice set off warning bells. "How am I to trust you if you keep such things from me?"

"I fully intended to inform you. I didn't want your emotions to cloud your judgment."

Brinnie winced. That was not the right thing to say. Tension in the room spiked, and she took the opportunity to slip the key ring onto the peg.

Mordred gave Vorath an icy stare. "My reason does not leave me when I meet a distant relation. Some of us have risen above familial ties."

Brinnie scooted back toward the alcove.

"Fine." Vorath dropped the papers in his hand onto the table. "What do you want?"

"Bring him to the meeting chamber tomorrow. I'll bring Nimue. If anyone can ascertain his true identity, she can."

"Is that wise?"

Mordred looked at him expressionlessly until he nodded. "Of course. Noon tomorrow."

"Good." Mordred turned to leave right as Brinnie reached the wall leading to the alcove.

"Wait," Vorath said with a sigh. "Keilrie's been bothering me about the Ludovic girl. Apparently, she can't find her. Have you seen her?"

Brinnie's heart stopped. She dove for the tapestry and through the door, easing it shut as quickly as she dared. Then she turned visible and gestured furiously to Marcus. "Hurry, we need to get out of here as quickly as possible."

His eyes widened, but he didn't ask questions. He led the way at a run. Seconds later, Brinnie felt the coolness of her scar intensify. Mordred must have pulled out the blade.

She darted after Marcus down a long passageway and the glow slowly faded to a cool tickle. She stopped, grabbing his arm. "Okay, I need a reason to be in this part of the fortress, and fast."

"Why? What happened?"

"Mordred came to see your father. He has the enchanted blade with him, the one I'm connected to. He knows I was nearby, and they're both looking for me."

Marcus pressed his lips together. "I have an idea. Follow me."

He led her through a short series of twists and turns before they came to a door similar to the one leading into Vorath's chambers. Marcus pushed it open and stepped through, then beckoned for Brinnie to follow him.

She stepped out and looked around the sparsely furnished room with a table covered in books and papers on one side, an upholstered chair in front of an empty fireplace, and a rack of weapons on one wall. "Where are we?"

"My chambers." He shut the door after her and pulled a curtain over to hide it.

Does everyone around here have secret passageways to their bedrooms? She paused. The scraping she'd heard her first night at Mordizan. She'd thought the noise had been rats, but was it possible someone had been slipping by in a secret passage on the other side of the wall? Even if she hadn't found any escape, could someone have been watching her?

She shuddered at the thought. Thank goodness she wasn't living in that room anymore.

Marcus pushed the upholstered chair out of the way and kicked the rug on the floor into a corner to create an open space in the middle of the room. He pulled two swords off the weapons rack and handed one to Brinnie. "Blunt. Good for practice."

She took the blade, turning it over. "Um, why?"

"You came up here because you wanted to improve your swordsmanship." Marcus flipped his sword to his other hand. "And I offered to help."

"Oh! Good idea."

He rotated his shoulders. "We better get started to make it convincing."

They began running through the basic motions of thrusting, blocking, and slicing. "Why do you keep weapons in your room?" Brinnie asked.

"For this very reason. I like to be able to practice without going down to the training arena." Their swords clashed as Brinnie made a slice and he blocked. "So you didn't find anything helpful in the scrolls?"

Brinnie swung her sword up for her turn to block. "Nothing. They're mostly guides to magic that aren't applicable anymore, from back when wizards could learn all kinds of magic. I didn't find anything about Mordred."

"There has to be a reason they're restricted, something that could help us."

"Well, if you got a spellcaster together with another wizard, you could in theory come up with some pretty scary curses." She pushed loose hairs that had escaped her ponytail out of her face. "Maybe we can curse him."

"Dark magic?" Marcus swiped left.

She blocked. "Magic is magic, right?"

"No." He stopped, his expression grave. "The magic we possess—we're born with it. It's a talent, something natural and inherent. Dark magic comes from the outside, from dabbling in things you shouldn't." He swung again, and she blocked. "Besides, we can't do dark magic anymore. That's part of Myrddin's curse."

Interesting. She imagined Keilrie would beg to differ.

Just then, her scar flared. "They're coming."

Moments later, a knock sounded at the door. Marcus went to open it, sword in hand, leaving Brinnie breathing heavily in the middle of the room from the exercise of bladework.

The door swung open to reveal Mordred on the other side with his glowing blade. Brinnie's scar burned cold, blazing with light.

"Hello." Marcus left one hand on the doorknob. "Can I help you?"

Mordred looked past him to Brinnie. "What is she doing here?"

"We're practicing. She wanted some extra training with the sword, so I offered to help."

Mordred raised an eyebrow, not taking his gaze from Brinnie. "At midnight?"

Marcus shrugged. "Why not?" He held the door open wider. "Would you like to come in?"

"No. I was only looking for the girl. Keilrie said she was missing."

Brinnie strode closer. "Keilrie's looking for me?"

"Yes." Mordred looked at her impassively. "For the past two hours."

"Oh. Whoops." She tried to keep her tone lighthearted. "Do you know where I can find her?"

"She would be in her chambers under the fortress."

"Thanks." She handed the sword to Marcus. "Thanks for the help. I better get going."

"No problem. See you later."

Brinnie grimaced to Mordred as she slipped out the door. "Sorry about that."

Their eyes met, his cold and stony, and for a moment Brinnie was afraid he would call her bluff. But instead he simply nodded.

She wanted nothing more than to bolt, but she forced herself to say, "Um, this is kind of embarrassing, but I don't remember how to get down there."

"I can show you," Marcus offered, leaning the swords against the wall.

"Thanks."

Marcus nodded to Mordred. The ancient wizard didn't move as Marcus closed the door, then led the way down the hall, watching them with an inscrutable expression.

They walked in silence until they rounded the corner. Under her breath, Brinnie said, "Well, that went almost too smoothly."

"It's fine." Marcus's tense shoulders began to relax. "He has no reason to suspect us. Especially me."

"I guess."

But she had a nagging feeling Mordred knew more than he was letting on.

CHAPTER TWENTY-SIX

She was in the same place again, the dark path with the skeleton trees. A gust of wind pushed her forward, down the crooked path. With each step as she drew closer to the fiery red blaze lighting the distant sky, her feeling of dread increased. As the lightning flashed, the skeleton beasts seemed to grin at her with their jagged teeth. She was being drawn along, unable to resist, farther down the dark path . . .

She awoke to the sound of someone moving around. She cracked open her eyes to see Lana dressed and ready, a sword strapped to her hip. Brinnie pushed up on one arm. "Where are you going?"

"Morning drill with our new unit. It's required. Except for you, of course, what with being Keilrie's apprentice. Do you want to come?"

She dragged herself into a sitting position. "I think I might impale myself if I try. Keilrie had me up until three in the morning 'becoming one with the darkness,' also known as sitting there bored out of my mind while she chants weird stuff. That woman's a lunatic."

Lana laughed. "Okay. I'll see you later then."

Brinnie waited until Lana left, then threw off the covers and forced herself out of bed. She shook herself out to get rid of the jitters left over from her dream. *That witch is messing with my mind.* She pulled on a tunic and sturdy leggings, finishing the ensemble with a belt, and stuffing the translator stone in the pocket of her tunic. The clothes here still seemed strange, but they were functional. After a trip to the bathroom, she headed out the door with teeth brushed and hair pulled into a tidy ponytail, feeling more put together than she had in a while.

She found Marcus in the library, sitting at the same table as the day before. When he saw her, he stood and bobbed his head toward the stairs. She took a different staircase to follow him.

This time, he'd found a secluded table on the second floor, with two books already open and waiting. Today, he wore a fitted red jacket emblazoned with Mordizan's emblem and gold braid with tailored black trousers. *He really does look like a prince today.*

"You look terrible," he remarked as she approached.

Illusion broken. "Well, thanks."

"I mean you look exhausted."

She slumped into a chair. "Between this and Keilrie's obsession with late nights, I haven't had much time for sleeping." She leaned against the table. "Do you have the keys?"

"No. My father took them with him."

Brinnie sighed. "Fabulous. What's the plan?"

Marcus pulled out a pocket watch. *Wizards and their pocket watches.* "There's a council session starting in fifteen minutes, the trial of a prisoner. I'm required to be there." He stuck it back in his pocket. "I'll lead you there, then you turn invisible and follow me in. You can snatch the keys off my father's belt, and if he notices that they're gone, I'll convince him that he forgot them. We should have a few hours after the meeting to search the scrolls before he'll be able to return to his chambers, and by then we'll have put them back."

She could hardly keep up with the precise timing that would take. "That sounds awfully risky. Shouldn't we wait for a better opportunity?"

"Mordred is leaving for the fifth stronghold in just a few days." Marcus turned a page in one of the books. "I'd like to find a way to defeat him before he leaves. Who knows when we'll get another chance, especially with you leaving in less than a week."

"Well, that is inconvenient." She stood. "Okay, then. Let's go steal some keys."

As they descended the stairs, Brinnie glanced down at Marcus's high black boots polished to a shine, finishing off his princely ensemble. "You look fancy."

Did his cheeks redden? "I'm supposed to for council sessions."

"Right." They reached the bottom of the stairs. "I haven't figured it out yet. What exactly is the style around here? Late medieval? Fantasy novel?"

He raised an eyebrow. "Do you usually wear something different?"

"Usually a t-shirt and jeans."

Marcus didn't speak for a moment as they exited the library. "I've heard of those, I think. Human fashion. It's a short-sleeved shirt and blue pants, right?"

Brinnie couldn't contain a surprised laugh. "Have you ever been someplace non-magical? As in, not an estate or stronghold?"

"No," he admitted. "But I've seen humans before."

She laughed. "You say it like they're some sort of strange creature. Aren't there plenty living here? Back at Wraithwood, wizards are the minority."

"There are humans here and there." They rounded a corner. "They've just usually lived here for generations."

Brinnie shook her head. "After we defeat Mordred, you should go on a vacation to the real world."

"Let's focus on defeating him first. You should probably turn invisible now."

They approached the entrance to the main fortress, and she did as he said. They passed through wide pillared corridors until they arrived at the familiar doors of the council chamber. The guards opened the doors without question, and Brinnie followed Marcus inside.

He made his way up the aisle and around the semicircular table until he was seated at his father's side. Brinnie kept her distance, staying out of the way pressed against the wall, circling the room toward Vorath as various members of his council came to take their seats.

Mordred entered from a side door and sat on the other side of Vorath from Marcus. Brinnie watched him pensively. If for any reason he decided to draw his blade, she was in trouble.

Nimue entered from the main doors and took a seat next to Mordred. "Why did you want me here?" Brinnie heard her ask as she moved into position closer to Vorath.

Mordred folded his hands on the table. "There is to be a trial I believe you will want to see."

Servants, guards, and council members milled near the table.

Brinnie didn't dare venture closer yet. She couldn't afford to collide with someone.

Finally, the crowd died down. Brinnie edged closer to Vorath. About fifteen feet spanned between his seat and the wall, but it felt like a football field.

"Bring in the first order of business," Vorath said.

A herald stood at the end of the aisle. "The prisoner known as Antony Drakon, captured two days ago outside the border of the protection spell, seeking asylum in Mordizan from the alleged captivity of enemy forces."

"Bring him in."

The doors opened, and in walked Brinnie's father, hands bound, flanked on either side by a guard. His feet were bare, and his beard had grown in scraggly to match his dirty, tattered clothes. *Nice job on the outfit, Dad.* He really did look like he'd been in captivity for the past few decades.

Nonetheless, he held his head high, taking even steps as he walked up the aisle with poise.

Nimue gasped and rose. "What . . . what is this?"

"This man claims to be Antony Drakon." Vorath leaned back, mouth in a thin line. "The traitor who deserted our ranks three decades ago."

Dad bowed. "If you'll pardon my saying, that isn't the full story."

From her vantage point, Brinnie could see Nimue's face pale. "Antony. Is it really you?"

Dad straightened from his bow, and his gaze turned from Vorath to Nimue. Shock flashed in his eyes, then his expression melted to joy. "Nimue."

"Antony!" Nimue shook off Mordred's restraining hand on her arm and vaulted over the table in one fluid motion. The council erupted in exclamations. She ran and threw her arms around Dad. "I thought you were dead! I searched all over for you—"

"I'm so sorry." Tears welled in his eyes as he leaned into her, as much of an embrace as he could manage with his bound hands. "I never should have left you."

The guards shifted, hands hovering over their sword hilts, but they couldn't threaten Nimue Drakon.

"What happened to you?" Nimue cupped Dad's face. "Where have you been?"

"The enchantment wizards. I went to them first. I was young and confused. I tried to join them, but they didn't believe me. They put me in prison."

"But you escaped." Nimue dropped her hands. "They said you got away."

"No." He shook his head. "That was a lie the enchantment wizards told so that no one would try to free me. They moved me to a different cell, the dungeon below Wraithwood. But when Merlin died—"

"Enough." Vorath stood. "Nimue, this man could very well be an impostor."

"An impostor? Just look at him!" She turned and threw out an arm toward him. Her eyes shone with unshed tears. "He looks exactly like our father."

"He could be a shapeshifter," a council member shouted.

"That isn't my power." Dad's hands burst into flame, fire dancing around the iron cuffs.

The guards drew their swords.

"Stop!" Nimue stepped in front of them. "He's not hurting anyone." She turned to Dad. "Let's prove this once and for all. Tell me something only Antony would know."

His gaze drifted around the room in thought, then snapped back to her. "You were always following me to the training grounds. You thought you were sneaky, sitting up in the rafters, but I saw you. Eventually I made you promise that if I taught you how to use a sword, you would stop risking your neck climbing up there."

"This is a waste of time." Vorath sank back into his chair.

"Wait." Nimue nodded to Dad. "Go on."

"Father didn't want you training yet—you were only eight years old—so we had to keep it a secret. One night, it was getting dark when I was teaching you, and my sword slipped. I cut you right there." He nodded to her shoulder. "We told him you tripped and cut yourself on a rock. We never told anyone the truth. At least, I didn't."

She grinned. "I didn't either." She turned to the council and pushed her sleeve off her shoulder to reveal a thin white scar. "It's really him."

Mordred and Vorath exchanged a look. "That may be," Vorath conceded, "but there's still another matter to address. He's a traitor."

Nimue opened her mouth in protest, then closed it and bit her lip.

"It's true." Dad stepped forward. "I did betray you when I was young. I tried to join the enemy. But I quickly saw the error of what I had done." He inclined his head to Vorath. "To prove my loyalty, I have come here instead of returning to Dirklon. Without any powers of the Mastership, I offer myself to your mercy and judgment." His expression hardened. "Believe me, after thirty years imprisonment, I hate the enchantment wizards more than ever before."

Mordred leaned forward, one eyebrow slightly raised. "And how *did* you escape, after so long?"

A rumble of approval washed over the room. Many expressions remained hard or skeptical.

"A fair question. The dungeons below Wraithwood were closed up for years. The only person I ever saw was Merlin. But now, with the Key being kept down there, it was only a matter of time. Security grew lax. And finally, Merlin died. His spell keeping me there was broken, and I escaped." He nodded to Mordred. "I understand I have you to thank for that."

Mordred sat back. "And your intentions?"

Dad faced Vorath. "To offer my allegiance to you, my lord, as did my father before me. Dirklon has always been a faithful servant of Mordizan." He looked from Vorath to Mordred. "I understand your hesitance. But I assure you, decades of imprisonment have purged any confusion of loyalties from my youth. My only regret is that I didn't finish the job when I burned Wraithwood—that I didn't kill Merlin long before now."

Brinnie winced. She knew it was a ruse, but the murderous glint in Dad's eyes was a bit too convincing.

Vorath glanced at Mordred. "We will need to confer."

"Really?" Nimue exclaimed. "This is my brother. If anyone can vouch for him, I can. So he had some doubts after his first major battle. We've all been there. The important thing is that he's here now, and with his help, we can finally get Dirklon up and running again as a hub of military power. We need that now more than ever."

Vorath nodded slowly. "I might not fully be convinced of his loyalties, but I could never doubt yours, Nimue. Antony is not to return to Dirklon yet. Don't let him out of your sight, though I doubt that's a hard task. You." He pointed to Dad. "You're on probation. Convince me that you're truly committed to Mordizan, and you could very well find yourself leading the charge to destroy our enemies. Convince me otherwise, and . . . well, I'm sure your Drakon mind is full of the tortures I could inflict."

Dad bowed. "That's all that I can ask for."

At that moment, Brinnie realized she had completely neglected her task. She darted forward and crouched behind Vorath's chair. As expected, the key ring hung from his belt. Ever so slowly, she eased her fingers onto the key ring and began rotating it to remove it from the belt. *Don't jingle, don't jingle, don't jingle.* With a final twist, she had them off. She pressed the keys to her chest to prevent any noise as she slunk back into her corner.

With the doors to the council room manned by guards, she had no way to slip out until the meeting ended. Dad and Nimue had gone, presumably while she was focused on the keys, so she couldn't sneak out behind them. She eased to the floor in a cross-legged position, spread her tunic across her lap, and gently splayed the keys on the ring over the muffling cloth so she could examine each one.

The key she needed turned out to be easily recognizable, with a unique jagged edge and circular base. With agonizing care, she slipped it from the key ring and tucked it in her pocket.

The rest of the council meeting consisted of far less interesting conversation concerning battle strategies, rations for the troops, and inter-estate politics. Brinnie sidled up behind Vorath and threaded the key ring back through his belt.

One of the keys slipped and clacked against another. Brinnie froze.

Vorath didn't look down, instead nodding along to a council member droning about numbers for something or other. Marcus, however, glanced toward her, then quickly averted his gaze.

Once she had replaced the key ring and taken up her post by the wall again, she breathed a sigh of relief. With luck, stealing one key instead of the entire ring would give them days to search instead of hours.

When the meeting concluded, Marcus loitered, chatting with his father and other council members. Brinnie pressed against the wall, out of the way of the crowd, until Marcus exited. Then she followed.

Once he had taken a few turns, far enough away from the council chamber, she turned visible during a quick moment when Marcus was the only one in the hall. "I have the key."

To his credit, he barely startled at her sudden appearance. "You had me worried for a minute when you put the key ring back. Are you sure it's that one?"

"Trust me, I memorized it." She fell into step beside him. "I didn't want to have to try all those keys again."

"Good thinking. That will give us more time." He paused as they passed a couple of what appeared to be messengers in the hall. "By the way, did you know Drakon was down there in the dungeon at Wraithwood?"

She chose her words carefully. "As far as I was concerned last summer, Wraithwood didn't have a dungeon. I never had any reason to go down there."

"So do you think he's telling the truth?"

She shrugged. "Sounds reasonable."

He hooked a thumb in one of his pockets and looked at her sideways. "There's something you're not telling me."

Her mind whirred, looking for an excuse. But one look at his earnest expression and she gave up. She wouldn't be able to convince him she had nothing to hide. So she gave a nonchalant shrug. "You have your secrets, I have mine. I'm sure there are things we both don't want the other knowing once our interests aren't aligned anymore."

His expression darkened. "Right." They walked in silence for a moment before he said, "I do intend to make peace, you know. Someday."

"I know." *I think.* She hesitated. She trusted him to help her defeat Mordred. But after that? They were on opposite sides of a war. He wanted to destroy the very thing she and her family were trying to protect—the Enchantment. As much as he might want peace, it would never happen as long as his goal remained the same. "But I don't think you'll be the Master anytime soon."

"Fair." His expression melted into neutrality. "I suppose we really are only temporary allies then."

She wanted to argue, but what could she say? She winced. *That could have been worded better.* "I mean, not necessarily, but—"

"Good afternoon," he interrupted her to greet an oncoming wizard.

Excellent going, Brinnie. You better hope you don't figure out how to defeat Mordred too quickly or your cover is going to be blown before Dad can get you out. She tried to push down her feelings. *He's not your friend. You have to remember—this is enemy territory.*

And thanks to her lack of tact, she may have just gained another one.

CHAPTER TWENTY-SEVEN

Brinnie strode across the courtyard leading to the library with Marcus, relishing the warmth of the sun's rays on her shoulders after the chill that permeated the fortress. "Okay. So are we pulling the same trick as yesterday?"

"Not quite. We can't wait for night again, or Keilrie's going to be looking for you, and I doubt we can bluff our way out of it this time. Here." He pulled an hourglass out of his pocket—how deep were those pockets?—and handed it to her. "The sand runs out after an hour. After the third hour, you get out of there. I'll be in the library at the same time, creating a distraction."

"All right." She hesitated. "Marcus, about what I said earlier . . ."

"Let's just focus on what we're doing. We should enter the library at different times to cause less suspicion. Follow me in ten minutes."

Before she could say anything else, he strode ahead, his longer legs eating up ground faster than hers could.

She reduced her speed to an ambling pace, nodding to passing guards, scholars, and members of Vorath's court. By the time she entered the library, Marcus had taken up position browsing the shelves. She went in the opposite direction, scanning shelves where she could watch him, but she was out of sight of the guard at the entrance.

Marcus meandered to one of the shelves nearest the entrance. He reached up as if trying to grab one of the books on the highest shelf. His foot grazed the base of the bookshelf, and Brinnie briefly saw sparks shoot out under the shelf from the toe of his boot. Then he stepped on the bottom shelf and pulled on the top one. With a creak, the entire shelf began to tilt. He jumped out of the way just in time before the shelf smashed into the one next to it and books crashed all over the floor.

The security guard hurried over, and Brinnie seized her chance. She yanked shadows over herself and ran for the door.

"I am so sorry, I don't know what happened," she heard Marcus saying.

She slipped the key in the lock and was inside with the door closed behind her within seconds. She turned visible again, set down the hourglass, and flipped it over.

She pulled out the translator stone and hurried to where she had left off. *Techniques for Slow and Painful Death . . . A Guide to Creating Diseases . . . One Hundred Uses for Dead Bodies . . .* She shook her head. *Wizards are messed up.*

After flipping the timer twice, she still had found nothing. *It's like there's everything* but *stuff about Myrddin in here.* Her eyes widened. *Almost like someone took it all out.*

She checked the shelves. Every space was occupied, and nothing looked like it had been disturbed in years. The only fingerprints in the dust were her own. *Which is kind of bad. I should probably wipe those off.* It would be odd for a room full of important scrolls not to contain any works concerning one of the most important magical events of all time—perhaps a record of how Myrddin cast the spell, or at least what kind of spell he used. No one had ever told her how he did it, only that he had. No one seemed to know, other than that such magic couldn't be performed anymore by post-Myrddin wizards.

But now we have a pre-Myrddin wizard on our hands. One who may be trying to break Myrddin's spell.

Sure enough, within a few moments she had found it. In a back corner, she discovered an empty place on the shelf. A thick coating of dust surrounded it, but in the shape of a scroll, the dust was thinner.

A scroll had been removed.

She shoved the translator stone in her pocket and sped down the rows, blowing on the dust on the shelves in order to remove her fingerprints. By the time she finished, her head spun from lack of oxygen and the sand in the hourglass had almost run out. She waited until the last grain fell through and took a deep breath. *Well, Marcus, I hope you really are creating a diversion out there.* She turned invisible and stepped through the door.

Her mouth dropped open when she saw what was going on. The shelf had been set back up, and most of the books had been put back, but Marcus stood in the middle of a flaming pile of books on the floor that had yet to be returned to their places.

"I'm so sorry—*achoo!*" He sneezed and sparks of flame flew everywhere. "It's the dust, it's making me—"

"Hurry, hurry, outside!" The security woman herded him toward the door. "Thank you for your help. I can finish from here."

"Thank y—*achoo!*" Sparks showered the floor. "I'm sorry for the mess."

"No problem, really." She nearly shoved him toward the doors. "Go get some fresh air. Really, don't worry about it."

Brinnie held in her laughter until she'd safely slipped through the doors behind Marcus and made it outside. "*That* was your diversion?"

"Come along, my imaginary friend. I have to seek medical attention." He fake-sneezed again, showering sparks.

She followed until they turned the corner out of sight of the library. She scanned the area, then turned visible. "Was it really necessary to burn books?"

"She wasn't much for conversation. I had to get her attention." He chuckled. "Besides, that was a shelf dedicated to arithmetic."

"Okay, I guess I can forgive this great sin once." She sobered. "I think Mordred removed the scroll we need from the library. There's an empty space, just one, and it was taken relatively recently. My guess is he's using it to figure out how to break Myrddin's spell."

He stopped under an overhanging buttress. "We already know how to do that. Destroy the strongholds."

"Maybe there's more to it. That just destroys the protection spells and Mastership limitations."

"What do you mean?"

She hesitated. If she told him her true suspicions, that Mordred was trying to destroy what Myrddin had done and bring back magic as it once was, would Marcus still be on her side? "All I mean is that the scroll probably tells what his bane is, too. He's probably trying to keep it from falling into the wrong hands."

"True." Luckily, he didn't press her more. Instead, he continued walking. "So we need to find where he's keeping it."

"That sounds like a job for someone with full access to the fortress." She gave him a cheesy grin and a thumbs up.

He laughed. "Okay. But taking it would be a job for someone who can turn invisible."

"You find out where, and I'll snatch it."

He nodded. "I'm on it. But it might take a while."

"Can't be helped." They reached the main courtyard in front of the fortress. "Meet you tomorrow in the library?"

"I think we need a different meeting spot. If we keep meeting in the same place, it might look suspicious. And Kepler is going to be watching me like a hawk after that fire scene." He pondered for a moment. "Meet me by the gate, noon tomorrow. I'll let you know what I've found."

"Got it." She started off on her own. "I'm going to go try to take a nap before Keilrie catches me."

"If I see her, I'll steer her in the wrong direction."

She turned away smiling. He made it awfully hard to remember they were enemies.

"Pay attention!"

Brinnie refocused her eyes on Keilrie. "I'm listening."

"No, you're not. You're falling asleep." She picked up a roll of paper from the low table and whacked Brinnie upside the head. "Wake up!"

Brinnie flinched. "Sorry." She resisted the urge to complain about the late hour. At least this way, she would have most of the day free to work on defeating Mordred.

"Now reach out with your mind and listen for what the darkness is trying to tell you. Become one with the shadows."

Brinnie sighed and closed her eyes. It didn't matter how many times she said she wasn't going to dabble in dark magic. Keilrie insisted. So she had come up with a new strategy. "I think I hear them."

"Yes?" Keilrie leaned forward. "What are they saying?"

Her voice came out low and gravelly. "'Join the darkness, our sister.'"

"Yes. And what do you reply?"

"Sounds like fun," Brinnie said in her normal voice. She switched back to the other. "'Good. You must perform the ritual darkness dance.'" She switched voices again as she stood. "Yes, of course." She hopped in a circle, waving her arms, performing a dramatic grand jeté, and flailing. She began humming what she hoped was a sinister-sounding tune.

The next thing she knew, she was being whacked upside the head with the angry roll of paper. "Ow!"

Keilrie glowered at her. "Stop this foolishness!"

Brinnie went for a look of wide-eyed innocence. "You interrupted the ritual darkness dance."

"Sit down. Have you no respect?" Keilrie collapsed onto the cushion and sighed. "That's enough. Go. I'll not waste any more time on you tonight."

"Thank you." Brinnie was out the door in seconds.

She made her way through the fortress, retracing her steps with exacting precision. *Right. Straight. Left.* Inordinate pride swelled within her as she reached the door to her room. She tromped inside and collapsed on her bed, feet hanging off the edge.

Lana lifted her head from the pillow and squinted at Brinnie. "You *are* alive. I haven't seen you since this morning."

"Been a little busy." She kicked off her shoes. "I think I'm going to sleep until next year now."

But her mind had other ideas. Again, the dreams haunted her, of the red sky and the dark path. She slept fitfully, always awaking before she had a chance to continue down the path.

Morning came all too soon. Brinnie's head nodded throughout her lessons with Keilrie, learning to better shape the shadows into convincing forms. But she perked up as she headed for the gate at noon to meet Marcus.

She found him waiting in the courtyard in front of the inner gate, chatting with one of the guards and laughing. Brinnie didn't recognize this guard, but he seemed to be about the same age as

Marcus. She watched as Marcus's eyes crinkled with laughter and a dimple appeared near his chin. Or maybe the guard was older than Marcus. When the son of Vorath didn't have a pensive furrow between his brows, he looked much younger—maybe even Brinnie's age.

He made eye contact with Brinnie, said a few words to the guard, and clapped him on the shoulder before passing through. Brinnie followed a moment later.

She emerged into the outer courtyard and approached him where he loitered near the gate's entry. "Did you find anything?"

Under his breath, he said, "Not here. Follow me." Then he grinned and said more loudly, "Glad you can make it! It's a shame no one has taken you on a proper tour of the city."

They didn't exchange any more real conversation until they had passed through the outer gate and into the busy street. Marcus leaned closer while leading the way down the avenue. "Apparently word has gotten back to my father that we've been spending time together the past couple of days," he said. "You know, in the library, going to Goddensfeld's, practicing sword fighting. He was asking me about it. I thought it best for us to get out of the fortress entirely."

Brinnie's heart beat faster. "What did you tell him?"

"I said I was teaching you about wizardry and fighting before you're sent off." Marcus hesitated. "I don't think he quite bought that that was all there is to it."

"Definitely best to stay away from the fortress, then." She wove around a child chasing a ball.

"We can talk once we catch a broom." He sidestepped a man toting a large package. "No listening ears high above the rooftops."

They joined the line for brooms heading northeast. Brinnie stood on her toes, watching the brooms take off over the main street to the opposite direction of the University. "I haven't been in this direction."

"Right. I'll tell you more about that in a moment."

They reached the front of the line. Marcus boarded and she got on behind him. As the broom left the station, he turned around to sit sideways in the way that made Brinnie cringe. "You're going to fall off."

"I haven't yet." He brushed his palms on his pants, making her cringe even more. "So last night I pretended to need to talk to Mordred, and I managed to get into his room."

Focus. "Did you find the scroll?"

"Nothing that exciting. I had to carry on a conversation, so I couldn't search very well. But when I came in, I interrupted him reading something and making notes. I couldn't tell what was written on it, but it was a scroll. When I started talking to him, he put it in a drawer in his desk."

Brinnie sighed. "So either that was it, or just one of millions of other possible scrolls that he could have been reading."

"Exactly."

"Well, it's worth a shot." She clung to the broom as a breeze lifted her hair. She still hadn't gotten used to this method of transportation. "Is there a way to get into his room through the secret passages?"

"No. He's too smart for that." Marcus scowled. "He may have more spies in this fortress than even my father does. There's only one way in—right through the door."

They passed a broom stop, but Marcus didn't lean on the broom to lead it to land, so they kept flying. *Where on earth are we going?* "Does your father have the key?"

"To Mordred's room? Hardly. Only Mordred has it."

She drummed her fingers on the broomstick. "Do you know any lockpicking?"

He let out a surprised laugh. "If these locks could be picked, I would have done so for the library. Around here, keys are enchanted to fit the locks. And Mordred most likely keeps the key on his person."

Enchanted locks, special guards, secret passages. Nothing around here can be easy, can it? "I can't just sneak up on him invisibly and start giving him a pat down. He's going to notice."

"That leads to what we're doing today." Marcus took a deep breath. "Today and tomorrow, the Allied Masters are coming to Mordizan for the Masters' Gathering, before Mordred leaves for the strongholds. The Gathering is Thursday morning, but before the Gathering there's always a great feast. It's tomorrow night. It's going to be busy with people everywhere, so it will be the perfect time to scope out the situation, and Mordred won't be as likely to notice if you take the key —he'll just think one of the many people bumped into him."

"Wait, all the Masters?" Brinnie's heart thumped. That much power in one room . . . "How did I not know about this?"

"Technically, I shouldn't be telling you. It's kept quiet until it's actually happening, that way spies don't know and aren't able to plan any attacks or assassinations. It should be quite a Gathering—Mordred's formal introduction, the revealing of Antony Drakon's return. The point being, it will be crazy. The perfect time to act."

"So I'll sneak into the feast, swipe the key, then we'll have all night and the next day to figure out how to defeat him before he leaves for the fifth stronghold."

"Yes, except for the sneaking." Marcus waved off a leaf blowing by on the breeze. "There's a spell protecting the entrance to the feast so only those invited can enter. It's meant to keep the Masters safe from assassins. To get in, you need an invitation."

"Oh, great. And how am I supposed to get that?"

He fidgeted with the seam on his shirt. "It's customary to bring a, uh, guest. As my father's heir, I have to be there, and as a matter of tradition, I'm supposed to bring someone. I can bring you."

Brinnie snapped her fingers. "Perfect!" Then she paused. "But won't that look suspicious? Why would you bring me?"

"Well, um." Marcus kept his gaze flitting over the rooftops. "My father seems to think that our relationship is not purely . . . academic."

It took Brinnie a moment. "He thinks you have a crush on me?"

"Yes." His cheeks reddened. "I hope that doesn't bother you."

She laughed at the absurdity. Spies and assassinations and wars, and the Master of Mordizan thought his son was involved in some sort of middle school romance. "Of course not. That's the perfect cover. If he thinks that, he won't suspect a thing."

"Okay, good." He seemed unnecessarily relieved. "In that case, we should get off at the next stop. The feast is a very formal occasion, and you'll need something to wear."

She bit her lip. She didn't exactly have much wizard money, whatever they used here. "I have a black dress Nimue gave me."

"That was fine for a dinner." He leaned the broom toward a station. "Not a Masters' Gathering."

"How do you know?" She tilted her head. "You haven't seen it."

"I was there at the dinner where you were introduced to my father. I don't think you saw me." The broom came to a stop at the platform. "There's a shop down here. We should be able to find something. And no worries, it's on me."

Brinnie couldn't suppress a giggle as she hopped off the broom. "You're taking me shopping?"

He looked flustered. "For the sake of the mission."

"Of course." She quirked an eyebrow. Where had this awkwardness come from? "Lead the way."

The street they entered was paved with light stone. Colorful shops fronted a wide road with much fewer pedestrians. However, those who did stroll by wore fine garments and often elaborate hairstyles. Cultural differences aside, Brinnie knew upscale shopping when she saw it, or in the human world what she would call the window shopping only district.

Marcus gestured toward an upcoming shop with an elegant emerald ball gown in the window. "It's this one."

Brinnie couldn't resist the opportunity. "Is this where you get your favorite dresses?"

"Only my party gowns." Marcus maintained a serious expression. "But don't tell Gerd, he wouldn't understand."

She clasped her hands behind her back and gave a look of wide-eyed innocence. "No judgments. I think fuchsia would suit you."

He wrinkled his nose, feigning horror. "Not with my skin tone." They reached the front of the shop. "In seriousness, Nimue told me about it. I . . . asked her where women usually go to get formal clothes."

Brinnie laughed out loud. "That must have been an interesting conversation."

His cheeks reddened. "I worded it a little differently than that." He held open the door. "After you."

A bell tinkled above the door as Brinnie entered, followed by Marcus. Her eyes widened at the sheer amount of tulle, lace, satin, and velvet on display. She felt mildly proud of herself for knowing the names of those fabrics.

A large pink dress housing a petite woman came bobbing around the corner. The woman's shock of red hair topped the getup like a cherry on a pink cupcake. "Welcome to Lily's Boutique! How can I help you today?"

Brinnie couldn't stop staring, so Marcus supplied, "We're looking for a formal dress."

"Of course. Give me just a moment." The woman sidled up to a stool, stepped onto it, then somehow shimmied out of the dress so that it hung from the hanger above the stool while she emerged out the bottom wearing the simple loose shirt and pants Brinnie had found typical in Mordizan. She brushed her hands together. "I was trying it on for a customer. I'm Lily. Now, tell me more about this dress. What's the occasion?"

Marcus hesitated. "A formal feast and ball."

She tapped the side of her nose. "Ah, the Masters' Gathering, no?" She smiled. "Not to worry, my lord. You must be Marcus Vorath."

"Er, yes." Brinnie saw him glance down at his attire, as if wondering what gave it away.

The dressmaker turned to Brinnie. "And you must be the one the dress is for. May I ask your name, my lady?"

"I'm Brinnie." She awkwardly stuck out her hand. "Nice to meet you."

"A pleasure." Lily stood back, surveyed them up and down, and clapped her hands together with a grin. "You two are beautiful together. I'm going to love this. I must warn you, though, I can't create a custom gown with only a day to work."

Marcus's eyes narrowed. "How do you know when it is?"

"I'm in the business of fashion, my lord—it's my job to know everything. The ladies all come to see me." She laughed. "Don't worry, I'd hate for my biggest sales of the year to be ruined by loose lips. I don't tell."

"Right." His shoulders remained stiff. "We understand it can't be anything custom. We're just looking for something suitable."

"A last-minute arrangement, is it?" She winked at Brinnie. "I assume you already have something to wear, my lord? Probably in the traditional colors of Mordizan?"

"Yes."

"Good. Oh, good, good, good!" She accentuated her words with little hops and clapping. "I might have something. It's one of my latest works. Brinnie, if you'll come with me, and my lord, there's a place to sit right over there." She waved to a pastel pink settee nestled between displays.

Brinnie allowed Lily to herd her into a back room, giving one uncertain glance back at Marcus. Lily directed Brinnie through racks upon racks of clothing to a position near a low pedestal in front of a panel of mirrors. "Stay right here. I'll be back." She scurried away into the maze of fabric.

Brinnie tilted her head, examining herself in the mirror. Her shoulders seemed broader, her muscles more defined. A month of brutal conditioning and sword work appeared to be paying off. On the other hand, the dark circles under her eyes weren't doing her any favors.

And she was still as pale as ever. She smiled ruefully to herself.

Lily bustled back in, a mass of red and black fabric billowing behind her. "Here it is! Let's have you try it on."

Lily had no qualms about stripping Brinnie down to her undergarments then tossing underskirts over her head and fastening a bodice around her waist. The speed at which Lily buttoned and laced and tugged almost made Brinnie dizzy, until Lily fastened the final piece on the back of the dress. "Oh, it's wonderful! You make it look even better." Brinnie began to turn toward the mirrors, but Lily stopped her. "Not yet! We need the full look. Eyes closed."

Brinnie kept her eyes shut as Lily brushed lipstick over her lips and what she assumed was eyeshadow and eyeliner over her eyelids.

"You don't even need foundation. Such smooth, pale skin, like a doll! Open."

Brinnie opened her eyes, blinking.

"It's time." Lily spun her toward the mirror.

Brinnie looked at herself with a raised eyebrow. The deep red skirt of the floor-length dress split in the front from waist to bottom forming an upside-down V that revealed the black underskirt. The ruby bodice matched the skirt, both adorned with intricate designs of red and black crystals like tiny drops of blood flowing through obsidian. The bodice dipped, exposing Brinnie's throat and collarbones, to reveal more of the black underneath and flowed into sleeves that started tight and fanned out until they gradually matched the easy flow of the skirts.

With the dress, the red lips, the eyeliner winging from her lashes, she hardly recognized herself. Awkward Brinnie had turned into this, this *woman* who looked every bit a Drakon heir, a mistress of shadows . . . a dark wizard.

Lily gave Brinnie's hair a twist and pinned it with a fastener bejeweled with red stones. "It even fits you perfectly," she breathed. "Maybe just take in the hem slightly. Some shoes to go with it. I've been so wanting someone to wear this, but I only get the older women in here, and they can't pull it off." She waved a hand. "Nimue Drakon could, but she won't. It would kill her to buy a new dress. But look at you!"

Brinnie shook her head. "It's lovely, but isn't it a bit much?"

"Of course not, milady. The Masters' Gathering. The most important wizards. It's impossible to overdress." She spun from behind Brinnie to stand in front of her, looking her up and down. "And more importantly, your young man won't be able to keep his eyes off you." She gave a sly wink. "The fastest way to the top is through appealing to the men in power."

Brinnie's eyes widened.

"If the rumors are true, you're Brynna Ludovic." She adjusted the drape of the skirts. "You're smart to go after the heir of Mordizan." She smirked. "But I'm sure it has more than political benefits. All the young women of Mordizan would love to be in your shoes."

Brinnie opened and closed her mouth. "I want to see what Marcus thinks," she said finally. She didn't necessarily trust Lily not to try to sell her way too fancy of a dress.

"Go right ahead."

Brinnie held up her skirts and made her way out to where Marcus perched on the settee, fiddling with a ball of fire between his fingers.

She let the skirts drop and turned from side to side. "What do you think?"

He looked up and froze with flames dancing in his hand, eyes wide.

Brinnie felt her cheeks heat. "I knew it. I said it was too much, but Lily insisted."

"No," he protested. He clamped one hand over the other, putting out the fireball. "No, it's perfect. Great. Not too much. Definitely good."

She fiddled with the crystals on the skirt. "Really? I could go with something a little less fancy."

"Not at all." He blinked, eyes running down the dress and then snapping back up to her face. You're, I mean, it's, it's beautiful."

"Okay . . ." She felt the sudden urge to flee. The back of her neck heated to match her cheeks. "I'll go tell Lily." She lifted her skirts and made a hasty retreat.

After Lily had pinned where the hem was to be taken up and found matching shoes, she helped Brinnie out of the dress and they joined Marcus in the main room.

Lily curtsied. "I'll have it sent to the fortress by tomorrow afternoon, my lord, plenty of time before the evening. She'll be the talk of the Gathering."

"Thank you." Marcus stood stiffly. His gaze flicked from Brinnie's lips to her eyes, then quickly away, and she wished she could scrub off the makeup. Why had Lily insisted?

While Marcus settled the bill with Lily, Brinnie scanned the premises for any tissues she could use on the makeup. Nothing.

Lily waved to them as they exited the shop. "Make sure you tell everyone who made your gown."

Marcus breathed a sigh of relief once the door shut behind them. "I thought I would suffocate in fabric in there."

Brinnie's mouth quirked. "So we're ready for tomorrow." They maintained a leisurely pace toward the broom stop. "Is there anything we can do in the meantime besides twiddling our thumbs?"

"No lessons with Keilrie?"

"Not until tonight."

"I don't have any obligations until this evening. But I can't think of anything we can do toward the plot . . ." He stopped talking and changed his tone. "Don't look, but there's someone trailing us."

She forced herself not to glance back. "How do you know?"

"He got on the broom behind us near the fortress and got off at the same stop. I figured it was a coincidence, but he's behind us again. It's not one of my father's men, so he must be Mordred's."

Brinnie's heart skipped a beat. "Do you think Mordred is on to us?"

"I don't know. But he's at least suspicious."

Brinnie took a deep breath. "Then we have to give him a reason not to be. Do you think the same trick we're playing on your father will work on Mordred?"

"How?" Marcus chuckled. "Should I go confront that man and profess my undying love?"

She gave him a shove. "You know what I mean. What would you do if you liked me?"

"I don't know." He scratched the back of his neck. "I've never had to think about something like this before."

He'd never had a girlfriend or been on a date before? Of course, she'd never been on one either. "Okay. Let me think about this." She racked her mind and thought back to movies she had seen. "All right, here's the deal. You're going to take me someplace special to you, someplace cool, and it will be 'romantic.' Can you think of a place?"

His brow furrowed in thought, then he nodded. "I've thought of somewhere. But we need to catch another broom."

The breeze whistled softly as their broom glided over businesses and homes. Before long, buildings trickled off and gave way to grassy space, until the street below abruptly ended at an empty broom stop. Marcus angled them toward the platform.

As they descended from the platform, Brinnie scanned the sky for their follower, but saw nothing. He would likely give them a while before venturing into such an open space.

Marcus stopped at the end of the road. "The protection spell is only a few yards out from here. Follow me."

They tromped through the weeds past the end of the street and into the trees on the other side. When she turned back around, Brinnie exclaimed. Where there had been a bustling city, instead she saw only small farmhouses dotting rolling fields of crops, many which seemed to have been recently harvested.

"I forgot about the double space." She inhaled the sweet smell of grass and hay, mixed with woodsmoke drifting on the breeze. "So this is what the double looks like?"

"No, we were in the double before, in the city." Marcus stood with one foot propped on a fallen log, gazing at the rustic landscape with a small smile. "It's better protection to have the only entrance to the city through the fortress gate."

They re-entered the protection spell. As they walked along a ridge beside a field of dry corn, Brinnie could see the fortress looming in the distance, the dark walls familiar, yet strange set against pastureland dotted with the tiny white specks of sheep, and tall trees growing in a dense line beyond the castle. "This dimension is much prettier."

"It's mostly populated by humans." Marcus ran his hand through the rustling stalks. "Honestly, I think they get the better end of it, not living in the city."

He led her through the cornfield to where a line of trees clustered along a small stream. Tall grass edged the grove, waving in the slight breeze. "This stream doesn't exist in the double—we blocked it. Here." He held aside a branch to allow her to pass. "This way."

A few rocks poked up from the streambed, and Marcus hopped from one to another. He offered a hand, which she took—with her coordination, she'd likely slip on moss or something and plunge straight in. She focused on her footing, not looking up until she took a final step onto dry land.

Marcus's voice was hardly more than a whisper. "This is what I wanted to show you."

They stood in a small meadow on the bank of the stream, surrounded by trees. A butterfly flitted through a beam of sunlight and a squirrel scampered away, but Brinnie's attention was drawn to the stone in the middle of the glade.

She drifted closer. The white slab seemed to have been chiseled out of marble. She leaned closer until she could see what was engraved. *Leticia Vorath*. Not quite making the connection, her eyes moved down to the dates. Leticia Vorath had died almost ten years ago.

The hairs on the back of her neck prickled. She turned toward Marcus slowly. "Is this . . ."

He stared straight ahead at the stone. "My mother always loved to come here. She would take me with her. I knew, at the end, she would want to be out in the sunlight, near her favorite brook."

Brinnie put a hand to her mouth. "Marcus. I'm sorry."

"I thought you should know." He turned to look at her, eyes hard. "She wasn't killed by the enchantment wizards. She was killed by my father's men."

CHAPTER TWENTY-EIGHT

Brinnie stared at Marcus in shock. "What do you mean?"

He rested his hand on the stone. "She was caught smuggling prisoners out of the fortress and setting them free. My father tried to cover it up, and she promised she wouldn't do it again . . . but she did." He sighed. "She was too tender-hearted to let them suffer. And one day, it caught up to her. The guards didn't recognize her in her disguise, so they killed her as she was crossing the border."

Brinnie pressed her fingers to her lips, unsure what to say.

"My father had the guards put to death, of course. But he was angry at her, too, and her betrayal." He gave a half-smile. "She's the one who first showed me the secret passageways. He found everything she had been doing right under his nose, organizing rescues, even sending advance notices to the enemy about our planned attacks." He ran his fingers over the memorial. "He loved her more than anything. He's never been the same." He removed his hand from the headstone. "A traitor couldn't be buried in the ceremonial crypts, but I was glad about that. She would like this place much better."

"I'm so sorry," she breathed.

Her mind spun. Ten years ago, Leticia Vorath helped prisoners escape Mordizan. Twenty years before that, Antony Drakon burned Wraithwood, then abandoned the dark wizards. And here she and Marcus stood, decades later—for the first time, perhaps able to do what their parents couldn't.

He knelt in front of the headstone, dusting debris from the letters. "When I was a child, she always told me that people are just people. There's no such thing as an enemy. She didn't believe in this war. She told me that she was happy with me and my father, and that was all she needed. She didn't need to be free to wander the earth, or regain the powers of the pre-Myrddin Era, or even have magic at all. She just wanted us." He pulled a few weeds from the ground in front of the stone. "Her mother was a human. I imagine that's where she got a lot of her ideas. She always told me that when I grew up and became a Master, I was going to help bring peace."

Brinnie knelt beside him and placed a hand on his shoulder. Their gazes met, and she could see the pain, the hope, and beneath it, the resolve in his eyes. "She was right. I know you will." *And when you go up against the dark Masters, you'll have Dirklon and Wraithwood on your side.*

Hesitantly, he took her other hand and squeezed it. "Thank you. For being the first ally I've had in ten years."

She blinked back unexpected moisture.

He leaned down as if to say something else meaningful. Instead, he whispered, "The man who followed us is hiding in the trees over there."

She swallowed and forced a smile. "Then we better give him a show."

"Well, come on!" Still holding her hand, he pulled her up and tugged her toward the edge of the stream. He let go, kicked off his shoes, and splashed into the water.

She gave what she hoped was a convincing giggle—probably made more realistic by her surprise at his quick shift—and pulled off her shoes as well. She stopped to roll up the hems of her pant legs. Then she shuffled down the bank and gasped as her toes met frigid water. "You're getting your clothes all wet."

"Oh, you think yours are going to stay dry?" He grinned, cupped his hands, and splashed water at her.

She squeaked, flinching away. "Cold!" She planted her fists on her hips. "All right, it's on."

She kicked water at him in retaliation, and he laughed. Soon a full-on splash battle had commenced, leaving both of them dripping.

Marcus ran splashing away in water reaching above his knees, then stopped and looked down, sobering. "Hey, come look at this."

"What?" She sloshed over, wincing as the cold water hit her middle. She joined him looking out toward the center of the brook. "What is it?"

He pointed. "You see how deep it is?"

"Yeah."

"It would probably be over your head." His serious expression gave way to a fiendish smirk. "Perfect for dunking."

She shrieked as he grabbed her and tried to toss her toward the water, but she clung to him in a move she'd learned in her classes, dragging him down with her. They hit the water with a mighty splash and came up gasping and laughing.

"Everything is soaked, even my hair!" Brinnie treaded water, trying to look angry. "I will never get those thirty seconds of styling back."

He bit his lip, holding in laughter. "Well, maybe not the hair, but . . . you did still have that eyeliner on."

Brinnie gasped, hands flying to her face. Her fingers came away smudged with black. "How dare you!" she shrieked, launching another splash attack.

Thoroughly waterlogged, they finally sloshed out of the brook and found a large, flat boulder in the sun to sit on. After such an epic splash battle, Lily's outlandish makeup had been washed away for good.

Brinnie sprawled on the rock. "That's the most fun I've had in a long time."

"Me too." Marcus sat, his clothes hitting the stone with a wet slap, and they both laughed at the noise.

As she squeezed out her hair, Brinnie's teeth began to chatter. A cool breeze had come up, ushering in the evening.

"Here." Marcus spread out his hands, and a smokeless campfire burst to life on the rocks in front of them. A wave of heat washed over her a moment later.

She held her hands in front of the fire and sighed in contentment. "Well, aren't you handy to have around?"

He snorted. "I try."

When he smiled back at her like that, she couldn't help noticing the warmth in his deep brown eyes. She wasn't used to it, someone around her age knowing her this well. Friends at home had been superficial, exhausting. Enjoying hanging out with someone other than the Wraithwooders felt . . . strange.

It felt dangerous.

She cleared her throat. "What do I need to know about this feast?"

He leaned back on his hands. "It will last for hours. There will be dancing, and you'll be introduced to way more people than you can remember, but that's okay, because no one will expect you to know all of them. The Masters and their wives will be there, the Masters' heirs, and maybe a few other family members. Some of them will have a lot of hatred toward a Ludovic, so you would do well to convince them as quickly as possible that you're on our side."

The Masters and their wives? "Are there any Masters who are women?"

"Not currently. It doesn't happen very often."

She set aside her girl power annoyance for a moment as more questions surfaced. "Okay, Mastership goes to the sons first, then daughters. But if the Master doesn't have any kids, it goes to the Master's siblings, right?"

"Yes." He twisted the edge of his shirt, squeezing it out. "Why?"

"Then why isn't my mom the Master of Wraithwood?"

His brow furrowed. "We don't know. I would have suspected Merlin wasn't actually dead, but his body was seen by our own spies. The only way a Master's sibling couldn't become a Master is if they themselves were already married to a Master." He shrugged. "But obviously that's not the case."

Brinnie tried to control her expression of surprise. "If you marry a Master, you lose your claim to a Mastership?"

"Yes. For example, if two heirs marry, the first one to become a Master cancels the other's ability to become one. It's meant to keep one family from accumulating all the Masterships." He chuckled. "I'm sure the previous Masters of Mordizan would have changed it if they could, but it's part of the curse."

Her pulse raced. *I really am the Master.* It wasn't that Mom didn't inherit the Mastership because Uncle Merlin wasn't really dead—it was because Dad was already a Master. Her heart plummeted as her last hope was lost.

But Marcus couldn't know her relations or her Drakon heritage, not if the plan for Dad to break her out was to work. She feigned ignorance. "Then who is the Master?"

"We're not sure." He gestured to her. "It can't be you, since your mother would have inherited it first. Our only guess is that somewhere, Merlin has a descendant."

She dropped her hands from the fire, mouth falling open. "You think he has a kid?"

"What else could it be?" Marcus sighed. "I've been wracking my brain about this. It's driving my father crazy—it means you would have to kill your mother *and* whoever else came to claim Wraithwood."

Well, at least the theory kept suspicion of Brinnie's parentage off the table. "I never knew about an heir, but he was good at keeping secrets." She glanced toward the sky, tracking the progress of the sun. "Evening will be coming soon. We should probably go back. Keilrie will want me."

"I hope you don't mind a walk." He stood and offered her a hand. "We can't get back to the city except through the fortress."

She took his large, callused hand and pulled herself up. "It will be nice to be outside the city for a while longer."

They followed the narrow paths through the fields. A dog barked at one point, and from a distance, Brinnie heard children laughing. It all seemed so oddly normal.

"Do the humans out here interact with the wizards in the city much?"

"Trade representatives do business with representatives of the city. The farms, lumber, and raw materials from this dimension supply most of the city's demand. But other than designated officials . . ." Marcus looked uncomfortable. "Wizards and humans don't often mix. Most of the people out here have lived here for generations. There's a town down by the river, between where they harvest lumber and the quarry. They're fairly self-sufficient."

It didn't seem so bad, but . . . "Why don't they leave?"

"I thought you might ask that." He sighed. "As far as they know, anyone who steps outside the protection spell disappears forever."

Brinnie stopped walking. "You kill them?" she squeaked.

"Of course not." He caught her skeptical look and amended, "Not usually. But once they leave the protection spell, they become disoriented. They can't get back in. As far as I know, they wander off into the human world."

She started walking again, slowly. "So they don't know about the world beyond the protection spell. And the ones that leave . . ." She imagined the culture shock of finding the modern world. "People out there must think they're crazy, talking about magic and wizards."

"I'm ashamed to say it, but I don't know what happens to them. Most people who live on the estates have never really left. Wizards included." He glanced at her sidelong. "Your experience is . . . unique. Operatives train for months or years before being sent into the human world."

They continued in silence toward the fortress. Her mind spun with new perspectives, with possibilities. What would happen if the dark wizards did succeed? What would happen when cultures clashed?

Would this tranquil dimension still be a place of peace? Or would the humans be allowed to live at all?

As they approached the looming gate, Marcus glanced behind them. "He's not following us anymore. He turned off on another path."

It took her a moment to remember. Ah, their follower. "Probably thinks he's being sneaky." She paused in the shadow of the fortress, looking out at the rolling fields one last time. "Thank you. For today."

He took her hand and squeezed it. "No, thank you."

And despite everything she knew she had to do, the feast and their plan fast approaching, and the problem of Keilrie, all Brinnie could think about during her lessons that night was the way that for a moment, wars and battles and politics hadn't mattered, and her enemy had become her closest friend.

CHAPTER TWENTY-NINE

"You're *what?*"

Brinnie took the weighty beribboned package from the courier and thanked her. She brought the bundle back into their room, shutting the door behind her, and set it on her bed before responding to Lana. "I'm going to the feast with Marcus tonight."

"Excuse me. How did this happen?" Lana yanked off a boot and chucked it into the corner. "Why didn't you tell me?"

It was late afternoon, and Brinnie had spent an exhausting morning training with Keilrie. She hoped she would never have to summon so many shadow creatures at once ever again. She and Lana had arrived back at their room within moments of each other, Lana flushed and sweaty from . . . whatever it was the army had been doing that Brinnie really should have been participating in. "You were asleep when I got back from my lessons with Keilrie last night, and then we both had training this morning. It never came up."

Lana shook her head incredulously. "Okay. Tell me everything. When did he ask you? I didn't even know you knew each other that well."

"He asked me yesterday." She began unwrapping the package and the ribbons holding it shut, avoiding direct eye contact. "We've been hanging out lately."

"Hanging out." Lana pulled off her other boot. "Like how?"

"Oh, you know, he was helping me with some sword training—"

"I could have done that."

"—showing me around the city, that sort of thing."

Lana grinned and sat back shaking her head. "Wow. So he's taking you to the Masters' Gathering. Do you know how tight security is on that? I didn't even know about it until today, and my family's going to be there."

Brinnie paused her attempts to unfasten the packaging. "Your family?"

Lana raised an eyebrow. "Lana *Arion*? My dad's the Master of Ariondam."

Brinnie facepalmed. "I'm an idiot." How had she missed that? It should have been one of the easy estates to remember, unlike estates like Mordizan and Wraithwood where the last names had nothing to do with the name of the estate. If only she'd memorized those names in school instead of all the Roman emperors and U.S. presidents in order.

"Yup. Anyway, how serious is this relationship?" Lana waggled her eyebrows. "Do you *like* him?"

Heat rose to her face, and she focused on getting the dress out of the ridiculous amount of ribbons Lily had used to tie up the package. "We're just friends."

"Uh-huh. Well, he's not at all bad-looking, that's for sure."

"Lana!"

"Just saying." She smirked. "I'm a little jealous. He doesn't even seem like a jerk like most heirs are."

Brinnie rolled her eyes. "Not at all. He's very nice." She finally removed the dress from the wrapping and laid it on the bed.

"Oh my gosh." Lana stood straight up and gaped. "How did you get a dress like that on such short notice?"

"Marcus took me yesterday." Why did it embarrass her to say so?

Lana cackled. "Okay, it's serious. He is *smitten*."

She tried to convince the heat rushing to her face to calm down. *This is good. The more people think that, the better. Then they won't get suspicious*. She changed the subject. "Are you going to the Gathering?"

"No." She pursed her lips in a pout. "My parents took me last year, so they're taking my brother this year." Brinnie pulled out the shoes and hair pin to go with the dress, and Lana practically bounced up and down. "That is going to be *stunning*. Please let me help. I can do your hair and makeup!"

Brinnie laughed. "Okay, okay. I might need it. It's going to take me forever to get into this thing, and Marcus should be coming by in less than an hour."

Lana snatched a towel off her bed. "Give me five minutes and I'll rinse off the training grime. I love makeovers." She dashed into the bathroom.

Forty minutes later, Brinnie held up a mirror Lana had procured, admiring the elaborate twist Lana had somehow looped all of her hair into. Thank goodness. Brinnie couldn't do hair to save her life. "You did amazing."

"Forget the hair. Look at you! You are stunning." Lana grinned. "I doubt Marcus will be the only one wanting to dance with you."

As long as I have enough time to sidle up to Mordred.

She had just slipped on her shoes when a knock sounded at the door. They glanced at one another and Lana gave two vigorous thumbs up. "Go stun them all," she stage-whispered.

Brinnie giggled. "Thank you." Her heart gave a pitter-patter of self-consciousness. What if she looked ridiculous? What if this was over the top? She'd never had a reason to get all dressed up since Anna's wedding when she was a kid. And even then, her muted dress had seemed designed to help her fade into the background.

She took a deep breath as she opened the door.

Marcus stood outside in an outfit that made her feel much better about her own. He wore a black, long-sleeved coat with gold embroidery and fine buttons over a scarlet vest and white shirt with a black cravat. His pants were belted with a gleaming buckle and tucked into polished black knee-high boots, and his hair had been neatly combed.

It was stupidly, annoyingly dashing. She avoided romance books when she could, but he looked like some dark prince the girl would swoon over.

It made her want to muss up his hair and challenge him to a duel in the training ring.

She realized she had been staring, but it took him a moment to say anything either. He cleared his throat. "Are you ready?"

"Oh. Yes."

He offered her his arm, and she stepped out, dramatically taking his elbow like a fine lady. He tipped his head to Lana. "I'll take good care of her, madam."

Lana laughed and wagged a finger. "Make sure you bring her back by a reasonable hour, young man. Have fun!"

As they made their way down the hallway, Brinnie dropped the fine lady act and brushed at her skirts nervously. "Did anyone act suspicious about you bringing me?"

"Not at all. My father doesn't suspect a thing, and after yesterday, I doubt Mordred does either."

"Good." She took a deep breath. "Let's get this over with."

He laughed. "Not what most people would say about attending a Masters' Gathering."

She glanced up and down the hall. "Well, most people aren't trying to steal from Mordred while wearing a ball gown and heels."

"Point taken."

The heels clacked on stone, and her skirts rustled. She scowled. "This outfit was not designed for sneaking." She fidgeted, wishing she could rip the whole thing off and slip into the Gathering cloaked in shadows instead.

He gave her a reassuring smile. "That's good. No one will suspect you're planning on sneaking."

Instead of approaching the grand dining hall from the front, Marcus led her around to a back entrance. "It's customary for us to enter second to last, and then my father last of all," he explained. "A grand entrance and all that."

The hall leading to the back entrance was smaller, but just as elaborate as the front. Sentries stood guard on either side of the doors, while more guards unobtrusively lined the hall leading up to them. Brinnie's heart beat faster as she realized every one of those guards could kill her if they caught her. Luckily, Vorath was nowhere to be seen. She and Marcus stood alone in the hall lined with stoic soldiers.

Marcus seemed to sense her fear. He placed her hand in the crook of his elbow and leaned over to whisper, "It's okay. No one suspects us. It's only a feast. If we fail today, we'll try again another time. You can do this."

She forced a smile. "Right."

They stepped up to the doors and Marcus nodded to the guards, who opened them.

A crier in Mordizan livery stood on the other side. As the doors swung open, he proclaimed, "The heir of Mordizan, Marcus Vorath, and the heir of Wraithwood, Brynna Ludovic."

The crier stepped aside. Brinnie forced her feet forward, fingers digging into Marcus's arm for support.

They emerged onto the long, raised dais that had once supported the head table in the dining room. But the table had been removed, leaving the raised floor as more of a stage. In fact, all the tables were gone, transforming the hall into a ballroom of immense proportions.

Brinnie looked out upon a sea of faces and colors, glitter and fabric, wizards clad in their finest of every cut and style. They clapped politely, though music continued to play, undercut by a buzz of conversation as the attendees leaned close to whisper to one another. Whisper about her, about them.

Marcus gave a slight bow, so she followed suit with a little curtsy.

Music from the quartet playing on a stage in the corner increased in volume, most likely a result of magical amplification. That seemed to be a sign for the crowd to return to their previous conversations.

Clutching Marcus's arm as if for dear life, Brinnie let him lead her down from the dais to mingle with the crowd.

Nimue met them the moment they stepped down. Her sleek black dress glittered under the light of the chandeliers, and Brinnie wondered if Nimue still managed to get around the rules and hide a knife on her person somewhere. Nimue without knives didn't seem natural.

Nimue smirked at Marcus. "So that's why you wanted to know about that dress shop."

The tips of Marcus's ears reddened. "I told you it was for a friend."

Nimue continued to smirk, but the expression shifted as she raised a questioning eyebrow at Brinnie. "Settling into Mordizan well these days?"

"Can't complain." Brinnie gestured down to her dress. "You have good taste."

"Oh, I don't shop there. Lily drives me up a wall. But she is the best at what she does. Figured Marcus would want the best for his mystery lady friend." She gave a casual three-finger salute. "I won't keep you. You have your rounds to make."

As Nimue melted back into the crowd, Brinnie asked, "Rounds?"

"At some point in the night, I must greet all of the guests," Marcus explained, leading her deeper into the crowd. "It's customary." He turned to an elderly wizard wearing an emerald-green robe with a floppy wide-brimmed hat settled upon his head of long gray hair. "Master Bartimus. It's a pleasure to see you again."

"Young Heir Vorath." The old man smiled, wrinkles crinkling around his merry blue eyes. "And to see you."

"All is well at Verisfel, I trust?"

"Quite well, quite well." He absently combed his fingers through his beard and plucked out a leaf. "You should see it—soon the leaves will be turning. And the ivy is doing absolutely marvelously this year."

"Good to hear. Is Ignatius here?"

"Why, yes, somewhere over there, I believe." He gestured broadly in a way that encompassed nearly the entire room.

"Of course. Well, I'd love to hear about the forestry—maybe you can tell me about it later tonight?"

"Of course, of course. Off with you, young fellow." He winked. "I'm sure this young lady would rather be dancing than listening to me." He wandered on his way, calling out to someone about the state of the forest lichen, though Brinnie wasn't sure who he was talking to.

"Is he . . . ?" Brinnie began as they turned away.

"Quite sane?" Marcus finished. "Good question. He spends most of his time with the plants. His son Ignatius does most of the work of running the estate." He smiled and nodded to other wizards as they made a slow circle of the room. "I'm sure as soon as Ignatius gets a chance, he'll eliminate the nuisance of having to go through his father to do what he wants."

The meaning hit her, and Brinnie almost tripped over her dress. She forced herself to keep her voice down. "You mean he'll kill him?"

"Most likely." The rest of his reply was cut off as he stopped to speak with another group of wizards. Brinnie tried to keep her expression calm and smile politely at everyone to whom she was introduced.

On the other side of the room, the great doors she and Marcus had passed through were thrown open. The music stopped this time, and all went silent as the guard announced, "The Master of Mordizan, Master Septimus Vorath, and Lord Mordred of Arthrys."

Applause echoed over stone from throughout the room as Vorath entered in kingly garb with a smile. Mordred stood in stark contrast in his simple black robes, his steel gray eyes scanning the room coldly.

Brinnie whispered to Marcus, "It doesn't look like he has his blade."

"I suppose even Mordred has to respect the rules of the Gathering," Marcus said under his breath, clapping without looking at her. "Another reason why this is a perfect time to act."

Master Vorath stood on the platform raised above the rest of the room, Mordred by his side. "Good evening to all of you, fellow Allied Masters. It is with great joy that we receive you here at Mordizan. As you know, this year has been an especially prosperous one for all of us. For one, we acquired the Case of the Master Key." Applause. "Of course, of greater importance than the Case itself is the one who brought it to us." He gestured to the man beside him. "May I formally introduce Mordred, son of Myrddin."

This time, the thunderous applause was accompanied by cheers and a few whistles. Brinnie clapped along with the rest, glancing around to see wizards grinning, nudging each other, some even standing on tiptoe to see better.

Vorath waited a moment for the applause to die down. "Mordred has brought with him unprecedented success. In the past year, we have overtaken two strongholds and eliminated countless enchantment wizards, including Merlin Ludovic."

The hall rang with cheers. Brinnie clapped along, cringing inside. Marcus shot her a sympathetic glance, but she avoided his gaze.

"Indeed, my friends. We certainly have much to celebrate. But before we do, I have one final announcement that should bring pleasure to us all." He exchanged a secretive look with Mordred. "Dirklon has long been closed and masterless, but no more. Dirklon will once again rise to its former glory as a producer of armies. May I present Antony Drakon, Master of Dirklon."

The room fell into stunned silence as Brinnie's father stepped through the door.

He looked like a different person from the ragged man she'd seen only days ago. Clean-shaven, wearing a black formal ensemble with a green serpent crest emblazoned on the right breast, he stepped forward with an imperturbable expression, gazing out upon the room.

He looked every inch a dark wizard.

Antony Drakon gave a slight bow, and the room erupted with questions.

Vorath held up a hand for silence. "Master Drakon has been held captive these three decades by none other than Merlin Ludovic. Upon Ludovic's death, he was able to escape and return to us. With the might of Dirklon behind us once more, the strongholds do not stand a chance."

Some wizards clapped, but others whispered to one another and exchanged confused glances. Vorath ignored the buzz and held out his arms. "That is all. May the festivities begin!"

The musicians began to play once more, and wizards moved away from the center of the floor.

Brinnie's mind spun with objectives. Get the key from Mordred, shake Marcus long enough to talk to Dad . . .

Marcus interrupted her thoughts by bowing and holding out a hand. "May I have this dance?"

She blinked, realizing the reason the center of the room was suddenly empty. "Oh, uh, no thanks. I don't really know how to dance, like, ball dance. I mean, I can hokey pokey or macarena or whatever, but . . ."

"It's fine. I'll teach you." At her hesitance, he explained, "My father has no one to dance with, so it's my job—our job—to start the dancing."

"That's really unfortunate." She took his hand as he led her toward the center of the room. She kept a smile pasted on her face, aware of people watching her. "Can't he dance with Mordred or something?"

Marcus barely contained a guffaw. "I want to see that." He put one hand on her waist and one on her shoulder. "Now you do the same, and just step the way I step."

Conscious of the many eyes upon them, Brinnie focused on her feet. After a moment, others joined them on the dance floor, and she began to relax as she realized the dance was simply a repetition of the same steps, over and over. She finally looked up to meet Marcus's eyes with a sigh of relief. "It's not as hard as I thought it would be."

"I really should have taught you how beforehand. My fault for not thinking of it." He directed her into a spin, which she managed to complete without stepping on his toes or falling on her face. She looked up to see that instead of roaming the room, keeping track of Mordred, his gaze was fixed firmly on her. "You look beautiful."

"Well, someone gave me this awesome dress."

"Not just the dress. No one can keep their eyes off you." He seemed to hesitate for a moment, not speaking until the dance called for a spin. "Including me."

She felt heat spread over her face and wished Lana had been able to find makeup pale enough to match her skin in addition to the dusky eyeshadow and a lipstick that matched her dress. Nothing to hide her blush behind. "Hey, you don't have to keep our little ruse up when it's just the two of us. No one can hear you."

His smile faltered and he looked down as if to focus on his footwork. "Right."

Oh. Wait. Was that a real compliment? How awkward. She wanted to melt into her shoes. How was a person even supposed to respond to something like that? *I want to go back to the library.* Books didn't do silly things like give compliments.

Not a relevant train of thought. She instead focused on keeping an eye on Mordred. When the song ended, she stepped away from Marcus with a feeling of relief.

"My lady, would you do me the honor of this next dance?"

Brinnie turned at the familiar voice. Dad gave a bow, holding out an arm.

Brinnie glanced at Marcus for confirmation, and he nodded. Apparently, this was proper form.

She took Dad's arm. "Yes, indeed."

She wanted to throw her arms around him and ask him a million questions, sink into him and have him fix all of her problems, take her away from Mordizan. He needed to know so many things about Mordred's bane, and Anna, and the plan. But she calmly took up position for the next dance and followed Dad's steps in a new sequence.

His eyes twinkled with mischief. "So you are this Brynna Ludovic I hear of."

"Yes. But I've renounced the ways of my family. Vorath knows I'm fully committed to him. Mordred . . . I'm sure he'll come to accept the truth in time."

"Interesting." He weighed his words. "Have you found a special way to endear yourself to Mordred?"

"I almost did, but I think that secret lies only within his inner heart." She gave him a significant look, willing him to understand.

He did. "A feast is a fine place to find the key to a man's heart."

She suppressed a grin and nodded. "So I hope."

"I see you've come with the son of Master Vorath."

"Yes. He and I hope to, ah, learn more of Mordred together." She took a moment to cobble together another phrase. "Mordred has a very special gift in mind for him, but he prefers other pursuits than his father and Mordred."

Dad nodded. "Like pretty young shadowmasters."

"Da—!" Brinnie quickly caught herself from exclaiming. She shook her head. "Vorath wondered why we were spending so much time together."

He gave her the unmistakable Dad Look. "Did I hear you were to take a trip soon?" he asked in a reminding tone.

"Yes, as soon as I deliver a gift to Mordred," she confirmed. *I know, Dad. My goodness, in the middle of enemy territory and he's being protective about a guy.* "And after I, uh, pick up some goods from the cellar."

His expression darkened. "I thought those goods might be here." He hesitated. "I'll be taking a trip soon as well. Maybe I'll need to bring some goods with me to stock my cellar. I leave for Dirklon the day after tomorrow."

She didn't know how he would manage it, but at least he knew Anna and David were there. "I might have to visit sometime."

"Maybe after you find the perfect gift for Mordred. You wouldn't want to give it to him alone."

"True." She paused for a moment, concentrating on a new step. "Do you have a need of shadowmasters at Dirklon?"

"As a matter of fact, I might." He raised an eyebrow. "I just have to remember why."

There was so much more she wanted to say and ask. She worded her question carefully. "I'm sure you were overjoyed when Merlin was found to be dead, and no Master to succeed him."

"I was indeed overjoyed, though I'm sure your joy must have been much greater." His expression remained neutral, but his eyes grew tender, and she swallowed the lump in her throat. He cleared his throat. "Strange how his sister did not succeed him. It's not as if she married a Master. How strange to think that if he had no descendants, there would be an enchantment Master at this very gathering of Allied Masters."

She nodded. "I wonder what the state of the estate would be in that case."

"Stable, I would imagine—the rules of the old Master still stand until the return of the new." The dance ended and Dad bowed to her once more. "It was a pleasure to meet you."

"And you as well." She tried to convey all of her emotion with her eyes.

He released her hand and stepped away, leaving her with a void in her heart, wishing more than anything that she was home at Wraithwood with her family all around her, Uncle Merlin still alive, no deception between anyone.

"Pardon me, my lady."

The voice jolted her out of her reverie. She turned to see a tall, blond man, probably in his mid-twenties, with sharp features and piercing blue eyes.

"I wanted to introduce myself." He gave a serpentine smile. "Ignatius Bartimus."

Ignatius. The one who would kill his father, given the chance. Her eyes widened, but she quickly gained control of her expression. "Brynna Ludovic. A pleasure."

He bowed. "Might I have the pleasure of a dance?"

She didn't see any way she could politely refuse. *Sorry, I don't dance with patricidal creeps.* She couldn't even make the excuse of being tired yet—she had only slow-danced twice. "Certainly."

As the next song began, he led her in the steps of what seemed to be a waltz. Once she got used to the steps and stopped focusing on her feet, she realized that his gaze was fixed on her, a corner of his mouth quirked. "I hear you're a helper."

"That's right." She kept her eyes on the room, disconcerted.

"You can amplify anyone's power?"

"Pretty much."

"How fascinating." His smirk grew to an oily smile. "Did I tell you yet how absolutely lovely you are?"

She resisted the urge to raise an eyebrow. *What does he want from me?* "Thanks."

"Pardon me for asking, but I'm very curious. This talent of yours—can you deplete power as well?"

There it is. "I've never attempted to do such a thing."

"Pity. That could be an excellent weapon against the enemy."

Or your father. She gave a tight smile. "You're right. Too bad I don't know how to do it."

"No matter." His chilly hand twitched in hers, the only sign of his annoyance as he offered another smarmy smile. "You know, I bet your powers as a shadowmaster would go along perfectly with my line of work here in Mordizan."

This song couldn't be over soon enough. "Oh? What do you do?"

"I'm an extractor of information. Of course, I also help people indoctrinated with harmful ideas."

It took her a moment. "You're a torturer."

"Well that's a bit of a rude way to put it." He sniffed. "That would imply that what I do isn't for their own good."

She searched his face and shuddered. For the first time, he looked completely sincere. "Of course. How silly of me."

The song ended and she stepped away.

He bowed, smiling. "Thank you for the pleasure, Brynna."

She nodded, unable to formulate a response. Instead, she scanned the room for Marcus. There he was, bowing politely to a matronly woman with whom it appeared he had just danced.

She made her way to him as casually as she could, but once she arrived, she whispered urgently, "Ignatius wants me to help him kill his father."

"I figured." He stopped to shake a man's hand. "I'd avoid him as much as possible."

"You're not going to report this to your father or something? Shouldn't he be stopped?"

Marcus shook his head. "That's not how it works. If he succeeds his father, all the better for my father. Ignatius is a stronger ally."

Brinnie's mouth dropped open. "But you don't think that!"

He took her arm and directed her away from the crowd. "Of course not. But there's nothing I can do about it right now. We have more important things to take care of." He lifted a flute glass from a table of refreshments and handed it to her. "We need to get Mordred down into the crowd so that he won't notice when you . . . you know."

She glanced at Mordred, standing stiffly upon the platform, monitoring the festivities. "Yeah, that's not looking too promising right now."

"You could ask him to dance." He picked up another glass for himself.

"Are you crazy?"

"He's your protector, your rescuer from the enchantment wizards." Marcus batted his eyelashes, faking a swoon. "Play it up. Get him down there."

"You're ridiculous." She rolled her eyes. "Or I could act concerned that he's lonely and ask him to come mingle."

He took a sip and shrugged. "If you want to be boring."

She would have been annoyed at his flippant behavior if she didn't appreciate how his body language expressed ease to anyone who might be watching—ease that didn't quite reach his eyes. *All part of the game.* "I'll wait a dance or two to make it more convincing that I'm worried about him being bored." She sipped from the glass he had handed her and almost spat it straight out again. She coughed. "What on earth is this?"

He held it up to the light. "This one is a raspberry vinegar tonic, I believe."

Her eyebrows shot up. "Do you guys drink this regularly?"

"On special occasions." He took another sip. "It's a substitute for alcohol. No one wants a room full of powerful wizards all intoxicated."

"Well, I appreciate the thought." She set her glass on a tray of discarded flutes and scanned the gathering. She spotted Dad across the room, smiling and apparently making pleasant conversation with the Master of Mordizan. All was still well.

"Brinnie?" She glanced back to see Marcus giving her a questioning look. "What's going on between you and Drakon?"

"Nothing." That came out way too fast.

An eyebrow rose. "Are you sure?"

"Of course." She took his arm. "Do you want to dance?"

She doubted that he was convinced, but he let her distract him. She led him back onto the dance floor and they joined an upbeat number, spinning and twirling. The dance involved switching partners, and Brinnie found herself with several young heirs, seeming to range in age from twelve to thirty. Marcus took the opportunity to talk with the young ladies he danced with, obliging his role of greeting all guests, and Brinnie hoped it was enough to make him forget their conversation.

At the end of the number, they ended up together once more. "It might not be long before the feast begins," Marcus warned.

She nodded and took a deep breath. "All right. I'll go get Mordred."

CHAPTER THIRTY

Many of the older wizards had sat out the lively number, talking and laughing with goblets in their hands. Brinnie attempted to scoot by a gaggle of middle-aged ladies, but the matronly woman Marcus had danced with earlier spotted her. "You're Brynna Ludovic, aren't you?"

She gave a small curtsy. "Yes, I am."

"Matilda Bathgot. We were all just saying how exciting it is to have you here." She gestured to the four other women standing in her circle. "It's quite a tale. A pretty young thing like you, escaping the enemy, coming to Mordizan, and of all things catching the eye of the heir of Mordizan. It's a perfectly heartwarming story."

Brinnie smiled and glanced downward, playing at the demure young girl. "I never thought of it that way."

"But you do know, dear, that you can't be with Marcus."

Brinnie looked up, surprised by her change of tone. "Pardon?"

The other women glanced at each other. One snapped open a fan to whisper to another.

"Do you see that young woman right there?" Matilda Bathgot pointed across the room at a girl wearing a silver dress who looked a bit older than Brinnie. "That's Eris Skrisgard, the daughter of one of the most prominent Masters." She leaned in conspiratorially. "Their line is one of the few untainted bloodlines left—not a drop of human blood in them. Everyone knows she's the one to be the future Master's wife." She looked down her nose. "Not some halfling former enchantment wizard."

Brinnie's eyes widened at the antagonistic tone. She wanted to snap back that she had no intention of becoming a Master's wife, thank you very much. Instead, she checked out the other girl. Eris

Skrisgard was certainly pretty, willowy with long hair so white-blonde it almost seemed silver, reaching out a delicate hand to greet an elderly man. *Not too bad, Marcus. Could be much worse.* She ignored the slight pang at the thought of Marcus with a girlfriend. She pasted on a sweet smile. "Thank you for letting me know."

Matilda gave a sharp nod. "Of course. Wouldn't want you to break your heart over the young man."

Brinnie moved away, intent once more on her target. She resisted the urge to roll her eyes at gossiping women. Matilda had to be the wife of some Master—did they have nothing better to talk about in the face of war?

She took a deep breath to prepare herself, then stepped up onto the platform. She crossed to Mordred.

He watched her approach with only a small nod.

She joined him looking out over the crowd. "You're not joining us, my lord?"

"I don't dance." He kept his eyes on the room.

"Not even in your youth?" Brinnie ran a subtle eye over him, wondering where the key could be kept. "Weren't there grand dances with lords and ladies and knights in shining armor and all that?"

She knew the picture she painted was off by about a thousand years—the Dark Ages of Britain hadn't reflected typical Arthurian imagery at all. But she'd learned that playing dumb helped put people at ease.

"Not quite in that way. But I was never invited. We wizards were outcasts."

"Then isn't it about time you learned how to party?"

His head finally turned toward her as he raised a brow, but she kept the friendly smile on her face. "Come, my lord. You look lonely up here by yourself."

She noticed a flicker in his eye. He gave a small nod. "One dance."

She hadn't expected to succeed. Her heart thudded as she led the way to the dance floor. They joined a dance of moderate tempo, and she tried not to flinch at his touch. Keenly aware of his closeness, it took all of her effort not to stiffen when he took her hand in his icy cold grasp. But the song didn't call for the closeness of a waltz, only clasped hands.

She offered a smile. "You dance pretty well for never having done it before."

"I have danced."

She cocked her head, trying to keep the conversation going between stolen glances, searching for pockets or telltale bulges that might be keys. "When did you learn, then, if you didn't go to dances?"

He was quiet for a moment, then said, "I danced with my wife, Nimue. We had festivals all our own."

She was distracted temporarily from her search by the hint of wistfulness in his voice. "You miss her," she observed softly.

Anger flashed through his eyes for a moment, but then his expression softened to sadness before returning to its usual stoic state. "She was so young when I left her. When I returned, she was gone, with only distant grandchildren in her place."

For just a moment, Brinnie saw things through his eyes. He had awoken into a time so different it might as well have been another world, everyone he knew and loved dead for more than a millennium, to a new magic system and wizards in hiding with weakened powers.

What would it be like to lose everything and everyone? Did he even have time to grieve before the dark wizards turned to him to lead them? When all was said and done, if they won, where did that leave Mordred? Alone again? "I'm sorry," Brinnie breathed.

"You do not need to be sorry." He blinked, and if she hadn't known better, she might think she saw moisture. Then his expression hardened. "It was Arthur's doing, not yours."

The statement jolted her back to reality. No matter his inner feelings, he was a man bent on revenge and destruction. "But Arthur was my ancestor. Why have you helped me, after all he did to you?"

"You didn't choose your lineage any more than I chose Myrddin as my father. Revenge on you would accomplish nothing." He paused as the dance called for Brinnie to spin. "We are not so different, you and I. Our families betrayed us. The world feared our power and called us evil. We were trapped in a society that hid us as if we were a shame to the world instead of embracing our power as their salvation. Simple minds fear what they do not understand."

She forced words past the sick feeling in her stomach. "Imagine what you could do if not for the Enchantment."

"No. Imagine what *we* could do." He sought her eyes. "Brynna, I saw it immediately. No wizard like you has been born since the time of Myrddin. You are young, but I could teach you all that I know." His gray eyes sparked with blue. "Together, we could rule all the earth and create the world as it is meant to be. None of this pain has to exist anymore."

"I don't know about ruling. But a new world . . ." She thought of ending the fighting, of returning to Wraithwood, of her family living in peace. She channeled all of those feelings into her words. "There's nothing I want more."

She held his gaze unwaveringly as they rotated to the music until at last he nodded. "For now, you must prove yourself to Vorath. I have full confidence in you. Once you overtake the seventh stronghold, we can begin."

She didn't know which question to ask first, so she asked the stupid one. "Not the fifth?"

"I will be headed there." His lips twisted into a half-smile. "They do not need the both of us. You will go to the seventh. Your task will be to slip inside invisibly and open the gates for our forces. You will be hailed as a hero and your loyalty will be unquestionable."

Her stomach turned. How was she supposed to fake her way out of that? *He knows you can't. That's why he's telling you this. He's toying with your emotions. Just get the key, find his bane, and get out of here before that happens.* She smiled and put a hand on his shoulder, feeling for a cord of some sort that might be holding a key. "I look forward to that."

The dance ended and she stepped away, frustrated with her fruitless search. She curtsied and smiled. "Thank you, my lord."

"The pleasure was mine." He started as if to leave the dance floor.

"Wait," Brinnie said quickly. "Stay a while. You might not be able to dance with your wife, but there's another Nimue I'm sure would be happy to dance with you." She gestured toward her aunt, willing Nimue to look over.

Mordred turned his gaze to Nimue, engrossed in conversation with Brinnie's father. Brinnie saw her wide smile, the way she looked at her brother with adoration. She hadn't seen Nimue look at anyone that way before. *She missed him.*

Mordred shook his head. “She seems quite content. I believe I have had enough for one evening.”

Brinnie watched him stride back toward the platform, away from the crowd, to take up his post as a solitary figure once more.

As Mordred left, Marcus drew her off to the side. “Well?”

“Nothing.” Brinnie shook off any lingering sympathy. “I didn’t see it anywhere, and I couldn’t keep him down here in the crowd.”

He frowned. “He must have it on him somewhere.”

“Where? No pockets, no cord around his neck, nothing.” She paused. “You’re certain we can’t pick this lock?”

“Positive. Even with a spellcaster, I don’t know if it would be possible.”

She sighed. “Wonderful. What are we supposed to do?”

His gaze wandered around the room as he thought. “I don’t know,” he said finally.

“We’ve got to come up with something. He’s leaving tomorrow, and I’m leaving two days after that. Apparently, I’m supposed to take down the seventh stronghold as some sort of grand plan to prove myself to your father.”

Marcus snapped his fingers. “That’s it. We don’t need to sneak into his room. You need to be invited in. He’s taking you into his confidence. If you keep playing along, soon he’ll trust you.”

“I can’t wait that long.” Her heart squeezed. “If we don’t figure this out in the next two days, I’m going to have to reveal myself. I can’t take down the stronghold. People will die. He has to have the key on him. I’ll have to turn invisible and try.”

His brow furrowed in concern. “While he’s up there alone? He’ll notice right away. You’ll be caught.”

“One way or another, he’ll find out the truth. Either it will be now, or two days from now when I don’t open the gates of the stronghold.” She took a shaky breath. “At least right now there’s a chance. I’m going for it.”

“Wait. You can’t just disappear right here.” He offered his arm. “Come with me.”

She concentrated on keeping a vapid smile on her face as he led her through the crowd. “Where are we going?”

“On a romantic moonlit walk.”

"Excuse me?" The mask cracked as she shot him a glare. "How is that helpful?"

He reddened. "No, I mean that's where everyone will think we've gone. Then you can turn invisible and sneak back in."

"*Oh.* Got it." She smiled up at him in what she hoped seemed to be a flirtatious manner, glancing around simultaneously to see who was watching. Not surprisingly, Matilda Bathgot pinned her with an icy glare from across the room. Brinnie caught her father's gaze for a moment and quickly looked away. That was enough scanning the crowd. She would just have to hope that whoever did notice would fall for the ruse.

Marcus led the way to the side of the room, to a small door nearly hidden behind a pillar. He nodded to the guard standing beside it and pulled open the simple wooden door, gesturing for Brinnie to exit first.

She stepped into a small courtyard bathed in moonlight. It consisted of only a few hedges, a bench or two, and a small fountain in the middle, closed off on all sides by walls. The only entrance was through the door from which they had come. "You weren't kidding." Brinnie looked up at the sky. "Literal moonlit walk. What's with this random courtyard?"

"It's meant as an escape from the ballroom, if it grows too warm or loud or crowded." Marcus closed the door behind him and joined her. "More often it's used as a place for couples to be alone."

She plopped onto one of the stone benches and began pulling off her shoes. "Okay. You stay here. I'm going in."

"Whether you get the key or not, come back out here in twenty minutes and we'll go in together." His gaze roved the courtyard, as if worried someone would pop out of thin air and point an accusing finger.

Which, in the world of wizards, wasn't an unreasonable fear.

"And if I'm caught?" She set one shoe on the bench and pulled off the other. "What will your cover-up be?"

"My cover-up?"

"Yes. We don't both need to go down with the ship. If I don't get back here, return to the party after the twenty minutes is up and claim that I tricked you and left shadow wolves to guard you."

"And what if you get delayed?" He took a solid stance. "I'll be out here until you come back."

"Marcus." She took a deep breath. "If I don't come back, and you're caught, Mordred will kill you." He began to protest, but she gave him a look. "A traitor to the greatest good that's happened to Mordizan in centuries? No one will be able to protect you."

"Then you better not get caught. If it's looking too dangerous, abort mission."

"It's the only chance I have to stop him." She stood, gravel stabbing her bare feet. "I'm not helping him take down a stronghold. In a couple days, my cover is blown. And then you'll be on your own to defeat him."

"Brinnie." He took a step closer, hesitated. "Your safety is more important to me than finding Mordred's bane."

She opened her mouth to protest before the full meaning of the statement hit her. Her heart skipped a beat, and her face warmed. But his concern was unwarranted. "It's fine. He doesn't want to kill me."

"I know. But I also know the sort of things they'll do to you to force you to do their bidding. I can't let that happen."

She shook her head and tried not to meet his gaze. How much could she reveal? "I have an escape. What I mean is that once I get out, I'll have to leave you to find his bane alone."

"What escape?"

She finally looked him in his eyes, full of concern. Did she trust him? Could she? How far apart were their goals, really? *Or does that even matter? He's not looking out for his own interest—he's looking out for mine.* "My father. Antony Drakon. He's here to get me out once I find Mordred's bane . . . or get into trouble."

His mouth dropped open. "Drakon? Your father? How?"

"It's a long story. He wasn't really held captive by Uncle Merlin. He married my mom. He's part of the plan for me to escape."

"How didn't I see it? You look just like him." Tension melted from his face. "Brinnie, that's great. If you're caught, you can be sent to Dirklon for 'rehabilitation.'"

"And he'll set me free," she finished. "I know."

He grinned. "You have no idea what a relief that is. Why didn't you tell me earlier?" As he saw the look on her face, his smile faded. "Oh. Dumb question."

"It's different now, you know."

"I know." He hesitated. "If we don't see each other again, I wanted to say—"

If they didn't see each other again? She cut him off. "That's not going to happen. You're going to reform Mordizan, remember? We're going to make peace."

He shook his head. "Maybe. Maybe not. Maybe Mordred will kill me before I get the chance. I just thought I should tell you." He gave a bashful half smile. "You've been more than just an ally to me."

His sincerity, the warmth in his eyes . . . she had never really had a friend like him. In some strange way, they understood each other. She nodded. "This isn't just an alliance. Whatever happens . . ."

"We're in it together," he finished. "Mordred or no Mordred."

With a deep breath, she stepped away. "I need to go. Say a prayer."

He nodded. "Good luck."

CHAPTER THIRTY-ONE

"Oh, silly me, we don't want to return yet." Marcus shut the door, giving the confused guard a wink.

Brinnie slipped through, invisible. She held back a hysterical giggle at the guard's confusion. *Pull it together.*

The music still played, wizards still danced and chatted as if everything was normal, as if they weren't all plotting each other's deaths and warring in an effort to take over the world.

Brinnie hugged the wall, working her way toward where Mordred still stood on the platform. The stone felt cool beneath her feet, now quiet without clacking heels. As she stepped onto the platform, shadows trailing her in an attempt to blend in the way Keilrie had shown her, Vorath strolled up from the other direction, heading toward Mordred.

Good. Distraction. She lifted her skirts, landing lightly on her toes, and hurried to reach Mordred while Vorath made conversation.

Vorath waved a grandiose arm. "A fine party, isn't it?"

Brinnie slowed, coming to a halt directly behind Mordred. She hooked one feather-light finger around his collar and gently pulled it away from the back of his neck, looking for a hidden cord.

"Indeed." He reached back to touch his neck and she jerked away, her heart pounding. He rubbed the skin where her fingers had grazed him. "Have you seen your son and Brynna lately?"

"I can't say I've paid much attention." He chuckled. "I hardly need to ascertain my son's loyalties."

Brinnie leaned, sliding her hand ever so slowly into the pocket slit in Mordred's robes.

"Perhaps you do. I watched him leave not long ago with the shadowmaster."

She paused. He saw? *Of course he did. There's a reason he's standing up here watching.*

Vorath laughed. "Ah, yes. He's taken a fancy to her. I don't blame him—any boy his age would be a fool not to."

Well that's creepy, old man. She wriggled her fingers deeper, feeling for anything beyond fabric and pocket lint.

Mordred remained unmoving. At least his sometimes-unsettling stillness worked in her favor. "It doesn't concern you that your heir has taken up with a Ludovic girl?"

"It can't last of course, but for now he can have his fun." Vorath gazed out over the crowd. "Besides, it should be good for her. If she gets attached to him, she'll be more likely to abandon her old ways."

"Or will he abandon his?"

Brinnie removed her hand and reached for the pocket on the other side.

Vorath turned toward Mordred, brows furrowed in offense. "My son would never be so stupid." He shook his head. "Besides, he's told me about this girl. He admitted that she isn't completely on our side, but he thinks he can persuade her. It seems she thinks he's as confused about his loyalties as she is. He thinks he can stage their coming to the right conclusion together. He's a clever one."

Brinnie pulled her hand out of the empty second pocket a bit too quickly, causing a slight tug. Was Marcus lying?

No, silly. He's lying to his father. He told you that.

She leaned back and considered the situation. No key. If only she could see underneath the layers of his formal clothes.

Her eyes widened. *Maybe I can. The only problem is not getting caught.* She remembered what Keilrie taught her—again. She hated admitting the lessons had been helpful. *Imagine what I want. Believe it's real. Bring it to life.*

She pictured the creature—nose like a peppercorn, whiskers fine as spider's silk, small feet peeking out beneath soft fur. In her hand, the shadows converged, and the creature's tiny claws tickled her palm. "Find the key for me," she breathed.

The mouse hopped out of her hand and onto the stone floor. It scampered toward Mordred, clawed its way up his boot, and peeked inside. From there, the creature moved to the next, checking inside, before it slipped beneath his robes.

Brinnie had lost track of the conversation, but Mordred remained conversing with Vorath. Mordred twitched. Every muscle in Brinnie's body tensed as she waited for him to react, casting aside her mouse, recognizing it as hers.

Suddenly, Mordred slapped at his side and a spark went out from his hand. It took Brinnie a moment to realize that he had used magic. Any normal mouse would be dead. She forced the mouse to stiffen as Mordred shook his robes and the corpse fell out onto the floor. Mordred nudged it with his boot, nose wrinkled in distaste.

Vorath stepped back. "Where did that come from?"

"It seems you have a rodent problem. It crawled right up my leg." He examined his robe. "And slipped past my enchantments. What sort of vermin do you have here?"

"My apologies." Vorath waved a hand toward a hovering servant in Mordizan livery. "I'll have someone take care of it."

"No need." Mordred pointed a finger and fire shot out toward the mouse.

Brinnie struggled to quickly reduce her creation to a pile of ash. Mordred scuffed the pile and Brinnie caused it to disperse, forcing the shadows to splay into tiny particles. They fought, seeking to coagulate. Rather than allow that to happen, she released them altogether, hoping Mordred wouldn't notice the ash had disappeared.

"Evidently I need to add new species of vermin to my charms." He gave Vorath a hard look. "You know how I feel about crawling things." He brushed his hands on his robe and returned to the conversation. "Now, what were you saying about the third stronghold?"

Brinnie's heart pounded. Even though part of her wanted to laugh that Mordred hated pests enough to cast magical repellents, the rest of her mind raced. *That could have been me.* The last time she saw Mordred's power displayed was at the Battle of the Master Key. He didn't use it lightly. *Did he suspect? Was that his way of making sure the mouse was real?*

She didn't know what to try next. He didn't appear to be carrying a key at all. But would he leave it somewhere?

A thought struck her. What if there wasn't a key?

As soon as the thought crossed her mind, she couldn't believe it hadn't occurred to her earlier. He had a spell because he disliked *vermin.* With something like his private research and the secret to his bane, it wouldn't make sense for him to resort to ordinary measures like enchanted keys that could be stolen. Someone like Mordred would cast a spell.

She scowled. That made things even more complicated. To break the spell, they would need a spellcaster.

She practically stomped back to the door to the garden. She tapped the guard on one shoulder, causing him to look away, and slipped through the door.

She found Marcus sitting on a bench facing the door, shredding a leaf into tiny pieces. "There isn't a key," she announced, turning visible.

He jumped and reached for the sword that wasn't there. "Brinnie." He clasped her shoulders. "Thank goodness you're all right." He stepped back. "But maybe next time, turn visible a little earlier. I was about ready to take your head off."

"Sorry." She waved off his concerns. "I couldn't find a key on Mordred anywhere. But I witnessed some of his power. He's not bound to any one talent like we are. Mordred wouldn't use a key that could be stolen, not when he could cast a spell instead."

His eyes widened. "You're right. I'm such an idiot."

"Do you know any spellcasters who we might be able to convince to our side?"

"The only one I know personally is Ignatius." Then he snapped his fingers. "Ignatius! That's perfect, actually. He doesn't need to agree with us. We have something he wants."

A way to kill his father. Brinnie stepped back. "That's horrible! We're not helping him with that."

"Oh, I don't intend to." He raised a brow. "But what if he thought he could find something to help him in Mordred's room?"

She nodded slowly. "You have a point."

"I'll talk to him."

"You? Why would he trust Mordizan's heir in a murder plan? That sounds like a set-up to get an admission of guilt if I ever saw one."

He laughed mirthlessly. "Not around here. He would be a stronger ally than his father, remember? The key is keeping the other estates from knowing that Mordizan had a hand in it so that the Masters continue to trust my father."

That's terrible. She bit back her unhelpful condemnations of Mordizan. "Can you get him alone?"

"Give me a few minutes."

Brinnie sat to wait on the bench, playing with the straps of her discarded shoes, trying to decide between pinched toes or frozen toes. She shivered in the night air. *Pinched toes it is.*

Instead of a few minutes, the door swung open within a few seconds, and Marcus and Ignatius entered, Ignatius laughing heartily about something. "I was just heading out for some fresh air anyway."

As soon as the door closed, Ignatius's laughter ceased, and his expression grew serious. Another reminder of how many liars and secrets filled Mordizan. He glanced from Marcus to Brinnie. "What is this?"

Marcus hooked his thumbs on his pockets. "We would like to discuss with you a matter of some sensitivity."

He smirked, watching Brinnie's approach as the three converged between the door and the bench. "Does it happen to do with my father?"

"Ah, your father." Marcus nodded. "Not the man he used to be, is he? We all know that you do the real work of running the estate. It's a shame that you aren't recognized for it."

Ignatius raised an eyebrow. "What are you saying?"

"It would be unfortunate if someone undid the spell on Mordred's chambers and retrieved details on an item used to kill powerful wizards, wouldn't it?"

"It certainly would." He and Marcus shared a conspiratorial look. "But two wizards would have had to be working together—a spellcaster couldn't do that alone."

"Of course." Marcus shrugged. "I would never be an accomplice, of course—I'm impartial as a representative of Mordizan. But some people aren't as impartial." He glanced toward Brinnie. "Some might have their own reasons for wanting to access Mordred's room."

Ignatius grinned at Brinnie. "I knew you were holding out earlier. What do *you* want with such a weapon?"

She tried to adopt a smooth persona like Marcus. "That's my business. The important thing is that the two of us work together to get in. You get what you want, I get what I want, and we never speak of it again."

He nodded. "Sounds fair. When do we act?"

Brinnie and Marcus looked at each other. "How long are you staying?" Marcus asked him.

"Until after the Masters' Gathering. We'll leave tomorrow."

"And we both have to be present at the meeting." Marcus frowned.

"We'll slip out early tonight," Brinnie suggested.

Marcus shook his head. "With all the spells cast over the Gathering, no one can leave without my father knowing."

"Isn't that normal?" She hated looking unknowledgeable in front of Ignatius. "He's a Master. As far as I've noticed, he hasn't paid much attention."

"He can't usually keep track. There are too many people in Mordizan. But these spells are specific to the Gathering."

Ignatius shrugged. "Tonight, then, after the feast."

"When Mordred is in his room? Suicide." Brinnie tapped her foot. "There has to be another way."

"What's your hurry, sweetheart?" His thin lips stretched upward. "I have business here next week. We can do it then."

"Good!" Marcus said, at the same time Brinnie said, "That won't work." They looked at each other for a long moment.

Brinnie gave a sweet smile. "Ignatius, will you give us a minute?"

She pulled Marcus off to the side near the burbling fountain. Hopefully the sound would drown out their voices. "Two days, remember?"

"For you. But we have a way in now." Marcus glanced back toward Ignatius, who leaned on one leg, hands tucked in his pockets, the picture of cool arrogance. "You can escape, I can get the bane, and it will all work out."

"Did you forget the part where Mordred would kill you if you're caught?"

"I just won't get caught."

She wanted to shake him. "That's too risky. We need you in power at Mordizan—"

Ignatius cleared his throat loudly. "Sorry to interrupt, but we've got to get back in there soon before people get suspicious, and I can hear everything you're saying anyway. There really isn't an option—I'll need the girl to get in there."

"How do you know that?" Marcus demanded.

"She's a helper, which means she can also negate magic. I can use that to form a spell to neutralize the other spell. You, on the other hand." The smirk returned. "I don't see fire doing much good against Mordred's spells, no offense to you."

Brinnie's mind raced. She couldn't think of any other way. Implications flashed through her thoughts. Say yes, and she would have to fight against the enchantment wizards. Say no, and Mordred would be free to continue his conquest. "Deal," she heard herself say. "When are you coming?"

CHAPTER THIRTY-TWO

The rest of the Gathering passed in a blur. The enormous feast featured exotic dishes Brinnie had never seen before, but everything tasted the same to her. She sat beside Marcus, who was seated at his father's left with Mordred on his father's right. She tried to focus enough to make an appropriate amount of conversation, but her mind kept spinning. There had to be another way to stay in Mordizan to help Ignatius without taking down any strongholds.

Finally, once the feast ended and conversation had dragged on for an eternity, people began to leave. Marcus glanced at Brinnie, then broke in during a pause in Vorath's animated discussion with a bearded wizard. "Father, if you don't mind, I'll take Brynna home now."

Vorath nodded and waved a hand distractedly. "Of course."

Marcus offered his arm, they paid a few respects, then they headed for the door.

Brinnie glanced over her shoulder at Dad as they left. "Can we say goodbye?"

Marcus shook his head. "Probably not a good idea. You don't know him, remember?"

Her gaze lingered on her father, but Marcus was right. She wished she could talk to him, ask him what to do, gain some fatherly wisdom.

Instead, they exited the hall.

As they strolled through the corridors of the fortress arm in arm, Brinnie sucked in a breath. "Idea. What if I got sick?"

"What?" Marcus's brow wrinkled.

"Right before going to the seventh stronghold." Why hadn't she thought of such a simple ploy sooner? "What if I got a terrible fever? I wouldn't be able to go."

His brow smoothed and his lips twitched. "Have you ever been sick before?"

She thought for a minute, filtering through memories. She blinked. "Not that I can remember." Odd. "But they wouldn't know that."

"Yes, they would." He chuckled. "I don't mean to laugh, but wizards don't get sick. Cursed, wounded, poisoned, sure, but not sick."

"Oh." She scowled. "That's dumb. Does poisoned include food poisoning?"

He tilted his head. "I mean, usually when you poison someone, you poison their food."

She facepalmed. "I'll take that as a no."

"We'll think of something. Don't worry."

She shook her head and took a deep breath. "We don't have long."

Back at her room, they stopped in front of the door. Marcus straightened his shoulders in a mockery of poise and bowed to her. "Thank you for a wonderful night, my lady."

Despite her situation, she couldn't help a smile. "A rather unsuccessful night."

"Not entirely. We learned things, came up with a plan. And, you know . . ." He trailed off and cleared his throat. "Anyway, good night."

"Good night." She cocked her head as he strode away quickly. Strange.

The moment she stepped inside her room, she kicked off her shoes and collapsed into the room's singular chair. *What am I going to do?*

"Well?" a voice asked from under the covers.

"Lana." Brinnie lifted her head. *Right. I have a roommate.* She stretched out her feet, wiggling her aching toes. "Why are you still awake?"

Lana sat up, clutching the blanket to her chin with a grin. "You went to the feast with the heir of Mordizan. You didn't think I'd be a little interested in how it went?"

Brinnie patted her hair, pulling out pins to keep her hands busy. "It was fine."

"Fine? Details, please."

"There was a lot of dancing." Another pin. *Plunk.* "Then a feast." *Plunk.* "Everyone was dressed really fancy. I met a lot of Masters and heirs." She tried to come up with more, but her brain was too tired. Too many thoughts of plans and battles and strategies floated through.

"I know all that." She waved a hand. "What about Marcus?"

"Oh, he was Marcus. Fun. Gentlemanly. We danced a lot." She plucked the last pin from her hair and shook it out. Then she stood and reached behind her back to struggle with the dress, trying to escape from the bodice.

Lana climbed out of bed and began helping to free her. "So? What went wrong?"

Brinnie shimmied out from the first layer of fabric. "Wrong? Why would you say that?"

"You're in a state." Lana paused to put a hand on her hip, scrutinizing Brinnie. "You should be glowing with happiness, but you're all . . . brooding."

"I don't *brood.*" Lana gave her a look, and she shrugged. "Okay, maybe I brood a little." She wriggled, trying to free herself from her skirts. "It's complicated. But Marcus . . . that part was good."

Lana sighed and helped Brinnie escape from the last of the skirts. "So you're not going to tell me any details?"

Brinnie tripped and flopped backward onto her bed, wincing at the hard thud on the mattress. "I'm sorry. I know I'm not making much sense." She grimaced. "My brain is mush. Can I tell you more in the morning?"

Lana crossed her arms and gave an exaggerated pout. "You'll have lessons with Keilrie."

"For once, no. She gets to be at the Gathering for some reason."

"Fine." Lana giggled. "But I want to hear everything."

"I'll tell you more than you ever want to know. Including what Matilda Bathgot wore."

"Oh, I can't stand her!" Lana plopped onto her bed, grinning. "I hope it was something hideous."

Lana climbed under the covers and Brinnie breathed a sigh of relief. At least tomorrow morning, she might have better answers and more success with a chipper tone.

She rolled over and tried to sleep, but her mind wouldn't stop spinning, mulling over the situation with the stronghold, the key, Ignatius. She tossed and turned as no solutions came to her. Finally, she began to drift off.

She floated, disembodied, in the dungeon where her sister was being kept.

Mordred stood over Anna as she lay on the stone floor, dirt streaking her face and highlighting her protruding cheek bones. "Your sister will not free you."

Anna glared at him. "Even if she doesn't, I'm glad she escaped from you."

"Escaped me? It is not me you should fear, but her." He smiled, a slow, sinister smile. "Haven't you heard? She could have stopped me, but she didn't. She knew where my bane was to be found. Yet she chose to flee. She is darkness at loose on the world."

"And now I'm here." Brinnie's view shifted to see herself standing in the doorway, smirking. Yet, it wasn't really her. This Brinnie's hard eyes glinted, and her black cape seemed to float with an unearthly force. "I won't join you, Mordred. But I'll allow you to do your work. I have my own work to attend to."

"Brinnie!" Anna pleaded. "What are you doing? What has he made you?"

She gave a harsh laugh. "Him? He hasn't made me anything. I've become what I am—I am the Mistress of Shadows, the Vessel of the Dark Ones."

Brinnie sat up with a gasp. She pressed a hand to her heart as if to keep it from pounding out of her chest. She glanced over at Lana. Her friend was fast asleep, curled under the blanket.

Was the dream a sign? *Not that any of my dreams have been particularly pleasant since Keilrie started messing with my head.* She took a deep breath. *No. It was just a nightmare. You have a lot on your mind.*

She lay back down, wrestling with the blanket to get into a comfortable position. She concentrated on pleasant, calming thoughts, of the Wraithwood gardens, of sunsets on Arizona mountains . . .

She found herself in the middle of Wraithwood's circular drive. In front of her, where the house once stood, smoke rose from beneath piles of rubble. "No!" She ran forward, stumbling over the wreckage, tossing bricks aside in a frantic search.

"They're all gone."

Brinnie whirled around to see a familiar form standing behind her. "Uncle Merlin! But . . . you're dead."

"Yes." He folded his hands serenely. "We all are."

"No." Tears rolled down her cheeks. "What happened?"

"You found Mordred's bane."

"What?" Hot tears obscured her vision as she gazed at the singed lawn, the trees fallen and splintered. "Then how did this happen?"

"There was a terrible cost."

"But why? Was it because I took down the stronghold?"

He shrugged. "I'm dead. I can't tell you."

Everything began to fade. "Wait! Did we defeat him? How did it go wrong? What can I do?"

The next thing she knew, she was staring at the ceiling, her eyes wet with tears.

She sat up and looked at Lana's bed—empty.

Only a dream. It didn't really happen. None of it happened. She rubbed her temples. *So, what, my options are either turn into something even worse than Keilrie or have everyone die?* "Thanks, brain," she said aloud. "You're really helpful with tough decisions." She rolled over to get out of bed.

"What tough decision?"

Brinnie jumped, rolled off the edge of the bed, and hit the floor. Lana scooted out of the way with a squeak.

"Lana? Why on earth are you down here?"

"I was stretching." She leaned forward and grabbed her toes. "I thought you were talking to me. Guess you were talking to yourself." She giggled.

"My bad." Brinnie stood and dusted herself off.

Lana twisted her torso in a contortive stretch. "Okay. It's morning. Now I can ask. What's going on with you?"

Brinnie bit back a sigh. "Well, first things first, it isn't guy related, so I'm sure it's a lot more boring than you think it is."

"Okay." She assumed the butterfly position. "So, what is going on? And please don't brush it off. I want to help."

Brinnie hesitated. *I could use all the allies I can get right now.* Especially if something happened to her and Marcus, if Dad was discovered . . . there were some things someone else needed to know. "You know how I said I thought Mordred still had my sister somewhere? I was right. She's in a cell down in the dungeon under the—"

She was cut off by banging on the door. She glanced at Lana, who shrugged. Brinnie stepped over her and went to open it.

A young messenger stood outside, looking nervous. "Brynna Ludovic?"

"Yes?"

"You are requested in the council chambers immediately." His awkward posture reminded her of Quentin.

"What? Why?"

He rocked on his heels. "I was told they're strict orders from Master Vorath and you must come at once." His hands fidgeted. "Er, my lady."

"Okay. Hold on two seconds and I'll put some clothes on." She shut the door and turned around, her heart pounding. Had they somehow found out about the plan? Should she run now, while she still could? *No, they wouldn't send an awkward message boy. They would send armed guards.*

"Hey." Lana gave her a reassuring smile. "You look like you're going to your death. People call for you all the time."

"Right." She threw on a tunic and pants, yanked on her shoes, and stuck her hair in a ponytail. "I'll be back soon."

She followed the message boy through the corridors to the council chamber. The guards threw the doors open, and she was announced by the herald. "Brynna Ludovic, as requested by Master Vorath."

As she stepped through the doorway, her eyes widened. Today, the rows of seats of the council chamber were filled. Vorath sat at the head table with his key advisors, Mordred, and Marcus by his side, while Masters and their heirs filled the benches.

I'm so dead.

Vorath nodded to the assemblage and banged a gavel. "Five-minute recess of the Gathering."

As the crowd welled around her and the room buzzed with conversation, Brinnie made her way down the aisle to the front. As she wove around distinguished old wizards and dashing young heirs, she realized that she was significantly underdressed. *Well. Nothing I can do about that now.* She came to stand in front of the head table, acutely aware of her messy hair. She bowed to Vorath. "You summoned me, my lord?"

"Yes." He stood. "Come up here. I want to stretch my legs."

She rounded the table. Vorath stood a few feet away from the table, Marcus beside him. Vorath nodded to Brinnie. "You said you wanted to prove your loyalty to me. Today is the day."

She forced herself to give a calm bow of her head. "What can I do, my lord?"

"Our informants have brought word that enemy reinforcements are being sent to the seventh stronghold. They'll be arriving in four days."

"Yes, my lord." Thank goodness, nothing new. "Mordred informed me last night that I'll be going to the seventh stronghold soon."

"Plans have changed. You're going today."

Brinnie felt her mouth drop open and quickly snapped it shut. She shot a panicked look at Marcus, but he gave a slight shake of his head, eyes wide. He hadn't known either. "Today?" she repeated.

Vorath gave her a calculating look. "You have to be there before the reinforcements arrive. We want time for our forces to secure the fortress before having to deal with the reinforcements."

"We have four days," Marcus interjected. "Why leave early?"

"Why wait?" Vorath countered. He turned back to Brinnie. "Keilrie recognized the urgency of the situation. You're temporarily released from your apprenticeship."

She nodded dumbly.

Marcus found his voice before she did. "Father, do you really think she's ready for battle? I don't doubt her loyalty, but what about her safety?"

Vorath held up a hand. "Enough. She's ready. Don't let your emotions cloud your judgment." He nodded to Brinnie. "A squadron leaves in two hours from the west outer courtyard. You leave with them."

"Y-yes, my lord."

"Dismissed."

He returned to his seat, leaving Brinnie standing dumbfounded, staring at Marcus in horror. He brushed past her, headed back toward his seat. She almost didn't hear his whisper as he passed. "There's a recess in half an hour. I'll meet you at your room."

She nodded and descended from the platform, her mind whirling. As she made her way back to her room, she considered making a run for it. *No. Marcus and I will figure something out. It isn't time to run yet.* She needed a better plan than just *flee*.

Her face must have said it all as she walked into the room. Lana paused, sword belt half buckled. "What happened?"

"I'm leaving in two hours for the seventh stronghold."

"Why?" Lana cocked her head. "We have two more days."

"Reinforcements are coming. Vorath wants an attack before they get there."

Lana cinched her belt. "But you said your sister is still here? What is going on?"

Brinnie reached under the bed, pulled out a knapsack, and began stuffing in her meager belongings. "I don't know." Somehow, she'd been outplayed.

"Brinnie, please." Lana grabbed her arm to stop her rapid shoving. "Tell me. What's going on? Remember when we talked at the beginning? And you told me about your sister and I told you about my friend? I want to help you."

Brinnie turned and faced her. "Do you? I'd give anything not to be headed out there, but you're dying to get on the battlefield, which honestly, I don't understand at all, since you're such a sweet person. Where does the bloodlust come from? Do you really not understand why I don't trust you?" Lana stared at her with round eyes. Brinnie winced. "I'm so sorry, I didn't mean—"

"I think you did," Lana broke in. She rubbed her forehead. "And I understand. It does seem contradictory. But it isn't bloodlust. I want to change the world, do the right thing, be at the forefront. To me, that's always meant becoming a warrior."

"I shouldn't have said it that way." Brinnie clutched her knapsack, unsure what to say after such an outburst. "I understand your goals. I know you mean the best. But is war really the way to do it?"

She sighed. "I know it's hard. Trust me, the more battle training I receive here, where it's more about killing than finesse . . ."

Time was running out before Marcus came. "Lana, you don't have to do this. You don't have to fight this war."

Her open, concerned expression closed into a reserved, suspicious one. She stepped back. "Oh. No, Brinnie, I wasn't saying I wanted to quit. At all. I just understand why *you* don't want to fight." Her brow furrowed. "Is this only about being averse to violence? Or . . . are you concerned about things other than your sister?"

Brinnie's chest squeezed. So this was it with Lana. She was understanding, to a point. But within that tender heart resided a deep loyalty to a faulty cause. "No. You know me. I don't mess with politics or wars or anything like that. I'm just a girl trying to keep my sister alive and trying not to get killed in the process. You know that."

She nodded. "I think I do."

There was a knock at the door. Brinnie grasped Lana's hand. "Please. If something happens to me, remember my sister. She's still down there. If I'm not around to get her out . . ."

Lana clasped both of Brinnie's hands. "I will do whatever I can to set them free." She offered a weak smile. "Wars are meant to be fought by warriors, not civilians."

Throat tight, Brinnie nodded and released Lana's hands. She hurried to open the door.

Marcus stood outside, breathing heavily. He must have run all the way from the council chamber. "We don't have long. We have to go."

"Go where?"

He glanced over her shoulder at Lana, looking at them both in confusion. "Away," he hissed. "To escape."

"No."

"What?" He pulled her outside and closed the door.

"If I run now, your father will ban me from Mordizan. It will be impossible for me to get back in, impossible to get the scroll. It *has* to be me and Ignatius."

He stared at her. "That doesn't matter now. You need to get out. We can talk with your father, or I can get you over the border, or—"

"No." She cut him off. "I'm going. Somehow, I'll find a way to keep their trust *and* keep anyone from dying. My safety, me getting caught, none of it matters if we don't take out Mordred."

They looked at one another for a long moment. His warm brown eyes gazed at her from beneath a furrowed brow. "I'll come with you. Protect you somehow."

Brinnie's heart warmed. "You know you can't. Your father wouldn't let you go in the middle of the Gathering. Besides, neither side wants me dead right now." She glanced around the corridor. "Don't you have to be back soon?"

"I have a few more minutes." He hesitated. "Please be careful. In battle, political strategies don't always matter. People get killed." He took her hands, gently. "Live. No matter what. If not for you, then for me."

She felt tears welling. This was it. She was actually going into battle. Everything else had been child's play, sneaking around, acting innocent. Now, things would really be decided. "I will."

He seemed about to say something, but instead, he wrapped her into a hug.

She hugged him back. For just a moment, she allowed herself to feel warm, protected. With her ear against his chest, she could hear his heart beating, beating too quickly with worry, but his strong embrace diffused confidence into her.

She could stay in an embrace like this for a long time.

She forced herself to pull away. "Don't worry. I'll be back." She gave a half-smile. "Maybe we'll even have a second chance at the whole ball thing. You know, without worrying about sneaking around and trying not to get killed."

He mirrored her hesitant smile. "I'll hold you to that."

She backed toward her door, where a knapsack waited to be packed for battle. "I'll see you again—in this life, or, God willing, the next."

He raised an eyebrow. "Did you come up with that line?"

Time was running out. He had to get back before anyone knew where he had been. "It's what Uncle Merlin told me." She turned the doorknob.

He stepped back, headed for a curve in the wall. "This life, or the next." Then he pushed aside a pennant hanging from the wall and disappeared into a narrow crevice, to dash through the hidden passages of Mordizan once more.

In her room, Brinnie gave Lana a quick hug. "I'll see you soon."

Her friend nodded. "I have full confidence that you will."

She shouldered the pack and hurried down to the courtyard. Men and women scurried about packing bags, gathering weapons, shouting to one another.

"Shadowmaster," a voice boomed.

She turned to see a tall, brawny man in the Mordizan colors looking down at her. "Um, hi."

"I've been waiting for you." He frowned, but Brinnie got the feeling that was his usual expression. "I assume Master Vorath informed you of your task?"

"Yes, I think so."

"Good. You report directly to me. Commander Rand Ernst."

"Yes, sir, Commander Ernst."

"Toss that bag and get a kit over there. Assemble your weapons and fall in." He turned to walk away.

"Excuse me, sir. Are we . . . marching there?"

"Of course." He gave her a longsuffering look.

She couldn't help blurting out questions. "Won't we be seen? You know, by humans?"

He barked out a laugh. "How do armies get anywhere? We'll have spellcasters, shield spells. We could almost march through New York City and no human would bat an eye."

"Right. Thank you, sir." She made her way across the courtyard to two women passing out packs, weapons, clothing, and leather armor and helmets. Brinnie didn't feel too bad ditching her sack, since it only contained a few borrowed items anyway. She shrugged on the new pack and stepped into the boots the woman gave her.

Those around her began falling into two lines. All fell in except for a few spellcasters, wands in hand, who flanked the columns. There seemed to be around fifty wizards in all. Unsure of exactly what to do, Brinnie stood toward the back of the formation. Commander Ernst called out the command and the lines began to move. The formation marched out of the courtyard.

Brinnie tried to keep time as they marched through the front gate and out into the city. People moved to the sides of the streets as they passed, hardly seeming to take notice of the warriors carrying swords, knives, and spears. They marched along the main thoroughfare through the city, all the way to the end, and then out through the protection spell.

Brinnie looked back as they crossed the boundary. All that lay behind were the rolling fields she had seen once with Marcus.

Then she turned her eyes forward, toward the seventh stronghold and the battle that lay ahead.

CHAPTER THIRTY-THREE

They marched for two days.

The first day, the rain soaked Brinnie through. Her feet stayed relatively dry within her boots, but the unfamiliar shoes gave her blisters. They marched wordlessly until dark, when Commander Ernst called a halt for the night. At least, Brinnie assumed it was dark, since those in front of her stumbled over roots and called for other wizards to light the way. Brinnie crawled into her canvas, zipper-less sleeping bag and pulled it over her head to keep out the rain, feeling like a potato in a potato sack, but the oiled fabric kept her dry. Those around her chatted while fire wizards started campfires and others cooked, but she didn't feel like trying to be friendly. The last thing she needed to do was get attached to more dark wizards.

The next day, the rain stopped, and the sun slipped through the cloud cover from time to time. They marched through forest, making Brinnie wonder where in the world Mordizan was located. She didn't even know which continent she tramped across. She guessed as far as wizards were concerned, countries and oceans didn't really matter, winging about through portals and gates.

They marched all day with a quick break for a midday meal. Brinnie sat alone, watching the wizards laugh and joke with one another. She knew they had to cope with war. She knew this was normal soldier behavior. But she couldn't join in. Not when their task loomed before them.

They arrived long after dusk. Brinnie almost ran into the back of the soldier in front of her, half asleep in an exhausted trudge. She blinked, looking up, then her eyes widened as she crested a small hill and gawked.

Dozens of tents spread across the plain in neat rows. Under an awning, a blacksmith pounded near a forge, while across the way another wizard fed scraps to what appeared to be mountain lions. Sacks of provisions floated behind some wizards while others sparred. The camp bustled with activity, just out of projectile range of the enormous fortress.

The stronghold itself loomed in the distance. There was no elegance to its design—thick stone walls topped with crenellations rose high above the ground. No windows broke up the wall, not even arrow slits that might allow footing for those attempting to scale its heights. The wall jutted outward at a ninety-degree angle at what seemed to be five feet below the crenels, making climbing even more difficult. The gate offered little hope either. A sturdy iron portcullis shielded the heavy doors several feet behind.

How exactly do they expect me to get in there?

The new arrivals were assigned to tents. Brinnie found herself in a tent with two other women, both of whom gave her a passing nod before bedding down. She quietly rolled out her sleeping bag and lay down beside them, though the last thing on her mind was sleep. As she mulled over possibilities, she found herself wishing the woman beside her was Lana.

Instead, she considered her next order of business. She didn't have a choice about infiltrating the stronghold if she wanted to retain the dark wizards' trust, but that didn't mean it had to be a successful attack. It wouldn't be her fault if the enemy somehow received a warning, after all.

Glancing at the women to make sure they were truly asleep, Brinnie turned invisible and slunk out of the tent.

Campfires glowed as embers. The blacksmith had left his forge, and the sound of metal on metal had ceased. A few sentries roamed between the tents with torches, but they posed no threat to Brinnie, cloaked in shadows.

She sighed to herself. *This ranks pretty high on stupidest things I've ever done.*

She left the camp and headed across the plain toward the stronghold, stepping carefully over tussocks of grass dotting the ground, perfect for twisting an ankle. As she continued, the stronghold loomed higher and higher, until it blotted out her full frame of vision. Eventually, she stood in front of the gate, gazing upward. She had no hope of getting in there without wings.

Luckily, she had a plan for that. An idiotic, potentially deadly plan.

She closed her eyes, focusing only on her imagination. She pictured plumage, talons, a curved beak. She imagined the bird growing, larger than any she'd ever seen in real life. But that was the beauty of imagination—it didn't need to be real.

The shadows swirled and coalesced. She could feel them beyond her, beneath her fingertips. Taking a deep breath, she opened her eyes.

A dusky eagle cocked its head at her, looking down from nearly a foot above her. It was enormous. Tentatively, she reached out to touch it.

Her fingers sank through the eagle's beak like molasses, the creature not fully physical. She closed her eyes, focused on deep breaths, on infusing herself into this creation. She more carefully imagined the strength in its wings, the interlocking fibers of its feathers, and the curve of the beak. She reached out again, fingers stretching until she felt a smooth beak under her fingertips.

She opened her eyes, meeting the obsidian gaze of her creation.

Her heart beat quicker in her chest. She had made this.

Sometimes, her own power frightened her.

She patted the eagle. "Okay, buddy. You know what you have to do."

The bird spread his massive wings and took off with a lurch. She tensed, ready, as its talons curled around her shoulders, lifting beneath her arms and ripping into her tunic. If she could better picture what a bird looked like with a rider, she would have picked a more comfortable mode of conveyance, but she wasn't sure of logistics. She'd seen plenty of birds carry their prey in their talons, though. With a yank, the eagle lifted her into the sky.

She bit back a cry of pain at the wrenching feeling. As the ground fell away, stars danced before her eyes. This was so, so much worse than a broom. All that stood between her and a fall to her death were the claws of an imaginary shadow bird.

In tandem with her thoughts, the claws of the eagle began to slip. Keilrie's grin flashed across her mind. *"You have to make me believe."*

Frantically, she imagined the rustling of feathers, the prick of the talons, the beat of its wings. The eagle solidified once more.

The enormous raptor wheeled toward the rear of the stronghold. As it circled, approaching the back wall, one of the sentries pointed to her and shouted. *Great.* She could turn invisible, but her shadows, if they were to have form, couldn't do the same.

More sentries came running, two from either side, one each holding a torch while the other nocked an arrow to their bow. *This is a stupid way to die.* She directed the eagle into a steep swoop into shouting range so she could reassure them of her friendly intentions, but as it began to dive toward the congregation on the wall, the two archers loosed their arrows. Brinnie cried out as the arrows passed through her shadow creation and narrowly missed her.

More soldiers swarmed to the wall. She could hear alarmed calls for reinforcements at the seeming invincibility of the beast. Before they could loose another shower of arrows, Brinnie dropped from the talons of the eagle onto the wall, bending her knees to absorb the impact that stung her shins. "Wait! I come in peace!"

The eagle flapped to a halt, perching on the crenellation. The dozen soldiers on the wall hesitated, bows drawn, swords out. One of the men nearest to her glanced at the others. "It speaks!"

"What sort of creature are you?" another shouted.

"Oh." Brinnie dropped her shadows and turned visible, eliciting a shout and swords turned in her direction. "No, it doesn't talk. That was me."

The soldiers formed a semicircle, backing her against the wall. One man stepped forward, his breastplate metal instead of padded leather. Presumably a leader. "Who are you?"

She took a deep breath. "That doesn't really matter right now. I'm here to deliver a message. The dark wizards have brought someone to infiltrate the stronghold, probably tomorrow, but definitely soon. That person is going to open the gate and let the enemy in. You have to do something to stop that person and send them out of the fortress."

He gestured to the wall they stood upon. "No one can infiltrate the fortress—it's impossible to scale the wall, and we have eyes on the skies."

She raised her eyebrows. "Uh, but I'm here."

One soldier emitted a nervous giggle. The man shot him a glare before turning back to Brinnie. "What do you want?"

"I wanted to warn you. Guard the gate from the inside."

"And you bring this news out of the kindness of your heart?" He snorted. "Our forces are on high alert. No infiltrator will make it through our defenses alive."

Her eyes widened. "No need to kill anyone. Just, maybe capture them? Or stop them and send them back?"

"We will kill dark wizard infiltrators," he said firmly. "Thank you for the warning."

She bit her lip. "Okay, well, here's the thing. You can't kill the infiltrator. The infiltrator is actually on your side."

"You're not making any sense, girl." He motioned to the soldiers behind him. "Detain her."

"No, wait! Listen, I was supposed to infiltrate—"

The sound of a horn cut through her sentence. The leader swiveled toward the front of the fortress in confusion. Then his face cleared. "A diversion. To the western wall! You four, take her."

As he and his division ran for the front of the fortress, four men charged toward Brinnie.

She turned invisible, and her eagle snatched her in its claws, wheeling away. She squinted toward the front of the stronghold. What was going on?

Soaring away from those intent on her capture, she directed the eagle to the western wall, arriving ahead of soldiers scrambling for the walls. There, she saw what the fuss was about.

Dark wizards swarmed up ladders propped against the walls as fireballs and arrows flew into the fortress. *How? Why are they attacking now?* Understanding dawned. They noticed she was missing. They must have assumed she deserted. *They're trying to attack while they still have the element of surprise.*

Her mind whirred as the eagle wheeled. Should she assure the enchantment wizards of her innocence, or the dark wizards? At this point, she couldn't do both. The only course of action that would convince either one was to fight against the opposite side.

We have to get Mordred's bane.

And Marcus and Ignatius couldn't do it without her.

A plan began to form. A terrible plan, even worse than the first that had backfired.

She'd always hated chess. She hated a game predicated on sacrificing pawns in order to win. A game where if the "important people" were left standing, it was considered a victory, no matter the numbers remaining on either side.

Yet she found herself in a tournament of master chess players. To win their game, she had to play by their rules.

She swooped downward and landed in a roll in a side yard of the open courtyard in the middle of the stronghold as the eagle released her. She dismissed the creature, coming out of the roll running. As she emerged into the wider courtyard, the crowd of warriors charging for the front swept her along. A stray sword swiped her arm, and she bit back a yelp as she dropped her shadows, becoming visible. A fireball sailed from the sky, and she dove out of the way, though some weren't quick enough. Their screams rang in her ears. Everywhere around her, people screamed, shouted, ran toting weapons, dragged the wounded toward the inner wall, tossed buckets or conjured water to put out the flames caused by fireballs.

She scrambled to her feet, stumbling again toward the front. "Surrender if you want to live!" She coughed on smoke. "They're going to win! If you surrender, you can live!"

"Shut up," one woman growled, pushing past her with several quivers over her shoulders. "Don't demoralize the troops."

She nearly tripped over a prone soldier, pushing her way toward the front. She kept up her shouting. "The enemy is going to win! Surrender peacefully and live. You'll be spared if you surrender!"

A man pointed at her. "That's the girl from the wall. Stop her! She's the enemy."

As several wizards ran toward her, she quickly turned invisible and ducked out of the way. They spun, swords swiping at air.

She kept up her beseeching. "I warned you. Please listen to me! I'm not your enemy. Surrender peacefully." If they would just listen, she could plead their case. If they would listen, she would be lauded as a hero by the dark wizards, ushering in a painless victory. And she would be in position to bargain for their lives.

"Never surrender!" someone called. The shout was taken up by others until it became a battle cry as wizards charged up onto the walls. Brinnie clenched her fists and whirled toward the gate. She had warned them. They were going to lose.

Hopefully they would heed her words before it was too late.

The door to the gatehouse was a simple wooden affair just to the left of the gates. And it was completely unprotected. Brinnie wove through the milling troops and slipped inside.

The interior reminded her of the guardhouse at Mordizan with gears, ropes, and chains, but the guards were noticeably missing. *I guess you don't need anyone guarding the inside of an "impenetrable" fortress.* Within only a few seconds, she found which crank to turn—the huge wooden screw with push-bars in the middle of the floor. She took slightly longer to find the levers and stops keeping it in place. Her heart pounded, waiting for someone to come in and stop her. Shouts rang from outside, but no one thought to protect the gatehouse.

She positioned herself behind one of bars of the screw and pushed with all her might. Her arms trembled, and blood dripped from the cut on her arm. Just when she thought she wouldn't be able to move the massive winch, it slowly began to move, picking up momentum. With a great deal of creaking and groaning, she heard the metal grate outside begin to lift. As gears turned and chains clattered, she continued her slow circles until she felt the thud of the portcullis hitting the top.

The cries from outside grew louder as the dark wizards cheered. She threw the levers, locking the screw in place. The door to the guardhouse burst open, but she pressed herself against the wall, invisible, as soldiers dashed for the winch.

I'm sorry. She summoned wolves to guard the screw. *Don't let them get to it.*

She slipped out of the guardhouse in time to see the heavy wooden doors of the gate shaking from the battering without. The three massive crossbeams shuddered. She gulped in a deep breath. Time for more physical labor designed for someone much larger.

She reached the left holder for the lowest crossbeam and heaved the huge board onto her shoulder. Stumbling, she managed to take a wobbling step to the side just far enough to drop the board and allow it to crash to the ground. Her breath came in ragged gasps, her hands stinging. As she summoned her strength to reach above her head for the next crossbeam, a grating, sliding sound came from somewhere above her. That was when she heard it—the whoosh of fire and the screams of the dark wizards beyond the doors.

She staggered back from the heat she could feel through the doors and looked up. Through holes in the top of the thick wall, fire wizards rained down flames on the dark wizards trapped in the tunnel underneath the wall. Brinnie's stomach churned. She gripped the next crossbeam above her head, easier now without the gate shaking from a battering ram, and shoved upward with all her might, diving out of the way as the second beam fell, thundering onto the stone.

She forced her legs into a run as more wizards charged toward the gate, some pushing braces on carts to reinforce the doors. She scooted along the wall, out of the way.

But they were too late. The last beam splintered, and the dark wizards came rushing in with a roar.

Brinnie pressed herself against the wall to avoid being crushed. Swords flashed and magic exploded all around her. Fire, water, wind, flying vines and vegetation, snarling animals. She squeezed her eyes shut and shielded her head. She couldn't even tell who was who.

After a few moments of chaos, the sides soon became apparent. The attackers far outnumbered the defenders. The dark wizards surrounded the enchantment wizards, herding most of them into the center. Smaller dispatches of dark wizards spread out, chasing down straggling resisters and fighting the soldiers on the walls.

It had all happened so fast. Brinnie lowered her trembling arms from her head. A few dark wizards lay in the tunnel between the raised portcullis and the splintered gate, clothes smoking, presumably dead. Defenders littered the courtyard, some still, some moaning, bleeding or otherwise wounded.

Her knees buckled, and she realized power still flowed from her, animating wolves in the guardhouse. She dismissed them, and strength began to return.

The dead confronted her from both sides, the bodies she wasn't sure still had life. She pushed herself to her feet. She didn't have time to panic, to mourn, to scream. Now she had to make sure that death toll didn't rise. She turned visible and came to join the dark wizards surrounding the kneeling defeated defenders.

At Brinnie's footsteps crunching over debris behind him, Commander Ernst turned from overseeing the gathering. He scowled, and her eyes darted to his sword, dripping in a dark substance. "You dare show your face, traitor?"

"Traitor?" Brinnie forced her shoulders back, chin up. "I opened the gates!"

"After deserting." He stomped forward, and his hand shot out, wrapping around her throat. "I should have you beheaded," he snarled.

"I didn't desert." She tried to keep calm, infuse her voice with indignation. "I came to scope it out, figure out a plan before the attack." She glared at him, summoning the confidence of Nimue or Marcus. "But instead of thinking for a few seconds, you panicked and attacked, and I had to get in here without a plan—which was pretty hard, by the way."

She felt his fingers begin to loosen and kept going. "Do you think I would have let you in if I were deserting? I would have turned my powers against you, not forced my way into the guardhouse and singlehandedly opened the portcullis *and* removed two out of three crossbeams on that gate." She threw out an arm and pointed at the splintered wood. His hand dropped from her throat and she stepped back, straightening her shoulders. "I am loyal to Mordizan."

His red face relaxed, then his severe expression morphed into a stunned half-laugh. He swore. "Gave me a heart attack, Ludovic. Don't you dare act without consulting your superiors again." He shook his head, exposing broad teeth in a grin. "But for now, well done."

As he walked away, Brinnie's shoulders wilted in relief. She watched as the dark wizards gathered up the weapons of the enchantment wizards and forced the last of them onto their knees.

Commander Ernst swaggered forward. A few of the dark wizards clapped or cheered. He held up his sword, acknowledging victory. Then he flicked it beneath the chin of a young man cowering on the ground.

"You have the Enchantment?" The commander's voice boomed through the courtyard.

Brinnie could see the boy's throat bob from yards away. He swallowed and nodded. "Yes."

"Are you willing to give it up and join us?"

Sweat trickled down his pale face. "No."

"You would give your life to protect *humans*?" Commander Ernst sneered.

He said nothing.

The commander kicked him. "Answer me!"

Brinnie winced and drifted closer. *If they had only listened. If they had only surrendered.*

"I'd give my life to defend against you," the young man spat.

Commander Ernst bared his teeth. "Then I grant your wish."

With one slash, he slit the boy's throat.

Brinnie bit back a shriek as the young wizard's blood splattered the ground. She stumbled forward and threw her arms out in front of Commander Ernst. "We've won. Surely this isn't necessary."

He gave her a hard look. "Don't make me question your loyalty." He turned to the rest of the kneeling wizards. "I would ask if any of you would consider my offer, but I know your kind." He nodded to his troops. "Kill them all."

"No!" Brinnie leaped in front of the nearest woman, shielding her from the man whose sword arced toward the defender. Instead, the man growled and snatched Brinnie's arm. She struggled, but two more soldiers joined him, grabbing her by the arms and dragging her off.

The woman's back remained ramrod straight. She tilted her head up, icy eyes boring into Brinnie. "You would try to protect me? You brought this upon us."

Then the man's sword slashed.

Brinnie screamed and yanked against those holding her back. Hot tears burned tracks down her cheeks. She turned invisible and summoned shadow wolves. They leapt upon her guards, but the wolves simply passed through—as if the guards knew how to see through the illusion. No one but Keilrie had ever done so before. She flickered back to visibility, gasping.

Commander Ernst stepped forward, his eyes hard. "Keilrie informed us of the limits to your power. I suggest you behave, shadowmaster."

She should have known. Keilrie wouldn't keep Brinnie's weakness to herself. They had to have a way to control her. These weren't just ordinary soldiers—they were guards intended specifically for her.

The enchantment wizards fought back with flashes of magic, fists, and anything else they could find, but the dark wizards marched on, scything them down. The metallic tang of blood filled the air. Brinnie screamed and struggled. Bodies carpeted the ground. "This is not victory! This is a massacre!"

"Only extermination will free the world," Commander Ernst responded, posture relaxed as he watched his troops mow down the weaponless enemy. He nodded to her guards. "Take her away. She's an embarrassment."

The slaughter continued as the guards dragged her away screaming. Then something smashed into the back of her head, sending stars through her vision. She slumped in their arms, consciousness fading.

What have I done?

CHAPTER THIRTY-FOUR

Marcus squeezed her hand. "You did it!"

Applause filled the hall. Across the room, Vorath stood on the raised platform smiling magnanimously, Mordred noticeably absent—gone to the fifth stronghold. Along with Lana. Brinnie searched the crowd for her father, but she didn't see him either. He must have left for Dirklon. Both of her other allies, gone.

As her gaze passed over Keilrie's smirking countenance, she quickly looked away. She wasn't sure she could control her emotions if she met Keilrie's eyes.

Marcus hooked his arm through hers. Her arm ridiculously clad in ceremonial armor. No dress tonight—she wasn't a lady anymore. She was a war hero.

He led her forward through the path left by the crowd to the platform, then stepped aside with a grand gesture. "May I present Brynna Ludovic, conqueror of the seventh stronghold."

The crowd cheered. Brinnie bowed.

"Well done, Brynna Ludovic." Vorath beamed. "You have shown yourself to be a true friend of Mordizan." He paused to allow for applause. "Tonight, we celebrate the fall of the seventh stronghold. And you are the guest of honor."

She bowed again. "The honor is mine."

By the sound of the applause, the crowd approved of this statement. Vorath waved to the musicians, and they struck up a chord.

Music played, dancers whirled, and dozens of wizards came to congratulate her. Some shook her hand, while others slapped the pauldron on her shoulder in congratulations. The ridiculous, stupid armor. She'd been lucky to have a leather breastplate, spaulders, and vambraces as army issue, with a simple helmet and no chainmail or armor below the belt to speak of. Not that she'd been wearing any of it when she set out on her disastrous mission. Yet now, they dressed her up in chain and plate mail from neck to toe, so she looked like some dashing warrior instead of an army grunt.

All a show.

How many of these wizards had ever truly seen battle? How many of these members of the upper class even knew what happened at the strongholds?

Marcus interrupted her thoughts, disentangling himself from a nearby conversation. He offered an easy smile. "Remember when you said we might have a second chance at the whole ball thing? How about a dance?"

She nodded. He led her onto the dance floor, and they joined a festive, flowing waltz. Her feet remained sore from marching, her head still occasionally gave a pang from the blow to the head the two guards had given her to shut her up, and the wound on her arm stung. The detachment had only arrived back at the fortress a few hours earlier, giving her barely enough time to clean up and change into this chosen attire before appearing at the celebration.

She'd come to a mutual pact of secrecy with Commander Ernst. She promised not to reveal his rash attack—if he promised not to divulge her weeping.

"I'm not willing to allow my queasiness over my first time witnessing mass bloodshed to tarnish my reputation." She'd glared at him. "And if you plan to share, I'm more than happy to explain to Vorath and Mordred precisely how you panicked and threw your forces against an 'impenetrable' fortress. We both know you would have broken your army against those walls without my intervention." She'd even summoned a nasty smirk. "As much as it pains you to no end, we both know I have many more friends in high places than you do. I'll survive if you tell on me—but I'm not sure you'll make it back up if I drag you down with me."

With that, all reports stated that the joint effort for the attack had been planned. And ever since, she hadn't managed anything more cheerful than the slight smile for Marcus as he greeted her at the door to the hall.

Bile rose in her throat as they spun. She hadn't eaten since the massacre three days ago. The smell of food made her ill, every scent somehow reminding her of blood. Every noise in the night sounded like a scream, keeping her awake. But she had to stay strong. She couldn't show a single sign of regret.

"Brinnie." She focused on her surroundings to see Marcus's furrowed brow. "You've hardly said a word all night. Are you okay?"

She nodded but didn't dare open her lips to speak. She didn't know what would come out of her mouth if she did.

She danced. She smiled at congratulations, pretended to eat, sipped at a bit of water. Somehow, she made it through the night. She left as soon as was polite, claiming exhaustion. Marcus insisted on walking her back. She didn't try to argue, though she knew he would press her for what was wrong.

Instead, he didn't say a word as the sound of music and voices faded away and they wove through the corridors of the fortress. They walked for a while in silence before she noticed they were going the wrong direction to be heading to her room. "Where are we going?"

He smiled slightly. "It's good to hear your voice. You'll see."

He led the way through the halls and up a flight of stairs into a wide, roomy corridor. Finally, he stopped in front of a door and pushed it open. "Welcome to your new room."

Brinnie stepped in with surprise, taking in the full-size bed, a desk, a wardrobe, an upholstered chair, even a window draped with scarlet curtains looking out on an inner courtyard. "Why?"

"Well, Lady Brynna, presumed heir of Wraithwood, we couldn't have you staying in army barracks. You're a trusted special agent of the Master of Mordizan, not a foot soldier."

Brinnie shook her head, unable to summon words. The red curtains seemed a waterfall of blood, the crimson blankets a pool of luxury bought in bloodshed. She couldn't bring herself to turn, to face him. "I can't."

"You don't have to be humble with me." She saw him shrug out of the corner of her eye. "Besides, it will be easier to work on the mission without having to hide it from Lana once she gets back."

Easier to hide it from Lana. He was more right than he knew. She would never be able to hide this from Lana. "Thank you."

"Brinnie." She didn't turn to look at him, so he came to stand in front of her. He put his hands on her shoulders, that accursed armor clanking, and attempted to look into her eyes. “What happened at the stronghold?”

She pulled away. “The objective was achieved. When do we meet Ignatius?”

“Brinnie—”

“Don’t.” She took a deep breath and strode across the room to look out the window. “It’s done. When do we meet Ignatius?”

“In two days.”

“Good. Have a good night.”

She waited for him to leave, but he didn’t move. The awkward moment of silence dragged on.

He cleared his throat. “I’ve heard some rumors,” he said softly. “But I would rather hear from you. I want to know what really happened.”

“You’re the heir of Mordizan. You know everything. You know what happened.”

Another pause. “Okay. But I’m here for you.”

She couldn’t stand it anymore. She whirled around. “Stop it.”

His brow furrowed. “Stop what?”

“Don’t be nice to me.” Hot tears squeezed out as she held back sobs. “I need you to hate me.”

“Why would I ever hate you?”

“You know what happened.” Her voice cracked. “You know what I did.”

“Do I?” He shook his head. “I know the reports that came back to Mordizan.”

“Then you do.” She turned back around, gripping the windowsill.

“But I know you better than that. And I know better than anyone not to trust what I hear when it comes to you.”

“This time you can trust the reports. They’re accurate.” She brushed away tears. “I’m tired. Thank you for everything. Have a good night.”

“Brinnie . . .”

“Good night.”

She waited for the sound of his boots walking away, the opening and closing of the door.

The moment it clicked shut, she began tearing at the straps of her armor. She yanked off the pieces, tossing them onto the bed in a clanging pile. Her breathing grew heavy as she ripped off every piece, every bit of the outfit celebrating her crimes.

Down to a simple tunic and loose pants, she paced the cold stone barefoot. Her eyes threatened to close, but she dared not sleep. She knew the dreams that would come if she did. She thought of nothing. Anything, and she would break out weeping.

She stubbed her toe on an uneven stone and tripped, falling to her knees. Instead of standing, she curled over herself.

Forgive me.

If only she could rip out her heart so it wouldn't feel, turn off her mind so it couldn't remember.

She thought she would cry. Instead, she couldn't move. If she held still long enough, would she cease to exist? If she didn't make a sound, would she fade away into the mindless embrace of darkness?

But she had to defeat Mordred. She had to make sure the defenders of the stronghold hadn't died completely in vain. She could never atone for what she had done, but she at least didn't want anyone else to die because of her.

Finally, she couldn't keep her eyes open. She drifted off on the floor, so exhausted from days of marching and sleepless nights that she fell too soundly asleep to dream.

Brinnie opened her eyes slowly, blinking. Every muscle groaned as she raised herself up on one elbow. She bit back a grunt of pain, pushing into a sitting position. *Note to self—never sleep on a stone floor again.*

She hauled herself up to sit in the chair near the window. A knock sounded at the door as she was combing her hair out with her fingers. "Come in!"

The door opened and Nimue peeked her head in. "Mind if I join you for a while?"

"Sure." She snapped a hair tie off her wrist and stuck her hair in a ponytail. Stretchy hair ties were a precious black-market commodity at the University, but she couldn't live without them.

Nimue stepped in and closed the door behind her, smiling broadly. "I'm so proud of you."

Brinnie stood. "Oh, um, thanks."

She came and put her hands on Brinnie's shoulders. "Really, though." She shook her head. "I know how hard of a time you were having with the transition, and I'm sorry I got distracted with my brother. But I'm so impressed with what you did. I know it couldn't have been easy."

Brinnie's eyes prickled with tears. She wanted to tell her aunt. She wanted Nimue on her side. With Nimue, Dad, and herself, Mordred wouldn't stand a chance.

But Nimue was Mordred's right hand. And Nimue had no idea she and Brinnie were related. "It wasn't."

Nimue frowned, eyes going to the dark circles rimming Brinnie's eyes. "Not getting much sleep, huh?"

"Just kind of tired."

She made a sympathetic noise. "It's okay, kid. Your first major battle is rough. It will take time. But you come to terms with it, especially when the cause is something you believe in."

How can she actually believe that? Brinnie gazed into Nimue's sincere eyes and lied straight to her face. "I don't know if I'll get used to it. But I know that right now, I'm doing the right thing."

Nimue nodded. "I'm glad you've come to that realization." She put her hands on her hips and looked down. "What are you wearing? Have you changed since you got here?"

"Uh, not really."

Nimue laughed and hooked a thumb toward the wardrobe. "You'll find that stocked with clothes. You're one of Vorath's favorite people right now. Speaking of Vorath." She raised an eyebrow. "You and Marcus. Is this a real thing, or are you trying to get on Vorath's good side?"

"Nimue!"

"As your mentor, I feel I have the right to know." She smirked.

Brinnie sighed. "We're just friends."

"Mm-hmm. Notice that wasn't one of the two options." Nimue gave her a knowing look. "Well, such topics aside, there's something I want to prepare you for." Her expression grew serious. "Vorath's going to call you into the chamber today. He's going to ask you to do something. And I want to tell you that you can say no. It's taken me years to accept this sort of thing."

"What is he going to ask me to do?" *What could be more horrible than what I've already done?*

"He thinks you're ready. He wants you to go back to Wraithwood and assassinate Eira." Nimue bit her lip. "I know before you told him you would do anything to convince him you were on our side, and I told you to bluff, but—"

"I understand." Brinnie inwardly breathed a sigh of relief. If it was soon, all the better. As long as she had at least a couple days to break in with Ignatius and find Mordred's bane. "But why? She isn't the Master."

Nimue visibly relaxed, probably relieved Brinnie didn't burst into protests or tears or . . . who knew what she expected. "Supposedly. But you knew Merlin. Did he have a secret heir?"

She wasn't sure what to say, so she decided on the truth. "Highly doubt it."

"Right. So what if your mother is only pretending not to be the Master, so we won't send you to do this very thing? Better to make everyone believe the true Master is somewhere out there, undiscovered, making the taking of Wraithwood by assassination impossible."

Brinnie's eyebrows shot up. *This is perfect.* "I didn't even think of that. But it makes sense."

"That's why I'm warning you ahead of time." She hesitated. "It took me a long time to come to terms with fighting Lydia, and I've never even lived with her. But if you accept and become the Master of Wraithwood . . . Imagine what we could do with the power of Wraithwood stripped from Castelon and working for our cause."

Brinnie held back a shudder. She could imagine only too well. "I'll think about it."

She nodded. "Good. I advise you have your decision ready in two hours." Nimue headed for the door. "Put some clothes on, then you can join me for breakfast—Miss War Hero."

Any appetite she may have had left. But as she rifled through the wardrobe for suitable council chamber attire, a hard shell grew around her heart.

She could lie. She could pretend. She could become the cruel shadowmaster they thought she was, the deadly weapon they had forged.

And then she would flip the tables and turn that weapon against them.

CHAPTER THIRTY-FIVE

Brinnie entered the council room feeling nauseated. She had forced herself to eat at breakfast, but her ungrateful stomach wasn't thanking her for it.

The chamber felt empty without the visiting Masters and heirs crowding the benches. After being announced, Brinnie made her way up the now-familiar aisle and came to stand in front of Vorath and five members of his council, Mordred noticeably missing—and, surprisingly, Marcus.

"Brynna Ludovic," Vorath greeted her.

"My lord." She bowed. "May I ask why you have summoned me?"

He smiled. "It's a great day for you. I know how much you hate your family. How would you like to get revenge for everything they did to you?"

Brinnie snapped her head up from her bow as if in eager anticipation. "Very much, my lord."

"Good. We've come to the conclusion after your deeds at the seventh stronghold that you are ready, despite your lack of training. You will return to Wraithwood under the pretense of realizing just how wrong you were to ever leave." A few of council members laughed. "Then your mission is to kill Eira Ludovic—and whoever else stands in your way of taking the Mastership for yourself."

She allowed a slow smirk to form. "It would be my pleasure."

"You will be a valuable addition to our illustrious guild of Allied Masters." A couple of the council members nodded in agreement.

"Thank you, my lord." She bobbed her head in gratitude. "When do I leave?"

He laughed. "So eager! Soon. We must pull together a cohort for you to command once you conquer the estate. With Wraithwood's door and your future abilities, we anticipate it being a center of transport."

"It's an honor, sir."

"Good." He leaned back, obviously pleased with himself. "You may go. I'm sure you want to celebrate the good news with better company than a bunch of old men."

She decided to go in for the kicker. "Very astute, my lord. Do you happen to know where your son is?"

All five members of the council roared with laughter. "He's reviewing the troops in the eastern courtyard." Vorath raised an eyebrow. "I'm sure he'd welcome a break."

She left the councilmen to their crude jokes and reminiscences, exiting the council chamber with her head high. *And the Oscar goes to . . . Brynna Lane!*

She strode through the corridors so focused on replaying the conversation that she jumped when a voice said, "I imagine he shared his plan with you."

She whirled, then her eyes widened as she registered the identity of the speaker standing in a shadowed niche. "Mordred! I didn't know you had returned. You surprised me."

"I apologize." He emerged from his lurking alcove. "The fifth stronghold shall fall shortly and no longer needs my assistance." He stopped in front of her. "I have not spoken with you since your return. You seem pleased."

"I just heard the news from Master Vorath. I'll be sent on a mission to Wraithwood soon."

"Indeed." His brow rose. "But is that truly what you wish?"

How much did he sense? Would lying make her look worse or better? "I love Wraithwood. For all its . . . *quirks* . . . it's still home. I'm happy to return."

"I understand." His dark eyes seemed to pierce her soul. "You were disturbed by what happened at the stronghold."

Her heart began to pound at the abrupt change of subject. *He knows. He heard about what happened.* "Did you speak with Commander Ernst?"

"No. I see the ghosts in your eyes." Their gazes met, hers

transfixed by the steel gray of his. "Dozens have died by your hand. It leaves a mark."

Brinnie felt her face grow hot as she held back tears. She looked away. "It was necessary."

"Yes." His demeanor shifted, and he made a dismissive gesture. "The pain will soon pass. Once you have seen hundreds, even thousands, fall, it will no longer affect you."

Her stomach churned with revulsion. "I hope not." She clenched her jaw and forced herself to look straight into his eyes. "I hope I remember every one. I never want to forget the cost."

The corner of his mouth turned up. "I knew you were different." He nodded slowly, appreciatively. "I have chosen well. Only you will understand what we must do to right this world."

"And what's that?"

"Come with me. It is time I show you." He leaned back into the alcove and pressed against the wall. Something clicked, and the wall rolled back into itself, stone grinding on stone.

Brinnie's eyes widened. *He knows the secret passageways.*

He smiled. "This way."

A small part of her panicked, wondering if he would lead her into the depths of the fortress only to murder her and leave her body where no one would find it. But that made no sense, not after she'd proven herself. She shook off her paranoia and followed him into the passageway.

The moment she'd stepped over the threshold, the wall ground shut behind them. Mordred waited. He formed a light orb and tossed it into the air in front of him, then gestured for her to follow. The sphere hovered, lighting the way as they continued.

She followed him through twists and turns, up and down stairs, across stone and beams. She realized he intended to make sure she couldn't follow the trail—a wise move. Although with her navigational skills, he could put in half the effort and she'd still be hopelessly lost.

At one point, she heard voices and bent to look down through the boards. She looked up at Mordred sharply. "That's the council chamber!" she whispered.

He nodded wordlessly and motioned for her to continue. *Marcus wasn't kidding about ears everywhere.* Who knew how many hiding places like this housed Mordred's spies?

Soon the general trend turned downward. They descended staircase after staircase and spiraled down sloping tunnels. Eventually, they came to an iron door with no handle. Mordred pressed his hand against it. "*Agoraf.*" The door clicked and swung open. Brinnie followed as he stepped inside.

Light orbs illuminated the room. Scrolls, papers, and books overflowed from tables onto the floor. A quill pen floated in aimless circles over one table, slightly cleared to offer writing space. In the center, on a dais, sat a small black chest.

Brinnie stepped forward. "What is this place?"

"Wait." Mordred waved his hand. "*Sefyll i lawr.*"

Slight twanging sounds drew Brinnie's gaze upward, where crossbows affixed to the ceiling and pointing toward the entrance released their tension.

He nodded. "Now you may step forward. They are primed to shoot anyone who approaches."

"Thanks." She eyed them, wondering if Mordred got his ideas from *Indiana Jones*. She didn't trust magical ceiling weapons. "Where are we?"

He strode into the room. "You will remember last year when Castelon lost both the Master Key and the Case of the Master Key."

She nodded. "When that scientist guy stole it."

"And, you will recall, he gave us the Case in order to distract Castelon and confuse their spies. We were unable to acquire the Master Key, thanks to a certain young wizard." He glanced back at her, and she smiled sheepishly. "But we were able to keep the Case."

She looked at the chest with new eyes. "That's the Case of the Master Key."

"Yes."

Her heart thumped. Was this Mordred's secret trove? Had they been wrong? Did he keep the prophecy here as well? She tried to keep her tone light. "I would have thought you'd keep such a powerful object closer to you."

"Perhaps, but one should never keep all their valuables in one place." His gaze remained on the Case, but the corner of his mouth lifted. "Something Castelon should have learned."

Great. No prophecy here.

She approached the dais. The chest appeared to be covered in black leather with an iron clasp. It was the perfect size to hold the Master Key. A rogue impulse compelled her to reach for the clasp to open it, but Mordred held her hand back, cold fingers curling around her wrist. "Don't. The force inside is unstable without the Key."

She blinked, surprised at her own impulsivity, and stepped back. "What is it for? Other than keeping the Key stable, of course."

He circled the dais. "For years, it was thought to have no other purpose. But I know my father. He was a master of hiding magic's true power under the guise of a lesser power." He picked up a scroll from one of the tables. "Does this look familiar?"

"Not that I remember." She cocked her head. "Should it?"

"*The Case of the Master Key.* I acquired it at Wraithwood."

Her eyes widened. The scroll he had stolen after the battle the summer before. The one the Wraithwooders had hoped meant nothing without possessing the Key.

He smiled. "I see you remember now. Good. It explains the workings of the Case in great detail. By careful study, I have found the true power the Case possesses. With it, the war could end almost instantly."

Her gut sank like she'd plummeted over the hill of a rollercoaster. *Please, not a weapon of mass destruction.* "How?"

He set the scroll back on the table. "It is both unnecessarily complex and brilliantly simple—exactly like my father. You see, despite appearances, the Key does not suck away magic. Rather, the Key is raw, chaotic power, which makes our tidy little spells and powers spiral beyond our control. The magic is not taken away—it is simply untethered." He stepped closer to the dais. "The Case balances the chaotic power of the Key by absorbing its magic. But this is not limited to only the Key. When open, if properly channeled, the Case can absorb any magic." He stopped and looked at her as if this explained everything. "Don't you see? The Case can be used to drain a wizard's power—permanently."

It took a moment to sink in, another moment for her to form words. "You want to use it on the enchantment wizards."

"Exactly. Once they have no magic, they will be powerless to fight back. Our victory will be swift."

Her mind whirled. "But how? How do you steal someone's magic? How can a wizard become . . . not a wizard?"

"That was the problem." He shuffled through papers on one of the desks. "On its own, the Case's pull is not strong enough to permanently rob magic. However, by studying the writings of the past millennium and a half, I discovered that one special division of wizards has historically had the power to alter the magic of others."

"Helpers," Brinnie breathed. *Oh, please no.*

"The *liniadi*." He spread his hand over a yellowed page covered in numbers and diagrams. "So much more than 'helpers.' Such wizards are the strange, ah, side effect of Myrddin's curse. He thought he could limit power, but he unwittingly created those who had complete power over the rest. As a *liniad*, you can amplify the power of others, but you can also suck it away. In this, you and the Case are made of the same sort of magic. I've made calculations based on the strength of the Case and the strength of historic *liniadi*. If you were to wield the Case, you could strip the magic from hundreds of wizards simultaneously and completely."

She ran a trembling hand through her hair, setting her ponytail off-kilter. "But why are you telling me? Your magic isn't limited. You could do it yourself."

"I am immune to the effects of the *liniadi*, but I don't have your power." He made a fist on top of the papers. "I do not understand why—I have tried."

"So this is why you wanted me." She stared at the Case, the unassuming leather. "I'm literally the only person who can do this."

"Not originally. I suspected the powers of the Case before I met you, but I wasn't certain." He rested his fingers lightly on the chest. "I believed I might be able to wield it myself. However, at that time I was weak from my slumber. Last summer, I had hoped your power might sustain me if you saw the rightness of our cause. But you did not, and as I soon learned, you would not have been able to help me anyway in my immune state." He removed his fingers from the Case, turning fully to her. "I purposed to leave you in peace in the human world after you left Wraithwood, but I soon realized you are vital to the success of our mission." He placed a hand on her shoulder. "I hated to use the tactics that I did, but they brought you here. And now you are finally ready to save the world."

Her stomach turned. "This could change everything."

He smiled. "Yes. With their magic gone, the Enchantment would have nothing to attach to in the enchantment wizards. They would be powerless, the Enchantment would be destroyed, and we would finally be free."

She forced a grin. "When do we start?"

"One final test." He removed his hand from her shoulder, expression hardening. "I must be sure of your loyalty. Kill your mother. Take Wraithwood as your rightful inheritance. Then we will proceed."

Okay, murder, then world domination. Won't let you down.

"You can count on it."

CHAPTER THIRTY-SIX

"Formation! Forward march. Halt! Defensive formation."

Brinnie squinted in the bright sunlight that belied the chill in the air. In the courtyard, a cohort of warriors ran through their sequences. At the front stood Marcus, shouting commands.

"Return. Offensive formation. Half charge. Halt." Marcus scanned the group, expression impassive. The sun glinted on plate armor, and he rested a hand on his sword hilt. "Good. At ease! I'll turn it back over to Commander Urgal." Marcus nodded to the man beside him and stepped away.

His gaze traveled the courtyard until he spotted Brinnie standing near the wall, out of the way of the columns. He made his way over to her, cutting an impressive figure in well-made but scuffed armor, indicative of a good deal of use. "Hey."

"I have to tell you something."

"Okay." He pulled off his glove and wiped sweat from his brow. "Let's get out of the courtyard first."

"Where is it safe from eyes and ears?"

"Your room." He tucked the leather glove into his belt. "I chose it for you for a reason. No connection to the secret passageways."

"Good. Let's go."

He raised an eyebrow. "You look awfully worried for someone who just heard wonderful news."

"Right." She forced a smile. "Everything's great. I'm bringing good news."

"Exactly." He smiled back. "Let's go."

She forced herself to maintain an unhurried pace as they made their way through the fortress. To keep herself from fidgeting, she asked, "So you get to go out there and command the troops?"

He chuckled. "I was only inspecting them to report to my father."

"Right." She looked at him sideways. "Not to be rude, but how are you qualified to do that? Aren't you still in the University?"

He gave a surprised laugh. "No."

"But you tried out the same day I did."

"Oh." He rubbed the back of his neck. "I was never actually being assessed. I help Gerd out from time to time. I was sent to scope you out."

She stopped short. "Taking me to the dorms, talking to me on the university grounds—you didn't just happen to be in the area."

"Right. I came to see you."

She shook her head and continued walking. "You tricked me."

"Not directly." He fiddled with his gloves. "I never said I attended the University. But I had my own motives for the things I did."

Even then he had played double agent, giving her warnings when he was supposed to be reporting on her. "Are you still 'scoping me out'?"

"Supposedly. I tell my father about you." He shrugged, giving a half smile. "But only in ways beneficial to both of us."

She tried to shake off how deeply that disconcerted her. How much *had* he told Vorath? "So you've already passed all that University stuff. That's a good quality in an ally."

"I didn't, technically. I was privately trained. I completed my training when I was sixteen and began taking over duties for my father."

"Oh, no, privately trained. What a disappointment." She flashed a grin.

He smiled. "Sarcasm. I take it you're feeling better?"

Guilt punched her in the gut. "I'm coping," she said shortly.

"Brinnie." His empathetic look was almost too much. "What happened is not your fault."

The woman's glare flashed through her mind. *You brought this upon us.* "Wait until we get there, remember?"

Once in her room, Brinnie filled Marcus in on Vorath's instructions and on everything that had happened with Mordred.

He sank into the chair and rubbed his forehead. "With that sort of power, he won't just be stripping the Enchantment. He'll be capable of massacring any enchantment wizards you can get close to."

"Yes." She plopped onto the bed, folding one leg under, the other left to dangle and tap nervously.

"And not only enchantment wizards." He stood to pace. "Have you thought what he could do if he turned that on my father? He could take over Mordizan, easily. He wouldn't even have to kill him—he'd just have to make him look incompetent. As bad as you think my father is, Mordred would be worse."

"You'd still be next in line."

He shook his head. "You think he would spare me? He wants me dead, too."

She put a hand on his arm as he passed, halting his pacing. "But that's never going to happen. He needs me to work this thing, remember? And I would never do that."

He pressed his lips together. "Mordred wouldn't let his entire plan rest on your cooperation. He must have a plan B."

"Plan B is already in motion—destroy the strongholds, open up the estates to attack. It'll take longer, but it would still work."

"You're right." He took a deep breath. "When Ignatius comes tomorrow, we'll get that scroll. Then you can escape to Wraithwood, and none of this will matter without you there to help Mordred."

"Hopefully," she said bitterly. She looked away. "Last time I thought I could outsmart Mordred, dozens of people died."

"That's not your fault." He knelt in front of her. "You had no idea they would do what they did. Those must have been Mordred's orders. If I'd only have known . . ."

A tear squeezed out. "It doesn't matter. They died because of me."

"No." He held onto her shoulders. "They died because of Mordred. Not you."

What did he not understand? "I sacrificed them, like pawns." He needed to hate her. Someone needed to hate her. His comforting made it worse, made her feel even more guilty. She didn't deserve comfort.

She bit back a sob and tried to pull away, but he retained his grip on her shoulders. "*You* didn't. You can't blame yourself for forces outside of your control."

She shook her head violently. "I made a calculated decision to open that gate."

"You were dealt a bad hand. There *was* no good choice, and you did your best with limited knowledge to minimize damage." He sighed, his hold loosening. "Our circumstances of birth, of being shadowmasters or heirs or the sons of tyrants"—he gave her a small smile—"are beyond our control, not our fault. Some people have the luxury to make all good decisions, choices they won't regret. We aren't those people. We're playing with a low hand and the cards on fire, but we're going to play out that hand to the very last card, so that even if we lose, we'll leave scorch marks on the table to remind our opponent not to take the win for granted—because someone else will take our seat. And since we burned through the bad hand we had, they'll be bringing better cards to the table."

She blinked, gazing into his serious countenance. Mom had always made her regret the circumstances of her birth, wish she weren't born a shadowmaster or a wizard—or maybe not even born at all. Meanwhile, Marcus had been born to expectation—the expectation that he would one day lead armies of evil to victory over humanity. Neither of them choosing this life, this path. Their very existence an affront.

"Not just scorch marks." She stood, and he stood with her. "We're setting the table on fire." She met his eyes with lips upturned. "And Mordred will burn with me."

He snapped his fingers, a spark leaping to life above them. "I'll bring the matches."

"You've got this." Marcus gave her an encouraging smile.

Her heartrate kicked up a notch as she stepped toward the door in the secret passageways that led toward the entrance to the council chamber. But she still gave a cocky salute. "See you on the other side."

He hesitated, then embraced her. "I believe in you."

Before she could even properly return the hug, he released her and melted into the labyrinth. She shook herself and faced the door. *I believe in me, too.* She slipped out into the corridor.

Cloaked in shadows, Brinnie peered through the cracked door to the council chamber, open to allow members entrance for the day. Mordred sat at the high table, conversing with Vorath. Occupied and accounted for.

She took a fortifying breath. *Today's the day.*

She turned and ran, snapping to visibility out of breath in front of Ignatius in their chosen alcove behind a tapestry near Mordred's room. "He's occupied."

Ignatius pushed away from the wall. He wore nondescript clothes, no insignias to speak of, but featuring the red and black of Mordizan. If anyone saw him lurking where he shouldn't be, hopefully their gaze would skip over him instead of recognizing an heir. "Good. The corridor is empty." He pulled aside the tapestry and checked the hall one last time, peeking around the corner. "Coast is clear. I haven't seen anyone in half an hour." He rolled his eyes. "Which is an excessively long time to wait in a corner."

"So sorry." She gestured for him to follow. "Let's go."

He didn't move. "Where did Marcus go again?"

"He said he had to appear to welcome a visiting Master who hadn't been able to make it to the Gathering." She huffed in frustration, pushing aside the tapestry.

Luckily, Ignatius followed. "Do you believe that?"

She scowled, forcing him to keep up with her near-jogging pace, though his longer legs ate up the ground in an easy stride. "Of course."

"Fine." They came to a halt in front of the unassuming wooden door. He hovered his hand over the lock, frowning at it for so long she began to fidget. "This is a really strong spell."

"Can you undo it?"

"We'll see." His casual demeanor made her want to scream. "Put your hand on the lock."

She did as he said. "Now what?"

He laid his hand on top of hers. "You do your magic, and I'll use it to cast a neutralization spell."

"I need a bit more instruction than that."

He shrugged. "I don't know how your magic works. I've never worked with a helper before."

"I've never worked with a spellcaster either. I'm not sure how mine interacts with yours."

"Now might be a good time to figure that out."

She scowled and closed her eyes to concentrate. She knew what helping felt like—an off-balance sort of feeling, like her magic was open. Maybe neutralizing magic felt the opposite.

She concentrated, tugging her magic inward, closing it off. As she pulled, it created a force like a vacuum. She could feel the outside magic being sucked in.

"Good! Keep doing whatever you're doing. I'm going to bind the spell."

She kept her eyes clenched shut, focusing on pulling the magic in. Everything else faded as she held tightly to her concentration. She could almost see the strands and ropes of magic sucking out of the door, flowing toward her. In her mind's eye, she could sense Ignatius gathering the ends, knotting them to one another before they could reattach to the door.

"I'm done."

She opened her eyes and looked up to see that Ignatius had removed his hand. At his nod, she gave the handle a twist and pushed. The door swung open.

She stood staring for a moment. *We did it. Oh my goodness, we did it.*

"Come on." Ignatius pushed past her into the room. "We don't have long."

She jolted into action. The large room was surprisingly spare. A simple bed stood in the middle of the room across from one narrow window, accompanied by a massive, many-drawered desk with a stiff wooden chair.

She made a beeline to the desk. "It must be here." She began pulling out drawers, rifling through stacks of paper, jars of ink, and rolls of parchment.

Ignatius flicked through the drawers on the other side. "What exactly are we looking for? Weapon schematics? An incantation?"

"I'll let you know when I find it." She scooted over to his side and continued the search.

"I could help look if you would tell me."

"You helped enough with getting in. Don't worry, you'll get your information once I get mine." Although Mordred's bane probably wouldn't work against anyone else—but they would let Ignatius figure that out on his own. She sighed in frustration as none of the drawers turned up the scroll. Her last option was the locked drawer underneath the writing surface of the desk. She yanked, but it didn't open. "Do you pick locks?"

"I suppose." He pulled a wire out of his pocket and inserted it into the keyhole. Within seconds, the drawer popped open. Brinnie held her breath as she pulled the narrow drawer out.

A scroll sat in the middle next to a piece of paper covered in handwriting.

She snatched up the scroll and unrolled the parchment. "Ancient language." She spread it out on the desk and retrieved her translator stone from her pocket.

"Is this your special-weapon scroll?" Ignatius leaned over.

She waved him away. "I don't know yet. Let me read it."

Pulse pounding, she lowered to stone to the scroll and ran it over the first words. She gasped at the lines, heart ricocheting in her chest.

Myrddin's flesh and Myrddin's blood
Shall destroy the world he built.
The line of Myrddin here must die
Or all we wrought shall be in vain.
But Mordred, with his dread talent
Has cased himself in sleep.

"This is it," she breathed.

She scanned the scroll. Several lines down, the words were underlined. She ran the stone over them.

Mordred's bane, his final doom,
The heir of Arthur doth supply
With sword Excalibur in hand
His magic to destroy.

"Well?" Ignatius asked impatiently.

She glanced at him with a grin. "Just a minute." She snatched up the handwritten piece of paper from the drawer, presumably written by Mordred. Under the heading *"Remaining Descendants of Arthur,"* Merlin Ludovic's name was crossed out, followed by the unmarred names of Eira Ludovic and Brynna Ludovic. Small scrawl beneath read, *"Br kills E, only Br to watch."* Below that, a map marked with X's and circles was titled *"possible locations of Excalibur."* The rest of the paper seemed to be covered in notes on the scroll concerning how to destroy Myrddin's system and methods of finding and destroying Excalibur.

Brinnie threw the paper on the desk on top of the scroll and rolled them up together. *We did it. We actually have it.* "Okay. Let's get out of here."

"Wait." Ignatius grabbed her arm. "Do you hear that?"

The sound of boots on stone echoed down the hall. Her eyes widened, but she tried to calm her racing heart. "It's fine. It could be anyone. But we should hide."

"Agreed." Ignatius dove behind the bed and Brinnie turned invisible.

She stood by the desk, hoping, praying those footsteps would continue. Instead, cold bloomed on her arm. *No.*

The door swung open, revealing Mordred flanked by several wizards, swords drawn. Brinnie stifled a gasp. How did he know to arrive with soldiers?

He drew his blade, and Brinnie's scar burned as she caked it with shadows, trying to cover the light. "Brynna Ludovic." His glare seemed to pierce through her. "Show yourself."

Her mind raced. *He knows I broke in. How?* Her eyes widened. *Ignatius.* She scanned the doorway. No way she could break through—even if she pushed past the first line, those behind would undoubtedly cut her down. *Fine, then. Two can play at betrayal.* She darted toward Ignatius's hiding spot, dumped the scroll in front of him, then appeared in the center of the room. "Good, you're here! My lord, I discovered a thief."

The wizards moved instantly to form a circle around her. "You are the thief," Mordred said coldly.

"Oh, no." She forced a smile. "I can see how you would think that. But I was walking by when I saw Ignatius breaking in." She pointed to the spellcaster as he stood from behind the bed, hands up. "I turned invisible to see what he was doing." She shrugged. "I would have gone for you first, but I didn't want to risk him getting away without figuring out what he was up to."

Mordred continued to frown at her. "Interesting. That does not match the report I received from Marcus Vorath."

"From Marcus?" He must have misspoken.

"Yes." Mordred moved closer. "I received a messenger from him half an hour ago. He sent word of your plot."

"I hope he mentioned me." Ignatius crossed his arms.

"Of course." Mordred gave him a look of distaste. "He assured me that you were part of the plan to reveal her wrongdoing."

Her mind whirled. Marcus thought Ignatius was slimy. Why would they work together on anything? Much less betray her. "There has to be a misunderstanding." She pointed to Ignatius. "Marcus doesn't even like him."

Ignatius shook his head. "I don't know where you got that idea." He grinned. "Marcus and I have always been good friends."

She turned, meeting Mordred's cold gaze and the malicious stares of the swordsmen around her. "Don't you see I'm innocent? Do you really think Marcus would betray me? Obviously, Ignatius sent a bogus message to set me up." She appealed to Mordred. "You know what happened at the stronghold. Would I ever betray the cause I've done so much for?"

"Perhaps not as much as you would have us believe." His expression remained hard. "I spoke with Commander Ernst. And asked him for the truth."

Time seemed to stand still. No one else knew how much trouble she'd had at the stronghold. No one except Marcus—who had abandoned them for some sort of important work a little less than an hour before, leaving just enough time to send a messenger. *No. That's insane. He's on my side.* Yesterday, he had been comforting her. They had hardly seen each other this morning, but . . . "It's a lie. Even if any of it were true, Marcus wouldn't betray me."

"Why? Because he likes you?" Ignatius laughed. "There are plenty of pretty girls in Mordizan."

The garden conversation from the night of the Gathering raced through her mind. Ignatius had just happened to be close by when

Marcus had suggested including him in the plan. Were they in cahoots even then? *No. Don't be ridiculous.* "Mordred, my lord, please believe me when I say I'm innocent."

He shook his head. "I gave you every opportunity. But you've squandered it." He nodded to the swordsmen. "Arrest her."

She had no choice. She turned invisible and raised a pack of wolves around her. She sent them howling and snarling toward the men, who broke ranks, slashing against the shadow wolves. She dove through an opening, racing for the door. *Get out. Run for Wraithwood.*

Something hit her like an explosion. She flew backward, whacking her head against the stone. She blinked, willing her eyes to see. She felt as if she had looked directly into the sun.

Mordred stood over her, a ball of light in his hand. He held his shining blade to her throat, and her scar pulsed with its closeness. Panting, she gaped up at him. In the depths of his cold, dark eyes, Brinnie caught a glimpse of something strange—something bordering on regret or pain.

Then his gaze hardened again. "Bring chains," he ordered. "Take her down to the dungeons."

CHAPTER
THIRTY-SEVEN

The chain links clanked and rattled as the guards clamped them to rings in the wall. Panic overtaking reason, Brinnie fought, yanking and squirming, trying to break free of the cuffs around her wrists. She called to the shadows, tried to summon a shadow wolf, but nothing happened.

"Magic will not work here." Mordred stood in the doorway of the cell. "It wouldn't be a proper prison without containment spells."

She ceased her struggle, panting. "Please let me talk to Marcus. I'm sure we can get this straightened out. He'll tell you he never said those things."

The guards finished their work and exited. Mordred stalked forward and cupped his hand under her chin, staring deep into her eyes. "I should have known. Any descendant of mine would be a master of deception." He released her and turned away.

Descendant. Her heart seemed to freeze. "Wh . . . what?"

He turned and looked her up and down in appraisal. "Brynna Drakon. I should have seen it. A shadowmaster, from Arthur's line?" He shook his head. "You look just like Nimue."

Her mouth opened and closed. She didn't even have the presence of mind to deny it. "How did you find out?" she breathed.

"It was part of the message from Marcus Vorath." He pulled a piece of paper on Mordizan letterhead from his sleeve and unrolled it. "'She's counting on her father, Antony Drakon, to save her if you discover her,'" he read. "'Antony is not on our side. Rather, he married Eira Ludovic and is here for the express purpose of rescuing his daughter and seizing Dirklon. This, too, is why Eira is not the Master of Wraithwood.'" He rolled the paper up again and tucked it away.

The words hit her like a punch to the gut. She dropped to her knees. Outside of her own family, no one but Marcus knew about her lineage. Tears came to her eyes, and she buried her face in her hands, chains clanking. "No."

"My 'bane' is it?" Mordred paced the cell. "You would go to such lengths to kill me? And I suppose you were in a hurry to do it before you went home to Wraithwood."

Why? Why would Marcus betray me to Mordred? Not an hour ago, he'd given her a warm, encouraging smile, a spark of amusement in his eyes at her salute, even an embrace of seemingly genuine concern. How could this have happened?

Mordred stopped in front of her. "I am sorry it had to come to this. I thought we trusted one another."

She couldn't stop the tears leaking onto her cheeks, but she glared at him, trying not to show how badly her hands trembled. "I guess you're going to kill me, then. Fine. Add me to your long list of murders. But someday, someone will come along who will stop you, and all this bloodshed will come back on your head. And I hope I get to watch."

She tensed for a blow, but it didn't come. Instead, he knelt in front of her, voice soft. "Brynna. I don't want to kill you. I do not *want* to kill anyone. But there is death in war. Sacrifices must be made." His face was a mask of tender concern. "You are so young. You, Nimue, and Antony are all I have left. There is nothing I would rather do than share a perfected world with my family. You only have to let me."

She scowled and opened her mouth to retort, but reined herself in. Maybe she could still get out of this. "What do I have to do to regain your trust?"

He stood. "It is simple. You must only do what I should have required of you long ago." He folded his hands behind his back. "You must stand for an interrogation from the guards of the gate."

Her heart plummeted. Mordizan's one check against lies and deception—and a checkmate against her. "I can't tell them I support you."

"Perhaps not yet. But soon, you will." He exited the cell, closing the door. The lock clicked, and she could only see his face through the barred window. "I look forward to that day."

Then he left, and all light with him.

The darkness taunted her, reminding her of her powerlessness. She hated it—how did people stand not being able to see?

The chains clanked every time she moved, scraping over the stone floor. She'd felt every link for imperfection and twisted at the cuffs until her wrists were raw, but to no avail. She had yanked at the rings in the wall and chipped at the stonework, but they remained unmoving. Now, she slumped against the wall, staring into the darkness. She had no way to escape, no one in the fortress on her side. Marcus had betrayed her. Her father was far away at Dirklon, and with their secret revealed, Vorath had likely barred him from Mordizan. Her only hope was to convince Mordred that she was on his side, but the gatekeepers would pick up her lie in an instant.

Tears squeezed from the corners of her eyes. The reality of her situation hit her in the chest. In everything she had done so far, she'd known she had a safety net. She could flee if she needed to. Now, there was no easy way out.

Now, if she fell, she would die, spattered on the hard ground.

Not the most important thing right now. She had found Mordred's bane —the sword Excalibur. Somehow, someone needed to know. She had seen his power and experienced the ineptitude of Castelon. Mordred would win, with or without her. It was just a matter of time. She needed to pass the knowledge to someone who could defeat him.

For hours—at least, she believed it to be hours—she tried to come up with a solution. At some point, she fell asleep on the cold stone.

She was sitting in the cell, but now she could see. Dark forms swirled around the ceiling. One dropped from the vortex and partially materialized in front of her. Somehow, she knew the nebulous figure was grinning at her. "You seem to be trapped in an impossible situation." The voice wasn't so much a voice as a transmission of thought. "You have no recourse, creature of darkness. Embrace your identity, your destiny."

Brinnie awoke with a start. The door clanged open, and Mordred stepped in, carrying a plate of steaming food and a tin cup. A guard set a torch in a sconce right outside and closed the door after him.

Mordred halted in the middle of the cell, beyond the reach of her chains. "Good morning, Brynna. Or rather, good afternoon."

She sat up, wincing. Everything hurt—her muscles from sleeping on stone, her wrists from the manacles. "You left me in here for a whole day?"

"I thought it best to let you think for a while. Here." He handed her the plate and cup. "I imagine you must be hungry."

She squinted at the food, a stew with meat, potatoes, and carrots. It smelled heavenly. Her stomach rumbled, but she set the plate aside. "Sorry, but I find it hard to trust you at the moment."

"In all this time, have I ever tried to hurt you? You know better." He sighed. "I welcomed you here. I gave you every opportunity. I gave you an education and allowed you to do as you pleased. I never forced you to do anything. Was any of this so bad? You made friends here—even a friend who was perhaps more than a friend."

"Who then betrayed me," Brinnie said dryly.

"Was it really betrayal?"

She held up her manacles. "Well, seeing as I'm sitting in a cell in chains, I'd say yes."

"I regret that you must be in this position, but I know you." He put a hand to his heart. "You are much like me. Though I would rather keep you in comfort, you would escape anything less. For your own well-being, you must stay here for now."

She snorted. *Yes, obviously being kept in a dungeon is for my own good.*

He knelt beside her. "I know you feel the pain of betrayal. But Marcus didn't see it that way. He cares about you. He saw that he had no hope of convincing you of the truth. So he contacted me. He, too, wants what is best for you."

She raised an eyebrow. "Clearly."

Mordred stood. "What more can I do to convince you, child? Why do you persist in your delusions?"

"Why do you persist in yours?" she shot back. There was no point in acting anymore—the guards of the gate would detect any deception.

"Why can't you accept the world the way it is? Why do you have to have power? Why do you have to kill people?"

"Because I believe in something better." He folded his hands calmly.

"For who?" She hauled herself to her feet. "It seems to me that for most people, it will be a lot worse."

He shook his head. "You studied this at the University. You know what we believe and why. You and others like you are all that stand in the way of a perfected world."

"You *can't* perfect the world. You're not God." She clenched her fists. "And I don't think He would take kindly to you purging the parts of His world you don't think are good enough."

"Now you sound like my mother." He sighed. "Humans with their fragility, their petty squabbles, their hatred, prejudice, stupidity—they're dragging this world down, destroying it. Even Myrddin's curse, meant to protect them, instead hurts us, destroying our magic." He swept out an arm. "If humans were eradicated, there would be peace on earth. Without fighting, we would never die. No one would need to be sick or suffer. In a liberated world, we wizards would be gods."

Her mouth opened. He had a literal god complex. There was no reasoning with him. "You're insane."

"I'm right." He strode forward and put a hand on her shoulder, making her shudder. "Don't you want to rule a perfected world?"

"No. Not in the slightest." She huffed in frustration. "If you or me or any of us ruled, it wouldn't *be* a perfect world. Wizard, human—none of us were meant to rule like that."

His expression grew stony, and he stepped away. "I do not want to hurt you, but I will if that is what it takes."

"If you kill me, it won't make a difference. I still won't join you."

"There are worse fates than death." His steely glare made her blood run cold.

She forced her back straight. "You don't scare me."

"I give you one last chance." He held out his hand. "As my granddaughter. Won't you join me?"

She closed her eyes briefly. "And as your granddaughter, I give you another chance. Won't you give up this insanity?"

His jaw set. "You have made your decision. What will happen to you is not my fault. Tomorrow, it begins. One way or another, you will do my bidding." He took the plate and cup and knocked on the door. The guard came to open it, taking the torch from the wall.

Mordred turned to glare at her one last time. "May all the vengeance due Arthur fall upon you."

The cell door slammed open. Brinnie struggled to her feet as Ignatius stepped in, grinning. "Good morning, beautiful."

She glared at him and said nothing.

He laughed. "I'm looking forward to this. I like a challenge." He looked her up and down. "What's your weakness? Bribes? Physical pain? Psychosis? Phobias?" His grin grew wider. "I guess we'll find out." He gestured, and four guards entered the cell.

Brinnie couldn't bring herself to make any retort as the guards took hold of the chains connected one each to her wrists and ankles. She wanted to give a smart response, maybe ask Ignatius if hurting others helped him feel better about himself, but it wouldn't change anything.

She was alone, betrayed, without hope.

The guards surrounded her as they followed Ignatius through the damp stone tunnel outside her cell. They emerged in a spacious room filled with strange equipment. Chains hung from the ceiling, racks of weapons lined the walls, and a table was covered with whips and other unidentifiable instruments of torture next to a brazier filled with glowing coals.

Her heart began beating faster. Her imaginings hadn't quite prepared her for this. She attempted to summon shadows, but still nothing. This place must also be protected by containment spells.

Ignatius turned to her. "Welcome to my reeducation chamber." He smirked. "Are you ready for your first lesson?"

CHAPTER THIRTY-EIGHT

She huddled on the cold stone with her back to the wall, trying to stay warm in the shreds of her clothes. She pulled her knees in closer to her chest.

Days, years, months, she didn't know. Didn't know how long the terrible cycle repeated itself in the reeducation chamber. It always started simple—Ignatius offering her warm clothes, freedom, anything she wanted if she would give in. He waved steaming soup in front of her and ate it in her sight, offering the food to her if she would pledge herself to Mordred. After she refused, he would move on to his darker imaginings. He was an artist of misery, concocting new "lessons" each day. As long as he didn't think she would die—and he liked to push it as close as he could—he would then dump her in her cell, sometimes bleeding, sometimes burned, sometimes broken, and often all of the above. He would leave her there until right before the next session, when the guards would escort her to a healer so that she would be able to withstand the next round.

After the first session, she had been barely conscious, but after the second, she was able to recognize the healer. "Leslie!" she had gasped out.

The blonde woman said nothing and began her work, laying Brinnie on her stomach to magically seal the wounds on her back left by Ignatius's whip.

"Do you remember me?" Brinnie's breath rasped in her lungs. "I saw you that day with Marcus, when I accidentally broke his nose."

Leslie pressed her lips together and didn't make eye contact.

Brinnie was too weak to try any further. Once her wounds were healed, she gave a grateful smile. "Thank you."

Leslie glanced at her quickly, gave a sharp nod, and left. The guards yanked Brinnie's chains and led her back to her cell.

After several visits with Leslie, Brinnie learned not to try to make conversation. The healer refused to even make eye contact. Brinnie wondered if she had been ordered not to speak. And so the days slipped into monotony, a single blur of pain and darkness.

Now, shivering in her cell, Brinnie felt she was waking from a terrible dream. Ignatius had told her that he would be gone for a few days and didn't want her dying while he was away, so he'd had her healed. She didn't care what his motives were—she was just glad to have a precious few days free of pain.

If I could have some food, it would be a regular party. She was given plenty of water, but food came so sporadically she couldn't keep track of the frequency. She felt like she had been there for an eternity, but it might have only been a month. She had lost track of the days during week three, but that felt long ago. *We'll call this the Brinnie diet. Guaranteed to help you lose weight, or your freedom back.*

She sighed and closed her eyes, determined to enjoy this reprieve. The first couple of weeks, she'd cried, tried every means of escape, argued with Ignatius. She eventually learned that crying only wore her out, escape was impossible, and Ignatius couldn't be persuaded. The only time she had any magical power was when she went to the healer, but four guards held her down, each holding a chain leading to her arms and legs. When she'd tried to turn invisible and escape, she found herself with a knife to her invisible throat in seconds.

Instead, she slept for hours on end, drifting in and out of feverish dreams. With nothing else to do, nothing to distract her from her pain, she replayed the plots of her favorite books in her head. Tales of hope, tales of heroes, tales even of small magic and found family and everyday concerns. And when she ran out of stories she could remember, she made up more of her own. With the clearer mind afforded by these few days of reprieve, she remembered more tales, storing them in her memory to retell to herself when the pain threatened to overtake her again.

She had to hang on to the stories, let them hold her mind, keep her sane. Sane until the day finally came when Ignatius pushed her too far, and she could join Uncle Merlin in the next life where he'd always promised he would see her.

A restful cycle of pain-free sleep continued. She didn't know for how long. It could have been one day or three. But at some point, as she lay on the hard ground, the door clanged open and she sat up, expecting that Ignatius had returned. Instead, she blinked at the figure in the doorway, trying to make sense of the dark hair, the Mordizan colors—the devastated, horrified expression. Her eyes widened. "Marcus?"

"Brinnie." He took two lurching steps forward as if he would run to her, then stopped himself short as two guards followed him into the cell. His voice wobbled before he brought it under control, straightening. His expression morphed into a stone mask. "I'm sorry. I would have come to see you sooner, but I've been away at the strongholds ever since . . . *this* happened."

"*This*?" She gave a rasping laugh. "You mean your betrayal."

She refused to feel guilty for relishing the pain that flashed across his face at her words. "I would never betray you."

"Oh, really?" She held up her chains. "I guess you'd call this a friendly intervention?"

He looked at her for a long moment, jaw clenching, unclenching. His fingers twitched. What, was he angry? Did that hurt his *feelings*? She couldn't summon the energy to roll her eyes.

One of the guards cleared his throat.

Marcus shifted. "Yes, well. I brought you something." He held out a hand to the guard on his left, taking a plate.

"No, thank you."

"Here." He held out the dish. On it were two pieces of toast and a huge lump of butter.

She made no move to take it. *Yes, Marcus, toast makes all of this better.*

He set the plate down in front of her. "I hope you enjoy it. Be careful. The butter's kind of slippery."

He hesitated, taking a second longer to rise than was necessary, and for a moment she could have sworn she saw tears in his eyes.

But then he nodded to the guards, and they exited. The door clanged shut behind them.

Brinnie stared after him. She hardly believed his story about being away the whole time. It sounded like a convenient reason not to face what he had done to her. *What sort of peace offering is this? Weird toast? Real touching, Marcus.*

She wasn't sure how much time had passed since Ignatius left, but she knew she hadn't received any food in that time. She dipped her finger in the butter and began to spread it on the toast. Then she froze. *"Be careful. The butter's kind of slippery."*

No way. He wouldn't.

She had a plan.

"Wonderful to see you again." Ignatius stepped into the cell with a grin. "Have you heard the news? Of course not. All but two of the strongholds have fallen."

"Two strongholds and twenty-three estates to go. Or is it twenty-four now, counting Dirklon?" She rolled her eyes. "Yes, sounds like you're very close to taking over the world."

He snorted. "You can't change my mood. But I can certainly put a damper on yours." He glanced down at the floor. "Why do you have a plate of butter?"

Brinnie glanced at the guards, different ones than had entered with Marcus. She scowled. "Someone thought it would be funny to give me only butter to eat while you were gone."

He laughed. "Good, looks like you have enough rations for this week. Guards, you know what to do."

She returned to the cell two hours later, bleeding and bruised but grinning. Instead of sleeping off her pain, she stayed awake, trying to keep track of the time. When she thought she had waited long enough, she dipped her fingers in the butter—or rather, a coating of butter over an even more slippery, lubricating substance.

She began slathering it on her wrists. One at a time, she carefully rotated the cuffs, wiggling and pulling. She tucked her thumb and slathered on more around the joint, twisting and yanking. She grimaced as the cuff scraped and pushed at the stubborn joint. Finally, with one last pull, the cuff ripped the skin from her thumb and popped off her slippery, emaciated hand and almost clattered to the floor before she caught the shackle and set it gently beside her chains.

She continued to the other hand and after that began working on her ankles. Her feet cramped as she pushed and contorted them. Blood trickled from her heels. She began to sweat even in the cold dungeon. *Please, please don't let two heels keep me trapped in this dungeon.*

Her teeth gritted, she shoved one ankle cuff with both hands with all her might. Slowly, it skidded until the shackle finally slid past her heel and clanked around her toes. She almost cried in relief. She did the same to the other, slathering it with the slippery substance and setting pain aside in her quest for freedom.

Finally, she sat panting with four empty cuffs around her. Step one complete. Now for the hard part.

She slid the cuffs partially over her hands and feet. If anyone looked, it would be obvious they weren't actually on, but she hoped the guards wouldn't notice. She hid her feet underneath her and buried her hands in her lap. Now it was time to wait.

Not long after, the door swung open and four guards entered as usual. Looking somewhat bored, they took hold of her chains and yanked her off toward the healing room. She held on tight to the cuffs. Her ruse would be blown if she accidentally let one drop.

She took her time on the way, shuffling more slowly than usual. Luckily the rattling of her chains masked the clanking of her ankle cuffs on the stone. One of the guards gave her a shove, smashing her tattered clothing into her wounds. "Hurry up." She stumbled and said nothing, picking up the pace for only a few seconds before slowing down again.

She needed all the time she could get for her powers to return.

Her vision expanded. Shadows twitched in the corners. *Soon.*

Once in the alcove with a stone table that served as the healing room, Brinnie's heart pounded at the risk she planned to take. Her legs could barely hold her up—she would never make it out of the fortress in this state. Instead of running, she would wait to be healed. She could only hope Leslie wouldn't register the loose cuffs.

Leslie entered, stoic as usual. She placed a hand on Brinnie's head, sensing her injuries. But once she opened her eyes, she didn't step away as she usually did. She met Brinnie's gaze, and their eyes locked.

She knows. Brinnie's heart stopped, completely at Leslie's mercy.

Instead, she winked.

Leslie healed Brinnie's wounds, closing up the major gashes. Brinnie wasn't sure, but it felt like Leslie did a more thorough job than usual on even the smaller wounds.

Once she finished, the healer nodded to the guards. Her eyes turned one final time to Brinnie, and she scratched her nose.

Her nose. She'd treated Marcus's nose the first time they met. She was Marcus's cousin.

Were they working together?

Before Brinnie could think on it further, Leslie turned and left. The guards pulled on her chains and Brinnie stood. As she walked out the door, she allowed the cuffs to slide down her hands and feet until they rested on her toes and fingertips.

Then, right as they dropped, she turned invisible.

The guards all yanked at the chains, but they only dragged empty cuffs swinging through the air. Brinnie took off at a stumbling run. Behind her, the guards yelled and snatched at nothing. She rounded the corner, mapping out the way in her mind. The path was somewhat fuzzy—she had been more focused on struggling than planning an escape route when she'd been dragged down to the dungeon in chains. But even then, part of her had been putting her limited navigational skills to use, committing as much as she could to memory.

Most of that memory told her to go up.

Two guards came charging after her, shouting. No doubt the others had gone the opposite direction. She couldn't outrun them, so she pressed herself against the wall as they passed. One yelled, "I'll keep chasing her. You get Lord Mordred!"

Brinnie stumbled along the hall to the stairs spiraling at the end and clambered upward. With each ascension, her legs shook more violently. Leslie might have healed her outer wounds, but that only did so much for an emaciated, beaten body.

After several turns and flights of stairs, she came to a hall with a window. *Ground level.* She could cry for delight.

Instead, shouting sounded behind her. She flattened herself against the wall as a squad of six guards quick-marched past her. From somewhere overhead, a bell began to toll. A bell for her.

She ricocheted through the halls and corridors, finally bursting out into blinding sunlight. She threw her hands over her eyes and heaped more shadows upon herself to hide from the penetrating rays. She recognized the inner courtyard and ran half-blind through the first gate, past the oblivious guards. Her bare feet pounded into the outer courtyard. She could almost taste freedom. She flew toward the outer gate.

And squinted up in shock. It was closed.

She should have known. Of course they would close the gate to prevent her escape.

You'll have to try harder, Mordred. Her gasps for air rattled in her chest as she ran for the guardhouse and stumbled inside.

Sitting at the table were none other than Betram and Stephan. *Thank goodness.* The very guards who had joked about how ineffectual they would be against someone trying to open the gates. Tiptoeing, she slunk past them.

"Haven't caught her yet, sounds like." Stephan looked upward, presumably toward the bells. "Crazy to think we had Brynna Ludovic sitting at our table—what, a few months ago?"

Betram leaned back in his chair. "Too bad about her being thrown in the dungeon. She seemed nice. Didn't seem evil or anything."

Brinnie examined the many gears, chains, cranks, and ropes. Why was it more complicated than the one at the stronghold?

The bells continued to clang. "I liked her." Brinnie glanced back in time to see Stephan shudder. "Glad she didn't kill us."

"I don't think she'd do something like that." Betram drummed his fingers on the table. "You know, everyone hated Merlin, but he sounded like an honorable sort of fellow. I heard he let an entire squadron of human soldiers go after he defeated the wizards—said he didn't have any quarrel with them."

"That's decent."

Brinnie leaned against an important-looking lever, pushing with all her might.

"Yeah," she heard Betram continue. "They say he's too weak to kill anyone, but I've heard the stories of what he did to some wizards. Seems he could do it just fine, but preferred not to."

The lever lurched forward with a screech, something grated, and Brinnie fell, tripping onto her hands and knees.

Betram and Stephan both stared at the wall of gears. "What was that?" Betram asked.

"You don't think . . ."

"Nah." But he didn't seem convinced.

Brinnie remained absolutely still until they turned back around. Then she examined the other levers and cranks. *Which one is it?* She yanked on a promising crank, but instead of anything happening, a rope released, and a sandbag fell to the floor.

This time both of them jumped up. Stephan grabbed a coffee mug and held it up like a weapon. "She can turn invisible, right?"

"Hey!" Betram put up his fists in a fighting stance. "We know you're in here. You'll never figure out that gate—it takes two people to open it. You might as well show yourself."

She weighed her options. Mordred would be coming quickly with the blade. If opening the gate really was a two-man job, she needed help. They had been kind to her once. It was a long shot, but maybe they would do it again, just as Leslie had unexpectedly decided not to blow her cover.

Even better, these men would know she wasn't lying when she told them what horrible things Mordred had in store.

Holding onto the crank for support, Brinnie returned to visibility. "Please. I'm not trying to hurt anyone. I only want to get out of here before Mordred finds me."

"Not exactly the truth," Stephan remarked. "I'll call the guards."

"Wait." Betram stepped forward. "Look at her. She's skin and bones."

More truth, give them more truth. "Please don't turn me in. They torture me, every day, and then they heal me again so they can torture me some more. I'm lucky to get bread once a week. Please let me go."

"She's telling the truth." Betram's brow furrowed.

"Betram!" Stephan waved his mug. "She's an escaped prisoner."

"I don't want to hurt you. I'm trying to escape because I care about people like you. Mordred wants to kill you all—all humans. He wants to take over the earth for wizards only. I have a way to stop him. But I need to escape to do that."

Betram and Stephan looked at each other.

"She certainly believes it to be truth," Stephan said finally.

"It *is.*" Brinnie held back tears of frustration. "Can't you tell? That's your job!"

Betram rubbed his chin. "That's the funny thing. We can't tell when someone's telling the truth—we can only tell when they're lying. A lie is on purpose, but a person can be completely wrong about the truth without knowing it."

Ridiculous. Absolutely ridiculous that she would be playing a high stakes game of Truth or Dare for her life. "I swear to you I've heard from Mordred himself about these plans. You don't have to help me. Just don't stop me."

"Now that is pretty compelling," Stephan admitted.

Betram plopped down in his chair. "I'm not helping a fugitive escape." He tapped his chin. "But if I was, I'd tell them there's a rope ladder on the other side of the guardhouse for guards who need to get up there fast. A person could climb up the wall and use it to get down the other side."

"I wouldn't tell anyone I don't like Mordred, but I don't like Mordred," Stephan piped up.

Betram waved him off. "You're not doing it right. You have to say it like—"

"Thank you so much!" She cut them off. "You've been kind twice. Hopefully someday I'll be able to properly thank you."

"Just keep Lord Mordred from killing us all. That should be enough." Betram winked.

She returned to invisibility and dashed outside. Guards lined the gate and marched to and fro around the courtyard. She skirted the guardhouse, ducking into the alcove between the protrusion of the guardhouse and the wall.

As promised, a long rope ladder led up the wall.

Brinnie set her foot on the first rung and painfully hauled herself upward. The ladder swayed, rope biting into her palms. She heaved herself up again, and again, and again.

By the time she reached the top, her breath came in gasps like she was breathing shards of glass, and every muscle trembled. She fell prone onto the top of the wall.

Guards stood stationed along the wall in regular intervals, but the closest was at least ten yards away. She rolled to her feet and pulled up the rope ladder hand over hand before unfastening the rope from the iron pegs driven into the wall holding it up. She dragged the ladder to the other side of the wall and tied the ends around a crenel. She yanked on her knots to make sure they were secure. She didn't know much about knots—knitting techniques didn't come in handy here. She would just have to hope for the best. She pushed the ladder over the edge.

The rope ladder slapped against the wall, but luckily the sound of the bells drowned out the noise enough that the nearest guards didn't turn to look. Brinnie slipped over the edge and stepped one foot gingerly onto the first rung. The rope creaked, but the knots held. She descended as quickly as she could.

About a quarter of the way down, she felt the ladder sliding. She looked up to see the rope slowly pulling out of the knots. Her heart raced. At this height, if she fell, she would be a Brinnie pancake.

She descended faster. She made it about halfway down when the knots on one side of the ladder fell through completely. Her weak grip wasn't enough to keep her hanging as the ropes jerked and swung. The ladder rotated and she thudded into the wall. The force dislodged her, and she fell toward the cobblestone, crashing down into the street.

She tried to bend her knees as she made impact. Her ankle buckled with a horrendous popping sound, and she collapsed. As the wooden slats in the rope ladder clacked against the wall, she looked up to see one of the guards leaning over. She saw him shout something over his shoulder. Invisible or not, the ladder provided a dead giveaway. They knew she was outside the fortress.

She pulled herself up using the side of the wall. Her foot felt both numb and on fire at the same time. She decided not to look at it. Instead, she held onto buildings, carts, and stalls, bouncing off passersby, hobbling into the city. Behind her, she heard the gates begin to creak open.

She pushed through the crowd, not caring who felt her strange, invisible presence. "Clear the streets!" someone yelled. Wizards began flowing into the nearby shops, out of the way of a unit of soldiers. Brinnie's scar tingled.

Mordred was coming.

There was no way she would make it out of Mordizan in this condition, let alone escape from Mordred's blade on foot in unfamiliar territory.

But someone else might be able to.

Though wizards had cleared the street, the brooms kept their usual path, stopping, starting, flying off again. She scrambled onto the platform and grabbed the first broom headed for the northwest—the artisan's quadrant.

After taking a breather while riding the broom, Brinnie managed to dismount and resume her hurried waddle until the eclectic storefront came into view—Oswald's Emporium.

She burst inside and the bell jangled madly. To her dismay, a handful of shoppers browsed, creating an unwanted audience. Hanging onto shelves, she made her way to the counter where Goddensfeld stood discussing his wares with a customer. She slipped behind the counter, hobbling up beside him until she could lean over and whisper in his ear, "If you're a friend of Merlin, meet me in back right now."

He gave no indication that anything strange had occurred. "Well, I think I might have something in the back like what you're looking for," he told the customer. "Let me go check."

Once he entered the back room, Brinnie followed him in and slunk into a corner between shelves of odds and ends, waiting.

He scanned the room. "Brynna Ludovic?"

Relief coursed through her. She turned visible.

His eyes widened. "Rumor had it you were dead."

"Not quite." She held onto a shelf for support. "I don't have much time. What side are you on, and why are you here in Mordizan?"

"Merlin's side." He stepped closer. "This shop is my cover to collect information that I pass along. I haven't been able to get any information out since Mordred's takeover, though. Security increased —the messengers were all killed."

"Thank goodness." She slumped against the shelf. "Er, not about the messengers. About you being on our side." She leaned forward.

"Mordred is going to find me soon, so you have to find a way to pass on this information. I found Mordred's bane. It's the sword Excalibur. The ancient prophecies say that a descendant of Arthur will use it to destroy his magic. It's all written down in his room, in a drawer."

His mouth dropped open. "That's better news than I could have hoped to hear. I'll do everything I can to get the message out." He stepped forward, reaching out an arm to steady her. "But what about you? You're injured. We have to—"

Cold ripped through Brinnie's scar. She cursed her aching body that hadn't noticed the coolness slowly growing. "I have to run. Before they find you too." She glanced around and limped toward the back door of the shop. She threw it open, poised to run.

Only to find a blade pointed directly at her chest.

"Quite the escape." Mordred looked down his nose at her stonily. "Congratulations. You have led us right to that last annoying little rat."

CHAPTER THIRTY-NINE

Mordred nodded to the soldiers behind him. "Take them."

Brinnie turned invisible, but Mordred grabbed her arm, nails digging into her skin. Before she could even summon shadow wolves to attack, he yanked her forward and slammed the hilt of his blade into her skull.

Everything went black.

The next thing she knew, stone scraped beneath her feet as rough hands dragged her. Chains clanked against the ground, the familiar dark stone of the fortress. As her vision cleared, she recognized the passageway. Within moments, the two guards shoved her into Ignatius' reeducation chamber and clamped her to the stone chair complete with rings for holding the chains of prisoners.

Mordred stepped in with a maddening grin. "I'm sure you thought you were clever. We'll see how smart you think you are after this." He motioned behind him, and two guards came forward, dragging a shackled Oswald Goddensfeld between them, his head bowed. They fastened his chains to loops in the wall, stretching out his arms above his shining bald head. Then they bowed to Mordred and left.

"Three months. I've given that fool Ignatius three months to change your mind. But it seems you have brought about your own doom in a matter of hours." He drew a short sword from a rack on the wall and smiled. "I seem to recall a certain aversion to harming others."

Brinnie's heart raced. "You think I care at this point?" she bluffed. "I watched dozens die at the stronghold."

"But you can stop this one." He held the sword to Goddensfeld's throat.

"That's not going to work. I don't care if you kill him."

"Lie." Brinnie turned her head to see a tall, angular man enter the room beside Ignatius.

"As you can see, I've asked someone to assist us." Mordred gestured. "Meet Irten, a guard of the gate."

Brinnie bit her lip. This just got a whole lot harder.

Mordred turned to Ignatius. "Now. Watch how this is done." He balanced his weapon and ran the blade along Goddensfeld's pale cheek until a trickle of blood dripped from his chin, never breaking eye contact with Brinnie. "This will be no easy death for him. It will be long and painful. But you can avert it. Do what I asked of you, and I'll let him live."

Brinnie glanced at Irten. "May I have a confirmation that your promise is true?"

Irten began to open his mouth, but Mordred interrupted. "I ask the questions. You must trust me."

Brinnie hesitated. Maybe, if she agreed to do what Mordred wanted, he would let Goddensfeld go free, and Goddensfeld would be able to defeat Mordred before she actually had to do the deed. "Fine. If you let him go completely free, I'll do it."

"Lie."

Brinnie's mouth dropped open. "What?"

Irten looked at her impassively. "You have no intention of following through."

Her mind raced. How could she fix this? How long would it take Goddensfeld to escape and relay the news, and for someone to find Excalibur, get to Mordred, and kill him? By that time, Mordred would have used her power to defeat the last two strongholds, if not some of the estates as well. How many lives would be lost? She shook her head. "You're right. I don't. I'm not going to kill hundreds of people to save one man's life."

"She's uncertain," Irten stated.

Brinnie opened her mouth to protest, but Goddensfeld rattled at the chains. "Don't comply. Whatever it is, it isn't worth my life."

"Silence." Mordred smacked him with the broad side of his sword. He looked at Brinnie. "So that is your decision. Shall I kill him, then?"

"No, wait!" Dizziness pierced her skull, nausea roiling in her gut.

"Please think about this. Why do you even need me? Just let him go. You seem to be doing fine defeating strongholds on your own."

Instead of replying, Mordred slashed downward. Goddensfeld cried out as blood gushed from his thigh.

"Mordred, please! Don't do this. Why would you do this?"

"Decide." He swung again. More blood.

"No!" Tears streamed down her face. Her throat burned. She couldn't let someone innocent die right in front of her when she could stop it.

"Will you cooperate?"

She hesitated, and Mordred slashed once again. Goddensfeld yelled and gasped, "Just let me die."

"Please, Mordred." Her chest heaved with sobs.

"Have you ever wondered what life would be like without one of your arms?"

Brinnie squeezed her eyes shut, screaming to drown out the terrible sound. How could she give in? How could she agree to something that would cause so much death?

Brinnie heard another noise and a cry of pain. "It's all right," Goddensfeld gasped out. "Brynna, I'll give Merlin your regards."

Brinnie forced her eyelids open and locked eyes with the bleeding, mutilated man. "I'm so, so sorry."

"Don't be." He smiled slightly. "I've fought the good fight. Now it's your turn."

Tears streamed, squeezing through her eyelashes and dripping from her chin as she turned away. Every stroke of the blade, every scream resonated in her ears. Finally, silence.

She waited until she heard footsteps approaching. She opened her eyes and Mordred grabbed her chin with a sticky, bloodied hand. "This is the blood of the man you killed."

She felt the heat rise to her face. She glared at him. "No. The man *you* killed. Tell me, do you feel good about yourself after that?"

"I will do whatever is necessary to ensure the future." He let go of her. "How long will you resist? How many must die before you give in?" He nodded as she clenched her teeth. "You didn't think he was the only one, did you? I'm not afraid to kill. Will you let *children* die for your stubbornness?"

She gripped the arms of the chair. *He'll do it. He'd send a thousand people to the grave if he thought it would help him get his way.* Her head fell. What choice did she have? No matter what she did, people would die.

"Consider that. I'm going to send for those who will die for you. In the meantime, you think about your choices."

Numb with the impossibility of her situation, Brinnie found herself staring ahead, left alone with Ignatius and the guards. Her tears mixed with the drying blood of Oswald Goddensfeld, running down her cheeks.

Could she really do it? Could she help Mordred defeat the final strongholds standing between the enchantment wizards and annihilation? Either way, people would die. Mordred wouldn't stop until she did what he wanted.

She had fought, had stayed alive hoping to pass on news of Mordred's bane, stayed alive as the Master of Wraithwood. If she died, it would go the way of Baronstead, a masterless estate. The dark wizards would take it over. They would kill her family—whoever remained with Anna and David somewhere else in this dungeon. So she had lived, for them.

The nightmares from before she went to the seventh stronghold haunted her mind, of the two alternatives where she stood either as Mistress of Shadows or among the burning remains of Wraithwood. Was there any other path?

Time slowed, sped, morphed, until she sat facing a saucer-eyed little girl at the end of Mordred's blade. "Stop." She broke down sobbing. "I'll do what you wanted me to do."

"Truth," Irten announced.

They left her chained to the chair for the night. Brinnie shivered against the cold stone, back aching. Each heartbeat pulsed in her chest like a wound, a reminder she lived while so many others did not.

That morning, the door clanged open. One guard nodded to the two others standing watch on either side of her. They stepped forward wordlessly and dragged her to her feet and out into the passageway.

As they made their way toward the surface, Brinnie saw a party approaching up ahead. Two guards dragged a figure with long blonde hair between them while another followed holding a torch in one hand and a spear aimed at the prisoner with the other.

Brinnie blinked. Were her eyes deceiving her? "Lana?"

One of her guards smacked her and ordered silence, but she ignored him. The figure lifted her head, then bounced forward, straining against her bonds. "Brinnie! Brinnie, they're free. Get away —save us all!"

"Shut up." The guard with the spear drove the spear butt into her back.

"What?" Brinnie dug in her feet, resisting as her guards tried to push her forward. "Lana! What do you mean? Are you okay?"

One of Brinnie's guards backhanded her. As she recovered from the slap, she saw Lana's jailers dragging her off into another passageway. "Lana! Wait! What are you doing to her? Why is she down here?"

"Enough." Brinnie's guards shoved her forward. "Walk."

Her mind churned. What was Lana, a faithful supporter of Mordizan, doing in the dungeon? *"They're free."* Who was "they"?

Her eyes widened. Was it possible?

She freed Anna and David.

The guards marched her out into the courtyard. She squinted in the bright morning sun, head spinning. Mordred stood alone in the center of the courtyard, cloak flapping in the cold wind, waiting for them. In one hand he held the Case of the Master Key, in the other his enchanted blade. Her scar burned with cold.

Once they were in earshot, Brinnie asked, "Where's your conquering army?"

"Pillaging, I would assume. Another stronghold fell last night. Only one remains, manned with the best warriors of Artema. An army waits for us there."

Brinnie's stomach turned. Only one stronghold left. "So we'll get there in a few days?" Maybe she could escape during transport.

"No. In a few moments." He sheathed his blade and pulled out a shimmering orb. A portal. "I suggest you don't try to escape. If you don't exit the portal, you will be lost forever in scattered pieces of matter."

Maybe that wouldn't be so bad. "Got it."

The guards positioned her close, and Mordred smashed the portal on the ground. The mist enveloped them, obscuring their surroundings. "This way." The guards pushed her forward to follow Mordred. As they walked, the mist faded away and grass tickled her toes.

A low roaring, crashing sound met her ears. As the mist faded, it revealed a dramatic landscape. They stood on a cliff jutting out into the ocean, surrounded on three sides by crags leading down to a rocky coastline and tumultuous waves. At the far end of the cliff, a stronghold of weathered stone loomed against the overcast horizon, like a castle ruin in Ireland or Scotland. But nothing about this castle had fallen into disrepair—the walls soared high and smooth, then jutted outward to discourage climbing. The two-layered gate mirrored that of the seventh stronghold, iron bars before a massive door of heavy timber. Arrow slits slashed the tops of guard towers, while tall crenellation offered protection on the wall. Brinnie could see figures peering over the crenels from time to time, while an arrow occasionally flew from an arrow slit.

In the foreground, a cohort of dark wizards worked war machines, catapulting boulders and fiery missiles at the stronghold. However, Brinnie had to glance over her shoulder to see the majority of the army. Lines of tents stretched all the way back to the mainland. The projectiles seemed to be a half-hearted attempt to keep the defenders occupied. The rest of the army was waiting.

Waiting for her.

"Two hundred warriors behind those walls." Mordred smiled. "Their power shall be mine."

Brinnie's brow furrowed. "What?"

"Did I not tell you?" His smirk grew. "Magic cannot simply disappear. Once absorbed by the Case, it must be transmitted. Ordinarily, it would be transmitted back into the Key. As it is, you will use the Case as a conduit to direct the magic to me."

Her jaw dropped. "You'll be the most powerful wizard to ever live."

"I already am that." His eyes flashed with a crazed glee. "Unlike yours, my magic is unlimited in possibility without the effect of Myrddin's curse. But the extra strength from their power will be most welcome." He turned and raised his arm toward the army behind them. "The time has come."

Trumpets blew throughout the camp. Hundreds of wizards poured forward, forming ranks behind where Mordred and Brinnie stood. She fought back nausea. Once the defenders had no magic, they wouldn't stand a chance against such a massive army.

One man strode forward, ahead of the ranks. As he approached, Brinnie recognized Marcus, dressed in chain mail with a sword on his hip. Her heart beat faster.

He bowed slightly to Mordred. "The army is ready, my lord."

"Very good. I appreciated your help the other day." Mordred glanced at Brinnie. "She did indeed lead us to the final spy."

"I knew she was clever enough to figure out what it was for." Marcus turned emotionless eyes on her. "She would never let others die for her."

Brinnie's eyes slowly widened. A trick. She'd been foolish enough to think he'd offered her help. Instead, her "escape" was planned? Her pulse pounded with rage. "You sick, twisted, deceiving—" She lurched toward him, but the guards held her back.

He nodded impassively. "Any opportunity can be used in more than one way." His gaze sharpened on her. "Motives aren't always what they seem."

Her blood boiled. Goddensfeld's death, her presence here—all Marcus's fault.

Before she could rail at him again, Mordred's voice cut through the air.

"My fellow wizards." Mordred addressed the assembly, his voice amplified, presumably by magic. "Today, the last stronghold falls!"

A roaring cheer crashed over the waves.

"Today, we will strip Artema of its strength. The magic of the enchantment wizards will be taken from them. Our enemy will be no more than human scum to crush beneath our feet!"

The cheers continued. Mordred wheeled, and Marcus signaled to the army. In a fluid motion, the horde advanced toward the castle. The wizards manning the siege engines fell back, melting into the army, leaving Mordred, Brinnie, Marcus, and her guards several dozen yards ahead.

When they reached the siege engines, Mordred halted and held out the Case to Brinnie. He leaned close. "Remember, if you do not do this, I will kill until you do." He straightened. "One way or another, people will die. You get to decide how many extra will die for your persuasion."

She glared at him as she took the Case in her manacled hands. Mordred put his hands on her shoulders, fingers digging into her skin. She winced.

"Now," he said softly, "Reach out. Sense the wizards in the stronghold. Find their magic. Then open the Case and drain that magic into me."

She felt tears trickle down her cheeks. *I can't do this.*

But she had to. She knew now. Mordred would get his way, no matter what. She couldn't stand against him. All she could do was try to keep the death toll to a minimum.

"Some people have the luxury to make all good decisions, choices they won't regret," Marcus had once said. *"We aren't those people."*

"I'm setting the table on fire," she'd said. *"And Mordred will burn with me."*

She closed her eyes and reached out with her senses. Inside the stronghold, she felt them, dozens and dozens of wizards with a score of different talents. Their magic pulsed, danced, called to her. With slow steps, she drew closer to the stronghold, Mordred and the guards keeping her tightly under rein.

Then she opened the Case.

CHAPTER
FORTY

Brinnie gasped and nearly fell backward at the force of the magic slamming into her.

Her magic grasped that force and pulled, flowing through the open Case. She felt her power amplify, flow like massive, snapping jaws, clamping onto the magic of the wizards in the stronghold, using the Case as a conduit to amplify her pull to an irresistible level.

Screams rang out from behind the walls.

Her whole body tingled. Her cells seemed to vibrate, and her skin burned where Mordred's fingers dug into her shoulders. She felt the instability of the Case, felt it spitting the magic back out into the nearest receptor, her. From her, the power flowed into Mordred, who cackled with delight, his hands searing into her skin like brands.

Then his grasp ripped away as he yelled. Brinnie tried to turn to see, but the magic was too strong. With a final burst, the last of the magic from the stronghold flowed into her and she whirled around.

The three guards stood in front of Mordred, who lay on the ground holding his bleeding side. The guards parried blows from a young man whose sword flashed and hummed through the air.

Marcus?

She didn't have time to think. She didn't have time to do anything. She acted almost on impulse, as an instinct.

She swung the Case around and directed it at the army of dark wizards.

The force of the magic exploded against her. It poured into the Case until the the chest began burning her hands, her skin reddening, cracking. It spat the magic back out into her, her entire body shaking with the tremendous power. Her veins seemed to run with lava, and she fell to her knees, screaming.

Every particle seemed ready to tear apart and explode, yet the magic kept coming. She was faintly aware of cries of distress from the dark wizards.

Then just like that, it was over. The Case snapped shut, and she fell to the grass, sweating and trembling.

A thud—the last guard hit the ground.

"Brinnie!"

She looked up with bleary eyes. Marcus's face swam in and out of focus.

He reached down. "Quick, we have to run."

Her brain burned. Had it melted? "You . . . you betrayed me."

"No. I never did. I can explain, but not now." He grabbed her arms and pulled. "Come on."

She tried to stand, but her legs gave out.

"No!" Mordred rolled, grabbed one of the chains attached to her ankles, and yanked. "Fool boy. You've sealed your own death." Clutching his side, he shot a bolt like lightning toward Marcus.

Marcus dodged and grunted as the bolt struck his arm, leaving a scorch mark. He flung a ball of fire back at Mordred. As Mordred shielded, Marcus yanked the chain away, pulling Brinnie with him. "Come on!"

Tripping and stumbling, she ran as he half-dragged her toward the edge of the cliff. She glanced back to see the army pulsing forward, wizards cutting them off on all three sides. "Marcus, we're surrounded."

"No, we're not." He tossed aside his sword, still running.

"I think you'll need that!"

"Better without it." He grabbed her, and she shrieked in surprise as swung her over his shoulder. She bounced with his pounding footsteps as he grabbed her cuffs and melted them in his hands, singeing her skin, but she hardly felt it as the chains fell behind them. "Hold on tight."

"Wait, wha—"

Her question was cut off as he jumped over the side of the cliff.

She screamed as they plummeted. Marcus curled his body around her in midair, and they hit the water with a smack. The icy waves stole her breath as her head went under. She kicked upward, Marcus pulling her up with him. As her head broke the surface, she gasped for breath, coughing up salty ocean water. She shivered, the fire inside her warring with the icy water around her.

"Hold on." Marcus wrapped an arm across her chest, under her armpits. "I've got you."

Shouting echoed from the top of the cliff. Brinnie looked up just in time to see an arrow sailing toward them. She threw up a hand to protect herself.

Fire flew out of her palm, incinerating the arrow.

She gasped as darkness threatened to overtake her. *What did I just do?*

"Stay awake for me." The arm around her tugged. "We're going to swim for shore."

Barely conscious, she held on as Marcus swam with powerful strokes parallel to the coast, away from the arrows. The water stung the flaming fingerprints of Mordred on her shoulders, the manacle-shaped burns around her wrists and ankles. But the fire within raged hotter. *I'm going to melt. Melt from the inside.*

As the shouts died away and Marcus began panting, Brinnie kicked feebly to try to help him along. They turned in toward the rocky coastline. Eventually their feet hit the bottom and Marcus supported her as they sloshed through the shallows to shore.

"A bit longer, all right? We need to get farther away before they come after us."

Brinnie nodded, too tired to question what on earth was going on. They clambered over the rocky coastline to the tufts of grass growing on the hills. She did her best to keep going, tripping on tussocks and stumbling over knolls. Finally, Marcus said, "We should be able to rest here for a minute."

Brinnie collapsed behind the larger hill hiding them from view of the stronghold, shivering uncontrollably.

Marcus knelt in front of her and pushed her hair away from her face to feel her forehead. "You're burning with fever." His jaw tightened. "I wish I'd killed Mordred with that blow. It would have killed an ordinary wizard. He deserves to die a hundred times for what he did to you."

"What?" She tried to keep her eyes from closing. "You're the one who turned me over to him. Why are you on my side again? Or is this another trick?"

His eyes filled with pain. "I didn't betray you. I would never, ever have done that. It was Ignatius. He didn't just happen to be near the garden that night of the Masters' Gathering. He followed us. He heard everything. He set us up so that you would be caught trying to find Mordred's bane."

Her firing neurons struggled to comprehend. "Then why did everyone think it was you?"

"Ignatius was trying to play to power. By betraying you, he got in with Mordred—by protecting me and making it look like I was part of the plot, he was trying to earn the favor of the future Master of Mordizan." He brushed the hair back from her burning face, tucking strands behind her ears. She closed her eyes at the gentle contact. "I confronted him, but it was too late. Anything I did would only incriminate me as well. I had to stay above suspicion so that I could get you out of there." His tone grew bitter. "But apparently my father didn't trust me to leave you in the dungeon. He sent me off to war the day after, before I could do anything. I returned as quickly as I could."

Her mind spun. What he said seemed to make sense—why Ignatius didn't get in trouble, how Mordred found out about her father, why Marcus supposedly sent a message instead of telling Mordred in person. "But then you set me up all over again. You made me lead them to Goddensfeld."

He sat back, shaking his head slowly. "You think I would ever want Oswald hurt? I set you up to escape safely, or so I thought. Once you escaped, I planned to send you word of what really happened and ask for Mordred's bane so I could kill him from the inside. But you didn't make it." He thrust a hand through his wet hair. "I was stupid—I didn't properly consider the blade's power to track you. Once you were caught, I knew they would eventually trace the escape back to me, so I made up a story for Mordred about helping you escape on purpose so that you would lead us to the last spy. He seemed to believe it."

She wanted to trust him. She wanted to think she had an ally, that their time together hadn't been a lie. But deceit had compounded upon deceit at Mordizan. "Did you plan today?"

He shook his head. "I didn't know what I was going to do. I saw my chance while Mordred was distracted. I still don't know if this will work, if we'll escape." He took her hand, and she let him. "Every day on the battlefield, all I could think about was you, alone in the dungeon. And then when I actually saw you, learned they had turned you over to Ignatius . . . it took all my willpower not to do something stupid and attack Mordred then and there." He blinked. Were there tears in his eyes? "Today, I realized saving you is more important to me. I should have rescued you immediately. Forget Mordred's bane and plans and secrecy and some sort of martyrdom delusion about saving the world. I'm so sorry."

Her heart softened, and she took his other hand. "No. You did the right thing. Defeating Mordred is more important. If things came down to it, of course I would want you to sacrifice me for the billions of others Mordred wants to destroy."

There were definitely tears in his eyes now. "I'm not making that choice anymore. You and I, we're going to live. *And* we're going to defeat Mordred."

She smiled, though it came as more of a grimace, every movement sending small fires through her skin. "You can't promise that."

"I can try."

She shuddered and stifled a moan as the inferno in her veins burned. "Marcus, what's happening to me?"

"You absorbed all that magic. No one was made to contain so much. It's destroying your composition."

The world spun. Her eyelids fluttered. "I'm dying, aren't I?"

"No. We'll get help. Just hold on a little longer."

"I'll try." Then everything went black.

She awoke to the beating of rain on what sounded like a tin roof. She squinted and shivered, trying to make out where she was. She could feel weathered, sandy boards beneath her. Her voice rasped. "Marcus."

"Here." He knelt beside her. Somewhere along the way, he'd dumped his chain mail. Sand and salt dusted his hair. "How are you feeling?"

"Been better. Where are we?"

"An old fisherman's hut, a mile or so from where you passed out." He glanced around the small space. "We should be able to hide here for now until you're stronger. I've heard there's an old spellcaster who lives around here somewhere, guiding the way to the stronghold. Maybe he can help us."

"And why would I do that?"

Marcus jumped to his feet and reached for the sword at his hip that wasn't there. Brinnie pushed herself into a sitting position, muscles screaming. A man with a shaggy gray beard stood in the doorway, a line of fish draped over his shoulder.

"Who are you?" Marcus demanded.

"Who am I?" The man snorted, shuffling into the hut. "Who are you, trespassing in my home?"

"I'm sorry." Marcus stepped back. "My friend is hurt. I was looking for shelter for her."

"Humph." He tossed the fish on a rough wooden table. "Heard you say spellcaster. I'm guessing you two are wizards."

"Yes, sir."

"What side are you on?" He shrugged. "Not that it matters much anymore anyway. Dark wizards just took over the last stronghold."

"No!" Brinnie squeezed her eyes shut. She should have known, but the confirmation sent pangs through her heart. Even without magic, the dark wizards had more manpower.

"Guess that answers that question. You two escape from the stronghold? I thought they killed everyone in there."

"Not from the stronghold." Marcus hesitated. "Do you think you could help us get away from here?"

"Nope." The man pulled out a knife and began lopping the heads off the fish.

"No?"

"Where do you think the dark wizards will come next?" He waved the knife between them. "Here, looking for you two. I'm not going to have them killing me for helping you. I'm strictly a neutral."

"But you call them dark wizards," Brinnie put in. "Only enchantment wizards refer to them that way."

"So what? You're not my problem."

"How about this." Marcus spread his hands. "When they come, tell them I tricked you into helping us by making you believe you were helping them. If the enchantment wizards come after you, you can tell them the truth. Either way, you're safe."

"Oh?" He sniffed, his knife thumping down, severing another fish head. "And how exactly would you trick me?"

Marcus straightened his shoulders. "I'm Marcus Vorath, heir of Mordizan. Obviously, I'm a dark wizard, as you call us."

The knife halted in mid-swing. "You aren't."

"He is," Brinnie said wearily. Her head spun, threatening to lose consciousness again.

"Well, then." The man set down the knife and wiped his hands on his pants. "Guess I might have something for you." He turned to a shelf and opened a wooden box, pulling out a portal orb.

Marcus accepted the orb in cupped hands. "Where does it lead?"

"No idea. I didn't make it, and the traveler who gave it to me didn't specify."

Marcus glanced down at Brinnie, concern written on his face. "Can you withstand more magic in a portal?"

Her bones ached at the suggestion, but she swallowed and nodded. "Anything to get away from here."

Thunk. Another fish head cleaved. "What's wrong with her?"

"She, ah, absorbed too much magic."

His eyes widened. "By the sea, you're Brynna Ludovic."

"Guilty," she admitted.

He wagged the knife. "You enter a portal with too much magic, and you're asking to get blown apart." He pointed it at Marcus. "I'd leave her if you want to escape."

"Not an option." Marcus glowered at him. He knelt again, taking Brinnie's burning hand and helping her into a wobbly standing position. "We can keep going on foot."

"No." She closed her eyes, opened them. "We'll never make it. Maybe I'm a traveler or something. Maybe that will help the portal hold together."

The spellcaster laughed. "There's no 'might.' You're not. You can't be a shadowmaster and a traveler."

"I'm not delusional." She turned back to Marcus. "The Case spits magic back out into an available recipient—usually the Key, but in this case, Mordred. He was taking all the power. But then I detached from Mordred."

Marcus's eyes widened. "The fire incinerating that arrow. I thought I did that without realizing. But . . ."

"It was me," Brinnie finished.

The spellcaster whistled. "Well then. If all that magic you absorbed isn't loose magic—if it's *your* magic now—you might actually survive the portal. Don't quote me on that, though."

Marcus held the orb out to her wordlessly. *Your decision,* his eyes said.

She took it. The magic within tingled in her palm but didn't hurt.

They had no idea where it led. They didn't know if they would survive the portal, or if she would blow them both to pieces.

But they had each other. They had the prophecy, locked in her mind. And she held the secret of Mordred's bane.

She held up the portal and nodded to the spellcaster. "Thank you."

"I didn't do anything. You remember that. I'm a neutral."

"Of course." She held out her other hand to Marcus, and he took it.

Fire blazed under her skin where he touched her, and she tried not to show her pain. *My insides are literally melting.*

Before it grew any worse, she smashed the orb on the ground.

As the cloud enveloped them, Brinnie gasped in agony. She didn't have enough breath to scream. Every particle felt like it was being pushed apart by rivers of burning hot magic. Marcus's hand in hers felt ethereal, his essence mixing with hers.

Through the mist, his voice spoke in her mind. *Hold on tight. We're almost there.*

Then the cloud cleared, leaving Brinnie and Marcus standing with both hands clasped, facing each other, alive.

Leaving her holding the world's most important secret.

"His bane is Excalibur." Brinnie met Marcus's eyes, her jaw set. "And I'm the one who has to wield it."

ACKNOWLEDGMENTS

I wrote the first draft of *Mordizan* during one of the most difficult times of my life. In many ways, Brinnie's story felt personal. As she overcame challenges and navigated a harsh environment, I hoped I could do the same. Many years later, upon the re-release of this series, I'm proud of both Brinnie and of a younger Alyssa, who made it through and came out the other side.

Thank you first to my family. To Maureen, to Mama and Daddy, to Steph and Juli, to Nana and Papa, and to my family all across the country.

Thank you to Miralee Ferrell and MBI for being my first publisher. To Hope and Nikki, constant supporters and biggest fans. And now, thank you to Teri and Jori at Torchflame Books, for giving this series a whole new readership.

And thank you to the readers! For the messages and posts and reviews and demands for book two the first time around, and for those of you, both old fans and new readers, who have picked up this new edition. I'm so excited for this book to be in your hands. None of this is possible without you.

About the Author

Alyssa Roat is an award-winning multi-published author and has worked in a wide variety of roles within the publishing industry. She has four black cats who allegedly have never been fed in their lives and occasionally help her write by walking across the keyboard. Her name is a pun, which means you can learn more about her at www.alyssawrote.com or on social media @alyssawrote.

THANK YOU!

Thank you for reading! The team at Torchflame Books hopes you've enjoyed this book and might consider leaving a review on Amazon, Goodreads, BookBub, The Story Graph, or anywhere else you like to track your recent reads. Alternatively, you could post online or tell a friend about it. This helps our authors more than you may know.

- *The Team at Torchflame Books*

Follow Torchflame Books for news about our authors and upcoming new releases @TorchflameBooks.

Find your next great read at torchflamebooks.com.

THE STORY CONTINUES...

WRAITHWOOD

Sent to Wraithwood Estate to live with an uncle she never knew, Brinnie Lane's quiet life takes a thrilling turn. The eerie mansion hides secrets of a hidden war, a tragic event, and ties to Arthurian legend. As Brinnie uncovers her family's mysterious past, she must confront the impossible: what if magic is real?

MORDIZAN

When Brinnie's sister is captured by the ruthless Mordred, she returns to the dangerous world of magic she thought she'd left behind. To save her, Brinnie goes undercover in Mordizan, seeking a prophecy that could destroy Mordred forever. How far will she go to defeat him? And how much of herself will she lose in the process?

CASTELON

Brinnie races against time to stop Mordred's reign of terror. With magic consuming her and the legendary weapon to defeat Mordred still lost, she must face war, political betrayal, and the allure of forbidden power. Only one man holds the knowledge of the weapon that could destroy Mordred forever—a man they already buried.

Get your copy at torchflamebooks.com/authors/alyssa-roat/

MORE FROM ALYSSA ROAT

DEAR HERO

Teen superhero Cortex and teen supervillain Vortex meet on Meta-Match, a nemesis pairing app for heroes and villains. But when darkness from the past threatens them both, they may need each other for the fight to come. Can a hero trust a villain to do the right thing? And can a villain trust a hero not to screw her over?

DEAR HENCHMAN

Kevin and Himari didn't plan to be heroes. Henchmen and sidekicks are supposed to brew coffee, take pics of their hero or villain for social media, and stay in the background. But when a taxidermy-collecting villain robs Kevin's hero of his powers and leaves Himari's villain wounded, it's up to the sidekicks and henchmen to save the world regardless of whether they have superpowers or not.

DEAR HADES

Freshly resurrected as 21st century teens, Medusa and Tiresias seek a second chance amidst meddling gods, murderous heroes, and a classic Greek bet. With pressure building on all sides, they must work together to save mortals and monsters alike.

Get your copy at torchflamebooks.com/authors/alyssa-roat/

www.ingramcontent.com/pod-product-compliance
Lightning Source LLC
LaVergne TN
LVHW050923080826
845145LV00001B/184

* 9 7 8 1 6 1 1 5 3 1 8 3 1 *